Books by Brenda S. Anderson

WHERE THE HEART IS SERIES

Risking Love
Capturing Beauty (coming February 2017)
Planting Hope (coming May 2017)

COMING HOME SERIES

Pieces of Granite
Chain of Mercy
Memory Box Secrets
Hungry for Home

Where the Heart Is, Book 1

Risking Love

A NOVEL

Minneapolis, Minnesota

Vivant Press

Risking Love
Copyright © 2016
Brenda S. Anderson

ISBN-13: 978-0-9862147-4-5

Scriptures taken from the Holy Bible, New International Version®, NIV®. Copyright © 1973, 1978, 1984, 2011 by Biblica, Inc.™ Used by permission of Zondervan. All rights reserved worldwide. www.zondervan.com The "NIV" and "New International Version" are trademarks registered in the United States Patent and Trademark Office by Biblica, Inc.™

This novel is a work of fiction. Names, characters, places, and incidents either are the product of the author's imagination or are used fictitiously. Any resemblance to actual events, locales, organizations, or persons living or dead is entirely coincidental and beyond the intent of either the author or the publisher.

Cover Design by Think-Cap Design Studios

Printed in the United States of America

16 17 18 19 20 21 22   7 6 5 4 3 2 1

To Marvin for taking a risk on loving me!

"Lord, I know that people's lives are not their own;

It is not for them to direct their steps."

Jeremiah 10:23

Chapter One

What possessed people to jump out of airplanes? Corliss Morgan slapped the Minneapolis newspaper down on her cube mate's desk and pointed to the headlines. SKYDIVING ACCIDENT KILLS NEWLYWEDS. "Insanity. If I ever think of dating a daredevil, remind me to run far, far away."

Just as she'd like to run far, far away from that fundraiser tonight. She was still hoping, praying even, for something to come up that would prevent her from going.

"Lissa," Rita Dunlap emptied the remnants of a bag of Pop Rocks into her mouth and continued typing, the candy's crackle vying for attention. "A little insanity is exactly what you need."

"No way." Lissa plopped down on her office chair and moved her mouse, chasing away the Fourth of July screensaver, as her eight coworkers' voices buzzed in the background of the bank office. They were all trying to accomplish the impossible: extract late mortgage payments from unemployed people. Talk about insanity. "Give me someone safe, someone who does things the right way, someone like Haven. Now there's—"

"Did I hear my name?"

Eyes growing wide, Lissa slowly swiveled her chair and looked up into her boss's indigo eyes. She swallowed hard, stealing a glance at her chuckling cube mate. Payback would be coming. "Um, we were talking about those skydiving newlyweds and how you'd never do something crazy like that."

"Hmm." He took the newspaper off Rita's desk and rubbed his

Romanesque chin. "Maybe once I would have." He gave the paper back to Rita then handed Lissa a stack of files. "My priorities have changed."

Lissa threw Rita a triumphant smile before thumbing through the files. "Foreclosures?"

"I'm afraid so."

"Gee thanks." She couldn't contain her sarcasm. How many of these foreclosures would be credited to her dad? Good thing he wasn't alive today to see what his generosity had wrought.

"Sorry about that." Haven leaned a broad shoulder against the edge of her gray cubicle and brushed a hand through surfer blond hair. Her heart did a two-step. Handsome wasn't complimentary enough. "But you're the best, Lissa. If anyone can keep those people from losing their homes, it's you." He smiled, lighting a spark in eyes as blue as a Minnesota evening sky.

Heat flooded her cheeks. Now, why did he have to go and smile? If only he weren't her boss. "I'll do my best."

"I have no doubt." He glanced at his watch and slapped the cube wall. "Looks like it's closing time. But before you go, can I see you in my office?"

"I'll be right in." After she regained her composure. The click of associates' fingers on keyboards quieted and the professional phone voices changed to excited personal tones. People couldn't wait to get away from the complaining and hideous words they heard all day. Not that she blamed her coworkers. Trying to collect overdue loan payments always brought out the ugliness in people.

She slid open her desk drawer and secured the files in the To Do slot. Why would Haven want to see her? She wheeled her chair to the left, peeked around her gray fabric wall as he walked past the end cube. His charcoal Hugo Boss suit perfectly accented his six-foot frame. Handsome indeed.

"Hey, sweets, I saw that."

Lissa gulped and focused at her computer screen. "Saw what?"

"Nothing but a little flirtation with the boss."

Lissa spun in her chair and glared at Rita. "I was not flirting."

"Right, and I'm a natural blonde." Rita twirled one of her curly locks as Pop Rocks crackled in her mouth.

"Okay, so the man's cute." More like gorgeous.

"How about hunkalicous?"

Oh yeah. That worked.

"And successful."

"Yeah, so?" Dad was successful too. Until . . . Chin quivering, Lissa snatched a small handful of the raisin, walnut, almond concoction from a bowl on the credenza that separated her workspace from Rita's. She cleared her throat and stilled her chin. "I've got an appointment."

"Uh-huh." Rita shut off her computer. "With a man so straight-laced, word has it his lips are still virgin."

"Please." Not that she hadn't imagined kissing those lips. "The boss is off-limits."

"Wouldn't stop me." Rita drummed a pencil on her desk. "Hmmm, I just might—"

Lissa laughed. "You'd be bored to tears."

"Ahh, but you're so right." With a sigh, Rita gazed at the ceiling and fanned a hand over her chest. "I crave heart-galloping adventure. Something you should try, by the way. Let's face it, the boss is too safe."

And safe is exactly what I need. Lissa clicked off her computer and picked up the college graduation gift from her father. A framed list with her sixth grade goals inked on crinkled, yellowing paper: graduate from high school, go to college, and find a job. Three tasks already completed. Next item was to become a boss. Buying a home, getting married, and having children would come in time. God's path for her life written in a tidy package. Step-by-step rules for assured happiness. She set the frame down. The plan had worked well so far.

"Sweets, you definitely need to get a life."

Lissa grabbed her purse from beneath her desk. "I intend to live, all right." If there was one thing her father's death had taught her, it was how to live the right way, and to treat her body as the temple God created it to be.

Rita rolled her eyes. "Mr. Boring is awaiting."

"Yeah, I better go. See you Monday." Lissa dumped the last drops of her water bottle into a bud vase that held a single pink carnation and then strode past the now deserted cubicles. It was amazing how quickly the place cleared out at closing time.

She stopped at Haven's door. 'Hennepin Bank and Trust' was etched into the door's glass, and a mahogany nameplate, engraved with Haven's name and title of Collections Supervisor, hung below the bank's name. The door framed him at his desk, his brows knitted in concentration.

She raised her hand to knock and held it still, nerves jitterbugging in her stomach. What was this about? A pink slip? Probably not. The collections department was the one area in the bank that wasn't lacking for work. Most likely more remnants of her dad's ghost that required exorcizing, more problems created from his granting unwise loans. Regardless, being summoned to the boss's office was never good news.

Gnawing her lower lip, she knocked.

He smiled and waved her in.

The dance in her stomach slowed but didn't stop. He wouldn't smile like that to give bad news.

Would he?

A lingering hint of minty cologne greeted her when she stepped into the room. Focusing on the waterfall photograph on the wall behind Haven, she sat in a chair opposite his desk, crossed one leg over the other, and clutched her purse in her lap, hoping to still her trembling fingers.

"Hi Lissa." He closed his laptop and leaned back in his chair, his face unsmiling.

Not a face bearing good news. She gripped her purse even tighter.

He pointed to a newspaper on the side of his desk. The headline read, JUNE FORECLOSURES IN HENNEPIN COUNTY AT ALL TIME HIGH. "Hennepin Bank and Trust made the paper again."

"Thanks to my dad," she mumbled.

Haven straightened, and a storm brewed in his eyes. "I know I don't always stress this, but with the bank's struggles, your dad's become an easy scapegoat. I'm guilty as the rest when it comes to laying blame, but he was a good man. Don't let anyone tell you otherwise."

She glanced down at her fisted hands.

"Sorry, Lissa, I didn't mean to jump at you, but if you ask me,

Theodore Morgan is the main reason this bank is still afloat today."

Lissa's eyes burned, and she blinked back sudden tears. She couldn't recall a time when someone had stood up for her dad.

"And he saved my rear more than once." He toyed with a plastic Snoopy paperweight. "Like you, your father had a heart for helping people."

And if her dad had taken care of that heart, he might still be here for her.

Lissa cleared her throat, reining in her emotions. Breaking down at work was bad enough, but in front of Haven? Sheesh! She squared her shoulders and donned her professional face. "You needed to see me?"

"Uh, yes." He glanced at his watch then set the paperweight next to a framed portrait of Haven's aging beagle, Schroeder. "I've got a commitment tonight that I'd love to avoid but can't." He shook his head and frowned.

"Me too." If raising money to build awareness for heart disease wasn't so vital, she'd gladly skip the evening event.

Haven slid his top desk drawer open and pulled out a sheet of paper. "The bank received this letter today from a customer."

Lissa slumped in her chair and eyed her crimson pencil skirt. It wasn't her fault people got in over their heads with their mortgages, but they sure always found a way to blame her. If it weren't for her occasional successes, the vile language and hate that spewed from people would probably drive her to drink. She didn't need one more vice to deal with.

"You want me to read it to you?" He held out the paper.

Through her lashes, she peered at the dour line of his mouth. "Please." Seeing and reading the words often implanted them in her mind. Maybe in only hearing them, the memory would fade sooner.

Haven took a sip of his bottled water. "It's addressed to the owners of Hennepin Bank regarding you."

"Get it over with." Keeping her head down, she closed her eyes.

"It says, 'Recently, our family went through a difficult time with hourly cutbacks followed by a job loss, then the threat of losing our home. Creditors hounded us, and many used bullying language as if that would somehow help us find a non-existent flow of money. But the collection call we should have feared most was the one that helped steer us out of our situation: the call from Hennepin Bank.'"

Helped them? She stared at Haven.

He winked. "'Your employee, Corliss Morgan, listened to us and sympathized with our plight. She took time to guide us through our finances, helped prioritize our bill paying, and offered ideas on how to save money. It took a few months to get back on track, but without Ms. Morgan's calm advice, we are certain we would have lost our home.'"

Relief washed over her. That was what made her job worthwhile.

"'So, thank you, Corliss Morgan and Hennepin Bank, for being the human side of banking. You have earned our business for a lifetime and we will gladly recommend you to others. Sincerely, Ted and Marla Cockran'."

They'd been a joy to work with. If all people listened like they had . . .

Haven handed her the letter. "We've placed a copy in our files, but you should have the original."

"Thank you." Now these were words she'd love to imprint on her memory.

"We don't get a lot of positive feedback in this department, but when we do, more often than not your name is attached to it. That leads me to another small piece of business." He folded his hands on top of his desk. "I've been offered a new position at a downtown Minneapolis mortgage company."

No. He couldn't leave. Seeing his smile every day always eased the stress of the job and fed her futile hope for something more. "You've decided to take it?"

He shrugged. "I'd be a fool not to."

Of course. "I guess congratulations are in order." Even if she wasn't happy about it. "When do you start?"

"Three weeks. Two weeks here then I'm taking a week off."

"Good for you. We'll miss you around here." *Especially me.*

"I'll miss it too, but it's time to move on. Before I leave Hennepin Bank, though, there's one more very important duty to perform, and that's to help find my successor." Haven slid a manila folder from the side of the desk and opened it.

Not Tyler Abernathy, please! Being unemployed would be better than working under that ogre. His bullying tactics gave all collection agents a bad name. No way would she work for him.

Haven rapped a pen on the open file. A copy of the letter he just read lay on top. "I'm recommending that you apply for my position."

"What?" Her heart sprinted. Others were far more qualified than she. "But I—"

"You, more than anyone in our department, have protected the bank and homeowners from foreclosure. You understand that we don't want to take people's homes away—that we want to find a way to save them. You understand that there's a living, feeling human being at the other end of letters and phone calls. I can't think of a better person to lead this department."

She peered upward and whispered thanks. If she got the promotion, she'd be personally responsible for eradicating her father's mistakes. Life couldn't get better.

No doubt she'd apply, but it was unprofessional to appear overeager. She curled jittery fingers on the edge of his desk. "May I think about it?"

"Absolutely." He closed the file. "I wouldn't expect otherwise."

"Thanks, Haven. Your encouragement means a lot to me." More than she dared let him know. She got up and headed for the door. To think she might be weeks away from achieving the next goal on her list. Owning a house wouldn't be far behind. Too bad she had a commitment tonight. Rita would have loved to celebrate this news with her.

"One second, Lissa." Haven's calm, professional baritone disappeared and was replaced with a wobbly tenor.

She turned on her heel as he stuffed the folder back in his desk drawer.

"One more little incentive to throw in, for you to ponder over the weekend." Resting back in his chair, he rubbed his hands over his thighs.

"Is something wrong?" Never had she seen him anything but confident.

He chuckled and looked toward her, but his gaze didn't meet hers. "I was wondering if, when I left . . ." He rubbed his hand over his chin.

"Would you mind if I asked you out?"

Would she mind? Lissa tried to hold in her smile but failed. "I look forward to it." Good thing he couldn't see her heart dancing a samba.

"Whew." He puffed out a breath and grinned. "I listen to people tell me no all day and it doesn't bother me, but if I'd heard it from you . . ."

He pushed away from his desk and shut off all his equipment. "I'll walk you out."

"I'd like that."

Side by side, they walked from the building across the parking lot, sharing small talk. Someday soon, maybe they'd hold hands. Maybe she'd get a chance to kiss those virgin lips.

Girl, you are getting way ahead of yourself. She pointed her remote at her Volvo. A clothing store stood out beyond her car. Shoot, she needed panty hose for the night. She nodded toward the store. "I remembered some shopping I have to do." Considering the mush Haven made of her mind, it was a good thing she remembered them now and not once she arrived home.

"Okay, I'll see you on Monday."

Maybe by then her heart would be dancing to its normal beat. With her purse slung over her shoulder, she watched Haven's car head down the road then she floated across the parking lot, imagining Haven's hand protecting hers.

"Watch out!"

Tires screeched. Lissa's body hurled through the air, strong arms tucked around her. With a scream, she landed.

Softly. On top of a woodsy-scented, leather-clad man. A dark-haired, gorgeous one at that.

His arms sprang away, and she pushed herself off the ground, making certain her skirt stayed at her knees. Murmuring shoppers gathered around the two of them

A trail of blood coursed from his temple down his cheek shadowed with whiskers. She retrieved her purse that had flown a car's length away, and dug out a tissue. "Are you all right?" She squatted and dabbed at the cut. "It looks superficial, but you should have it checked out."

He brought a hand to his temple, winced, and looked at his bloody fingers. "I've had worse." He turned in the direction of the sedan that had nearly plowed her down. The car was long gone. "Crazy driver."

And one daydreaming lady. That didn't make for a safe combination. She stood and wiped off her skirt. She was lucky her handsome rescuer happened to be passing by or she wouldn't just be cleaning road dust off her outfit.

The crowd dispersed as he helped himself up. "Are you okay?"

"Thanks to you."

He shrugged. "I happened to be in the right place."

Right, but how many other passersby would have watched the car ram into her? "In my book, you're a hero." She opened her purse and pulled out a couple of twenties.

He frowned and crossed his arms over his chest. "That wouldn't make me much of a hero now, would it?"

"I feel I owe you."

"Just watch where you're going next time." He winked a toffee-brown eye and grinned. "That'll be payment enough."

Be still my two-stepping heart. "I promise." Or was it her two-timing heart? She fanned a hand by her face as her savior sauntered across the parking lot to a bright yellow motorcycle, the streamlined kind that was made for speed.

And danger.

He donned a helmet and zoomed from the parking lot.

She hadn't even gotten his name.

Not that it mattered. He may have saved her, but the man oozed danger. He'd be perfect for Rita.

Besides, now she had Haven's attention—he was made for her.

So why did the thought of gazing into the stranger's deep-set eyes bring a grin to her face and make her heart dance a traitorous tango?

Caleb Johnson looked in the bathroom mirror and pried his lips into a smile, practicing for tonight. His mother-in-law said that was a terrific way to meet someone new, someone who could jumpstart his heart. But come on, not like this, where he'd have someone forced on him. That was insanity.

But if he could choose someone like that woman from the parking lot earlier today . . .

Where had that thought come from?

Nearly two hours had passed, and that woman still occupied his mind. "Traitor," he mumbled and slapped Stetson cologne onto his face, avoiding the superglued area of his temple. How could he betray Jeanette like this? Maybe his heart wasn't ready for a jumpstart. Maybe he wasn't ready to forget. He straightened his red cummerbund and bow tie and grimaced at the bathroom mirror. "I look like a bloodied penguin."

"And a *très beau* one."

Handsome? With a grunt, Caleb rolled his eyes at his mother-in-law. "This isn't me."

"Nonsense." Yvette McCarthy readjusted his tie. "Every man is *très beau* in a tuxedo."

"Jeanette liked me as I was."

"Jeanette never saw you in a tux, *mon cher*."

"My point exactly." Caleb pushed past Yvette into the hallway and stopped at his wedding portrait. The sparkling waters of Gooseberry Falls tumbled behind the bride and groom dressed in khakis and hiking boots. Jeanette held a rainbow bouquet of wild flowers. Who wanted a church when they could marry in God's sanctuary?

A marriage that ended years too soon, imprinting forever the image of Jeanette in a casket, dressed in her wedding outfit, clutching a bouquet of wild flowers in lifeless fingers.

He blinked, packing the memory away. For tonight. "Jeanette didn't need me in a tux."

He felt a tug on his trousers.

"Dada hansum."

Caleb chuckled and looked down into gray eyes so reminiscent of his wife's. Even the copper pigtails reminded him of Jeanette. "Handsome, huh?" He beeped his two-year-old daughter's nose and cocked his head, peeking at his mother-in-law out of the corner of his eye. "Sounds like Mémé's been doing some coaching." He scooped

Aimee up.

"No, no, no." Yvette stole Aimee from Caleb's arms then wiped cracker crumbs from his sleeves. "Our petite Amelia Earhart just finished eating. We would not wish to dirty your suit."

"Amelia Earhart, huh?" Caleb tickled his daughter's tummy, eliciting an infectious giggle. "Is my Aimee-doodles taking flying lessons again?"

"I fwy." Wide-eyed, Aimee spread her arms straight out from her side and flapped them up and down.

"Off of the picnic table this afternoon." Yvette carried Aimee around Caleb. "Right into her pool. Your wee explorer behaves like her mamma, and, dare I say, her dada."

He touched his temple and grinned while following Yvette down the maple-floored hallway. Yep, that was his daughter, all right.

A mouth-watering blend of chicken and vegetable aroma clung to the air as he stepped into the open-concept kitchen he and Jeanette had designed together. His father-in-law stood at the stove, ladling soup into plastic containers. Stomach growling, Caleb rested his hand on Aidan McCarthy's shoulder and eyed the delectable concoction only his father-in-law could create. "Leftovers?"

Aidan sealed a bowl. "Enough for a week's worth of meals."

Well, at least he and Aimee wouldn't starve. Not this week anyway. That woman this afternoon had no clue how tempting it had been to accept her offer of money.

But his conscience would never have let him live it down. Caleb slapped his father-in-law's back. "You guys are too good to me."

"Never." Aidan carried five containers to the refrigerator, and nodded to Caleb. "Could you slide open that freezer drawer for me?"

"Oh, yeah. Sorry." He knelt and opened the drawer, and his mouth dropped open. Food containers and Ziplocked chicken, fish, and beef nearly filled the drawer that, just this morning, had been empty. "When did you . . . ? Why did you . . . ?" His jaw stiffened. He wasn't a charity case. Yet.

"Say thank you." Aidan shuffled the frozen food around and squeezed in the soup containers. "Someday, you'll have the opportunity to help us."

With a sigh, Caleb stuffed his hands in his trouser pockets and whispered, "Thank you." No way could he ever repay what Jeanette's folks had done for him. He really was blessed.

"Tank you, Papi." Aimee ran up and hugged Aidan's back as he crouched by the fridge.

"Grab on, Calamity Jane." He stood with Aimee's arms circling his neck and legs wrapped around his midriff. He patted his granddaughter's hand. "Now hang on."

"Aiden McCarthy"—Yvette cuffed her hands over her hips—"you be careful with your wee granddaughter."

He winked as he skipped past. "I'll do my best."

With a bittersweet smile, Caleb watched Aidan gallop and neigh around the dinette. "It's like having a piece of Jeanette right here, isn't it?"

"Both you and Jeanette." Yvette wiped off the gas stove. "Wrapped in one *magnifique* package."

"So why do you want me to forget her?" Caleb flattened his hands on the kitchen island's granite surface and glared at Yvette.

Her lips parted, and she splayed a hand over her chest. Yvette excelled at putting up a stoic front, but he knew she still hurt like crazy from losing her only daughter. What he'd give to take those words back.

"Yvette, I'm sorry."

"*Mon cher*, you are speaking your mind. This is not about erasing Jeanette from your thoughts."

"Then why am I tucked in this monkey-suit trying to convince a bunch of hoity-toity women that I'm something I'm not? What could we possibly have in common?"

Yvette caught Aidan's arms as he galloped past. "Papi, I think it is quiet time, do you not?"

"I do believe you're right. Even Calamity Jane needs her rest." Aidan squatted and Aimee slid to the floor. "Why don't you go find a movie for Papi, Mémé, and you to watch tonight?"

Caleb crossed his arms and watched his daughter run to the stairs of their split entry home. She laid on her tummy and inched her way, head first, down seven steps to the landing then she turned disappearing down the next short flight to the family room.

Yvette pointed at Aimee. "That is why you are going out tonight."

"No one can replace her mother."

"And no one can replace your wife. That is not the problem."

"Then what is?" He plopped down on a bar stool next to the island and shuffled through three days' worth of unopened mail piled up on the island. No comforting letter from his parents who were doing missionary work in some unpronounceable African country. Only bills, most likely. Or worse, overdue notices. Maybe if he ignored them . . .

"Dear Caleb, it is time to let go of Jeanette." Yvette sat next to him and touched his heart. "We will always hold her here, and no one can fill the hole she has left, but she would not want you to mope through life. It has been over two years."

Let go? He clenched his fists. How does a person let go of their soulmate? Time had nothing to do with it.

Aidan rubbed his temples. "Jeanette would want—"

"She'd want me to be happy." Caleb shook his head. How many times had he heard that? "How can I be happy when I've already lost her and now I could lose . . . ?" Clutching his fists, he stared down at the island top, at the heart etched into granite—the piece he and Jeanette had chosen together for the heart of their home. He couldn't lose their house too.

Yvette's hand covered his. "That, you must leave in God's hands."

Easy for her to say. She wasn't about to become homeless.

"Now go tonight. Have fun. Smile." She patted his whiskered face. "The ladies, they won't be able to resist such a handsome man, and you will raise much money for heart disease awareness. And maybe some other husband will not become a widower so young."

"Mémé, Papi! I got Belle!"

Yvette pointed to the toddler hopping up the stairs with the *Beauty and the Beast* DVD tucked against her chest. "So another child does not grow up without her mamma."

He studied his rambunctious daughter and smiled. Yvette was right, as usual. Aimee needed a mother.

And he needed someone to hold again, someone who could breathe life into his comatose heart.

He gritted his teeth. Chances of finding that person tonight were slim to nothing, but for Aimee he'd give it a try.

Chapter Two

Red. Red. Red! Didn't these people know that accenting with red made a greater impact than wearing solid red?

Praying the evening wouldn't last long, Lissa led her mom through the chandeliered hotel ballroom, weaving through a sea of numbered round tables all draped in red, each adorned with a red rose in a crystal vase. Women, and a smattering of brave men, all dressed in varying shades of red, sat around each table.

As if she were any better. She grimaced at her ruby sheath and matching nails. At least her black shawl toned down her gown, and her lip gloss matched her lips, not her dress. Too bad she couldn't say the same for her mom.

"Here it is, darling." Adelaide Morgan steered Lissa toward the stage. Front row table, naturally. "Good evening, ladies." Adelaide extended a limp hand to her six Red Hat Club friends seated around the table. If their overabundant bling was any indication of the money they had to spare, Lissa wouldn't be successful at bidding tonight.

No way could her meager budget compete with theirs. Or her mom's, for that matter. But she wasn't about to take one red penny of her mom's fortune.

Not that she planned on bidding anyway, especially with Haven's office revelation that he wanted to date her.

Trying to hide the blush warming her cheeks, Lissa picked up the thick program with *Go Red Bachelor Auction* imprinted in garnet foil. Sheesh, she was as bad as a schoolgirl with a teenage crush.

Ignoring her mom's conversation with their tablemates, Lissa immersed herself in the program highlighting the bachelors.

What kind of man would subject himself to this kind of humiliation regardless of the money raised for a good cause? Not one she cared to go out with, that was for sure.

She turned past the cardiologist's profile on the first page. Sure, the man wasn't half-bad looking, but single yet at thirty-five and obviously wealthy. What was wrong with him?

The following two pages highlighted a lawyer and an accountant. Again, no prize catches. The lawyer was divorced. Twice. And the accountant? His favorite pastime was fishing, and he wanted a partner to join him, be it ice or boat. Please. Not in a quadrillion years would she even think of touching a scaly fish. She shuddered at the thought and flipped the page.

No. She stared down at the familiar face and read the name. This was Haven's commitment?

"Mom." She tugged her mom's sleeve, drawing her from an inane conversation about the best stores to shop in at the Galleria.

"Yes, darling?"

Lissa thrust the program at her mom. "He's here."

"Who's here, darling?" With fingernails painted the color of a fire engine, her mom bent back Lissa's program.

"Haven." Lissa pointed at the picture and accompanying description. "My boss, er, my former boss, or about to be my former boss."

"Really, now." Her mom slipped the program from Lissa's fingers and a smile slowly lifted the edges of her lips. "Hmm, I must say, you won't regard this evening as a waste after all."

Lissa squirmed while studying her nails. "I can't bid on my boss."

"For goodness' sake, why not?"

"It wouldn't be . . . proper."

"Proper, my foot." Adelaide lifted Lissa's chin and smiled. "It's clear you've got a crush on the man, someone your dear departed father approved of, as do I, by the way, and I can't think of a better way to let him know you're interested. Nor will he be able to back out."

"I don't know," Lissa muttered. She retrieved the program from her mom and skimmed through his bio. His mom died of heart failure when he was only nine, and his father raised him to be a man of honor. Hennepin Bank and Trust was still listed as his employer. His new position would make him even more valuable to tonight's bidders.

Only twenty-nine. Never been married. *Never been kissed*, her cube mate's voice intruded. Yeah, right. Lissa shook the absurd thought away and kept reading. Teaches confirmation at his church. Holds season passes to Orchestra Hall. Relaxes by playing classical piano. Loves moonlit walks with his beagle, Schroeder, around Lake of the Isles near his home. Would love to share those walks with the right woman.

Dear God, the man was perfect, and to think, he was interested in her. Maybe God had plopped the perfect opportunity in her lap. Well, who was she to waste a gift from God? "Mom, I do believe you're right. Maybe it's time I take a chance."

The lights dimmed as Lissa finished her baked apple topped with walnuts and raisins. Who said healthy eating couldn't be delicious? Oh, silly question. Her father, of course. If only he'd listened to her, maybe—

"Good evening." The voice of the evening's moderator echoed through the ballroom. She adjusted the microphone on the Plexiglass lectern set off to the right of the stage. "And welcome to our Go Red for Women Day's first annual bachelor auction."

Applauding, Lissa relaxed in her chair.

Lights glinted off the emcee's ruby sequined dress as she spoke briefly about heart disease's effect on women. "The good news is that this disease can usually be prevented by changing your lifestyle, by eating nutritious—and delicious—meals, and through exercise."

Applause rang throughout the room.

Did you hear that, Dad?

"And, of course, through eliminating smoking and stress. The choice is very often yours to make."

Lissa looked down at her clenched hands as more clapping ensued.

Well, some things were more difficult to change. If they only knew how stressful work could be sometimes. And now with the possible promotion . . .

"Thanks to all of you, we will get the word out and realize a healthier America. And now, without further ado, it's time to introduce our bachelors. Gentlemen." The emcee stepped back from the podium and gestured to her right.

Hoots and whistles sounded through the audience as ten tuxedoed men filed onto the stage. Standing fourth from the right was Haven, dressed conservatively in his black tux with the sunset red vest, tie, and pocket square. Not to mention his heart-stopping smile. She chuckled to herself. Was that really a good thing to have at a heart disease fundraiser?

As the applause faded, the emcee stepped back to the microphone. "Let me introduce you to these very eligible men."

Lissa tuned out the emcee and studied the group on stage, admiring their variety of suits. One bachelor wore stop-light red from shoe to top hat. He definitely needed someone who didn't mind sticking out. A couple of men donned red suits with black vests or cummerbunds. Perfect for the non-conformist. One wore a short tail coat, and another's jacket extended past his knees. There were double-breasted jackets and even one with red pinstripes. For the traditional with a twist.

She gasped when her gaze landed on the bachelor at the end, the one she could almost reach out and touch. It was him. Her rescuer from the parking lot. Her heart did a double-crossing rumba. The man looked even sweeter in a traditional black tux, red cummerbund and bowtie. But his intentional five o'clock shadow, the deep-set eyes that squinted when he smiled, and his short wavy hair with the renegade dark strand inking his forehead like a tattoo, spelled danger. He probably had one of those barbed-wire tattoos circling his bicep. She glanced at his biography on the back page and shivered.

Caleb Johnson. Loves skydiving and bungee jumping.

Yep. Absolutely not her type. Even if her heart jitterbugged every time she glanced at him.

"—Haven Carlysle."

Lissa sat up straighter, and she held her breath as Haven stepped into the spotlight. Now here was the perfect man for her. Whistles and cheers reverberated through the room. Apparently everyone else thought he was perfect too. *Settle down, ladies, he's mine.* She raised her hand off the table and waved with her fingers. *I'm right here, Haven. Please, oh, please see me.*

As if hearing her thoughts, his gaze connected with hers and his smile deepened, the spotlight glittering in those eyes. He gave a slight nod to her as he stepped back in line. That was all the approval she needed. She'd go a thousand dollars, if that was what it took.

Closing her eyes, she leaned back into her chair, imagining their first date: dinner at Chez Amélie in downtown Minneapolis, a symphony at Orchestra Hall, a moonlit horse-drawn carriage ride along the Mississippi River and across the Stone Arch Bridge, culminating with a kiss on those virgin lips. Worth every penny of that thousand dollars. Yes, she definitely owed her mom an apology for complaining about the evening.

"And finally, I'd like to welcome Caleb Johnson."

Lissa opened her eyes as the dangerous one on the end came forward, receiving light applause. No whistles. No hoots. Odd. A lot of women were attracted to risk. What was wrong with him?

He smiled, but his focus remained above the audience as if he were avoiding everyone. Keeping one hand in his trouser pocket, he tugged at his collar. The man was clearly uncomfortable in a suit and with being on stage. Not that she could blame him. No way on God's blessed earth would she put herself up for auction, no matter the cause.

She turned to the last page of her brochure and read the remainder of his biography. Ah, no wonder. The man was a misfit among the corporate types on stage. A small business owner who also worked at a home improvement chain. A truly successful businessman wouldn't have to take a second job. And what kind of date could he provide on that puny salary?

Besides, the man came with baggage. A widower with a child. Those were issues better left to someone desiring danger in their life.

He may have saved her today, but she had no intention of rescuing him tonight. Her heart was safer with Haven.

"He's rather cute." Her mom leaned over and whispered in Lissa's ear.

Lissa grunted. Sure, Caleb was cute. Gorgeous even. She preferred handsome. Someone with a real job, with whom she could have a long, safe, and happy life.

Someone *not* like her father.

Someone just like Haven.

So why did her gaze keep flitting back to Caleb?

Off stage, Caleb paced while glancing through the evening's program. Why hadn't he been more firm with his *no* when his mother-in-law told him about the fundraiser? That answer was obvious. All she had to do was throw around Jeanette's or Aimee's name, and he'd give in quicker than freefalling from an airplane.

The question now was, would he get any bids? No response would be the ultimate humiliation.

Heaving a sigh, he plopped down on a stool and listened to the auctioneer beg for higher bids.

"Five hundred. Who can give five hundred for an evening with a cardiac surgeon? Five fifty. Thank you. Six hundred? Think of what this man could do for your heart."

Oh, please.

"One thousand is the bid. Thank you! Can anyone go fifteen hundred?"

Fifteen hundred bucks. For one lousy date. Caleb rolled his eyes and read through the professions of the other nine bachelors. An MD, a PHD, a CEO, a CPA, and five other initialed positions.

"We've got fifteen hundred. Who'll go two thousand?"

Brother. What he could do with that kind of money. Buy him another couple months, at least, in his home. Maybe by then the housing industry would have turned around.

He flipped to the last page where his profile was listed, as if his addition to the program were an afterthought. Owner of Heart of the

Home Kitchen Designs, and kitchen design specialist at Home Mart. Failed businessman, big box home improvement peon would be more accurate. Maybe he should have listed his own initials: big box HIP.

"Two thousand dollars. Going once . . . twice . . . Sold to the young lady at table thirty six."

He clutched the program in his lap and looked up. *God, what am I doing here?* What kind of man sells himself to the highest bidder? What kind of lesson was he teaching his daughter?

Well, she'd never find out. He'd do his good deed and go on this date and treat his date well. Chances of a wealthy woman being interested beyond that were slim to zilch. Although it would be nice . . .

He squeezed the back of his neck. After tonight, after his date, he'd turn his attention back to the important things in life. On raising a daughter and keeping a roof over their heads.

Clearly, no one in this room would understand how truly difficult that was. Not if they could throw two thousand dollars at one date easier than he could treat his daughter to McDonalds.

"And now, for the evening's fourth very eligible bachelor, Haven Carlysle."

Lissa rested her elbows on the table, and tented her hands in front of her mouth as Haven strode onto the stage. She had to win the date with him.

"Haven is a man on the move, ladies, as he's just received a generous promotion to Minneapolis' largest mortgage company. Who wouldn't want to stroll arm in arm around the lakes with this man?"

"Oooh," a woman's high-pitched, nasally voice screeched behind Lissa. "I need him!"

Her eyes wide, Lissa couldn't resist looking back. Three tables away stood a curly-haired redhead whose body was poured into the neckline-plunging, wine-colored dress. She waved her number in the air and her Marilyn Monroe-esque body followed suit.

"Oh dear." Lissa's mom laid a hand on her arm. "Missy Coborn is quite the competition, and she has deep pockets. I don't know how you can compete."

Thanks for the vote of confidence, Mom. Lissa swallowed and looked back to the stage.

Haven's gaze settled on her, and he winked.

Her stomach turned somersaults. Please, oh please, don't let his bids go over a thousand. Who would've figured that the first three bachelors would go for nearly two thousand each? But they were doctors and attorneys. Haven was a Collections Supervisor. A bad guy to most of the world. Certainly, his bidding would be much lower.

"Who will start us out at two hundred?"

Good, they even started with a lower bid than the first three. Lissa raised her paddle and the emcee nodded.

"Three hundred?"

"Me!" That voice squealed again.

The emcee pointed beyond Lissa. "Thank you! How about three-fifty?"

No way was Lissa losing to that woman! Lissa raised her number again.

Haven grinned and gave her a quick thumbs-up.

More affirmation.

"Four hundred? Anyone four hundred?"

Silence. Yes! So, Missy Coburn's pockets weren't as deep as Lissa's mom imagined. Haven was hers and for only three-fifty!

"Come on ladies, the man is an experienced Collections Supervisor. Think of what he could collect on."

Oh, boy. Even with the spotlight bleaching Haven's face, his cheeks bloomed as bright as his tie.

"Yes, thank you, number fifty-seven."

Shoot. Lissa grabbed her paddle, ready to flash it up.

"Five hundred. Who'll go—?"

Five hundred? Lissa slowly raised her number. What happened to four-fifty?

The emcee pointed to Lissa. "Thank you number three. Six hundred? Thank you! Seven? Eight!"

Eight? Lissa bid and downed half her glass of lemon water.

Haven glanced at her again and nodded, wearing his toe-tapping smile.

"Ladies, this man has a million-dollar smile. Certainly, you won't let him go for a mere eight hundred dollars!"

They better!

"Nine hundred. Will anyone bid nine? Wonderful! One thousand dollars, who will—"

Lissa inched her paddle into the air. What she'd give to have an unlimited budget.

"Thank you! Eleven hundred. Anyone?"

Lissa closed her eyes. Please, God. She couldn't go any higher. Any more would dip into her home savings, and that would forestall her plans.

"Just eleven hundred for this Greco-Roman chin. Anyone? Okay, one thousand going once—"

Please, God.

"Going twice—"

A smile tugged at her lips.

"Going—"

"Eleven hundred!" Missy shrieked again.

No! Lissa gritted her teeth, forcing herself to look forward.

"Thank you, Missy! Now who will go twelve?"

Twelve? Lissa hunched in her chair and peered down. It was a measly two hundred dollars. Haven was worth it, wasn't he?

"Only twelve hundred for the cause ladies."

"Corliss, darling, bid!" Her mom tapped the program.

"Twelve? I'm looking for twelve."

"But I only budgeted a thousand," Lissa mumbled.

"Eleven going once—"

"For lands' sakes, Corliss, I'll give you two."

"Going twice—"

"Mom," Lissa growled in a whisper. "It's a silly date."

"You're so right." Her mom waved her hand. "That curvy redhead is more Haven's type anyway."

An invisible force seemed to launch Lissa's hand up in the air.

"Yes, number three, thank you. That's twelve hundred ladies. Not nearly enough. Who wouldn't love to drag their fingers through this man's hair?"

Leave his hair alone. It's mine.

"How about fifteen hundred for that privilege, ladies?"

Lissa grinned. She couldn't imagine anyone going fifteen for a collections agent, not even Missy.

"Fifteen? Ladies, that's mere pocket change for you. And this luscious man is a dog lover. How can you resist?"

Ladies, you better resist.

"That's twelve hundred going once . . ."

Lissa bit back a grin.

"Twelve hundred going twice . . ."

Her grin inched up.

"Twelve hun—"

"Two thousand!" Missy whinnied and then giggled.

No way! Lissa slumped. She looked up at Haven whose eyes pleaded to her.

"Sorry," she mouthed back.

"Darling, you're right to give up." Her mom patted her hand. "No man is worth that amount."

He is too worth it! Lissa tugged her hand away. But no way could she go two thousand. It would take months to build that amount back up in her savings. Haven would understand.

"Sold for two thousand dollars to Missy Coburn."

Wouldn't he?

Haven offered her half a grin then walked across the stage and down the steps to her left, into the audience. Going to sit with his "date" like the other men. Hmmph.

He detoured by her table and raised his eyebrows.

"Haven, I'm sorry. I don't—"

He swooped past without a word and wound his way to Missy. He aimed his lips for her cheek, but Missy turned and caught his lips with hers. The hussy.

Did that mean Haven's lips were no longer virgin?

And why was he smiling?

"Oh dear," her mom muttered.

"Mom, he's being polite. Missy is so not his type." Was she? *Don't be silly*. Still, disappointment weighted her stomach as she focused on the stage where the next bachelor was being announced.

"See what you've done." Her mom grabbed a program off the table. "Stubborn, like your father."

"I am not like my father." No way, no how. She was the responsible one.

Besides, Haven said he'd call. In just two weeks Miss Curvaceous Redhead would be a date of the past. And, even if she wasn't, it wasn't like Lissa needed a man in her life anyway. She could get by on her own, thank you very much. "I'm not worried."

Her mom glanced back at Haven's date as the emcee droned on in the background. "Darling, with that as your competition, I wouldn't be so confident."

Gee, thanks, Mom.

"Now, let's see who might make your man jealous." Her mom flipped open the program.

"Mom, don't you dare."

"Ah, yes, here we go. The cute one."

Naturally. Lissa rolled her eyes. The dangerous one. "Don't even think it."

"Darling, it's time you added a little adventure to your life."

Lissa's cheeks flexed, and she crossed her arms. "I'm not bidding."

Her mom grabbed the paddle. "Who said you had to?"

Chapter Three

And to conclude the evening, we've got bachelor number ten, Caleb Johnson."

Caleb sucked in a breath and prayed that at least one person would bid. Breathing out, he forced a smile. *Jeanette, this is for you.* How ironic was that? Going on a date to make his wife happy. She'd have told him to pretend he was jumping out of a plane. That would be much easier than this. And a ton more fun.

Clutching a red carnation, he took the first step beyond the curtain to mild applause. He squared his shoulders and strode to the center of the stage. They didn't need to see his insecurity.

"Ladies, this man is a true gem, a seeker of adventure. His hobbies are skydiving, bungee-jumping . . ."

Were, lady, those were my hobbies. He couldn't chance Aimee growing up without a dad too. Despite the emcee's deception, he pretended to smile. He tucked a hand into his front pocket and pictured Jeanette across from him, hands joined, freefalling from the plane. That was when he knew he'd fallen in love.

"We'll start the bidding at one hundred dollars. Who's adventurous enough to give me the first bid?"

Caleb squinted through the spotlight. He perused the crowd, looking for a raised paddle. Thousands had been bid tonight. Chances were, their money was already spent.

"Thank you, number twenty-seven. Who'll go two hundred?"

Caleb released a relieved sigh. At least he got one bid.

"Two hundred? Ladies, certainly an evening spent with this fine specimen of a man is worth two hundred dollars."

A side of beef. That was all he was. Jeanette would get a kick out of this. She was probably looking down from heaven, giggling.

"Wonderful. Three hun . . . make that three-fifty."

The last bidder sat at the table right in front of him. Yes, Jeanette would definitely laugh. The woman was at least twice his age, but the sophisticated brunette scowling next to the bidder . . . ? Perfectly straight chestnut hair. A fitted dress over a svelte build. One of the few women in the room who had chosen not to highlight her lips in blood red.

She reminded him of that woman in the parking lot this afternoon.

He stared at her, and she waved her fingers.

It was her! Now, she wasn't half bad. He wouldn't mind . . .

His stomach tossed. *Sorry, Jeanette.* How easy it was to forget.

Besides, someone like that brunette would never understand his world, what it was like to work your tail off just to be able to feed the family, not to mention keep a roof over their heads.

"Thank you. We've got four. Who'll give me five?"

The older woman bid again, and Caleb grinned at the absurdity. *That's at least five for heart disease research, Jeanette, even if it is someone the same age as our mothers.* Maybe that was a good thing. The woman wasn't ogling him like others. Maybe her goal was the same as his, raise money for a good cause.

"Six hundred. Six hundred. Ladies, this is your final chance this year for a date with this roguish bachelor."

Roguish? He clutched the carnation to his chest. If that was what these women wanted, they'd be mighty disappointed.

The emcee pointed out at the attendees. "We've got six. This man's worth at least seven."

The woman in front of him raised her paddle and stood up. "One thousand."

His jaw dropped.

So did the jaw of the parking-lot woman. A thousand bucks for a date. Unreal. But at least he wouldn't have to worry about this woman wanting more than an evening out. A relationship with her wasn't even on the horizon.

What a great answer to prayer.

"Adelaide." The emcee propped a hand on her hips. "Since when were you eyeing younger men?"

"Call the bid, Rosalyn."

Rosalyn cleared her throat and scanned the crowd. "Well, Adelaide's bid a thousand. Is there anyone who *dares* challenge her bid? A thousand going once . . . Going twice . . . Sold to number three. Adelaide Mor—"

Adelaide strode to the stage and stopped in front of the emcee. "Rosalyn, if you'll be so kind as to look at your list, you'll see that number three is not assigned to me, but to my daughter, Corliss."

Her daughter! No . . . There went that answered prayer.

His gaze shifted to the parking lot woman and a rebellious smile edged up the corners of his mouth. The woman with the chestnut hair and silky lips. And eyes narrowed in anger at her mother.

His smile flatlined. If eyes could shoot lasers, hers would be lethal. She clearly had no interest in him. Could this evening get any more miserable?

"Thank you, Adelaide, for enlightening me." With her mouth pinched, Rosalyn raised her gavel. "Sold to number three, *Corliss Morgan*."

He raised the carnation upward. *For you, Jeanette.* Compelling his lips to smile, and trying to spark one in his eyes, Caleb climbed down the stairs.

Adelaide greeted him at the bottom and took his hand, while Rosalyn concluded the fundraiser in the background. "It's a pleasure to meet you, Mr. Johnson."

"You too, Mrs. . . . ?"

"Morgan. But please call me Adelaide."

"Adelaide."

"Much better." She patted his hand. "Now before I introduce you to my daughter, I must explain that Corliss truly is a kind girl; she's just feeling slightly under the weather and wasn't in the mood for tonight's festivities. I assure you, she will make a most gracious date."

A thousand-dollar date, at that. How could he possibly give this classy woman the kind of evening she'd paid for, the kind of evening she was most likely accustomed to, when Burger King stretched his budget?

Keeping a grip on his hand, Adelaide led him to her table.

Corliss stood, wearing a smile as plastic as that Tupperware stored in his freezer. The lasers in her gold-brown eyes had cooled to a slow burn. "We meet again, Mr. Johnson—"

"Caleb." He released Adelaide's hand and reached for Corliss's. Her hand was small, tender, and felt good against his calluses.

"Please call me Lissa." Her icy hand shook his perspiring one and released it as if they'd concluded a business transaction. Maybe that was all this really was.

So why did he feel disappointed?

"For you." He held out the red carnation. There would be no kiss on the cheek, like the other bachelors offered.

Although he wanted to. Was that another betrayal of his wife?

"Why, thank you." A glimmer of a smile cracked through her plastic. "Mr. John . . . Caleb."

He pulled out her chair.

Her brows rose as she sat and more of a smile emerged. A very nice smile at that.

Adelaide settled her hand on Lissa's shoulder and gestured toward her open chair. "You two get acquainted while I visit the powder room."

The fire was back in Lissa's eyes, her gaze honing in on her retreating mother. Shaking her head, she turned to Caleb and whispered. "I need to apologize for my mom's behavior. I have nothing against you, but—"

He held up his hands palms outward. "No need to explain. I've a mother-in-law who seems to have the same agenda."

"So you understand."

"Absolutely. But I've also made a commitment, and I honor my commitments." *Like I committed to pay my mortgage on time?* He looked down, shoved that thought from his mind, then directed his gaze back to Lissa. He'd make his plea as sophisticated as possible, anything to appease this woman. "I can't, in good conscience, not fulfill my obligation to you, especially with your generous contribution to raising awareness for heart disease, and I would really like you to join me for an evening out."

Hmm. That was even the truth.

Warmth filled Lissa's eyes and the remainder of her plastic façade melted. "And how could I, in good conscience, not insist you fulfill that obligation? I would be honored to go out with you."

Honored? Really? Or was that merely a part of their transaction? A transaction he needed to complete as soon as possible. "Maybe we should set a time now. I've got next Friday open."

Laughter squealed behind Lissa, and her synthetic smile returned. Proof that she wasn't happy with this evening's results. "Friday . . ." She pulled her phone from her purse and scrolled through the screens. "Friday would work fine." Her gaze never left the screen.

"Where can I call to confirm?"

Lissa drew a business card from her purse and wrote on the back. "Here's my home phone."

"Thank you." He inserted the card in his jacket's inner pocket and found his own business card, the one that still read: *Heart of the Home Kitchen Design. Caleb and Jeanette Johnson, Proprietors.* "Uh, obviously it's just me now, but the number's the same. I'll call you to arrange a time."

"That would be fine."

Business transaction confirmed.

So why did joy sneak into his heart at the thought of going on a date again?

Yvette would be thrilled. Jeanette was probably clapping.

Why did he feel guilty?

Caleb looked down at his right hand perched on the doorknob to his daughter's room and imagined Lissa's hand joining with his.

It had fit so well.

And almost made him forget what Jeanette's hand felt like.

Almost.

Perhaps forgetting her touch was the next step in him moving on. Lissa's cold, then hot, then cold again attitude helped. He clearly wasn't the type of man she was accustomed to. And the date he'd take her on could no way measure up either.

With a grunt of frustration, he opened the door and peeked in on his daughter. The Lightening McQueen nightlight highlighted Aimee snuggled with her elephant, bear, and seal on a *Cars* toddler bed. Nothing was more precious than a sleeping child.

Was that how God viewed him as he slept? He tiptoed to her side, bent over and kissed her satiny cheek. So much like her mother.

Rubbing the fatigue in his eyes, he retreated from the nursery. Nursery? Was it still a nursery when the child was two and a half? Jeanette would know. That had been her job to know the details. All he'd had to do was create and love. That was easy.

He found his in-laws in the family room watching the final minutes of *The Tonight Show*, snuggled together on the couch as cozy as Aimee was with her animals. How wonderful for them to be able to grow old together and still have such affection for each other. If Jeanette had been allowed to grow old, they—

"Funny or not, that Jimmy Fallon is no Jay Leno." Aidan raised the remote and clicked the television off.

Caleb yanked off his bowtie, unbuttoned the top three shirt buttons, and slumped into the recliner. At last, he could breathe. "I like Fallon better than Leno."

"Well neither are Johnny Carson." Aidan slapped his thighs. "Well, my dearest Yvette, it looks like our boy needs some rest."

"Nonsense." Yvette leaned toward Caleb. "Tell us of your evening, *mon cher*."

It was dandy. Caleb bent forward, pulled off his cummerbund, and untucked his shirt. "How was Aimee tonight?"

Grinning, Aidan sat up straight. "Your little Nadia Comaneci learned to do somersaults."

"Guess I've got one talented daughter."

"You certainly do, and you know what else—"

Yvette patted Aidan's knee. "Enough, *mon amour*. I wish to know of Caleb's evening."

Frowning, Caleb lifted the footrest. "You'll be happy to know I'm going on a date next Friday with a very lovely young woman."

Joy lit Yvette's eyes as she clasped her hands in front of her heart. "Next Friday? So soon?"

"No need to prolong the agony."

Yvette's brows drew together. "Agony? You just said she was lovely."

"Very much so. And she wants to go out with me about as much as she wants to kiss a grasshopper."

"I hardly think someone would bid for you if—"

"Yeah, well, she didn't. Her mother did it for her, and the daughter was rather ticked off about it too."

"Caleb. I am so sorry. But you are still going out?"

"She paid a thousand dollars for the privilege." He rolled his eyes. "How can I afford to go on that kind of date? What are we supposed to do? I don't think dinner at Denny's is going to cut it, and I can't even afford that."

"Now Caleb Johnson, you hush that sort of thinking. There are plenty of ways to treat a lady to an elegant evening without costing a month's salary."

Aidan circled his arm around his wife's shoulders. "I'd be glad to supply the meal for you."

"Aidan, I appreciate that, but you've already filled my freezer—"

"That's for you and Aimee. If this young woman—"

"Lissa Morgan."

"—is as sophisticated as you claim, I'm certain she would enjoy a meal courtesy of Chez Amélie's sous chef."

Caleb rubbed a hand over his whiskered chin. Maybe that would work. Aiden's award-winning entrees were what drew people to Chez Amélie, Minneapolis' top French restaurant. "I like that idea."

"It's settled. And I know precisely what to make."

"Thanks." Caleb plucked a piece of lint off his trousers. If only an exquisite meal would be enough. "What else can I do? I need to treat her to more than a meal."

"That, Caleb dear, will be up to you." Yvette rose, walked over, and kissed his cheek. "And I am certain you will have a beautiful evening."

He quirked a half-hearted smile. "Yeah. It'll be one to remember, that's for sure." Probably as the worst date in bachelor auction history.

That had to be the worst experience in bachelor auction history! Lissa slammed the door of her Volvo and it echoed in her rental townhome's garage. How dare her mom put her in this situation? It had been two good weeks with no cravings. The longest she'd managed since high school. She couldn't give in now.

This relapse was all her mom's fault.

Not that Mr. Zipline wasn't completely gorgeous. And a total gentleman. On top of saving her life.

And why did he have to be so nice? For a moment, she'd even been excited about spending an evening with him. Then Missy's whinny cured her temporary insanity.

Now she was battling a more insidious insanity.

Lissa stared at her trembling hands and squeezed them into fists. It didn't help. Maybe a walk around the park would do it. She glanced out into the night's inky blackness as her garage door lowered. No. Too many crazies roamed at night. Wouldn't be safe.

Taking a deep breath, she walked into her townhome where music played from her kitchen radio. She folded her hands together, hoping to ease their tremors. *Please, God. I don't want to give in.*

Do something positive, something healthy. Drink water. That should do it.

She grabbed a bottled water from the fridge, downing the whole beverage in two gulps. Her hands still shook.

God, help me. How can I make it stop? In daylight, pulling weeds from her garden kept the cravings at bay, but in the moonlight, she'd likely uproot a marigold instead. Some people took up knitting. Others substituted food. Or a pet.

Now there was a good idea. A pet would curb the night cravings. Tomorrow, she'd go find that stray tomcat that kept her company when she gardened, and she'd coax him into the house, but that wouldn't help tonight.

Journal. That would do it. She thumped her water bottle on the cupboard and strode to her bedroom. Write down every screaming emotion. She pulled the journal from beneath the Bible on her bed stand, plopped down on her bed, and reclined against her pillows.

Gripping the pen, she stared at the lined page.

Just one wouldn't hurt, would it?

Don't be an idiot!

It'll stop the shaking. It'll bring that peace nothing else can give.

Sure, it'll kill you, too!

Her gaze strayed from the blank page toward her dresser drawer, and she swallowed hard. Why hadn't she gotten rid of them? Why had she kept temptation so near?

Just one. Only one won't kill you.

White-knuckling her pen, she scribbled on the page, *Mom made me do it.* She threw down the journal and slid off her bed.

Her whole body quaked as she opened her top drawer and reached in back, her quivering fingers searching. Ahh, there it was. Instant relief eased her shakes as she pulled out the box lined in plastic. Only two left. This, for sure would be the last. There would be no more driving miles away to keep her secret.

She grabbed body spritz off the top of her dresser and a freshly cleaned shirt from the second drawer. With her heart pumping maniacally, probably pleading with her to stop, Lissa carried the spritz, shirt, and small package to her back door. She hung the shirt on the hook next to the door, and set the spritz on the floor, in case someone decided to drop by and she needed a quick change and to freshen her hair. With her mom, even at this late hour, an impromptu visit wasn't out of the question.

If her mom ever found out her perfect daughter wasn't so perfect, it would probably send the woman to an early grave. Lissa couldn't be responsible for her mom's death too. Carrying her dad's death on her conscience was bad enough.

She stepped outside, made certain the door was shut tight behind her and that no windows hung open, and sat on steps guarded by two overgrown arborvitae trees. The perfect location to hide her one weakness. The butterfly weed and the prairie larkspur blooming in her garden should mask some of the scent too.

Of course her neighbors knew of her habit. That was why it was best to keep their relationships impersonal. By the time she could afford a home, this habit would be long buried.

She reached beneath the branches and pulled out a coffee can. *You can still stop, you know.* She glanced down at the pack. *One to calm your nerves.* Just one.

She tapped out the lighter plus what her mom called a coffin nail onto her palm. Her fingers shook as she flicked the lighter once, twice with no result. *This is God giving you an out.*

Read the Psalms instead. Certainly she'd find kinship in those words. She glanced at the lighter weighing down her hand. One more try. If it doesn't work . . .

Inhaling a deep breath, she flicked the lighter, and it flamed to life. That was affirmation, wasn't it?

A second later, orange-red embers shimmered from the end of her cigarette like the sequined dresses women wore tonight. She brought the cancer stick to her lips, inhaled, and held her breath.

For the first time in hours, peace stilled her body. She closed her eyes and slowly blew a wispy ribbon of smoke from her mouth.

What would Haven think if he saw her now?

What would Caleb think?

Why would his opinion matter?

Her mom would keel over and die. Lissa chuckled and drew more tobacco to her lungs. Not only her mom. She'd hidden this addiction from the world for ten years. The only person who had a clue was the one who taught her, and her father had taken the secret with him to his grave.

A mewling sound came from beneath the arborvitae on her right and a tiger-striped tomcat poked its head from beneath the branches. She tapped the ashes into the coffee can and switched the cigarette to her left hand. "You're a bit late, Tiger. I needed you about a minute earlier."

He jumped onto her lap, pressed his paws over her chest, sniffed at her face, and jumped back down by her feet. No kisses this time. Even he didn't like her smoking. Smart feline.

Lissa bent over and scratched behind his ears. "You hungry, boy?"

He meowed and nudged his head against her hand.

"Okay, I get the picture." She dropped her cigarette into the coffee can and then scratched the top of Tiger's head. "Be right back." She hurried into the house and filled a plastic butter container with a cup of cat food. It would be inhumane to let the poor thing starve, now wouldn't it?

She carried the container back outside, but Tiger had disappeared. "Here kitty, kitty, kitty," she whispered her call and placed the dish down on the steps. "Here Tiger, come kitty, kitty, kitty."

No sign of him. He was clearly off to make whatever other rounds he made at this time of night.

Now, back to her . . .

She looked at the top of the steps where she'd left the cigarette pack with its last remaining stick. The step was empty. She searched beside the steps. Nothing.

With a chuckle, she leaned against her house's door. That silly cat was probably sent by God.

One problem taken care of. Now, to handle the date next Friday with Caleb.

And that double-crossing excitement dancing in her heart at the thought of going out with him.

Chapter Four

Time to tackle the beast. With Aimee occupied watching Saturday morning cartoons, and U2 playing on his iPod, Caleb lay four days' worth of mail on the kitchen table and armed himself with his checkbook, a calculator, and a pencil. He downed his orange juice almost wishing he were a drinker. It would be easier to face these bills with a muddy head. Not that it would solve his problems.

He organized the mail into piles like Jeanette had taught him: bills and junk. There wasn't anything else. Ironically, the junk pile was the smallest. Not even credit card companies wanted his business any more. He carried the advertisements to the recycle bin and returned to the table where the bills waited like a stalking cat.

Get it over with, Caleb. With a knife, he sliced open the electric bill. The total due wasn't too bad, actually, and as long as he didn't turn on the central air, it should stay low. He put that in the *pay now* pile. The gas bill wasn't bad either, just the normal budget amount. That also went in the *pay now* pile.

Now for the cat's claws. Two envelopes had his mortgage lender's logo and address in the upper left corner. Ignoring them was no longer an option. The first letter, postmarked nearly a month ago, was almost kind, a standardized letter reminding him the mortgage was ten days past due. Their follow-up phone call, five days after the postmark, had encouraged, but didn't berate. He'd made them all kinds of promises he planned on keeping, but his dismal paycheck had turned him into a liar. He could imagine what this latest letter wanted.

Heaving a sigh, he slit open the envelope and read through the correspondence. Not so nice this time. Twenty-five days past due, it read. He glanced up at the calendar. Make that twenty-nine days now. Not even a month. They couldn't take away his home for being one month behind, could they?

He subtracted the energy bill amount from his checkbook. That barely left room for phone, water, garbage, insurance, life in general. A curse word slipped into his thoughts, but he didn't let it loose, not with Aimee so close.

There had to be something he could do, someone he could talk to that would help him through this. There must be some way to save their home. Asking his parents wasn't an option. They didn't have money to spare either, not with their life earnings poured into their mission trip. And his in-laws? They'd already done enough for him and they didn't have much to spare either. Not on a chef's wages.

The internet might have an answer. He'd have to bike to the library since he'd cancelled his home internet, but Aimee loved books, so no problem there. He stuffed the bank letter back in the envelope, put down his iPod, and walked to the stairs. Strains of *Scooby-Doo* filtered up from the basement. "Aimee-doodles, Dada needs you." He jogged down the short flight of steps to the foyer and smiled as he listened to little feet drag across the carpet.

"Hi Dada." She looked up at him, grabbed on to the railing, and jumped up one stair at a time. Oh, to have that kind of energy.

He kneeled as she reached his level. "How'd you like to bike to the library today?"

"I drive trike?"

"Not this time. You get to ride on Dada's bike."

"Okay, Dada."

He took her hand, pulled open the garage door, and his home phone rang. Bill collectors didn't work on weekends, did they? "Wait here, Doodles." He closed the door to the garage, then took the stairs, two at a time, to the kitchen. Why hadn't he cancelled his home phone service yet? On top of saving money, creditors would no longer have his number. *Tomorrow*, he thought as he picked up the phone then cleared nervousness from his throat. "Hello."

"Yes, may I speak with Caleb Johnson?" A very business-like, collector-like tone.

Caleb pinched the bridge of his nose. "Speaking."

"Caleb. Good to talk with you. This is Roland Harmes of Harmes-Ernst Homes."

Whew. Caleb collapsed on a bar stool and excitement tingled in his stomach. "Yes, Roland. What can I do for you?"

"With the economy as it has been, we've been doing some restructuring and plan on getting away from the distinctive home building. The market isn't there anymore."

"Don't I know it."

"Yes, I'm sure you do, and that's why I'm calling. We're getting a few bids for kitchen design. We've loved what you've done in the past and would like you to submit a bid."

Yes! "I'd be thrilled to, sir."

"Wonderful. Would you have an hour or so to drop by the office this afternoon so I can give you the details?"

"I sure do, but I'd have to bring my daughter along."

"Not a problem. I keep toys for my grandkids in the office."

"Great. I'll see you this afternoon." Caleb pumped his fist as he ended the call. This was an answer to prayers he'd been too afraid to breathe aloud. One client would give him enough for a month or two of mortgage payments, maybe more. That would lead to more clients as they'd see he could provide great kitchen design without Jeanette. After all, he was the artist to her brains.

Whistling, he strode to the entry where he'd left Aimee. She wasn't there, but the door to the garage was opened slightly. He sighed and stepped into the garage where Aimee was attempting to latch her helmet. His daughter was growing up too fast, becoming independent too quickly. Did that mean he was doing a good job?

"Let me help you, Doodles." He'd still make a trip to the library, but it would be for fun instead of research. No way was he going to let this new offer pass through his hands like others had since Jeanette's death. This time he'd give them what they asked for, not what he thought they really wanted. If he had to sacrifice his artistry and become a yes-man to put food on the table, then so be it.

"Your father's ghost is at it again."

A stack of manila folders dropped with a thud onto Lissa's desktop and she jumped. Clenching her jaw, she whirled in her chair and glared up at her coworker, Tyler Abernathy, praying her eyes flung darts.

He just chuckled.

The nerve of him, sullying her dad's memory. So what if Tyler was right? Why couldn't the jerk slink back to the slime pit he oozed out of?

Lissa sat up straight and glared at Tyler. "My dad brought more money into this bank than you know how to count and you better—"

"Abernathy, don't you have work to do?" A baritone voice spoke outside the cubicle.

Lissa blew out a relieved breath as Tyler slunk away. Good riddance.

Haven took Tyler's place in the cube opening and her heart did a two-step. He'd saved her more than once from Tyler's goading, and he looked darn good doing it too.

"Sorry about him." Haven handed her another folder. "Sorry about this too." His gaze met hers. "And about Friday night."

Her too. He'd never know how sorry, how she'd given in to her weakness. She shrugged. "It's all for a good cause, right?"

Except Haven ended up with buxom Missy while she was stuck with Mr. Menace.

"Yeah, a good cause." He cleared his throat and nodded toward his office. "Can I see you in five minutes?"

Now what? She manufactured a smile. "Sure." So he could tell her he'd changed his mind? That he'd made a mistake about asking her out?

Sheesh, lady! This was work, not social hour.

That didn't stop her mind from doubting.

With Haven gone, Lissa studied the stack of folders and sighed. Maybe someday this bank would join the twenty-first century and go paperless. But that took money this bank didn't have.

She opened the top file folder and skimmed through the homeowner's information. Naturally, another ill-advised mortgage approved by her father. What had he been thinking? Hadn't he realized that he wasn't doing the homeowners any favors by granting a dream they couldn't afford? How could he not have known that all dreams end?

Well, it was time to bring this homeowner back to reality. Calling on a Monday morning would give him all week to reset his priorities. With Rita's Pop Rocks crackling behind her, she punched in his phone number and waited as it rang once . . . twice . . .

At least this mortgage wasn't upside down like so many others. If this client couldn't make his payment, he could still sell, and even walk away with a little cash. Maybe purchase something more reasonable. No, the owner wouldn't be happy, but if he was willing to listen. Six rings . . . seven . . . No answering machine or voice mail. Not a surprise. Debtors excelled at avoiding collection agents.

She ended the call and made a notation of date and time of call in the folder. She opened the next file and grimaced. Now this homeowner wasn't so lucky. A short sale would net the bank only 85 percent of the loan amount. The cost of foreclosure wouldn't be any better. The best option would be for the owner to come current. If she could help him find a way to come up with the money . . . She began dialing the number then glanced at her computer clock. The call would have to wait. It was time to see Haven.

Please let it be good news.

She closed the file and hurried to Haven's office. A short week and a half more and he'd be free to date her. If he still wanted to.

Of course he did! But first, she needed to get Friday night's obligation out of her way. How dare her mom do this to her?

With a knock, she walked through his open door.

He gestured to a chair. "About last Friday . . ."

Uh-oh. Rejection was written all over his tone. "Yes?"

He leaned back in his chair and rubbed that sexy chin. "I'm sorry the auction didn't work out."

Tell me about it.

"But I want to let you know, that . . . that this date." He chuckled and rolled his eyes. "It's a one-night obligation. I've no desire to . . ."

She swallowed hard. "To do what?"

Peering down, he rubbed his nose. "This isn't terribly appropriate for work, but I want to get this out of the way so we can both get things done."

"Okay . . ."

His eyes rose and met her gaze. "I meant it when I said I wanted to ask you out. When I'm done here, of course."

She inwardly sighed her relief. "And I plan to accept."

"Whew." A grin spread over his face. "Who'd have figured asking someone out would be more difficult than saving homes from foreclosure?"

"I can't wait for you to officially ask." This next week and a half would be the longest in her lifetime. "Is that all you needed?"

"For now." He waggled his brows.

Containing her smile, she nodded toward his door. "Well, I suppose I should get back to work if I'm going to impress human services with my résumé."

"You've decided to apply for my position?"

"Absolutely. And I intend on getting the job too." Just like she intended on netting the perfect man. With her chin jutted high, she walked out of Haven's office to her cube. In fewer than two weeks she'd have her dream job and a date with Haven. She was living proof that when you followed the rules, life would go as planned.

Well, not counting the little hiccup this coming Friday night with Mr. Bungee-Jumper. But she wasn't about to let that get her down.

Wearing a grin that had to be permanently affixed to her face, she sat in her chair and flipped open the folder. She glanced down and a frown stole her smile. Where was the client's mortgage application? Worrying her lip, she thumbed through the remaining pages of the file she'd left open on her desk before seeing Haven. Tax returns, pay stubs, title insurance, promissory note, copy of loan, insurance and escrow information. Everything was there except for the application.

She lifted the file folder off her desk. Nothing. She thumbed through the remaining stack of folders from Tyler. Not there either.

Beneath the desk there was no sign of stray paper. Garbage can maybe? Her fingers tingled as she dug through the papers in her recycling pile and then through the wastepaper can.

"It was here. I know it was," she mumbled and slid open her file drawer.

"What are ya looking for?" Rita's Pop Rocks crackled as she spoke.

Lissa rummaged through the new files again. "The application from this folder. It's gone." It should be here, right where she left it.

"Sweets, it's no big deal. Probably got mixed in with something else. Print off another one for now."

"No big deal? You've got to be kidding! It has private information on it. Besides, I don't lose things." Her heart rate sped up, and she nibbled on a fingernail.

"Take a deep breath, Lissa. Things happen. It'll show up."

It had to. This made no sense. Lissa wiped the perspiration from her forehead and took a drink of water. What she'd give for one more cigarette. Thank goodness, she'd used the last two on Friday night. To purchase more she'd have to drive to the next county where no one would recognize her. That wasn't going to happen anymore. She inhaled a deep breath, held it for the count of four and blew it out.

Once she became supervisor, she'd have to deal with much worse than this. If she couldn't handle missing papers, what did that say about her coping ability?

"You're right, Rita." The application would show up in an obvious place and she'd laugh about it.

Right?

She didn't need another problem. The upcoming date on Friday was stressful enough.

Chapter Five

He's not here yet." Lissa held open her drapes as she talked into her cell phone.

"Aw, give him a couple more minutes." Rita's Pop Rocks snapped between each word. "He's not that late, is he?"

Lissa let the drapes fall into place. She glanced at her watch then at her khaki capris. "Five minutes of prolonged agony. You know, I should be dressed in an evening gown, ready to be picked up in a black limousine, and be treated to Chez Amélie before going to Orchestra Hall for a symphony."

"Don't expect much, do you?"

"I have a right to expect a thousand-dollar evening."

"Sheesh, woman, give the dude a break. I'm sure he's doing the best he can."

"Yeah, I know. It's just that—" A motor rumbled outside her window. She peeked out at a red Mustang convertible. Of course. The car oozed danger. "Well, it looks like he's here."

"I want the scoop."

"Give him a second to get out of the car."

"What's he driving?"

"A Mustang ragtop. Top up, thankfully." The last thing she needed was windblown hair.

"No way! I love Mustangs!"

"Good for you."

He stepped out of the car, and walked around the front carrying some kind of plant. A stray wave curled over his forehead, and he still hadn't bothered to shave that ridiculous whiskered shadow from his face.

"Well, what else?"

"The man can't even tuck his shirt into his jeans." And it looked way too good on him.

"Sweets, that's the style nowadays, in case you haven't noticed."

"Haven's style is good enough for me."

"I don't think you deserve this guy."

"After tonight, he's all yours." Besides, a guy like Caleb would never be attracted to someone like her.

"You know what, sweets? You are plain stuck up."

"Stuck up? Because I know what I need? It's certainly not Mr. Danger Zone."

"Maybe he's exactly what you need."

In an alternate reality maybe. Definitely not this one.

The doorbell rang, gratefully ending the ridiculous conversation.

She was not stuck up. No way. Tonight, she'd be more than gracious.

She curled her fingers around the doorknob and inhaled a breath. Good thing she was out of cigarettes. Tonight's date would likely send her cravings into overdrive. Pasting on a smile, she opened the door.

His squinty-eyed smile greeted her. Somehow, it looked good on him. He handed her the flowering plant, its scarlet petals dipped with white. "It's a hibiscus."

She nodded. "A red heart, Rose of Sharon." From the Song of Solomon, talking about a young woman's beauty. Her favorite flower. She fingered a blossom and her heart danced a disloyal jig.

"You know your plants."

"I do." Unwilling to subject her heart to more dancing, she kept her gaze on the flower. "Hibiscus tea is known for its heart benefits." Sucking on lower lip to hide the smile that wanted to jump out, she glanced up at him. "Thank you. This was very thoughtful."

"It's the least I could do." He shoved his hands in his pockets. "We should probably be going."

"I'll put this in my kitchen." So she could take a moment to breathe. How dare he come in looking all ruggedly gorgeous and give her, her favorite plant? The man was, in no universe, her type. After tonight, Rita could have him.

Why did that thought niggle at her? She set the plant next to her sink, smoothed her floral blouse and dandelion-colored blazer, and walked back to the entryway. "I'm ready." For this night to be over and avoid whatever temptation this rugged man placed on her heart.

Why did he have to be so considerate?

In one more week, the man who was truly her soul mate would finally be available. It would be total craziness to fall for Mr. Death-defying Adventure. That was the last kind of adventure she needed.

Caleb opened the passenger door to Jeanette's—change that, his father-in-law's Mustang now. Selling Jeanette's car so he could manage a few mortgage payments had been difficult, but worth it.

Lissa stepped in, and he closed the door behind her. So far, it wasn't going too badly. Yvette had been right about bringing a flower.

He slid in on the black leather seat, buckled, and glanced at Lissa to make sure she was buckled. Probably out of habit from checking on Aimee. Lissa sat up straight, eyes forward, her hands folded over a leather clutch on her lap as if challenging him to make this a memorable evening.

Who was he to back down?

He stepped on the brake and clutch and turned the key in the ignition. Now there was a sweet sound. The V8, 260 horsepower engine could gallop with any of the more expensive rides on the road. Jeanette had proven as much with him as a passenger enjoying the race. Aiden probably never experimented with speed. Today, Caleb wouldn't either.

He released the clutch and smoothly accelerated away from the curb. Truthfully, now that he lived for Aimee, the lure of adventure had nearly vanished. A reckless demonstration of manhood could leave his daughter orphaned. He wouldn't do that to her.

Besides, somehow he got the vibe that the pursed-lip woman seated next to him wouldn't appreciate a test of the engine's wild power. What he had planned obviously wasn't what she expected, but that didn't make it bad. Honestly, it would be far more enjoyable than donning a constraining monkey suit again, and Lissa looked just as amazing, and far more comfortable, in her outfit today than she had the other night.

He shifted in his seat. Was admiring a beautiful woman a betrayal of his wife? He shot a glance at Lissa sitting like a statue next to him. No, Jeanette wouldn't mind. She knew a woman's true heart beat on the inside and couldn't be measured by the luck of genetics.

Caleb had yet to see this woman's heart. But how could he even speak with someone who obviously didn't want to be in the car with him? Should he compliment her attire? Or was it too late for that? Maybe he should have said something when he first arrived. He was so out of practice at this dating stuff.

After shifting into fifth gear, he held his hand above the radio knob. "Would you mind some music?" Something to break up the silence.

"That would be nice."

"Any station preference?"

"I usually listen to KT95."

"Really?" Now, that was interesting. He pushed in the radio knob and pressed the fifth preset button. Mercy Me's harmonies sang from the car's surround sound.

Keeping his gaze on the road, he heard the leather in the passenger seat squeak as Lissa moved.

"You listen to this station?" Lissa said.

"Sometimes, if I want to mellow down. I usually tune to 101."

The leather squawked again. "Isn't that a Christian rock station?"

"You bet."

"So, you're a Christian?"

"Since I was born." He flicked the blinker and turned left onto the freeway ramp. Now he'd give this car a little test of power. It practically purred as he pressed down the gas pedal. "Some people have this aha moment, you know, some epiphany that leads them to faith. But not me. I've been tested and I've questioned, but I've never stopped believing."

"Oh."

That was all she had to say? Was conversation all evening going to be like dragging her onto a white water raft?

Remember, it's a challenge. "What about you?"

"Me?"

"Yeah, you know, are you a Christian?" Listening to Christian music didn't guarantee her faith.

More squeaking leather. "Since I was about sixteen. My dad, being interested in architecture, started attending a century-old, traditional church in south Minneapolis, more out of curiosity than anything. He'd made a lot of mistakes in his life before—"

"Don't we all?"

"—and got hooked on the message of grace. Eventually, I did too. As for Mom, I'm still trying to convince her."

"And your mom is the elegant woman who so kindly bid on me for you?"

Lissa laughed. Man, that sounded good. Maybe he was finally breaking through.

"Oh, yes. Mom can't stand the fact that I'm still single. She'd been married four years by my age."

"Isn't it funny how those who love us try to steer us down their chosen path? I'm afraid I'm not a terribly good at sticking to the norm." Jeanette hadn't been either.

Why did she keep poking her way into his thoughts? He clutched at the steering wheel as he turned right onto Rockford Road.

"I've been accused of being too inflexible, of never deviating from what's expected," Lissa said.

"The traditional church fits you." He glanced over and glimpsed a smile. A cute one, at that, with full lips framing in perfectly lined teeth.

"It really does." She closed her eyes. "To me it's a taste of heaven with the organ and hundred-voice choir. I find comfort, stability, in the repeated liturgies, and by singing hymns that have been sung for generations."

"Sounds beautiful."

"It is. What about your church?"

He laughed. "It's about as far away from traditional as it could get." He slowed and hung a left on Fernbrook. "Our Sunday meetings are held at a former movie theater."

"A theater?"

"If you think about it, it's the perfect place. We've got the built-in screen for lyrics, announcements, and stuff. Cushy chairs with cup holders. No one cares if you bring in your morning coffee. Nobody cares if my daughter talks too much. The people there view it as her form of worship. Nothing's planned—or at least it seems spontaneous. We've got a few guys who bring in their guitars. A gal who leads singing. Some high school kid is our drummer. There's even an eighty-something woman who adds her violin."

"I've never heard of such a church."

"Jeanette, my wife . . . my deceased wife." He swallowed the bitterness of saying that aloud. "Jeanette introduced me. I had the same background as you in a traditional church, and there's nothing wrong with them, but this service really touches my spirit, you know? There's a freedom to our worship. Sometimes the pastor wraps his sermon around whoever has a need for that day." He'd lost track of how many of those sermons had been directed at him over the past two years. "God doesn't care where you meet, but that you get together. He doesn't care how you worship, but that you do."

Silence answered back. He glanced over as Lissa turned her head toward the window and choked out a sad laugh. "Your church sounds like a gem, but it wouldn't be for me."

"Hey, I understand it's not for everyone. But it's right for me and Aimee, my daughter."

He turned right on 34th Street and followed a train of cars likely heading to the same event. Already, vehicles lined both sides of the street. Thankfully, the city center's parking lot still had openings. It would be the perfect location for capping off this evening.

"Well, this is it." He backed the Mustang into a parking space.

"This?" Heavy disappointment clung to her tone.

Didn't surprise him. He didn't think it qualified as a thousand-dollar evening either. "Just a little walk from here." He popped open the trunk and removed a wheeled cooler and a handled wood box the shape of an extra plump briefcase.

Sure, this date didn't look like much now, but she'd enjoy it.

And, if she didn't, that was her problem.

Lissa walked side by side with Caleb down a meandering asphalt trail. In one hand he wheeled the cooler, in the other he carried a mysterious wooden attaché. At least she didn't have to worry about him taking her hand.

He led her away from the city center, and toward a colorful garden blossoming around a pergola. Fountains, waterfalls, and a brick walkway accented the garden and called to her. Maybe this date wasn't going to be so bad after all.

But then Caleb strolled past the garden, away from civilization, down a gravel path surrounded by trees and green vegetation. Her heart thumped as the trees neared and shadows darkened the path.

What was she doing walking into a secluded area with a complete stranger who carried a strange oak box the size of a small suitcase? Had she completely lost all sanity? Her gut had told her from the beginning that this man wasn't safe.

With a shiver, she stopped and cleared the fear rising in her throat. "Where do you think you're going?"

He jerked to a halt and slowly turned toward her, his eyebrows nearly touching. "I wanted to surprise you."

"I don't need the kind of surprise lurking in those woods." Chances were, where Caleb was headed was perfectly innocent and safe, but taking the risk made no sense. She pulled keys from her pocket and clutched them in her hand as she took baby steps backward on the path. She'd hoped to never need her self-defense training, but was glad she had it.

His brows furrowed deeper. He glanced back toward the trees, then at her, before smiling and shaking his head. "You're right. You're absolutely right." He held up his hands palms out. "I never considered how this would look to you. Trust me, that path takes us right to a very populated park, but we'll take the long way around."

The thumping in her heart slowed to its normal cadence. "I would appreciate that."

"Hey, no problem." Dragging the cooler behind him, he jogged to her side. "You'll have to forgive me. I don't date much and forget about the bad guys out there. I'm not one of them, but how would you know?"

Precisely. She hugged herself as the trail led them past the garden to a concrete sidewalk teeming with people of all ages. Safety definitely lay in numbers. Trees still bordered them, but at least she and Caleb weren't alone on this path.

It was a pretty area, but she still wondered where he was taking her. Of one thing she was certain, it wouldn't be the kind of place that would give her any return on her—her mom's—investment.

If only she could have afforded the extra money to bid on Haven, she'd be dressed in sequins and seated beside him at Orchestra Hall instead of walking into an outdoor circus with Mr. Cheapskate. Only a few more hours and the evening would be over. She would have done her good deed by raising funds for heart disease awareness. Wasn't that what this evening was about in the first place?

Whispers of a jazz band bounced off the trees and grew louder as they walked. Giggling teens ran past, stuffing artery-hardening cheese curds and mini donuts into their mouths. Parents pushed mini-van sized strollers through the gathering throng, oblivious to the fact that their babies were screaming.

Talk about chaos.

Stop being a brat! She mentally kicked herself. Rita was absolutely right. Lissa was being just as snarky as her mom and her mom's wealthy friends, the very attitude she'd moved away from when she rented her townhome. Caleb deserved much better than she was giving him. *Lord, help me see the good in this evening and in this man.*

The trees peeled away, letting the band's emotional strands flow unfettered around an open park filled with picnicking families. Outdoor vendors lined the asphalt sidewalk that curved up a hill and meandered through a grove of trees. The trail circled around the picnickers and past a pond where a fountain spilled over like a Jell-O mold. Her gaze stopped on an outdoor amphitheater beside the pond. A live jazz band played on stage. No, they weren't an orchestra, but they were pretty good.

"I've got us a spot down there." His hands full, Caleb nodded toward the middle of the throng. He began weaving around stadium chairs and picnic blankets, some filled with people, others empty.

How could he have a place saved when he'd just picked her up? Puzzled, she followed him through the crowd.

When they were within a football field's distance of the stage, he stopped in a small clearing and rested the cooler. "Would you mind waiting here? I need to go kiss my daughter good night."

"Your daughter?" On a date?

Caleb pointed toward the stage, a grin sprouting on his face. "On the purple quilt up ahead, with the red wagon. There's a munchkin turning somersaults by that couple sitting on lawn chairs."

Squinting, Lissa peered ahead. "I see them." Add two more to this date. This guy was completely clueless. And why did he need her to wait here? Sorry, that wasn't happening. "Let's go." She grabbed the cooler's handle and charged forward. His family wouldn't see her anger, but when he drove her home, she wouldn't hold back.

"Lissa, please." He jogged to her side and brushed her arm. "I'll only be a second."

"For what?" She dropped the cooler and crossed her arms over her chest. "You're not making any sense, and I'm rather upset off that you've invited your whole family on our date."

"What?" With that now-familiar confused squint, he glanced at his family, and back at her. "You think they . . . ?" Wrinkles formed on his forehead as his squint deepened, and then he chuckled. "Boy, I'm messing up badly tonight, aren't I? They're not staying. They offered to save me a spot up close, that's all."

Lissa closed her eyes and wished she could sink into the ground. Not only was she snarky, she was an idiot for jumping to conclusions for the second—or was it the third?—time tonight. She was worse than her mom's snooty friends because she knew better. Or she should know better. "Caleb, no you're not messing up, it's all on me. And I'm so sorry. I tend to think in straight lines and that doesn't allow for other alternatives. Would you forgive me?"

He quirked that too-adorable smile. "If you can forgive me for being dense."

"Forgiven." She offered her hand and he gave it a firm, yet gentle shake.

Then he gestured toward his family. "I'll be right back." And he took a step toward them.

She grasped his arm. "Why can't I come with you? I'd love to meet your daughter."

Sighing, he laid the handled box on the grass. "It's nothing against you, but I don't want my daughter seeing women come and go in my life. She's lost her mom already, and I don't want her to become attached to someone who's not staying around."

"I'll only see her this once. There won't be time to become attached."

"Please respect me on this. Aimee is my priority. Period."

"I understand." Well, not completely, but she had to admire someone who put his daughter first. Not all dads did. Her own father certainly hadn't until his final years. She patted Caleb's arm. "Hurry back."

"I will." He winked and jogged off, weaving gracefully around picnickers while a saxophone soloist blew a rollercoaster of notes into the air.

She sat on the cooler, tuned her ears to the music, and wrinkled her nose. The group was talented, but jazz melodies were too unpredictable, dissonant, dark, and didn't seem to follow any set of rules. So unlike a symphony that was laid out with mathematical precision. Why didn't it surprise her that Mr. Skydiver would prefer jazz?

Biding her time until Caleb returned, she looked down at his strange wooden box. Grapevines were engraved into the top along with a Bible verse, "Taste and see that the Lord is good . . ." Psalm 34:8. Regardless of the mysteries this box held, it was a beautiful piece of artwork.

Not unlike the artwork God was painting this evening with. The sun setting behind her cast long shadows over the park. Warmth still clung to the air, and a cool front had taken much of the humidity along with it this morning. Really, it was a perfect evening to enjoy God's splendor, even if she had to do it with Caleb, not Haven. To be honest, there could be worse ways to spend an evening.

She took a seat on the wood box, and glanced toward Caleb's family seated in the center of the grassy park. His daughter, with pigtails leaping from the side of her head like a fountain, circled pudgy arms around his neck, and his laughter rang out as he rubbed his nose against hers. Even from this distance, Caleb's joy was evident. With a kiss to her cheek, he peeled her arms from his neck and handed her over to the woman. Caleb's mom? The toddler struggled to be released and the woman lowered the child to the ground, then grasped her hand. The older man took the child's other hand and they walked away.

With thumbs curled around belt loops, Caleb faced his family as they walked up a grassy slope, disappearing into the grove of trees. His shoulders heaved before he turned back to Lissa.

Oh, to have experienced that kind of love. Albeit, after her dad started attending church, things had changed, but during her growing up years she'd missed out on the kind of relationship Caleb obviously had with his daughter.

Shoving away her jealousy, Lissa grasped onto the handles of the cooler and the wooden box, and walked toward her date.

The music quieted as he jogged toward her, a smile lighting his eyes. Her stomach danced a rumba. It clearly didn't understand that Caleb wasn't right for her.

"Thanks for waiting."

"It wasn't a problem."

"I'm glad you understand." He relieved her of the box and led her toward their picnic quilt lined up nearly center with the stage. Probably the perfect location for viewing a concert. Not so close that her hearing would pop, yet near enough to read the expressions of the musicians. She looked behind her at the throngs of people reaching back to a tree line, with picnickers still arriving. His family must have arrived very early to secure the spot.

"I take it you've never been here before." He placed the box on the edge of the blanket.

"No." She wheeled the cooler next to the box and gazed toward the amphitheater. A new band walked on stage, dressed like the Pointer

Sisters with their big hair and 1940s style dresses. "Does this happen often?"

"I'm not sure how often they have concerts here. I've just come for this one that's close to the Fourth of July. It's this city's Independence Day celebration, and I think they party well."

He knelt next to the box and opened it near the handle. A large piece of Styrofoam filled the interior, perfectly fitting the box. He pulled out the Styrofoam, spread both sides of the box out until their bottoms touched, and then flipped it over creating a raised flat surface. Their own little table. Ingenious! Next, he dug his fingers into a seam in the side of the Styrofoam and split it open, revealing a complete place setting for two: two transparent acrylic plates, crystal wine glasses, flatware, plus a tablecloth and napkins colored with grapes and vines. He laid the tablecloth over the box's now flat surface and arranged the place settings over it.

Impressive.

The trio onstage harmonized on "Don't Sit Under the Apple Tree" as Lissa picked up one of the glasses and studied it. It wasn't crystal, as she'd first assumed, but the crackling acrylic gave it a rich appearance. "Where did you find this?"

He shrugged. "Target, I suppose."

"They sell this set at Target?" She splayed her arms over his table setting.

"Not as a set." He opened the cooler and pulled out a plastic food container. "I think the plates and glasses came from Target. Silverware too, I suppose. The napkins? I think Jeanette got them from some linen store."

"But what about the box you keep it in? I've never seen one before. It's such a clever way to carry a picnic."

Caleb stilled, his hands reaching into the cooler. "You think it's clever?"

"Absolutely. I like the idea of not eating on the ground. I'm sure ants can still get to it—"

"Believe me, they can."

"—but, it gives the whole picnic idea an element of sophistication."

"Really?" His squinty eyes were back as he set another container on the makeshift table.

She nodded. "I know some people who'd love this. Where can I buy one?"

With a chuckle, Caleb sat on the ground. "Amazing. Jeanette said the same thing. She loved *pique-niques*. Said I should market this."

She blinked with the realization. "You made this?

"Sure did." Again, he reached into the cooler and lifted out two smaller containers.

"What about the carvings on top of the box?"

He shrugged. "Mine."

Wow. The man was a gifted artist too. "Well, Jeanette was right. You've got a gift that should be shared."

He picked at his jeans. "Working with wood was a hobby before Jeanette died."

Uh-oh. "I'm sorry. I didn't mean to bring up hurts."

He stared toward the fountain. "She's part of my life that only exists in memories. My in-laws say I need to move on. They're right, but it's hard remembering all the good times, knowing we'll never share them again. And when I look at Aimee, I see so much of Jeanette."

A tear trickled down his cheek. How beautiful to see such devotion, and how wonderful that must have felt to be so in love.

Would she and Haven share that someday? "You really loved her, didn't you?"

He dragged his arm over his eyes. "Yeah. I guess I'm blessed that God gave her to me in the first place. And now I've got Aimee. That's more than most people ever have."

Mom has me. Was she a blessing to her mom, or a painful reminder of the death of Lissa's father?

"But hey." Caleb reached into the cooler again as "Near You" sang from the stage. "Enough of that. Tonight's about new beginnings and I don't plan on wasting time feeling sorry for myself."

Touché. Lissa glanced up at the cottony clouds floating overhead. *Okay, God. I get the message.* At least Caleb had a reason for having a pity party. Her only excuse was that she wasn't at Orchestra Hall.

As Caleb poured sparkling water into her goblet, she tried to peek through the seven containers spread over his makeshift table and cooler.

"I hope you like French cuisine." He pulled a cover off a vegetable dish. The scent of thyme filled the air.

"French?" Her favorite! She leaned over the appetizer and breathed in. "What is it?"

"Crudités." He pulled at another cover revealing a pasty dish. A rainbow of scents, from anchovies to garlic to cayenne pepper arose from the bowl. "And this is tapenade."

Lissa's stomach rumbled and she crossed her hands over it. Her mouth watered simply from breathing in the tantalizing scents.

From the top of the cooler Caleb picked up a baguette, a bread knife, and a small cutting board. Was there anything he hadn't thought of? He sliced off the end of the baguette, spread tapenade over the top and handed it to her. If it tasted as good as it smelled, she'd have to rethink her opinion of her date.

She bit into it and her eyes rolled back. Pure bliss. She spooned a small helping of crudités into her mouth. The tang of lemon complimented the touch of thyme coating the vegetables. Superb. This man should be creating dishes at an exquisite restaurant, not slaving at a glorified hardware store. She couldn't wait to see what else he brought.

"You made all this?" She pried the lid up on the largest container and peeked in. Two hand-sized baguettes sandwiching sliced tomatoes and what appeared to be a tuna mixture. She glanced up at Caleb who was taking a bite of the crudités. "This must have taken you hours."

He shook his head and placed his spoon on his plate. "Wish I could take credit for it, but let's say I have a very good connection."

"Indeed." She pulled out a tuna baguette and bit into it. Hints of garlic and onion flavored the albacore. Eager to see what other delicacies hid inside the food containers, she pried the remaining ones open. Cucumber salad, cheese cubes, and what looked like lumps of white chocolate. "What are these?" She took a chocolate out of the box and sniffed.

"Well, the chef calls it Corsican Mendiant au Chocolat Blanc. Me, I call them Grandpa's white chocolate cookies."

"Your grandpa made this?" She bit into the confection and dashes of walnuts, dates, and orange peel tempted her to eat more.

"Actually, my father-in-law did."

"My compliments to him." Completely ignoring her normal protocol of eating the main dish before dessert, she downed the remainder of her cookie, and then spooned servings of the rest of the meal onto her plate. This feast could easily compete with her favorite French restaurant. Maybe Mr. Hardware Store was deeper than she imagined.

As they ate, the slender reach of tree shadows crept over their blanket. Onstage the musical trio concluded with "Boogie, Woogie, Bugle Boy." A beautiful tribute to the troops and veterans for Independence Day. Lissa leaned back and caressed her full stomach. Maybe not all the food was good for the heart, but it shouldn't object too loudly. After all, she didn't normally eat like this.

"It was good?" Raising a brow, Caleb began packing away the few leftovers.

"It was delectable." She rose from the blanket and sat in a lawn chair. "I can't remember having a better meal." And here she assumed she'd be eating peanut butter and jelly.

Rita was right. She was a snob.

She sat up straight and faced Caleb. "And I owe you a big apology."

Holding a container in mid air, his brows narrowed. "Why?"

"I made assumptions about this evening, wrong assumptions, and I'm afraid I haven't treated you fairly."

"You haven't—"

"Yes I have. So, please accept my apology. I've had a perfectly enjoyable evening."

A grin spread across his face. "Thanks. Apology accepted." He nodded toward the stage where men and women, dressed in black, carried violins, flutes, oboes, and other instruments onto the stage. "But the best part of the evening is yet to come."

Her eyes widened. "The Minnesota Orchestra?" she whispered.

"You bet." With a twinkle lighting his eyes, he refilled their goblets with sparkling water and sat in the chair next to her.

Slack jawed, she stared at the stage and blinked away a tear. Oh, yes, she was a first-class snob. Caleb had given her the evening she longed for, but in a different package than she expected. Actually, a more beautiful package than she could have imagined.

Whoever ended up with this gem of a man would certainly be blessed.

Walking beside Caleb, pulling the cooler behind her, Lissa glanced up at the stars blinking in an indigo sky. She was even getting the moonlight stroll she'd desired. How could God be so good to her, when she'd been so nasty to Caleb?

He hadn't complained once, although he had every right to.

"Thanks, again, for the evening." She glanced over at the man she'd earlier defined as dangerous. In one hand, he carted his picnic box, and with the other, he pulled along the red wagon filled with lawn chairs and the quilt. Good thing his hands were full or she'd be tempted to hold one, but her hands were reserved for Haven.

"I'm glad you enjoyed it . . . so far." With a lopsided grin, Caleb tugged the wagon up the concrete trail leading to his Mustang.

"So far?" There's more?

He pulled the quilt from the wagon and spread it over the hood of his car. "What's a Fourth of July celebration without fireworks?"

Fireworks? Like the ones he was setting off in her heart? It was time to extinguish them. After all, people got burned by fireworks if they weren't careful.

He jumped up on the hood and offered his hand.

For a moment, she stared at his enticing invitation and swallowed. Was she betraying Haven by accepting it?

Don't be silly! This man was just being a gentleman, as he had been all night. She took his hand, callused and warm, yet gentle, and allowed him to pull her up on the hood. Disappointment surprised her when he released his grip. Still a gentleman.

Raising her knees, she settled on the hood. Only inches separated them now. His woodsy cologne crawled through the air and seeped into her senses.

Yes, he was definitely dangerous. She folded her hands and tucked them between her knees as the first rocket screamed upward and burst above them into a dazzling white chrysanthemum. Soon, the night sky was filled with a kaleidoscope of sizzling color, some even forming heart shaped explosions.

She clamped her knees tight against her hands that wanted to betray her and latch onto the safety that Caleb's had provided.

But there was no safety with him. So what if he was the perfect gentleman and a staunch believer? A man who loved skydiving and rock climbing could never be for her. She glanced over at Caleb staring wide-eyed like a child at the fireworks blooming above them.

Yes, he was definitely dangerous. Especially to her heart. She better guard it so she wouldn't get burned.

With sweaty palms, Caleb walked Lissa to her townhome's front door. Who knew he'd enjoy the night so much, especially the way the evening started with her acting cold as January? But she'd definitely thawed by the end of the evening. Maybe his in-laws were right. Maybe it was time for him to move on. He stole a glance at Lissa as she unlocked her door, and his heart rate accelerated.

Once she ditched the attitude, he'd enjoyed the evening. She'd savored Aiden's meal, which proved she had good taste. When the orchestra walked on, her eyes had lit with the same wonderment Aimee had when trying a new adventure. And when they watched the fireworks, Lissa hadn't hidden her glee. Beneath that stoic façade, there was something endearing, something childlike about her.

Yeah, she seemed pretty reserved, but he'd never find another life mate like Jeanette who'd shared his love for adrenalin drives. Besides, Aimee needed a father, so his risk-filled days lay far behind him.

Lissa cuffed her hand over the doorknob and looked back at him, her gray eyes sparkling like the firework display. "Thanks for the evening. I thoroughly enjoyed it."

"You're welcome." He stuffed his hands into his pockets and

swallowed what felt like a tennis ball. He was a risk-taker wasn't he? *Just open your mouth and ask.* "I, um . . ." He cleared his throat. "I was wondering if we could do this again. Um, if you'd like to do something else with me."

He held his breath as her eyes met his.

Raking her teeth over her lower lip, she peered down. "I'm sorry, but I'm not ready for a relationship."

Chapter Six

What Lissa would give to be a miracle worker. With her telephone headset on, she ran her finger beneath the Williams's enormous past due amount and knew she had to encourage an unlikable option. "Mr. Williams, I can appreciate the sentiment behind your holding on to the heirloom."

She picked up her family photo kept next to the vase of gladiolus from her garden and stared at her father. "I know, as well as anyone, how important it is to have that tangible memory of the deceased. But think about what your grandmother would want. Would she want you to lose your home if you had means to catch up on your mortgage by selling her lake cabin? Do you place the value of holding on to an heirloom above keeping your home?"

"I don't know." Mr. Williams' voice shook.

Lissa set the portrait back on her desk, tuning out the homeowner's excuses, all of which she'd heard before. She'd never understand people's priorities. "Well, think about it for the night, and I'll get back with you tomorrow. Remember, I have no desire to take your home from you, but if you can't make your payments, Hennepin Bank and Trust will have no choice but to begin foreclosure procedures. We'd much rather work with you to find an amicable solution. Thank you for your time, Mr. Williams, and I look forward to talking with you tomorrow."

With a huff of breath, Lissa punched the End button. At least Mr. Williams hadn't turned the air blue with his language, a rarity these days. She flipped his file shut, swiveled to face Rita, and, with a grin, rolled her eyes. "William Williams. Now what sane person would saddle their child with that name? No wonder the guy has issues."

And you don't? She swatted the thought away.

Rita snickered. "And sweets, you were laying it on awfully thick there."

"If that's what it takes. Here, the family has means to get themselves out of the hole and they're worried about sacrificing some dumpy old cabin." She raised her hands palms up and held them like a balancing scale. "House." She lifted her right hand. "Cabin." She lowered her right and raised her left. "It's a no-brainer, don't you think? Besides, he's the one who brought it up. If it wasn't a viable option, he wouldn't have told me about it."

"I s'pose so." Sucking her annoying candy, Rita handed Lissa a file. "Here's a new one for ya. Name's just as good. A Mr. Jonathan Johnson."

Lissa chuckled and accepted the file. What had his parents been thinking? She opened up the file and groaned. Another one of her father's charity cases. Well, she'd deal with it after lunch. She placed the Williams file in the front of her filing cabinet under Follow Up and the Johnson case in the back of the To Do folder, a folder that was far too full. Tonight she'd stay late and likely catch some of the homeowners during suppertime. If only they understood that she wasn't the bad guy here.

"Care to join me for lunch?" Lissa reached beneath her desk and retrieved her insulated lunch box.

"As long as you tell me about your date with Mr. Hunkalicious."

"Please." Lissa made an exaggerated wave. Rita had no clue how right she was, and how utterly bad Caleb was for her heart.

"Give me a sec to clean off my desk and I'll meet ya outside."

Perfect. This way Lissa could practice her stoic face and not let Rita see the blush that would certainly rouge her cheeks. She hurried past the cubicles, aiming for the back door.

"Lissa!" Haven's voice sounded behind her.

Warmth crept over her face anyway as she stopped. She took in a breath, forced down her grin, and turned toward him. "Hi."

He jogged up to her. "Got a minute?"

"I was heading to lunch, but that can wait."

"Well, it isn't company business."

She bit her bottom lip, desperately trying to keep her smile in check. "We'd love to have you join us." Certainly Rita wouldn't mind.

Glancing at his watch, Haven pushed open the outside door. A blast of ninety-degree heat and high humidity rushed into the building. "I've got a couple minutes before a meeting that's going to go till who knows when." He led her to a wooden picnic table that would make better kindling than seating. Who knew when it had last been sanded or stained, leaving it open to outdoor elements? But a new picnic table wasn't exactly a priority in this economy.

She pulled on the hem of her skirt so her legs wouldn't catch slivers from the wood, and sat across from Haven. "What do you need?"

He cleared his throat as he shifted on the bench. This certainly wasn't the confident executive she was used to sitting across from. "Thought I'd tell you, my obligatory evening out is mercifully over."

"Your date from the fundraiser?"

He nodded and rolled his eyes.

"It was that bad?" She clasped her hands together, hoping to hold in her glee.

"Gives me a whole new appreciation for what you ladies go through with ogling men. The woman didn't care about the limo ride or dinner at Mancini's or the opera. She had one thing on her mind and, by the end of the evening, was upset that she wasted her money." He shivered, even with the noon heat. "That woman had more tentacles than an octopus. I will never put myself through that again, no matter the cause. Please tell me your date with the skydiver went better."

Visions of Caleb's French picnic and the strength of his hand flashed through Lissa's memory. The evening had been well worth the investment in the cause, but Haven would never know that. She laid her hand on the table, palm up in invitation, hoping Haven's strength surpassed Caleb's. "Like you said, it was a one-time thing."

Haven glanced at her hand and scratched the back of his neck. "We are still co-workers, and technically, I'm still your boss . . ."

How stupid could she be? She jerked her hand off the table and winced as a sliver dug in. "I'm sorry. I don't know what I was thinking."

You were thinking about Caleb. She massaged her hand, trying to loosen the sliver.

Haven grinned. "Not that I would have minded taking your offer. Come this Friday, we'll see what happens." He winked.

This Friday? "Are you asking . . . ?"

He shifted on the bench and redness glowed from his tan cheeks. "You know, it's much easier demanding money from someone who's fallen behind on payments than it is asking you out."

"So you are—?"

"Would you?" Uncertainty hooded his eyes.

"I'd love to."

He blew out a breath and shook his head. "Friday night. We'll celebrate my new job. Pick you up around seven?"

"I'll be ready."

Standing, he glanced at his watch. "Gotta go."

"Thanks, Haven." She closed her eyes and imagined herself spinning cartwheels across the bank's lawn. She'd caught the perfect man, now to get the job. The cartwheels morphed into somersaults and then a pigtailed child took over her imagination. She saw a father lifting up that child, and hugging her with more affection than Lissa'd ever experienced.

No, no, no! Mr. Dangerous would not invade her thoughts. The sliver in her hand loosened and she tugged it out. That man belonged with someone else, someone who dared put up with a risky lifestyle.

"Hey, sweets, you sleeping?"

Rats! Lissa forced a smile at Rita. "Just in my happy place."

Rita nodded toward the bank door. "Passed a whistling man on my way out. What's up with you two?"

Lissa gnawed her lip. "He asked me out."

"No kidding. The Puritan and the prude." Rita giggled and plopped down across from Lissa. "Not exactly movie of the week material. Sounds like a match made in Dullsville, if you ask me."

"I'm not asking." Lissa unzipped her lunch box and flipped up the cover. "As a matter of fact, we're going out this Friday."

"I won't bother asking for details. You'd put me to sleep."

"Ha, ha."

"Now, what I want the four-one-one on, is the dude you saw Friday night."

Lissa bit into her sandwich, getting a mouthwatering blend of turkey breast, tomato, avocado, lettuce, and a hint of mustard on whole-grain bread.

"Aww, you're avoiding me." Waggling her eyebrows, Rita pulled a bag of chips from her paper lunch bag. "You must have had a good time."

Lissa swallowed and raised her chin. "I did." So what if she had fun? That meant nothing. Absolutely nothing.

"You liked him!" Rita's eyes widened and she grinned. "Well, if that ain't something. Guess I don't give you enough credit."

Mustard dripped from the sandwich strangled between Lissa's fingers. "He was a nice guy. A gentleman even, so he wouldn't be for you, but that doesn't mean he was right for me either."

"Man, oh, man. You got it bad for him!"

"I do not!" Lissa threw her mushed sandwich into the box and glanced up at two co-workers huddled in the building's shade, smoking cigarettes. What she'd give to join them right now.

"Dish it, sweets. I need to know everything."

"There's nothing to tell." Trying to squelch her fingers' need to caress a cigarette, she withdrew a carrot from her lunch box. "He treated me to an outdoor concert and fireworks."

"Woo, hoo. Fireworks already." Rita unwrapped a Hershey bar and bit off the end. "Please, please tell me you're going out again."

"We're not." The words whispered from her mouth as she peered down at the carrot embraced between two fingers. She dropped the carrot and clasped her hands in her lap. "He asked me but I . . ." *I really wanted to say yes.*

Rita squeezed her head between her hands. "Sweets, when it comes to men, you have no sense."

"What's wrong with Haven?"

"Nothing, if you don't mind being bored to tears."

"I think you're jealous."

"You're a hoot." Rita slapped her hand on the table. "I'm gonna give you one little piece of advice. If that hunk from Friday gives you another call, don't think, just say yes. Got that?"

"Yes, Mother." She'd say anything to get Rita off her back. So, why did she smile inside thinking about a second date with Caleb?

She picked up her mangled sandwich and bit into it. She'd already committed this Friday to Haven. Truth be told, she didn't know where that one date would lead to, but it, at least, held promise for the future.

"Hey Lissa!" Tyler's bossy bass woke Lissa from her reverie.

Keeping the sandwich in her hand, demonstrating to him that she was on lunch break, she glanced at him holding the door open. "What do you need?"

"Phone call. Some William Williams wants to find out where he can bring payment."

Yes. She dropped her sandwich and bumped fists with Rita before jogging toward the building. "Thanks, Tyler." She squeezed past him and speed-walked down the hallway to her cubicle. What perfect timing for one more success story. The bank board would see that she, indeed, was the right person to supervise the collections department.

Sitting down on her chair, she inhaled a breath then opened her file drawer and pulled out the Follow Up folder. She picked up the line as she flipped the file open. "Mr. Williams, this is Lissa Morgan. How may I help you?"

"You were right, about the cabin."

Of course she was. "I'm very glad to hear that."

"And, we've found a buyer already. A cousin, actually, so the memento will stay within the family. Given that, we'll be able to make payment in full tomorrow. So, if you'll tell me the exact amount owed, I'll bring it in."

"Certainly, Mr. Williams." Lissa glanced down at the Follow Up folder and blinked. Where was the Williams file? It should be right in front. "Um, one second, Mr. Williams, let me locate your information." Her heart rate sped up as she thumbed through all the files in the folder. It had to be here. She'd put it in right before lunch. "May I put you on hold for a minute, please?"

"Not a problem."

Okay. Breathe. It's in here. She'd just misfiled it in her hurry to go lunch. Maybe she'd mixed it up with Jonathon Johnson's information.

That had to be it. She thumbed through the To Do folder. The Johnson file was in back, right where she left it. This could not be happening. Again! She was always so careful.

"Got a problem, Liss?" Rita's Pop Rocks snapped as she plopped down in her chair.

"The Williams file. It's gone. Vanished. And the guy's on the phone wanting to make a payment."

"You sure? I mean, you're always so organized and all."

Apparently not organized enough. Okay. Calm down. The computer had all the information she needed. That was where she'd get the exact figure anyway. She moved her mouse, waking the computer, and located the Williams file. First she'd take care of Mr. Williams, then do a thorough search of her desk.

Forcing a smile, she pressed the blinking button on the phone. "Mr. Williams, thank you for holding." Hopefully, he didn't hear the nervous crack in her voice.

"No problem."

She relayed the amount due and hung up, but her hands still tingled with anxiety. This was not a mistake she made. She scanned the top of her desk. Follow Up folder, monitor, phone, flowers, family picture, life goals. Clean. Like it was supposed to be so things didn't get lost.

Could it have fallen beneath her desk? She rolled her chair back, bumping into Rita.

"Hey, girl, cool it. Unless that file grew wings, it's at your desk somewhere."

"But it's not where it's supposed to be." She glanced beneath her desk then swiveled and looked under Rita's. Nothing but cords, feet, and empty Pop Rocks wrappers. It had to be in her drawer. She pulled out one folder at a time and rummaged through each file, every single piece of paper. Nothing. It had simply vanished. If only this bank would join the twenty-first century and go paperless, missing paperwork wouldn't be a problem.

How would she explain this to Haven? How would it affect her promotion?

Worst of all, how would it affect what Haven thought of her? If he believed she was a flighty female, not only did they not have a future,

they didn't have a beginning.

Caleb's leg bounced as he waited for Roland Harmes in the Harmes-Ernst Homes lobby. Clutching the drafting tube to his heart, he smiled at the wall-length credenza opposite him that had oak trees and a winding brook etched into stained cherry wood. A backyard scene from Roland Harmes' cabin. One of the rare side projects Caleb had taken on a few years back. No, it wasn't for a kitchen, but that hadn't mattered to Roland. He liked Caleb's artistry and quality, and that was what mattered.

So, how could Mr. Harmes not like Caleb's kitchen plan?

The office door opened and Roland stepped out. He glanced at the credenza and smiled. "Get lots of compliments on your work there, son."

"Thank you, sir."

"Why don't you step on in to my office and show me what you've got."

Caleb backhanded the perspiration from his forehead and walked into the office. He pulled his designs from the tube, spread them across a drafting table, and handed over his estimate for the job. As Mr. Harmes studied the drawing, Caleb cleared his throat to talk about it, but all coherent thoughts fled his mind. The selling part had always been Jeanette's job, but his work should speak for itself, shouldn't it?

The estimate was reasonable. Even discounted from what he and Jeanette had charged as partners. Best of all, he'd be able to catch up on his mortgage and maybe gain new customers in moderate-priced homes as opposed to the executive clientele he and Jeanette once courted.

With a poker face, Mr. Harmes looked away from the drawing and paged through the estimate. "Nice work, son. Reasonable too."

Caleb held his breath. Finally, he'd catch his first break since Jeanette died.

"But . . ." Mr. Harmes rolled up the design, inserted it in the tube, and handed back the estimate.

"Is there a problem?" Caleb squeezed the back of his neck. "Do you want to discuss the design? Is the estimate too high?"

"No, no." Roland tapped the drafting tube. "Fact is, it's too good."

"Too good?" How could something be too good?

"Yes, son. Your work belongs in million-dollar homes."

"Is the estimate too much? I'd be glad to—"

"Now son, it's not a good thing to give your talent away. It'd be downright stealing if I accepted that bid from you, and you know it."

Caleb tightened his fingers around the tube. "I could rework the design, make it simpler."

"Son—"

"Please, Mr. Harmes, I really need this job."

Mr. Harmes turned away from Caleb and walked to his office window that overlooked the junction of Highways 55 and 169. "People are not buying new homes. What's selling are the foreclosures, and that's bringing the values down in a lot of areas. Why buy new, when you can get a steal elsewhere? The truth is—" Mr. Harmes looked back at Caleb, his jaw shifting. "The truth is, our plans fell through. You're not the only one needing work."

The tube fell from Caleb's hands and thudded on the low-napped carpet.

How could he possibly save his home now?

Clutching the Follow Up folder between her fingers, Lissa knocked on Haven's door. She still didn't know what to tell him. How would she explain that a client's entire file had simply vanished?

He glanced up from his computer, smiled, and waved her in. That smile would shift into reverse very quickly.

Well, here it goes. She opened his door and stepped through, ignoring his motion to sit. "I have a problem."

He leaned back in his chair and again directed her to sit.

This time she obeyed and laid the folder on top of his desk. "Right before lunch, I put a file away in here." She placed her palm on the folder and inhaled. "Tyler called me away from lunch, said this client wanted to make a payment. When I returned, the file was gone."

"Gone? I'm not sure what you're saying."

"Gone, as in, it's not in here."

"What about—"

"It's not anywhere in or on or under my desk." She clenched her teeth together. Tears were not allowed, especially if she wanted the promotion. There would be far worse problems than this.

Frowning, he rubbed his temple. "It's not like you to lose things."

"That's just it, I didn't lose it. I distinctly remember putting it away. Someone had to have taken it."

"Why would someone do that?"

"I don't know. And the thing is, it's not the first time." Oh no. Closing her eyes, she lowered her chin to her chest. Why did she have to blurt that out?

"Excuse me."

Lissa slumped in her chair. "Last week, the mortgage application from a client's file went missing. I haven't found that yet either."

Haven sighed and ran his hand over his mouth and chin. "We'll put out the word to watch for the file. In the meantime, be a little more conscious of what you're doing. If you think someone's taking them, for whatever reason, lock your drawer whenever you leave your desk."

"I will," she mumbled and stood, grasping the Follow Up folder. "I'm very sorry about this."

"Lissa." Haven rolled back in his chair, came around the desk, and sat on top of it, crossing his arms. "Stuff happens, okay?"

Subtle mint scented his cologne, tempting her to move closer, but she stayed still, maintaining professional propriety. "It won't happen again." Of that she was certain.

"You're forgetting your good news."

"Good news?"

"Tell me about the client. The one who wanted to pay. Did you talk with him?"

That's right, she did have good news. How could she have forgotten? "Yes, actually. He took the advice I gave him and will be bringing in payment tomorrow."

A broad smile framed Haven's perfect teeth. "Why am I not surprised? You keep doing what you do best, and I'll worry about the minutia. By the way, I appreciate your telling me about the missing file. Everyone makes mistakes, but it takes guts to admit them. And that's exactly the type of person this bank needs right now."

Wanting to engulf him in a hug, Lissa backed toward the door. "So, we're still on for Friday night?"

"Try to talk me out of it." He winked.

Breathing a relieved sigh, she walked out his door. Yes, she was still in line for the promotion, but only if she could keep a handle on her paperwork. Any more mess-ups and advancement wouldn't be the issue. Keeping her job would be.

She hurried to her desk and pulled out the To Do file. Mr. Jonathan Johnson was about to learn how to come current on his mortgage, giving her and Hennepin Bank and Trust one more victory. How could they think of firing their most productive worker?

But they would have grounds for firing someone who continuously lost files.

Caleb pulled out his phone, checked the caller I.D., and grimaced. No way was he answering that call. He jammed the phone into his back pocket while stifling a curse. The last thing he needed was for Aimee to parrot his profanity. He walked to her room and listened at the door. Not a peep. Thank God for naps. Too bad he couldn't take one.

He strode back to the kitchen and stuffed a piece of paper into his pocket. Another prayer answered with a "no." Did God ever say "yes" anymore? He grabbed the baby monitor and carried it into the garage, its three stalls now housing only a ten-year-old F150 pickup and Jeanette's baby—her Suzuki SV 650 motorcycle. Pearl, she'd named it, for its official color: Pearl Lively Yellow. What a perfect description of his wife.

Bitterness clawed up his throat as he walked toward the bike. Yvette called it the death cycle. If they'd known then what would be lethal for Jeanette, would they have made the same choices? He glanced at the monitor and nudged away a rogue tear.

Most likely. If Jeanette had known what would kill her, she would have challenged it and defeated death. But death had been cowardly and snuck up on her when she was alone.

He rubbed his hand over the cycle's black leather seat and aluminum frame and pictured Jeanette, almost becoming one with the machine, her copper locks flying from beneath her helmet as the cycle hugged mountain curves. "Sorry, Jeanette. I don't have a choice."

Selling his matching candy grand blue machine hadn't been nearly as difficult. But it was the house or this. One more piece of his wife being stripped from him. All he had left was the house and Aimee. And a few trinkets of value only to him. He'd do anything to keep the house—the home they'd built together.

And that meant making this phone call. He pulled the piece of paper and cell phone from his pocket and dialed the number. Perspiration puddled on his forehead as the phone rang once, twice before his friend answered.

"Caleb, that you?"

"Yep." He straddled the cycle and cuffed his free hand over the handlebar. In his imagination he squeezed the throttle and chased the wind up Duluth's slopes. "You still interested in my bike?"

"Hey, man, sure. You selling?"

"Yeah, I guess it's time to let go."

They talked further and agreed on a price. Come this afternoon, one more garage stall would be empty. No more bikes. No Mustang. Just a ten-year-old, gas-guzzling pickup no one else would want.

He sank down beside his pickup onto the unforgiving cold concrete and covered his face with his hands. Why was letting go so miserably painful? What else would God require from him?

Live. The word whispered in his ear like a soft April breeze.

Live. Just as his in-laws said. Perhaps they were right. Maybe now was the time to take a risk again and turn his grieving into living.

He glanced at the phone in his hand and scrolled through the listings. Lissa's number was still there. It had to be a sign. So what if she said "no" the first time. Her excuse had been that she wasn't ready for a relationship. Well neither was he, but that didn't mean they couldn't spend some time together. Later tonight, once Lissa got off work, he'd take one more risk and give her a call.

Chapter Seven

Lissa pulled on her walking shoes and double-bowed the laces. A brisk walk was precisely what she needed to erase Caleb from her mind and to chase the tension from her day. If she had found that missing file, it would have been a perfect day with three clients promising to bring in payments tomorrow. What a coup that would be for her to add to her résumé, proof that three more delinquent mortgages were now up-to-date. Her efforts alone could keep the bank solvent, when so many other banks were going under.

She stretched her neck to the side then rotated it forward and to the opposite side. Where was that file? Her mom would tell her not to cart around trouble. That was easy for her to say. She didn't have her potential future staring at her this week.

Lissa shook out her fingers that ached for smoking's hand-to-mouth action. Good thing her last pack was now empty, as today's temptation would be too great. Instead, she raised her left arm perpendicular to her body, palm out, thumb up, and circled her arm fifteen times. She rotated her arm so her palm faced backwards and her thumb pointed down. One . . . two . . . three . . .

The phone rang and she moaned.

Shaking out her arm, she walked to the phone, glanced at the caller I.D., and joy lifted the edges of her mouth. She forced the smile down. Haven was supposed to make her smile like that, not Caleb. She stared at the phone as it rang a third time. Just talking to him wouldn't hurt though, would it?

She grabbed the phone and hit the silver button in the middle before voice mail could pick up. "Hello."

"Hi, is this Lissa?" His voice was as smooth and creamy as whipped butter.

"Ye-es." And hers seemed to be clogged with gooey caramel.

"This is Caleb Johnson, from Friday night."

As if she could forget him. "Caleb, hi." Cradling the phone between her ear and shoulder, she raised her right arm, thumb up, and rotated it forward. How dare his voice sound so sweet to her ears? "Can I help you with something?"

"Actually, I know you said you weren't interested in going out again, but I guess I'm not one to give up trying."

"Caleb, I—"

"I'm going to Minnehaha Falls on Saturday, and was wondering if you'd come with me."

"Minnehaha?" Her voice cracked. Tempting her with one of her favorite places? That was downright cruel. How dare he? Wasn't 'no' a strong enough word?

"I love going there, but my daughter is too young to appreciate it, and I prefer not to go alone. No strings attached. I'd like to go with someone who appreciates nature, and clearly you do."

"This Saturday, you said?" No strings attached? She couldn't say yes, could she? That would be leading him on, and that was clearly wrong.

"If this Saturday doesn't work, no problem. I happen to have a rare Saturday off. Usually I work both weekend days."

"Saturday would be fine." She clamped a hand over her mouth. That didn't come from her, did it?

"Great. How about I pick you up, say nine o'clock?"

She nodded and jerked the hand from her mouth. *Tell him you can't.* "I'm looking forward to it." Oh brother. Since when had her mouth taken over her brain?

"Me too. See you Saturday."

She hit 'end' without saying goodbye. Oh, Rita was going to love this. But it wasn't a date. Not really. Caleb said he wanted a companion for the day, right? Arghh. She pulled her hair tight behind her head and slipped it through a ponytail holder.

It was time for that walk. Maybe she'd walk some sense into that brain of hers and call Caleb back with her regrets. That would be the right thing to do.

But a traitorous smile tugged on her lips as she pictured him sitting beside her on the hood of the Mustang, with fireworks bursting overhead. What would one more outing with him hurt?

Rain pounded on the bank's roof as Lissa strode toward her cubicle, folder in hand. She glanced at her watch and groaned. How could it be five o'clock on Friday already? What she'd give for one more hour today. Any other day she'd stay and finish this project, but today seeing Haven was priority number one.

She veered into her cube and tapped Rita on the shoulder. "You ready?"

"I am. The real question is, are you?"

Lissa puffed a breath upward and her bangs fluttered. All week long, she'd anticipated tonight's date with Haven but, naturally, just this morning the bank announced that they'd planned a going-away celebration following work. Their date would have to wait.

And then there was that ill-advised outing tomorrow with Caleb. What had she been thinking when she said yes? Well, tomorrow would be the last time. Any more, and she'd be leading him on.

She slapped the folder on the desk. Work would have to wait too. For tonight. But come Monday, ten-hour days might become the norm. That alone would solve the Caleb problem. There wouldn't be room in her schedule for him. She plopped into her chair. "You would think we'd see an end to all the possible foreclosures, wouldn't you?"

"Remember, all those foreclosures are job security for us."

"I suppose." She lifted her flower vase and retrieved the key to her file drawer. "Word has it, they're going to announce who gets the temporary supervisor job at Haven's party."

"That's what the grapevine says. You haven't heard anything, have you?"

"Not a word." Lissa slid open her drawer, thumbed through the files, and froze. No. It couldn't be. Swallowing the knot in her throat, her fingers trembled as she pulled the file from the drawer. She opened it and a groan creaked from her mouth. No . . .

"What's up, Liss?"

Lissa circled toward Rita and tossed her the file. "This."

Her Pop Rocks snapping loudly, Rita paged through the folder. "What's the problem?"

"The problem is, that's the William Williams file, the one I'd lost, plus the missing mortgage application. I've wasted hours looking for them, and voilà, they suddenly appear in my drawer."

Rita rolled to Lissa's desk and peeked into the drawer. "Where it was supposed to be?"

"No." Lissa whispered. They weren't there before. They couldn't have been.

"Well, there you go. They were just misfiled. Mystery solved. Let's go party."

Party? Now? When she was losing her mind? Lissa snatched the folder from Rita, filed everything correctly, then slammed the drawer shut and locked it.

"Come on, Liss. It ain't a big deal."

"Isn't."

"Whatever. You made a mistake. You're human. Now let's go." Rita stood and slid her chair beneath her desk.

But it was a big deal, especially if Lissa wanted the promotion. The bank would never want a manager who couldn't keep track of important paperwork. One little cigarette would ease her way through this. She wiggled her fingers, hoping to chase away the craving, then stood and grabbed her purse. "Okay. Let's go." Rita was right. This was one little mistake surrounded by years of superlative work and she wasn't about to let it ruin this evening.

She dug an umbrella out of her purse as they walked toward the back door and popped it open. Huddled beneath it, she and Rita jogged across the parking lot, a steady drizzle pattering overhead and dripping off the sides. They hurried into Patrick's Pizza Parlor. She gave the umbrella a little shake before folding it. Frowning, she glanced around the heart-disease inducing restaurant overflowing with diners from the evening rush.

"Back there." Rita pointed to a glass door at the back of the room. They squeezed around tables surrounded by families, parents training their kids early on the wrong way to eat, with their pizzas laden with cheese, and refillable pitchers of pop centered on each table.

They'd all end up like her dad.

Not her. She'd learned from his fatal mistakes. If only people would listen to what the medical experts told them.

Lissa opened the door to the party room spilling co-workers' laughter and conversation throughout the restaurant. Streamers waved across the ceiling, and bouquets of helium balloons softened the room's corners. Lissa glanced toward the buffet table where Haven stood greeting his guests, that ever-present smile gracing his face. A smile she would miss seeing every day. But if not seeing him daily meant getting to know the heart of the man she respected, it would be worth it.

Haven looked toward her, and a spark ignited in his eyes.

Butterflies waltzed in her stomach. His smile was for her. Life couldn't get better than that, could it?

Leaving Rita, Lissa wove between the guests toward the table. Her arteries hardened just looking at the cheese-burdened spread of pizzas and garlic bread.

"You made it." Haven handed her a plate already filled with two triangles of pizza, thinly coated with mozzarella. "It's turkey-vegetable. Ordered just for you."

"Really? Thank you." She bit into the end sprinkled with corn, broccoli, carrots, and mushrooms. Now this was mouth-watering. All these people had no clue what they were missing.

"As for me"—Haven chose a piece weighed down with cheese and several different types of meat—"I plan on living a little dangerous tonight. This evening, you and I can walk it off."

This evening? "We're still on?"

"Are you kidding? It won't be the dinner I planned, but if you save a little room, I know a cozy place that serves amazing berry and yogurt parfaits. We can walk it off with a stroll around Lake of the Isles, if you don't mind my dog tagging along."

"I love Schroeder."

"Yeah, me too." He ran a hand over his chin. "Arthritis is slowing him down a lot, so the walk could take a while."

Which meant more time with Haven. She grinned. "Is that supposed to be a problem?"

"You tell me." He winked at her. "For now, I better mingle, but I'll catch up with you as things wind down."

"May I have your attention?" The bank president's booming voice silenced the partygoers.

The president stood at the end of the buffet table, holding his beer glass in the air. "On behalf of Haven Carlysle, I welcome you all here tonight as we thank a co-worker for his exemplary service at Hennepin Bank and Trust, and wish him well in his upcoming endeavor."

Plastic glasses plunked against each other. Lissa surveyed the table for a beverage, and Haven offered a glass with clear, bubbly liquid. "Carbonated strawberry water," he whispered. The man had thought of everything.

Smiling, she clinked her glass against his.

"With Haven's departure"—the president placed his glass on the table—"we have an opening for a supervisory position."

Lissa clutched her glass and closed her eyes. This was it. Temporary job or not, whoever was assigned the position would have the advantage once the bank began interviewing for Haven's permanent replacement.

"We've given careful consideration to many of the bank's existing employees, and have decided the person who best fills our immediate need for a temporary Collections Department Supervisor is . . ."

Lissa closed her eyes. Please, God, please. The president's pause seemed to last as long as a trip to the dentist.

"That person is Tyler Abernathy."

A smattering of applause echoed throughout the room. Lissa clenched her jaw yet forced a smile. His appointment wasn't a surprise as he did have seniority.

"Don't worry." Haven whispered into her ear. "We expected this, remember?"

She nodded. Yes, it was expected, but that didn't mean she wasn't disappointed. It was temporary. She'd have plenty of time to prove she was the right one for the permanent position.

"These are nice, but . . ."

Affixing his the-customer's-always-right smile, Caleb watched the woman draw her finger down the front of the cabinet on display. "But?" He needed this sale today. The manager had hinted at as much this morning when Caleb clocked in.

She walked to another kitchen display and frowned. "They lack originality. Any artistic quality."

That's what you get in a big box home improvement store, lady. Now, to put that thought diplomatically. "Mrs. Nickels, I appreciate your thoughts. As you see, our cabinets are high quality. To maintain affordability for the customer, though, we don't do custom-designed cupboards, but I can design a kitchen that will be practical, yet have heart." His typical sell. Women usually loved that line. The growing smile on the woman's face demonstrated it worked with her as well.

"Give me a moment, and I'll show you what I can do." He jogged to his workstation, grabbed his graph pad and hurried back to his customer. "Now tell me, how do you use your kitchen? Beyond cooking, what is its purpose?"

As Mrs. Nickels explained, Caleb took notes and sketched as ideas flowed from his mind to his pencil. Satisfied, he showed her his rough draft.

"Lovely, you've captured precisely what I want." She surveyed the cabinet displays. "It's too bad your cupboards lack the same heart as your kitchen design. If only you could give me a changing motif on each cabinet face."

"What exactly are you imagining?" The words snuck out of Caleb's mouth, dragging him onto treacherous terrain. His creative flow refused to be stopped.

She closed her eyes and tipped her head toward the ceiling. "I'm picturing an inlaid T, a cross that moves from cabinet to cabinet."

"I think I know what you mean." Again, he put pencil to paper creating something this store, his employer could never supply. "You want people to notice the cross. If it stays in the same place on each door, it becomes stagnant and gets lost, but if we move it around, people will notice." He finished his sketch and held it up for her perusal.

"Yes, yes!" She clasped her hands together. "Finally someone who understands."

Thank you, God. He hadn't lost his talent.

"Now, how do I order this?" She touched his drawing.

All his joy plummeted to his stomach. How could he be so stupid? That was what he got for following his heart. Now, the customer would never be satisfied with what this store offered.

He set the pad on a Corian countertop and scratched the side of his neck. "Mrs. Nickels, I need to apologize. I was out of line and shouldn't have shown you something we can't offer. For a design like this, you should go through a master cabinet maker. You won't find specialized door design at a big box store."

"But this is precisely what I want."

Well, maybe he could give it to her. Maybe this was his chance to move on. He tugged his wallet from his back pocket, dug out an old business card, and handed it to Mrs. Nickels. "I do custom kitchens—"

"Caleb."

No, no, no. Bile gnawed at his throat as he swiveled toward his boss. "Vince?"

"What are you doing?"

"I . . ." Caleb's voice caught in his throat.

"Pardon me, ma'am, I need a moment with my employee." Vince narrowed his gaze at Caleb and pointed toward a workstation in the center of the store.

Like a robot, Caleb led the way. This was not happening. It had to be some maniacal nightmare. Hadn't he suffered enough the past two years? He studied the concrete floor as Vince neared and plopped something on the workstation's counter. Caleb's graph pad.

"Nice work, Caleb." Ice coated Vince's voice. Even July's heat couldn't melt that. "You were our best designer."

Were?

A frown seemed frozen on Vince's face. "We can't have you sending our customers away."

"I realize that, and I'm sorry. I got carried away."

"Again."

Caleb sighed. Yes, again. But his pencil couldn't be restrained. Would they ask a runner to stand still? A singer to remain silent? "I promise, it won't happen again."

"You are correct." Vince crossed his arms. "Because you no longer work here."

"But—"

"Gather your things, and I'll walk you out."

"Please. I've got house payments, my family—"

"Something you should have thought of beforehand." Vince shoved the graph pad into Caleb's hands. "Let's go. We'll mail your check."

Numbness overtook his whole body as he walked from the store, ignoring the stares of co-workers. Was everything going to be ripped away from him? Couldn't God allow him one victory?

Maybe tomorrow, with Lissa. Aw, who was he kidding? A successful date with her was as likely as paddling backwards up rapids.

Lissa banished all thoughts of Tyler's temporary victory as she walked side by side with Haven down Edina's France Avenue. The afternoon rains had whisked away the clouds and much of the humidity, leaving the air warm but not sweltering. Tonight was going to be the date of her dreams.

Though Haven's hands seemed rooted inside his pant pockets. Not once had he even brushed her arm, much less held her hand. He was being the perfect gentleman, just as she anticipated. Never had she had a date with someone who avoided physical contact so much. Rita was probably right. The man's lips were virgin. Oh, to be the one to remedy that.

"Here we are." He pulled a hand from a pocket and opened the door beneath a red and white striped awning.

The nauseating scent of sugar blasted her as she stepped onto black and white checkered linoleum squares. A waitress, wearing jeans and a T-shirt with the shop's name embroidered on it, brushed past them, holding up a tray overflowing with ice cream concoctions. "Be right with you." How could people stand to eat all that ice cream, fudge, and whipped cream? Lissa's stomach roiled at the thought of it.

Seconds later, the server returned. "Hi, welcome to Ye Olde Ice Cream Shoppe. Table for two?"

"Please." Haven deposited his hand back in his pocket.

"Inside or patio? It's a beautiful evening to sit outside."

He pointed to the outside door. "Patio sound good?"

"Wonderful." Anything to get her out and away from all that sugar.

They followed the waitress past a '50s style lunch counter, complete with red-cushioned swivel stools, and then outside where a gated patio fronted France Avenue. They sat on grated metal chairs by a matching white table, and she breathed in. The exhaust fumes smelled better than all that sweet confection trapped inside.

"Nice place, huh?" Haven spread a napkin on his lap.

"Outside is wonderful."

"That it is." He relaxed in his chair and looked toward the sidewalk. "I love the people watching. Seeing families walk together and . . ." Haven blew out a breath and peered down, his eyes hidden from her view.

"Is something wrong?"

"That family." He nodded toward the sidewalk as a man and woman passed pushing a stroller, a beagle puppy straining on a leash. "I remember when Schroeder was that little. He loved walking." Grimacing, he shook his head. "I don't think a first date is the right time to talk about my longing to be one of those families."

Could the man get more perfect? "I don't mind." She closed her eyes and pictured them walking down the sidewalk, a dog leading the way, and a toddler clinging to their hands, her copper pigtails bouncing as she skipped between them.

Copper pigtails? Caleb's daughter! Why hadn't she told Caleb no?

"My turn to ask you if something's wrong."

"Huh?" She shook her head, dispersing Caleb's image. "I guess it's something I want too. Someday." Whoa. Good save.

"Yeah, someday." He grabbed a menu off the table, and his true smile returned. "For now, let's have some ice cream . . . or yogurt."

"Good idea." She focused on the extensive heart-healthy dessert section of the menu that even included nutrition values. Pineapple-raspberry parfait, tiramisu, chocolate-dipped strawberries. More proof that healthy food could be delicious.

"Are you ready to order?"

Lissa startled and glanced up at the waitress. "Sorry. I didn't hear you. I was too busy admiring your healthy dessert selection."

"Ah, yes. The boss added that after his wife had a heart attack. She's fine now, but insisted that they add healthy items to the menu. It's become very popular, so the boss is always trying out new desserts."

"Good for him." Lissa studied the menu. "Why don't you bring me the berry cheesecake in a glass? That sounds divine."

"It is. You'll love it." The waitress turned to Haven. "And you, sir?"

He rubbed his chin. "After that build-up, I can't very well order the turtle sundae, can I?"

"We can make it with low-fat ice cream."

"I don't think so." He slapped the menu closed and grinned at Lissa. "Today, I'm celebrating, so bring me the unedited, original version and don't skimp."

"Good for you." The waitress gathered the menus. "I'll be back shortly."

Lissa suppressed a groan at the very thought of all the calories packed into a turtle sundae, but she smiled at Haven anyway. "You're living a little dangerously, don't you think?"

"One sundae won't hurt, Liss."

She looked downward. "I'm sorry. I've got this terrible habit of—"

"Of looking out for people's welfare, making sure we don't make life-changing, harmful, even fatal choices, like you do with homeowners every day. I'd say that's commendable."

"Not everyone sees it that way."

"People don't like to have their mistakes pointed out. Personally, I sometimes wish someone would have been honest with me." With glazed-over eyes, Haven looked back toward the sidewalk. "Some mistakes are irreversible."

Lissa followed his gaze, which seemed focused on a young family. What could he have done that was so awful? She sat silently, waiting for him to expound. If this weren't a first date, she might dare ask. But that question was better left for later.

"Your desserts." The waitress set their food on the table, drawing Haven's attention away from the street. Perfect timing.

Lissa scooped up a bite of cheesecake topped with strawberries and savored the subtle hint of orange. What a brilliant concoction.

"It's good?" Haven brought a spoon overflowing with ice cream, fudge, caramel, pecans, and whipped cream to his mouth and moaned as his lips closed around it.

It did look delicious, but she didn't dare try it. It would be addicting and she already had one addiction too many. Besides, there was absolutely nothing wrong with this cheesecake. "What are your plans for this week?"

He wiped a napkin over his mouth and leaned back in his chair. "A little putzing around the house, fixing some things I've let go. Probably spend a few days up in Duluth with Dad. I guess, just relax before I dive into the new job."

"That sounds wonder—" Lissa screeched as a mottled, whitish goo splatted from above onto the edge of her dessert glass. "Ewww." She shoved the glass away and struggled to keep down the food she'd already swallowed.

"Liss, I'm sorry." He jumped up and grabbed the dessert off the table. "I'll go get you another one."

Her body shivered. As if she could eat anything else now. "No. I think that did it for my appetite."

"I think you're right." With a sigh, he sat back down and glanced at his sundae. A smile slowly turned up the corners of his lips. "Well, maybe not."

"Go ahead and eat your dessert."

He shoved it to the middle of the table. "I'll get it to go." He waved at the waitress who had just stepped outside, and he pointed at Lissa's glass. "A bird added a bit more flavoring to her dessert."

"Eww." Lissa wrinkled her nose and shuddered. "That is not funny."

The waitress slapped a hand over her mouth and her eyes grew wide. "Goodness gracious. I am so sorry. Let me get you—"

"If you'd put my turtle in a glass to go, we'll be fine."

"Absolutely." She picked up both desserts. "And don't worry about the bill, this one's on the house."

"Thank you." Haven leaned back in his chair and chuckled. "Some first date this is turning out to be."

"I'll never forget it, that's for sure."

"Tell me about it. Who knew eating outside could be dangerous?"

She laughed. "Next time, we'll pick a place with an awning."

"Next time? So, you're willing to give us another try?" He sat forward, crossing his hands on the table, his thumbs doing a nervous dance.

Was he kidding? With a giggle, she folded her hands in her lap, and resisted the urge to lean toward him. "I won't blame you for the bird's lousy aim."

He shook his head. "I'm sorry. I'm not good at this. I can go toe to toe with corporate bigwigs, but become tongue-tied around beautiful women. Around you."

Heat flooded Lissa's cheeks. "I think you're doing fine."

"So, when I get back in town a week from Sunday, would you, maybe, consider spending the afternoon with me? Lunch. Maybe the Sculpture Garden?"

He seemed to stop breathing. How could this confident businessman be so uncertain around her? She was the one who should be shaking.

With a grin, she glanced up at the sky. "As long as we eat indoors."

Now, all she had to do was get through the afternoon with Caleb tomorrow, and let him know they had no future. A little bird poo was about all the danger she could handle.

The pound of Minnehaha Creek freefalling fifty-some feet below her was like a steady drum in her favorite symphony. With Caleb at her side, Lissa looked over the stone bridge at the moss-covered rocks being splattered with added percussion. Maples, cottonwood, oaks, and wild flowers climbed the limestone bluffs channeling the creek, all swaying to God's music.

"You approve?" Caleb shrugged his backpack into place and rested a callused hand on her forearm.

"How could I not? I love this place." She closed her eyes and breathed in the fresh water's scent . . . and Caleb's woodsy cologne. *Careful, there, girl!*

"Me too." His hand pulled away, leaving a chill on her naked arm. "Care to explore?"

"Explore?"

"Check out some of those paths below? Get a unique view of the falls."

"Depends on what you mean by unique."

He laughed. A wondrously deep tone that added to nature's melody. "Nothing harmful, I assure you." He stepped away from the stone barrier and held out his hand.

She stared at it as if it were poison. Maybe it was. If she took it, would it infect her so she wouldn't want to let go?

"I don't bite."

How dare he grin? And how dare her heart tango? "I'm certain you don't, but I am capable of walking on my own."

His grin faded a shade as he stuffed his hand in a pocket on his cargo shorts. "Please forgive me if I'm being too forward. I'm not used to . . . being with a woman other than family."

"You're doing fine. Really. I don't want to give you the wrong impression, though. After today I don't . . ."

"You don't?"

She stared down at the plunging water. Didn't want to see him again? No. That wasn't true. She was afraid to see him again. Afraid her heart would tumble for the wrong man when the right man was finally available and interested. After all, even the Bible claimed that the heart was deceitful. She wouldn't fall into that love trap of following her heart like myriads of other women did, only to plummet down falls of their own making.

Hugging herself, she glanced back at Caleb. "I don't know if you and I are such a good idea."

"I see." He shrugged. "And I guess I agree with you at this point."

He agreed? Why did she feel disappointed?

"Today is just one day. It's not a commitment of any sort. I wanted to spend a day with someone besides Aimee and my in-laws. So, why don't we have some fun and let tomorrow worry about itself? No strings attached."

What could possibly be wrong with that? "Okay. Lead on and I promise to enjoy the day."

His grin returned. So did her butterflies as she followed him down what seemed an endless cascade of stone steps leading toward the creek. Didn't matter. After today, she'd release Caleb and those butterflies and concentrate on getting that promotion and securing Haven's affections.

The steps plateaued out near an overlook with a head-on view of the falls. They stood side by side, resting against a stone retaining wall, with Caleb's backpack on the ground safely dividing them. What fun God must have had creating this view, sprinkling the diving waters with iridescent colors. "Thank you, God," she whispered.

"It's quite the gift, isn't it?"

She nodded. Words seemed inadequate.

Three young people, probably late teens, hugged the rocky side next to the waterfall and inched their way toward the plunging waters.

"What are those kids doing?" She held her breath as, one by one, the teens disappeared behind a curtain of water. What if they fell?

Caleb laughed. He laughed when those three fools were in danger? "Don't worry about them. I've done that a number of times. You take it careful and it's worth it to get the perspective from behind the falls."

Not at all worth the risk.

"Shall we go?"

"Behind the falls? No way!"

With a laugh, Caleb swooped up his backpack. "Not today." He slung the pack over his shoulders. "But I do know a perfect place for our picnic."

Relieved, Lissa slapped a hand over her chest, but she kept her focus on the waterfall until the teens emerged and made their way to safe ground. Now, she could go.

He aimed for the stairs leading away from the picnic area.

"Don't we need to go back up?"

He pointed ahead. "Why don't we use nature's table instead?"

Why didn't he ever do things the normal way? Even worse, why did that thrill her? "Lead the way." She followed him down more steps that eventually evened out to a gravel trail meandering alongside the creek. Then they crossed a boarded path built by scouts, followed by a dirt trail formed from human travel. A faint rumble of cars in the distance was overshadowed by a bird chorus and the calming trickle of water flowing over and around rocks.

Caleb stopped, pointed up at a tree rising beside them, and whispered. "See that?"

She glanced upward just in time to see a mother robin fly into her nest. But then, with widening eyes, she backed out of the bird's dropping range.

"Is there a problem?" Caleb stepped back beside her.

"Last night a bird decided to use my dessert as its dumping ground."

He pinched his lips closed, but a chuckle came through anyway. "Let me take you out of her path." He stepped off the trail and climbed a few feet up the rocky incline. "You coming?"

"Are we supposed to climb those rocks?"

He shrugged. "I do all the time. So do others." He pointed to the area around the rocks where weeds had been trampled by foot traffic.

Her feet remained rooted, and her heart rate accelerated. "Really, we shouldn't leave the path."

"I can't force you to follow me, but I guarantee you'll miss out." He climbed probably twenty more feet before settling on a flat stone next to a boulder, securing the backpack between his legs. A low whistle blew from his mouth. "Man, you should see the view from up here, but hey, if you don't want to . . ."

With her heart dancing faster, she glanced back on the trail they'd just travelled. No one in sight. She scanned the path in front of her. No people there either. She gazed up the hill at Caleb as he unzipped the backpack and removed a sandwich.

Her double-crossing stomach growled, but climbing that hill was against all her rules.

"Mmm, mmm." He held up the sandwich. "I make a mean albacore sandwich . . . if you like celery and tomatoes. Aimee doesn't like the celery, but I was certain you would."

"Albacore?" Nothing tasted better than albacore. Her stomach begged to be filled with it.

"Fresh." He bit into what looked like rye bread and rolled his eyes, clearly exaggerating his pleasure.

"Okay. Fine. But if we get into trouble, it's your fault."

"I'll take full responsibility." He grinned.

Grumbling to herself, she climbed up the incline toward Caleb. More proof that he was all wrong for her. Haven would never entice her to break the rules. She reached the boulder and her foot slipped, propelling her face forward to the rock. A screech escaped her throat as Caleb's arms wrapped around her torso, stopping her a caterpillar's width from banging her head. Why had she listened to him and climbed this stupid hill? This was crazy.

"You okay?" Keeping an arm around her, he helped her stand.

She shrugged out of his arms, but his rugged hand grasped hers, keeping her balanced as she sat down a few feet away from him. No way was she going to sit close to him. She tugged her hand from his. It had felt too safe there. "This better be worth it." Muttering under her breath, she leaned over and dusted the dirt from her knees.

"I think it is." He handed her a sandwich and pointed down at a tree limb.

Her gaze followed where he pointed and her mouth hung open. The fall and her hunger forgotten, she clutched her meal and watched the mother robin feed her babies. "Amazing."

"Thought you'd like it."

She nodded and took a bite. Her eyes rolled back with joy. Did this guy ever know how to satisfy her taste buds. "This is wonderful."

"Thank you." He reached into his backpack and pulled out an

insulated covered mug. "Care for some water? It's got just a titch of lemon in it."

Nodding her thanks, she accepted the drink keeping her focus on the bird family. "I can't believe I almost missed out on this." It was worth the climb and the dirty knees, and even the risk of getting caught by park employees.

"I've learned that oftentimes the best sites are off manmade trails. You have to take a chance once in a while. You won't always find such beauty, but when you do, it's worth the effort."

"I'm not good at stepping off the path."

He winked. "Stick with me and pretty soon you'll be the one pointing out a new way."

Exactly what she was afraid of. She took another bite while eyeing the bird family and its nest perched yards above the ground. Ironically, that was the safest place for them. Just the way God planned it. Soon, that mother would be nudging its chicks from the nest, encouraging them out of their safe zone into independence.

But Lissa was already independent. She'd already flown away from the nest. She washed down her sandwich with a gulp of water and glanced at Caleb. His woodsy cologne drifted toward her, and her hand tingled with the memory of his safely surrounding hers. Would it hurt to spend another day with him?

Caleb linked his fingers behind his head, leaned back against the hill, and gazed at the sky above. *What do you think, Jeanette?* He chuckled, just imagining her unrestrained laugh. Two women couldn't be more opposite. Before meeting Lissa, he'd always pictured himself falling for a replica of Jeanette: adventurous and outgoing. Aimee was the same way. Not once had he envisioned himself enjoying time with someone timid and fearful of straying beyond the lines.

He studied Lissa as she nibbled at the remnants of her sandwich, her eyes wide, observing the bird family. Was she any different from those chicks staying secure in the nest? It was so much fun watching

Lissa cling to the edge then slowly step beyond it and finally taste the wonder God created off manmade paths. Her insecurity gave him purpose when everything else important in his life was being gnawed away.

His fingers strained against his head and he held in a sigh. Now was hardly the time to consider dating someone. His priority was finding a job. Any job at this point. Flipping burgers, if he had to. But that wouldn't make his next mortgage payment, due in a short two and a half weeks. He closed his eyes, blocking in tears. *What do I do now, Jeanette?*

"Caleb? Are you all right?"

He blinked his eyes open and managed a smile. "I'm fine. Just enjoying the afternoon."

"So am I." She laid her hand on his arm. "Thank you for making me climb up here. It's amazing, but there is one little problem."

"What's that?"

She nodded at the bank they'd ascended. "How do we get down?"

A grin forced away his melancholy. How wonderful it felt to be needed instead of needy. "Pretty much the same way you came up."

She sat up straight, craning her neck as she glanced down the embankment. "I guess I can do it."

"No doubt you can." He stuffed the food and beverage containers into his backpack. "You ready to go explore some more?"

"There's more?"

"We've barely started. It's a big park."

She worried her lip. "Well, I guess we should check it out."

Atta girl. He slipped the backpack around his shoulders. Using trees as leverage, he inched his way down the hill back to the dirt path. He glanced up the hill. Lissa remained frozen at the top.

"Do I have to walk down?"

"No." He shook his head. "Turn around and pretend you're climbing, but come down instead."

"If you say so." She clinched her fists in front of her and half closed her eyes. "I can do this."

"I'm right here."

"You better be." She slowly squatted then turned till her soles gripped the dirt and her hands clutched rocks. One foot edged down seeking purchase. She lowered the other foot, followed by her right hand, and her left. She stopped and he heard her puff out a breath.

"Good job. Now do that same thing again."

She repeated her first steps. This time a bit faster. Again she stopped and released a breath.

Observing Lissa was like watching Aimee learn to walk. Incredible. Beautiful. "I'm here. You won't fall."

She nodded slowly before she again stretched a leg down, seeking firm ground. Her other leg and one hand followed close behind.

"Ten more feet, Lissa, and you're home."

"No problem." Confidence rang through her voice. Her leading leg stretched longer followed quickly by the other. Without hesitating, she descended another eight feet. With about two feet left to go, she stood on a boulder, turned around and pumped her fists in the air. "I did it!"

"Great job." He offered his hand.

Grinning, she reached for it and stumbled onto him, fear blazing in her eyes. He staggered, but kept his balance while hugging his arms around her waist. Shoot, she felt good, almost like she belonged there. But she didn't. Slowly, he lowered her to the ground.

Her heart thumped wildly into his chest as he kept his arms in place. She didn't fight him off as he expected, but instead she buried her face into his shirt and gripped shivering arms around him.

Massaging her back, he whispered, "Hey, you're okay." And he was okay too. He breathed in her honeysuckle perfume. Better than okay. It had been too long since he'd held a woman this close. Not since Jeanette . . . Jeanette! He released his arms and backed out of hers, wiping perspiration from his forehead.

Disappointment registered in her narrowed eyes.

"I'm sorry." He scratched the back of his neck.

Her foot paved circles in the dirt. "I didn't mind." Her voice came out low and soft.

He wiped suddenly moist palms on his jeans, "But I can't . . ."

"Can't?"

Betray Jeanette. Oh, was he ever a fool to think he could date again? Not so soon. "I'm not . . ." He crossed his hands over his chest, securing them beneath his arm pits. "Ready."

"To take a risk?"

"What?"

She stepped toward him, wearing a sly smile, and gripped his hands. "You just convinced me to get off the path, climb a cliff, and climb back down." Leaning over, she kissed his cheek. Heat rushed through his face. "Don't you think it's time you reciprocate?"

"But Jeanette—"

"Sounds like she was a risk-taker too. I never knew her, but something tells me she'd be cheering you on."

Would she? He peered upward. *Would you?*

He smiled and squeezed Lissa's hands. "You know, I believe you're right. Want to do some more exploring?"

"If you'll keep me safe."

"That, I can do." Linking his fingers with hers, he led her farther away from the falls.

He'd saved her falling. Now, who was going to rescue him?

And his house?

He clutched his open hand at his chest and stole a peek at Lissa.

Who was going to rescue his heart?

Chapter Eight

Humming, Lissa glided into her empty cubicle, spun her chair around and sat. She glanced at her goals frame and gave it a tap. Nothing had changed, really. Becoming a boss was still next in line and, despite Tyler's temporary promotion, there was no reason to think she wouldn't get the permanent job. Then she'd have no trouble financing her dream home, and she'd be in the perfect position to marry and have kids. Everything done in the exact right order.

She lifted her vase, picked up the key, and unlocked her file drawer. Holding her breath, she thumbed through the folders. Nothing missing. Whew. With a light finger tap, she rolled the drawer shut. Yep, things were definitely looking up for her. Not even Tyler could spoil this day.

"Hey sweets, someone sounds like they had a good weekend."

Lissa swiveled to face Rita, failing to hold back her grin. "You could say that."

"Oooh, this is juicy. I can tell. Let me get settled, then you can dish." Rita flung her purse beneath her desk, and threw a few Pop Rocks into her mouth before plopping onto her chair. "I take it your date—or was it dates—went well."

Lissa felt her cheeks burn and she stared down at her feet. "Why is it I go twenty-four years without one decent guy interested in me, and then bam, I've got two? Is it wrong to date two guys at once?"

"Wrong?" Rita leaned toward Lissa, her eyes wide. "Until someone puts that ring on your finger, you can date as many as you want. As for me"—Rita splayed a hand over her chest—"I need at least three going at a time." She leaned in closer yet and lowered her voice. "But this isn't about two guys is it? That blush was put there by someone special, wasn't it?"

Lissa clapped her hands over her face. "Is it that bad?"

"It's that good. Now, come on, dish."

Lissa looked down at her fidgeting hands and whispered. "I kissed him."

"You kissed him!" Rita bolted upright in her chair.

"Ladies."

Groaning, Lissa glanced up at Tyler. He tapped his watch. "Work started two minutes ago. You don't get paid for idle chatter."

Rita rolled her eyes so only Lissa could see. "Give it a rest, Tyler. Just because you're the boss now doesn't mean you can get all highfalutin on us. We get the job done and you know it."

"And just because 'temporary' is in front of my title, doesn't mean you don't continue to give the same respect and quality effort you showed Haven. As a matter of fact, I expect more from you. If you ask me, he was a little lax with his discipline."

"We didn't ask." Rita chewed her Pop Rocks, mouth open, and their crackling grew louder.

"And that's another problem." Tyler snatched the candy wrappers off Rita's desk. "Do you think it's appropriate to talk on the phone and chew these at the same time? This is a professional establishment, and I expect you to treat it as such."

Rita saluted. "Yes, sir."

"Rita." Lissa laid a hand on her arm. "Don't let him get to you."

"I wouldn't worry about her, Ms. Morgan. If I understand it correctly, you've been having a problem misplacing important files." He bent toward Lissa and narrowed his eyes. "It better not happen again."

Holding in a scathing comeback, Lissa clutched her fists in her lap. How dare he make threats? "I can assure you it won't."

"And I can assure you, that if it does, you'll be out of here looking for a job faster than the Road Runner flees from Wile E. Coyote. Understand?"

Clenching her jaw, she nodded.

He leaned closer yet. "And I know all about you and the former boss. Actually, I know more, and let me tell you, he's not the lily-white saint you think he is." Wearing a sardonic grin, he pulled away. "Do we understand each other, Ms. Morgan."

"Perfectly," she answered through gritted teeth. Clearly, Tyler was jealous of Haven and would say anything to tarnish his reputation.

"Tyler, why don't you go skulk back to your cave or whatever hole you writhed out of?"

"Rita." Lissa shook her head once. "Let him be." Sitting up straight in her chair, she swiveled around and pulled out the file drawer. But something niggled at her. What could Tyler have been talking about? Haven was the most transparent, and one of the kindest guys she'd ever met. How dare Tyler muddy her thoughts with doubts about Haven? She pulled out her current folder and slapped it on her desk. The bank's board of directors would see Tyler's domineering management style and compare that to Lissa's compassionate collections. Then, he'd be the one looking for a job.

"Mémé Yvette!"

With a shake of his head, Caleb handed his daughter over to her grandma and walked into his in-law's foyer. "You'd think she hadn't just spent all of Saturday with you." A Saturday that still left him confused. His heart said go for it, but his head was screaming stop. For the first time in two years, he was inclined to listen to his heart. But first, he had to make some money, even if that meant unemployment.

"How could she tire of me when we have so much fun?" Yvette kissed Aimee's cheek.

Caleb shut the door behind him and slipped off his shoes. "I hope you don't get tired of her."

"She is a delight, *mon cher.*"

"Yes, but your job as grandma shouldn't mean full-time care."

"My job as mémé is to spoil this beautiful child."

"You're doing your job very well, but you're also spoiling me." Caleb caught a whiff of something mouth-watering drifting from the kitchen. "Chicken?"

"*Oui*. Cordon Blue. Aidan thought you would appreciate a home cooked meal today."

"I already have a freezer full of his meals."

"And now you will have more for the future."

Just say thank you. Caleb kissed Yvette's cheeks. "*Merci beaucoup.*" Someday, when he got out of this valley, he'd repay them for their generosity. At least he had them to turn to. Others who'd lost their jobs weren't nearly as blessed as he.

"You are very welcome, *mon cher*. Now go, let me play with my little girl."

"And I'll get to work. I appreciate you letting me use your internet. Doing personal stuff at the library doesn't sit well with me."

"We are always glad to help."

But constantly asking for help was getting painfully tiresome. Still, he had one more favor to ask. This one required Yvette's female wisdom. "Could you help me with one more problem?"

"Another problem? You are piling them up, are you not?"

"Well, this one I have you to thank for."

"Aww, let me guess. It has something to do with a beautiful lady."

Caleb scratched the back of his neck. "I guess you could say that. Would Aidan mind keeping an eye on Aimee for a second?"

"I think they would love to go on an adventure together, *oui* Aimee?"

"I play with Papi?"

"Yes, my pretty." Yvette set Aimee on the floor. "He is in the kitchen and he may have a job for you to do. You may be the sous chef for today."

"I help Papi!" In a blink, Aimee ran toward the kitchen.

Caleb quieted until he heard Papi's voice.

"Well if it isn't Wilma Rudolph running to see me!"

Shaking his head, Caleb glanced at Yvette. "Where does he come up with all these names?"

"The computer is helpful for him as well, *non*?" She laid a hand on Caleb's forearm. "Now how may I help you with your new problem?"

Caleb stuffed his hands into his jeans pockets and stared down at the tiled entryway. "I think I like her."

"I see." Yvette's tone hinted at a smile. "And what is it that makes her special?"

He grinned, thinking back to Saturday. "She's this scared little bird, afraid to fly from her nest, but whenever she spreads her wings and leaps, joy spills out. It's like she's been waiting for someone to nudge her out of her comfort zone but didn't know it. She's blossoming right in front of me, and for the first time in two years, I feel needed."

"And this is a problem how?"

He sighed. "Now is not the best time to start dating someone."

"Another time would be better?"

"Yes." His gaze met hers. "When I have a job. When I'm not worried about losing my home. I can't even take her out on a decent date."

"She has been enjoying your time together, spreading her wings, *non*?"

He shrugged. "I know she has."

"Then what is your problem, my dear? If you wait for the right time, the right girl may not wait for you. Do not hide yourself. Be honest with her. I am certain she will understand."

He sure hoped so. Next time they got together, he would let her know about his employment and house problems. Maybe between now and then he'd actually be working again. Maybe by then he'd be secure in his home. "Thanks for the advice, Yvette. Wise, as usual."

"You are welcome. Now go, get your work done, later we shall have a feast."

Caleb brushed past Yvette and plodded down the steps to his in-laws' unfinished basement. He stopped at the bottom of the steps and glanced around. The walls were framed-in already. The computer looked lonely backed against the wall of a future office, sitting on a cheap area rug. With the exception of the bathroom, the basement just needed sheetrock and Yvette's decorating touch. With him out of a job, it would take no time to finish off the basement and give Aiden his man cave.

A man cave . . .

Yes, that would be the perfect way to repay his in-laws for all they'd done for him. Soon. At the moment he had other priorities.

He strode to the computer and Googled "Minnesota Unemployment." The top link was for Unemployment Insurance Minnesota. Perfect. Now to see if he qualified. He'd worked for his former employer for over a year and, sure, he'd messed up a few times. One time too many. He clicked on "How to Apply for Benefits" and held his breath as he read the part about being fired. Wonderful. Both he and his former employer would be asked why he wasn't working. He slouched and rubbed his eyes. Well, he'd fill in the application, and the rest was out of his control.

He continued reading about the benefit amount and slouched further. Fifty percent of his weekly wage? That was it? He massaged a headache building in his temples. At one hundred percent, his wage didn't come close to paying his bills. Fifty percent of that would get him food and gas and not much more. How were people supposed to survive?

Well, he couldn't change the rules. Fifty percent was better than zero. Now, assuming he actually qualified for money, and that was an extraordinarily optimistic assumption, when would he receive his first payment?

A Waiting Week? What was that? He read further. One whole week without any payment whatsoever.

He slipped further in his chair and hid his face in his hands. Now would be a good time to pray, but only words of anger filled his thoughts. Did God have to take everything from him? May as well say goodbye to his and Jeanette's dream home right now. Barring a miracle—and God certainly hadn't been in the habit recently of granting miracles for Caleb—the last remnant of Jeanette would be stolen from him too.

And what about Aimee?

Caleb steepled his hands over his mouth. Yes, he still had Aimee. No way would he ever let her go.

He wasn't helping her by sitting here feeling sorry for himself either. He sat up and filled in the application for unemployment benefits. Whether they accepted him or not was entirely up to them.

Once completed, he pulled his mortgage information from his

billfold and unfolded it. Banks worked with people who had temporary hardships, didn't they? Especially small banks like Hennepin Bank & Trust. He dialed their number and explained his situation to the receptionist, who forwarded him on. At least he talked to a person and not a computer. That was a good sign, wasn't it? They'd see him as a person, not a number.

"This is Corliss Morgan, how may I help you?"

His heart seemed to still. No, it couldn't be.

"Hello, is someone there?"

It was her, the same voice he'd enjoyed hearing on the phone before. He cleared his throat and the words squeaked out. "Uh, yes, this is Jonathan C. Johnson." He cleared his throat again and lowered it, adding a hint of French accent, praying she wouldn't recognize him. "I have recently lost my job, and wish to discuss ways to save my home."

"I appreciate you calling in, Mr. Johnson. I'll need some information from you then I'll see how I can help."

The headache blossomed in his forehead again as he answered her questions without divulging the most important piece of information, that Corliss—Lissa Morgan—knew him as Caleb.

Lissa ended the phone call and fingered moisture from her eyes. Some days this job was too dratted hard. Not misplacing files should be the easy part. That would not happen again. But telling customers they had no hope? She'd never get used to that. What she'd give to make it through the remainder of the day without conflict. In her job, that was an impossible wish.

She sniffled and felt a hand on her shoulder.

"I take it that was a hard one." The annoying crackle of Rita's candy accompanied her concern.

Lissa nodded as Jonathan Johnson's folder mocked her from her desk. "Doesn't it get to you sometimes? These are people's homes we're talking about. Their memories. And I can't do a thing to stop that being stripped away."

"Hey, sweets." Rita swiveled Lissa's chair around. "You do more than most. How many people have you helped? Huh?"

"It doesn't make it any easier."

"Talk to me. What was so special about this one?"

Lissa dried her eyes again. "This guy. Nothing's gone right for him. In the past two years he's lost his wife, his business, now his job. And we're going to take away his home too."

"A common story, unfortunately. So, let me guess, the dude has no savings, no family to lend him money till he gets back on his feet, he refuses to rent, and his mortgage is upside down."

"You're right on three counts, anyway. He's one of the few who could sell without selling short. But it's the home he built with his deceased wife and he refuses to get rid of it. He asked about getting a break on finance charges, but with no money coming in, what difference does that make? He begged for more time, and I gave him the pat answers about collection calls and letters and accruing legal fees, and that wonderful sheriff's sale after the sixth missed payment."

She sighed and stared at the dingy ceiling tiles. "And then, there's the false light at the end that gives him a six month redemption period to come current before being evicted. Sometimes I feel like the biggest heel on earth." She pinched a dead leaf from the rose on her desk. "Of course, I gave him the name of a mortgage counselor. Maybe they'll be able to talk sense into him. Sell now before the market gets worse. But this guy's so emotionally attached to the house, I have a feeling that nothing anyone says will get him to change his mind. He's going to stay on the sinking ship."

Rita hugged Lissa. "You've done what you can. No sense beating yourself up over someone else's choice."

She grabbed a tissue off her desk. "Here, go freshen up. Those mascara tracks are freaking me out. I'll meet you in the break room and you can fill me in on that kiss you told me about earlier."

With a light chuckle, Lissa accepted the tissue. "Good idea." Keeping her head down, she grabbed her purse, hurried to the restroom, and glanced in the mirror. What a fright. Shivering, she wet a paper towel and dabbed at the runaway mascara. This was more confirmation that things needed to be done in the right order. Purchasing a house if you had no savings for downtimes wasn't wise. She dried her face and reapplied her makeup. No sense showing her coworkers what she felt inside.

One more glance in the mirror, confirming she looked professional, then she walked, chin up, to the break room, empty but for Rita.

"You feeling better?" Rita handed her a cup of tea.

Lissa sipped at the tea, and the tension slid away. "Thanks. This is exactly what I needed."

"No problemo." Rita planted her elbows on the table and rested her chin on her hands. "Now I need to hear about that kiss. Do you really think his lips are virgin?"

Huh? Lissa blinked. Oh no. Rita assumed Lissa kissed Haven. "Uh, well, I couldn't tell you about that. You see, it wasn't Haven that I—"

"No way!" Rita's chin fell off her hands. "It was the dangerous one? You kissed Mr. Cliff Hanger?"

Lissa's face burned. "It wasn't planned or anything."

"I'll bet he knows how to kiss."

"Well, it wasn't exactly on the lips."

Rita leaned back in her chair, her face toward the ceiling. "So you go get me all excited about a kiss, and it's a peck on the cheek? Puhlease. That's not news. That's saying hello."

"I held his hand."

"His? Which his? Remember now, you're two-timing these—"

"I am not two-timing. It's way too early to be committed to anyone."

Rita grinned. "Gotcha. I love watching you squirm. I'm impressed that Ms. Do-Everything-Right has a little double cross in her."

Lissa stuck out her tongue then sipped her tea. "Do I have to choose one over the other right now?" No way could she make that choice. They were both very attractive men, inside and out.

"Who you going out with next?"

"Well, Caleb works weekends usually, and he's devoted to his daughter, so I might not see him for a month or so, and Haven's out of town this week. We might get together on Sunday." Lissa swirled her teacup. "Do you suppose I should tell them about each other?"

"Sweets. You are so dense sometimes."

"Come on, tell me."

Rita glanced off to the left. "Would you look at that? Break time is over." She pushed away from the table. "See you back at the cube." With a mischievous grin, she wiggled her fingers in a little wave and skipped from the room.

Arghh. Lissa pressed her back into the chair. *What is the right thing to do?* Silence answered. Figured. Well, fine. Until God told her one way or the other, she wasn't going to make a choice. Grasping her teacup, she strode back to her desk. No doubt, if she lingered a second longer than her allotted fifteen minute break, Tyler would keep a record of it. She wouldn't give him any ammo to kill her chance at the promotion.

She plopped into her chair and stared at her empty desktop. Okay, what had she been doing before the break? That's right. Mr. Jonathon Johnson's file. On top of everything else, the poor guy was burdened with a lousy name.

Hadn't she left his file . . . ?

She sat up straight. Yes, she had left it right on top of her desk. Her now empty desktop. With fingers trembling, she checked beneath her desk, behind the monitor, and finally her file drawer. No. No. No! She clenched her fists. It couldn't be happening again.

"Got a problem, Ms. Morgan?"

Not now, Tyler. Please not now.

"Well?"

She squinted up at Tyler standing arms crossed, chin raised, thumbing his nose at her. The nerve of the guy. "No problems, *Mr.* Abernathy."

"Make sure it stays that way." He slapped the top of the divider and walked back to his office.

The arrogance of that man! She grabbed a pencil off her desk and cradled it between two fingers. No, she would not give in now. She threw the pencil down. It had been over three weeks since her last cigarette. No way would she let Tyler be the cause of her fall. She opened her drawer and pulled out the To Do file. Maybe if she didn't tell anyone, maybe if she kept working, the missing file would reappear, just like the last one had.

Chapter Nine

"Okay, smile."

With cars whizzing past on the freeway beneath her, Lissa leaned against the Irene Hixon Whitney Footbridge's metal railing. She smoothed wrinkles in her cream sheath and posed for Haven. No doubt, this date would make up for the disaster of the previous one.

"Beautiful!" He flashed sparkling-white teeth and rested his camera against his chest. Was it a good thing that he wanted permanent memories of their day?

She turned around and watched I-94 traffic speed out of the Lowry Hill Tunnel and whistle below them. Truthfully, today couldn't have been better, and it wasn't done yet.

"What are you thinking?" Haven rested his back against the railing.

With a shrug, she spun back around and glanced off to the right where the near-century old granite Basilica of St. Mary proudly greeted drivers entering or departing Minneapolis. A stunning homage to the Twin Cities. "That I loved your church service this morning. The trumpets, violins, harp, choir were phenomenal. Thank you for inviting me."

"But the sermon . . . ?"

She cringed. "Well, for a young guy, he was a little dry and he seemed to really like hearing himself speak."

"You've got him nailed." Haven laughed. "But if you can keep from falling asleep, he's got some incredible insights. And aside from preaching, he's a great listener. Helped me through some rough times."

"Rough times, huh? Rumor has it, life has always been perfect for one Haven Carlysle."

He clucked her chin. "Since when do you listen to rumors?"

"Only the good ones."

"Those can be the most dangerous." A passing cloud shadowed his eyes.

"Well, all I know is that today's been nearly flawless." Almost making her forget the feel of Caleb's hand protecting hers.

"Just near?"

The day wasn't over yet. A breeze blew his minty cologne toward her. If he'd take her hand, maybe show some physical affection, then flawless could describe it. She glanced down at her hand hanging loosely at her side, and his hanging mere inches away. It would take barely a muscle to reach over. Her fingers twitched but refused to bridge the rest of the way. Haven should make that first move.

She cleared her throat and folded her hands in front of her to avoid temptation. "Let's see, lunch at that Loring Park bistro was divine and no bird decorated my dessert."

"Being inside helped."

"It usually does." She chuckled and peered up at a sky streaked with wispy clouds. "Right now, the sun is shining and it's only mildly humid."

"And may I add that I'm here with a beautiful woman."

She wished she could blame the humidity for her face overheating. "Now you're bribing me."

"Is it working?"

"I'll tell you when you take me home." Maybe then his virgin lips would meet hers. "But that's a ways off. Let's go check out the Sculpture Garden."

"I'd love to." He held out his hand.

Sucking in her lower lip didn't stop her smile as she glanced up at eyes that matched the blue of the sky. She entwined her fingers with his and her smile dipped ever-so-slightly. Warm and protective, but soft, no calluses. Hands averse to manual labor. So unlike Caleb's. Wasn't that what she'd always wanted?

With her free hand, she blotted perspiration from her forehead. It wasn't a decision she needed to make today. Was she being fair to Haven or Caleb? Didn't they deserve the truth? Maybe. Just not today.

Side by side they walked through the remaining bridge—a work of art in itself with its sky blue metal arching upward greeting the yellow arch scooping down—with Haven reading aloud the John Ashbery poem painted on the bridge's beams. The poem ended, as did the bridge, and she and Haven walked down the zigzagging metal stairway that flowed onto the Sculpture Garden's green and soggy grass.

"How about we save that for last?" Haven nodded off to the right where the outdoor gallery's most famous sculpture stood.

She'd never seen the Spoonbridge and Cherry up close. Only in a blur passing by on the freeway, or in photographs. What an amazing structure.

He squeezed her hand. "And then the Walker Art Center?"

"I'd love it." It had been years since she'd been through the art gallery with its diverse expressions of art. To walk through it with someone who wouldn't mock the artists' renderings but appreciate them would cap off this day. At least until he brought her home. Then, she'd see if today was perfect.

He led her through the four outdoor galleries with tables carved from sandstone and benches formed from basalt, granite, and cedar, taking pictures along the way. They walked through the glassed conservatory with vines scaling the walls and native and exotic plants framing the walkway. A stunning place for a wedding.

Now, where had that come from?

Shaking that thought from her head, she dragged him out of the conservatory and headed north to the arbor and flower garden with its flowered vines climbing over a stainless steel arched pathway.

Another ideal photo spot. Haven took advantage of them all. She almost felt like a runway model.

Two quick hours later, he led her back to the Spoonbridge, his hand leaving hers only for the occasional photo op.

"Still *nearly* flawless?" His thumb caressed her hand.

"Yep." She stole the camera from Haven. "I need a picture of you, then ask me again."

"How can I decline?" He walked a few feet toward the massive sculpture of a cherry resting on the tip of a spoon that sat in a pond. Haven turned toward Lissa and crossed his arms over his chest. "How's that?"

She glanced in the LCD screen, centered the spoon and snapped a picture. She studied the saved image with the spoon's reflection mirrored in the pond. Beautiful. "Stay there. I want to get one with the Minneapolis skyline."

Holding the camera in front of her, she backed up slowly. Minneapolis' glass towers came into view, and the Basilica. One more—

"Lissa stop—" Haven frantically waved his hands as Lissa took one final step back.

The ground disappeared and her foot sunk into an ankle deep, muddy puddle. Screaming, she lost her balance and tumbled backward holding Haven's expensive camera high to keep it from getting wet. Her backside landed in the puddle, splashing muddy water over her legs, staining her new dress with brown splotches.

No, no, no. That did not just happen!

Haven ran toward her, his fist covering his mouth, but not hiding his grin. She could smack the guy.

Keeping the camera suspended, she tucked the skirt between her legs and pushed up with her other arm. Tears threatened as she stood and shook the goo from her arms.

"Hey, it's okay." Haven took her hand and walked her away from the puddle.

She frowned down at her sandals. Ruined, just like her sheath. "That's easy for you to say." She shook one leg then the other. "Today was going so perfect, too."

"Who says it still isn't?" He took the camera and aimed it.

"Don't you dare!" That was all she needed to show up around work. Tyler would find some way to use it against her.

"Sorry, too late." Haven looked at the screen, grinned, and suspended the camera around his neck. He wiped her cheek and showed her his mud-streaked fingers. "I hear mud baths are good for the complexion."

"Oh you." She swatted his arm. How dare he make her smile now?

"I take it you'd like a rain check for the art gallery." With one eyebrow raised, his gaze scanned her body.

Any other time, she'd have been flattered. "Do you mind?"

"If that means you dare go out with me again." A grin spread across his face. "Somewhere safe next time."

A giggle rose up from her belly and couldn't be stopped. She wiped a filthy hand on his white button-up shirt. "Sounds like a challenge."

Just like it was a challenge choosing between these two men who suddenly vied for her heart. She scraped crusted mud from her arm. *God, what am I going to do?*

Tell them.

Sure, that would be the right thing to do. But not today. She didn't want anything else to stain this day.

Chapter Ten

Caleb turned on the oscillating fan then chugged down eight ounces of water. Even his in-laws' central air system couldn't chase August's humidity away. Still, this project was worth completing for Aiden . . . and was necessary for putting Lissa behind him.

"Ready?" He glanced over at his father-in-law.

"Whenever you are."

"Let's do it." Simultaneously, the men grasped the five-by-eight sheet of MDF that leaned against the basement's concrete wall and lifted.

They rested it on top of two sawhorses, then Caleb spread his in-laws' basement plans on top. He glanced around the framed-in basement. Two bedrooms, one full bath, a living room or rather, man cave, even a kitchenette. Wasn't Aiden's gourmet kitchen enough? Apparently not for a professional cook.

He pointed to the kitchen area on the blueprint. "What happened to the Irish pub you always wanted?" Now that would add character to this room.

"Aye, what's a man to do with a pub if he's no ale to put in it?"

"Your Irish brogue is awful."

"Can I help it if we McCarthys have been in the US for three generations?"

"Which is exactly why you need the pub. Regain a touch of your ancestry."

"But we don't drink."

"Who says you need alcohol? It's not the beer that gives the pub its character, but the dark wood with intricate carvings. You could add a table made out of a wooden keg for the base with a walnut slab top. Leather bar stools, antiques and bric-a-brac, stained glass." He glanced at the area marked out for the kitchen and ideas bombarded his thoughts. "Teak flooring, beamed ceiling, wainscoting, your McCarthy crest. You don't want Guinness? Have a root beer theme instead. Metal steins, glass and ceramic mugs—"

"Whoa, whoa there, Caleb. My pockets aren't that deep."

Caleb cuffed a hand to his chin and walked around the future pub. "Doesn't have to be expensive. The bric-a-brac you get from antique shops or garage sales. There's a construction re-use center in Minneapolis that has reclaimed wood, doors, appliances, most anything we'd need. Wouldn't take much for me to chisel a little design into the wood either." His heart sped almost as much as when he bungee-jumped for the first time. "I can see you and your poker buddies down here yelling at the Vikings on your fifty-inch screen. Of course, I might have to join you."

"Son"—Aiden clapped a hand on Caleb's shoulder—"that sounds like the perfect project for you. Yvette and I are very grateful that you're taking this on. I wish you'd let us pay you."

He had to be kidding. "What do you call all those babysitting hours, the freezer full of food? I'll never be able to repay you for all you've done for me. This . . ." He splayed out his hands and walked in a circle. "This is my gift to you." And he couldn't wait to get going on it. "I'll start pricing out materials tomorrow and give you a quote."

"That sounds dandy. Now come have a sit upstairs. Yvette's cooking today."

"Ah, we're having leftovers." Caleb rolled the blueprint and stuffed it in its tube. "Sounds delicious."

"I'll warn you, she's gonna be serving up some mother-talk with her soup."

"Guess that's the price I have to pay." Caleb headed for the stairs with Aiden right behind him. The tantalizing aroma from whatever Yvette was warming encouraged him to take the stairs two at a time.

"Dada!" Aimee shook the child-safety gate and tried pulling herself up on it.

"Aimee-doodles, down, now."

Her lip protruded from her mouth, but she backed away.

"Atta girl." He opened the gate, stepped through, and held it for Aidan.

"That girl could be the next Lynn Hill, I'm thinking."

"Huh?" Caleb secured the safety gate. "Who?" Where did his father-in-law come up with these names?

"Famous rock, rather, sport climber."

"And you know this how?"

Aiden just grinned. The guy must spend hours on the internet searching for famous women adventurers.

"Dada hold." She held her arms up.

He scooped up his daughter and blew a raspberry on her tummy. This precious child was the only woman he cared about. A vision of Lissa witnessing the bird's first flight swooped through his thoughts. Well . . . maybe. Although there couldn't be a worse time to become interested in someone.

Aimee lifted her shirt and pushed out her stomach. "Again. Again."

No thinking of Lissa today, and the fact that he hadn't talked to her in three weeks. Ending things before they began was for the best. He needed to focus his attention on the most important woman in his life.

"Dada, zerbert again!" Laughing, he raised Aimee up and blew on her stomach, then brought her down, resting her on his hip. "You being a good girl for Mémé?"

"Caleb, dear, does that precious girl ever misbehave?"

He rubbed his nose against Aimee's and whispered, "You've got your grandmother snowed."

"I heard that, Caleb."

Of course, she did. Chuckling, he carried Aimee into the kitchen and secured her in the high chair by the dinette. "What can I help you with?"

"You can help by sitting and eating. That will make me smile."

Him too. Both he and Aidan pulled out chairs and sat across from each other. Caleb's stomach growled as Yvette set a basket of baguettes on the table along with a spinach salad. She sat and extended one hand to Caleb, the other to Aimee.

"I pray." Aimee shook her mémé's hand.

"That would be lovely, *mon cher*."

"Tank you God for food. Amen."

"Amen." The three adults echoed.

"Now, that's what I call a heartfelt prayer." Caleb reached for the baguettes.

"*Oui*, a child knows God's heart." Yvette stood and walked to the stove. "Now you eat up. The food will be ready *rapidement*."

"No rush." Caleb bit into the bread and sighed. No hurry at all. Aidan's cooking was meant to be savored.

"Now, tell me, *s'il vous plaît*, what did you find out about your home?" Yvette laid two hot pads on the table and topped them with a beef platter and au jus.

But this conversation could spoil even Aidan's cooking. He dropped the baguette on his plate. "I talked with a mortgage counselor and she basically echoed what the bank said. If I don't get a job, I can kiss the house goodbye."

"What are your options?" Aidan served himself a plateful of beef while Yvette filled mini bowls with *au jus*.

Blowing out a breath, Caleb leaned back. "One, I can sell the place. We've got enough equity built up so I wouldn't lose money, although I wouldn't walk away with enough for a down payment on a trailer."

"Eat, Caleb." Yvette filled Caleb's plate then began cutting Aimee's meat into pea-sized pieces. "You need energy to fix our basement."

"And you don't want to sell?" Aidan forked a bite of beef and dunked it in his juice.

"Sell?" And give up his last tangible memory of Jeanette? "Uh-uh. Not happening."

"Okay. We'll take that one off the table. What else?"

"I can rent the place. With quick access to the interstate, it could draw a decent price."

"Where would you live, *mon cher*?"

"My point exactly. Besides, can you imagine what renters would do to the place? I've heard horror stories." He stuffed a hunk of meat into his mouth. "Let's face it, my only hope is to find a job. McDonald's,

Target, wherever. Contractors aren't exactly clamoring for kitchen designers right now, but that's still where my heart is."

"How may we help?"

"Yvette, you're already helping more than you should."

"We can give you money, no?"

"No." He dropped his fork on his plate. "You're not raiding your retirement." Caleb leaned back in his chair and raked a hand through his hair, raising his voice. "Listen, I can handle this. I'm a good worker, a good designer. Something's going to come through. Can we change the subject, please?"

"Dada mad?"

"No, Aimee, Dada's not mad. He's . . ." Well, maybe mad was the right term. Mad at God for taking everything away.

"Let us talk about Lissa. You will ask her out again, no?"

Caleb shook his head. Out of the frying pan into red hot coals. It had been three weeks since he'd learned what Lissa did for a living. Three weeks since he'd spoken with her. How could he possibly face her now? "I can't."

"You cannot?"

He forked a piece of meat and dipped it but didn't bring it to his mouth. "She's . . ."

"Yes, *mon cher*, she is what?"

"She's the one who's going to take away my house."

"I do not understand."

"That's her job. At the bank. Collect or foreclose."

"And this makes her a bad person?"

"No, Yvette. But dating her would be rather strange, don't you think? Besides, I already told her I wasn't going to be available for at least a month." But not that he wouldn't call.

"She knows she is about to take away your home?"

"No. She knows Jonathon Johnson just missed a house payment. To her, Caleb Johnson is a completely different person."

"You must tell her. She would be able to help you save your house, no? And maybe your heart too?"

He pushed away from the table. Not even Aidan's cooking tasted good. "I still don't know how you can expect me to forget Jeanette."

Aimee whimpered.

Clenching his jaw, Caleb leaned forward and kissed his daughter's forehead. "Doodles, Dada loves you." Not caring that he was interrupting her meal, he unstrapped her from her high chair and pulled her out. Yes, she needed her daddy, but he needed her even more.

"You have a big heart, *mon cher*." Yvette's hand rested on his arm. "We do not wish to upset you, but it was not your fault that Jeanette's heart stopped."

"What? I know that." He tucked Aimee's head into the crook of his neck and wrapped his arms around her back while her pudgy arms circled his neck.

"Then why do you insist on blaming her for stopping your heart?"

His heart? He caressed Aimee's back. What was Yvette talking about? His heart was perfectly fine. "I don't know what you mean."

"Dear Caleb, Jeanette would not want you to stop living, but you choose not to sell your house because of Jeanette. You choose not to date because of Jeanette. You have chosen to stop your heart . . . because of Jeanette. What would she say to this?"

Caleb ran his hand through Aimee's fine copper strands. "She'd give me CPR, give my keester a solid kick, then tell me to start living."

"*Oui*, now what are you going to do?"

He returned Aimee to her chair. "I guess I'm gonna give Lissa a call. Tell her who I am."

Chapter Eleven

Lissa's home phone chirped and she jumped from her prone position on the couch. She rolled over on her stomach and glanced at the caller I.D. A spinning wheel seemed to twirl in her stomach. Even after several dates with Haven, just seeing Caleb's name did loopy things to her heart. A definite sign that she needed to focus on being sensible.

She sat up, straightened her bangs, muted the television, and finally hit the answer button.

"Hello."

"Hi, uh, Lissa?"

His shyness sounded so sweet. "Yes, is this Caleb?"

"Yeah, um, hey I'm sorry about not calling, I've been—"

"You told me you were going to be busy for the next month. I didn't hardly give it a thought." Well, maybe a little bit. She lay back on the couch. "How've you been?"

"Keeping busy. Finishing off a basement, but uh, the reason I called is, well, I've got next Saturday open and was wondering if you'd like to tube down the Apple River with me."

Her heart stopped. Tubing? Her? "Isn't that dangerous? And we've had so much rain lately, won't the rapids be too fast?"

He laughed. "It's not like white water rafting, although that's fun too. I see families go down together all the time. You attach an extra tube for beverages and enjoy a relaxing afternoon."

Fully exposed to the sun with water reflecting it. Melanoma loved that behavior. "I'm not a sun-worshipper."

"Me neither, but a good waterproof sunblock'll take care of it. Believe me, after one macho day, when I ended up as red as a cardinal, I've learned my lesson."

Her stomach flipped again, but this time it made her feel queasy. "I don't know . . ." She walked to her kitchen, and poured a glass of water.

"Seriously, I know you'll love it. There's a sweet side of nature you see from the river, a perspective you don't get from driving."

Rats. Using nature to bribe her was completely unfair. "Next Saturday, huh?"

"If you're available."

She downed her water. Haven was going up north again to see his dad, so Saturday was wide open. Fear wasn't a good enough excuse. "Can I think about it?"

"Hey, no problem."

She placed her glass in the sink and her doorbell rang. Who could possibly be ringing her doorbell on a Monday night? "I've got someone at my door, so can I get back to you later?" She walked to her door and peeked through the peephole. Her mom. She rolled her eyes. Oh joy.

"As long as you say yes. I know you'll love it."

Right. "Yeah, I'll call you in a day or two." Maybe by then she'd have the brains to tell him no. She ended the call and opened the door. "Hi Mom."

"Lissa, darling, how are you?" She shoved past Lissa into her small living room, sat in the Queen Anne chair, crossing one leg over the other with beauty pageant precision, and placed her purse on the floor.

Clutching the phone in her hand, Lissa walked toward the kitchen. "Lemon water?"

"Please. That's precisely what I need for this humidity."

Lissa poured her mom water and perched a lemon slice on the edge. "Why the visit today?"

Her mom sipped at the water then put the glass on a ceramic coaster set on a lamp table. "It's been over a month since I've seen you. Since the bachelor auction. You haven't even told me about your date."

Aww, yes. Now the unexpected visit made sense. Lissa poured herself a glass and returned to the couch. "Caleb and I had a wonderful time."

Her mom's brows furrowed. "You did?"

Not the reaction she was expecting. After dishing out a thousand dollars, the last thing her mom would want was for Lissa to have a bad time. "He took me to an outdoor concert. The Minnesota Orchestra played, and there were fireworks." Lissa waggled her brows to tease.

"Fireworks!"

She swallowed her giggle. "Mom, he was a perfect gentleman, all the way."

Relief softened her mom's features.

"As a matter of fact, I just got off the phone with Caleb. He asked me out this Saturday."

"Caleb?"

"Yeah."

"Not Haven?"

"What are you getting at?"

Her mom picked up her glass and worried it between her fingers. "This is not good. Not good at all."

"Not good? Aren't you the one who bid for him?"

"Yes, dear, but that was to prove to you that you should have pursued Haven harder."

"You've got to be joking! You wanted me to have a lousy time with Caleb?"

"Is it so wrong to want the best for your only child?"

Lissa rolled her eyes. "Spare me."

"But what about Haven, dear? You've always liked him. Your father often talked about your crush. And now that he's interested, you date another man?"

Her mom was right. It didn't make a lot of sense, but try talking your heart into thinking logically. "For your information, I've been out with Haven too."

"Too?"

"You have a problem with that?"

"But why would you date someone besides Haven?" Her mom set the water glass down, and walked to the front window keeping her back to Lissa. "He's who your father wanted for you."

Lissa massaged her forehead. It was going to be an aspirin evening.

"But Dad's not here is he? And whose fault is that? Who's he to tell me, beyond the grave, whom I should date? The reason Dad isn't here is because he refused to take care of himself. So, why should I take any of his advice?"

Her mom spun around, her narrow cheeks drawn in even more. "You will not speak of your father in that manner. He was the most giving person I've ever known. Yes, he had his bad habits, but we all do."

And some people hid their bad habits. Lissa clutched her twittering fingers. "Those bad habits cost him his life. If he'd learned to eat better, exercise, anything. Try a little harder. But his health didn't matter. It was like he didn't care enough about himself to want to walk me down the aisle."

"Darling, your father was completely devoted to you. And to me. Our thirty years together weren't nearly long enough. Yes, I wish he would have taken care of himself better, but wishing won't bring him back." Her mom braced her hands on the back of the Queen Anne chair. "He never listened to all my wishing and nagging about what was best for him. You're all I have left, and I want the best for you."

"Well, you should stop interfering in my life."

Her mom puffed out a laugh. "Ironic, isn't it, that my unwanted interference is what introduced you to Caleb." She sat back down, recrossing her legs, regaining her composure.

"Touché." Lissa glanced up at the ceiling. Her dad would be very disappointed with how she was treating her mom. And him. Honor thy father and mother. Right. There wasn't a hint of honor in her biting words.

Her mom loved her. Meddling, be it good or bad, was one way she showed her love. "I'm sorry, Mom. That was uncalled for. Actually, I'm fortunate, very happy to have a mom who wants to be involved." Much less, not have a mom at all. Like little Aimee.

"Apology accepted. I should know better than to try to run your life. It didn't work in the past." She splayed her arms, gesturing to Lissa's living room. "You insisted on renting this . . . this hovel when your father and I had something so much better for you. I know I should keep silent, I can't seem to help myself at times. You've grown up well and I'm proud of you for all you've accomplished." She bent down and picked up her purse. "But if I may leave you with one word of advice."

Lissa grinned. Her mom's one word would most likely be an entire sermon, but a sermon based on years of experience. Yes, she was blessed to have her mom, interference and all. "I'd love to hear it."

"People always recommend 'following your heart'." She crossed the living room and sat down by Lissa. "It sounds so lovely, so romantic, and there's nothing more wonderful than those butterflies twittering in your stomach, and the dancing beat of your heart. But sweetheart, that's surface love that doesn't last." She took Lissa's hand and surrounded it with her own. "Look at all the people having affairs in the name of following their heart. True love, deep love, is when you love them through their smoking and overeating. When your father loved me through my nagging. It's an act, darling, not a feeling." She kissed Lissa's cheek. "In matters of love, don't forget to use your head too. Let head and heart work together. That was the secret to my marriage. I want the same for you."

Lissa squeezed her eyes closed. Head . . . heart. Haven . . . Caleb. It made sense, but something was missing.

Her mom patted her knee. "Now you keep me abreast of your love life, and I'll try to trust your judgment. After all, you have earned my trust."

"Thank you." She gave her mom a quick hug then escorted her out. After locking the door, she leaned against it and focused on the cross nailed above her couch. Yes, there was something missing in her mom's equation, Someone Lissa had also failed to include. Head . . . heart . . . Heaven.

Her heart was saying go with Caleb, but her head gave an emphatic 'no.' And Haven? He was everything wisdom said she needed. Still . . .

She sighed. "God, what do I do?"

An image of the baby bird being pushed from the nest flitted through Lissa's mind. Well, maybe her attraction to Caleb was more than murmurings of the heart. There was one way to find out.

Chapter Twelve

Lissa dipped her toe into the swirling current of the Apple River. A hint of chill. Just right for this sweltering August afternoon. She waded in knee deep and stopped to let her legs acclimate to the temperature. If she survived today without becoming more attached to Caleb, she'd be happy.

"Feel good?" Caleb dragged their three tied-together inner tubes into the water.

"It does."

He dove under, T-shirt and all. He sprung back up, the water straightening his dark hair, and his now transparent shirt clinging to a muscled chest. But there was no barbed-wire tattoo circling his arm like she'd always imagined. On him, the look would have been sexy. She couldn't believe steam wasn't rising from the water.

No way would she be diving in like Caleb and let her T-shirt plaster itself to her. She forced her legs to wade out to the tubes, the rushing water skirting the hem of her shorts. Around her, couples, families, even small children, climbed onto their inner tubes only to be whisked downstream by the current.

"Here, let me help you." He offered his hand.

She stared at it. "Are you sure this is safe?"

"What? My hand or the river?"

Even in the heat, she felt the blush. She accepted his hand, grasped the other one onto the tube, and tried to jump up. And again. *One more try.* She bent her knees.

His hand deserted hers, then was at her waist, along with his other hand, and he hoisted her onto the tube. A second later, he was reclining in his tube, his feet dipping into the water. "Comfy?" He yelled over the pounding water.

With him looking so sexy next to her? Hardly. She tried to sit up straight, but the tube threatened to tip. All she needed was for it to turn over, saturating her outfit, letting her shirt cling to her one-piece bathing suit beneath.

"Hey, relax. Enjoy the ride." He lay back, rested his head on his hands, and closed his eyes.

How could he relax when the riverbanks were rushing past? "Are you sure this is safe?"

He grinned, but didn't open his eyes. "We're fine. The only adventure is a few light rapids down the—"

"Rapids? You said there weren't rapids!"

"No. What I said was, it's not whitewater rafting. Now, those are real rapids. Once you get used to the little ones here, we can go try the ones up by Duluth."

Huh. The odds of her going whitewater rafting were smaller than her becoming president of the United States. Simply, not happening.

"Hey, that was a joke. You know, ha ha, giggle, smile."

The edges of her mouth involuntarily turned up. She tried to force them down and failed. "Okay," she yelled. "I'm relaxing." She reclined, resting her shoulders on the tube, letting her bottom skim the water. She dangled her feet in front of her, the river surging over them. It did feel rather good.

"There you go. Now, close your eyes and take in God's voice."

"But I might bump into some—"

"We're fine." He reached over and patted her hand. "To put you at ease, I'll watch for both of us."

"I'm sorry. You must think I'm the world's biggest wimp."

"No. If you were, you wouldn't be here with me. You'd have found an excuse to turn me down. You have more adventurer in you than you think."

If only he knew how many excuses she'd thought up. Still, he was right. Not a single justification had convinced her to stay home. Maybe she was braver than she gave herself credit for. She snuggled deeper into the tube, resting her shoulders and head on the rubber, and closed her eyes. Sounds floated on the air around her. Laughter from children and adults and those in-between. A symphony of birds sang, their twitters bouncing off the water. A lazy breeze whistled past. Even the gurgling river declared its amusement. Not just God's voice, but His laughter. His joy.

She completely relaxed. No clock. No phone calls. No missing paperwork. Three hours of this wouldn't be nearly long enough. To think she'd almost told Caleb no. She raised an eyelid and peeked at him. His eyes were open, as he'd promised.

He cocked his head toward her. "See what I mean?"

"You win."

And he grinned.

Butterflies weren't dancing in her stomach. No, these were hummingbirds, their wings flapping at an invisible pace. Her heart was definitely saying charge ahead. Who cared what her head said? And God? Wasn't that His jubilant voice she'd been listening to? She turned her arm over, exposing her open palm.

Caleb's hand immediately covered it, securing it warmly. Again, she closed her eyes. It didn't matter what Caleb did as long as he didn't release her hand. Never had she felt so protected. Her eyelids grew heavy. It didn't matter. She was safe.

Caleb pried his eyelids open and squinted at the sun high in the sky. Must be noonish. Nearly two hours on the river already. Maybe one hour remaining. Had he fallen asleep? *Not wise, Johnson.*

Just like getting too attached to Lissa was unwise. Far too risky.

He glanced over at her hand encased in his. He hadn't planned on letting Lissa sleep the afternoon away, let her miss out on the beauty surrounding them. He rolled onto his side, staying balanced on the tube, and squeezed her hand. "Hey Lissa."

Her eyes blinked open and she gave him a zipline-riding smile, just like Jeanette used to do when she awoke next to him. How he missed that. Maybe, someday, Lissa would . . .

Whoa, boy. Rein it in a bit. He wiped perspiration from his forehead. It was time for a quick dive into the water. He eyed the people floating around them, some off their tubes, wading in waist-deep water.

He squeezed her hand again and let go. "I need to cool off a bit."

Her face turned crimson, and not from the sun.

Great choice of words, Romeo. He swung his legs around the back of the tube and jumped off, his feet landing him waist deep. He grasped onto the tube. His legs floated up behind him as the river coursed past.

"That looks wonderful." Lissa rolled onto her stomach.

"Come on in. River's shallow here."

She looked around, apparently surveying the teens and even pre-teens playing in the water. Biting her lip, she glanced down.

That insecure look was so adorable. That meant she was about to take another leap from the nest, and he was privileged to watch it.

Seeming to hold her breath, she pulled her T-shirt over her head, rested it on the cooler in the third tube, and adjusted the thin straps on her swimsuit. She hung her legs over the side and jumped in.

And disappeared.

"Lissa!" He released his grip on the tubes as Lissa bobbed back to the surface, coughing, spitting, terror gleaming from her gold-brown eyes. He circled his arm around her waist and paddled toward the fleeing tubes.

"I'm okay." She coughed and wriggled from his grip.

"You sure?"

She offered a weak smile. "Let's catch our ride."

With broad strokes, he caught up with their runaway tubes then reached back for Lissa. He pulled her to safety. This would be it. The death knell of their relationship before it barely started. "Lissa, I'm so sorry. A second ago, the water was shallow, I didn't know—"

Giggles burst from her mouth.

He rubbed the back of his neck. "You're not mad?"

Joy lit her eyes. "I've never been so scared, but I'm okay. I'm actually okay. You're right, there's nothing to be afraid of." She pulled herself back onto the tube and flopped on her stomach, looking down at him with dancing eyes. "Thank you."

Never had he been so confused. "You're thanking me for nearly drowning you?"

She patted the empty tube. "No, for proving to me that I won't necessarily be hurt by taking a few risks. I know that's no big thing to you, but for me?"

For her, it was clearly a life-affirming experience. He climbed onto the tube and lay back, looking up at the sky. *Thanks, God.*

"Did you and Jeanette do this often?"

Jeanette? Eyebrows pinched together, he glanced over at Lissa balanced sideways on the undulating tube.

She shrugged. "You don't have to answer. I'm curious, I guess. She's such a big part of who you are, and if I'm going to be getting to know you better, I'd like to know about Jeanette. You sound like you really loved her."

Wow. Not a question anyone had ever asked before. So many of his friends tiptoed around Jeanette's name. "Yeah, I did love her." And he'd never imagined feeling anything like that again. But now, maybe . . .

"You don't have to talk about her if you don't want."

"No, no. I want to. You've caught me off guard, that's all." He sat up on his tube, crossing his legs over the top, balancing with the swell of the water. "I met her at college. We were both studying drafting. It didn't take us long to discover how well we complemented each other. I'm the artist and she did wonders with numbers."

"But she was more of a daredevil than I am, I take it."

Caleb chuckled. "She'd outdo me. When we went skydiving together, that was it. I knew she was the one for me."

"So, why do you like me? I'm nothing like Jeanette."

"And I wouldn't want you to be." He reached over and brushed a wet strand from her eyes. "Maybe you complement me in a different way than Jeanette. Different, but just as good."

"Do you mind me asking . . . ?"

"What?"

"What happened to her? How did she die?"

Caleb splashed water on top of the tube and steam rose. "No. It's an okay question. Something I need to talk about." He splashed more water. "She had something called peripartum cardiomyopathy. In a nutshell, it's heart failure brought on by pregnancy. It's treatable if diagnosed, but we had no clue. One day I'm at work, she's home alone with Aimee, and she calls on my cell and says it feels like she's having a heart attack." He wiped his eyes. If only they'd paid attention to the symptoms. If they'd taken the edema, the cough, the heart palpitations seriously.

"Caleb. I'm sorry."

"Yeah. Me too. I called 911 and they beat me there. Still, it was too late." He wiped his eyes again. "She was so healthy, so energetic. Never in a zillion years would we have figured she had a heart problem. So, now it's one of my goals in life to spread the word."

Lissa grasped his hand. "Will you let me help you?"

"I'd"— A growing roar stopped Caleb. He glanced ahead and his eyes grew wide. "Hold on!" He yelled. "The rapids are coming up."

She settled her backside into the tube, her hands white-knuckling against the sides. Holding on to his tube with one hand, he grasped Lissa's hand with the other. "This is where it gets fun," he shouted.

Color drained from her face and he clasped her hand tighter. "Don't worry. I've got you."

Seconds later they bounced from one swell to another, as the rapids thrust them down the river, jostling over and around boulders. Her hand squeezed his as tight as a vice grip. His tube threatened to tip, but the next bounce righted him. Water splashed over and around them, but her grip never loosened.

And just like that, it was over.

She'd survived the unexpected drop-off earlier. What would she think about the rapids? Holding his breath, he glanced over.

A wide grin covered her face. "I did it!"

Whew. "Yeah, you did."

She leaned toward him, her lips puckered, but her tube dipped nearly plunging her into the water face first, and spraying water all over Caleb. Recovering, her eyes widened and she covered her mouth. "I'm sorry."

"Nothing to be sorry for." As much as he wanted to, he refrained from attempting a successful kiss. For now, anyway. Instead, he clutched her hand as they flounced over a smaller rapid with her giggling over every bounce.

If Lissa could take a risk and come away not only unscathed, but full of joy, maybe it was time to unlock his heart and take his own risks.

Yvette was right. His heart had stopped. It looked like Lissa was exactly the brand of CPR God ordered.

He stared upward. *What do you think, Jeanette?* The sun disappeared behind a wisp of cloud and reappeared. A wink of approval. *Yeah, I think so too.*

"Lissa, you asked me if you could help spread word about heart disease."

"In women, especially."

"I'd love to have you by my side." But it all hinged on her response to what he had to tell her when he dropped her off later today. Before this relationship could go any further, he needed to tell her his full name. That could change everything.

Caleb squinted into the evening sun as he steered his pickup onto Lissa's street. "Hey Lissa." He reached over and squeezed her hand. "You're almost home." The excitement of the day, and probably all that sun, had wiped away her energy, but even in sleep, she wore a contented smile.

Now to keep her content as he spilled the truth.

She released a long sigh as she stretched. "Already? Didn't we just leave?"

"About two hours ago."

"Oh my. I'm sorry I've been poor company."

"I'm glad you enjoyed yourself."

"It was a beautiful day."

She was right. Everything about it had been beautiful: the steamy temperatures, the scenic river . . . Lissa. Watching her blossom gave him a thrill he'd never experienced before. It was different from riding white water rapids. Both jolted his heart, but riding the rapids gave him a temporary high. Being with Lissa? Just watching her spread her wings jumpstarted his heart. Precisely what his mother-in-law ordered.

"When can we do it again?" She laid her hand on his arm.

"The river?"

"Well, that too, but I was talking about seeing you again."

"I'd like that." The question was, would she still want to see him after she learned who he was?

He drove past Xeroxed townhomes that lined the road. The only way he could tell the difference was by an occasional flowerbox in the front window, like the one Lissa had with ivy and petunias spilling out like a waterfall. Should the need arise, this was probably an affordable area to rent in. But he wasn't giving up on his home yet. He had eleven months before Lissa's employer could kick him out of the home he and Jeanette had designed together. There was nothing cookie cutter about his home. How could he give it up for this monotony?

"Oh no." Lissa sat upright.

"Something wrong?"

"I've got company," she whispered.

A black, four-door sedan was parked next to her short sidewalk with a single person inside. "Is that a problem?"

Silence answered back as he pulled behind the sedan and turned off the ignition.

She worried her lip, again, but this time it made him uncomfortable. "What's the matter?"

"Nothing's wrong." She opened the truck door.

"Let me get that." He pushed down on his door handle.

"No, no. That's okay." She stepped out of the truck.

"But I have something—"

She flashed a smile, but worry resided in her eyes. "I'll call you later, okay? Thanks." The door slammed shut.

I have something to tell you. His shoulders hunched and he watched her run up to the other vehicle. A man stepped out of the car and squinted toward Caleb, his jaw set. The guy looked familiar, somehow. Young. Probably late twenties, early thirties. To a woman, probably good looking too. Jealousy pinched his heart as the man embraced Lissa with a hug.

Caleb turned the key in the ignition and pulled away from the curb. That man could be anyone. A cousin or neighbor maybe. He drove past them and peered into the rearview mirror. At Lissa holding the man's hand.

How likely was she to embrace a cousin's hand?

Chapter Thirteen

s Caleb's pickup cruised past, Lissa's heart raced faster than it had when sailing over the rapids. What was Haven doing here? Now, of all times, when Caleb had practically stolen her heart. She wrestled from Haven's hug.

"Hey, what's up?" He released her, stepped back, and took her hands. Concern etched his beautiful blues as he stared down at her, making her heart want to waltz and flee at the same time.

She averted her eyes and considered pulling her hand from Haven's, but that would make him suspicious. "I, uh, . . ." *Am cheating on you?* Didn't there have to be some commitment for that to be true? It didn't matter. He deserved the truth.

"You what?" He led her toward her door. "Something's obviously bothering you." He jerked a thumb toward the road. "Who was that guy?"

Someone who makes my heart tango. "Come on in, and I'll tell you." The keys rattled in her fingers as she turned the lock.

She pointed to the Queen Anne chair. "Have a seat. Can I get you something to drink?"

"Water's fine."

No it wasn't. Water reminded her of Caleb. She hurried to her kitchen. Leaning on the kitchen bar, she looked out at Haven seated in the middle of her couch. Well, she'd have to take the chair. "How about lemonade?"

"That works."

She poured two glasses of lemonade, dropped in ice cubes, and joined Haven in her living room.

"Thank you." He patted the space next to him.

Could he make this any harder? She sat pressed against the arm, trying to avoid any physical contact. That would make what she had to tell him even more difficult.

"What's going on, Liss?"

"Do you think it's warm in here?" Wiping her forehead, she rose from the couch and checked her thermostat. Seventy-eight. Exactly where it should be.

"Come on, Lissa." Haven wedged himself in the corner of the couch. That gave her a few more inches of separation anyway.

She returned to the couch and set her glass on the carpet. How could she do this to Haven? What would her dad think? She pulled her knees up to her chest, wrapped her arms around them, and peered at Haven through her eyelashes. "I like you, Haven. You know that, don't you?"

"I don't think I like the direction this is heading." His Roman jaw twitched.

How could she say this and not hurt him? How could she express her heart's confusion without losing him? "We never said we'd date each other exclusively, right?"

His jaw shifted again and he chuckled, but there was no mirth in his laughter. "So, you're seeing that guy. Is that what you're trying to tell me?"

"I never planned on it." Lame. She tucked her hands between her knees. "He was my date. From the bachelor auction."

Relief softened his jaw. "Ahh. The adrenaline junkie. I remember him. Seemed like a nice enough guy, but definitely uncomfortable in a suit."

Uncomfortable? Sure. Gorgeous? Absolutely. "Yeah, you could say that."

"So this was a one-time thing."

"No," she whispered.

"No?" He pulled his hand from hers and wiped it over his mouth. "Be straight with me."

Right. No more pussyfooting around. Haven deserved that

consideration. "The fact is, I like Caleb, but I like you too, and I don't know if I like one of you more than the other. I go all my adult life without anyone being interested in me and now, boom, I have two great guys asking me out. I don't want to lose you, but I can't say goodbye to Caleb either. Does that make any sense?"

He shook his head. "That's what I get for waiting so long. I should have said to heck with the bank's rules and asked you out years ago."

"I would have said no." She ran her teeth over her bottom lip. That would have broken a rule. Why did she always have to be so inflexible?

"Yeah, I'm sure you would have."

"Does this mean you don't want to see me anymore?" It hurt to think of it. But it hurt to think of not being with Caleb either. How'd she get herself into this mess?

He got up off the couch, walked to the kitchen, and set his full glass on the bar. "It feels like that silly bachelor auction all over again. If I didn't go out with—"

"It's not your fault. It's mine for being a tightwad. If I'd bid a little higher—"

"You would have stolen from your savings. I liked that you didn't, Lissa. I like that you stand your ground and do the right thing."

The right thing? Right, dating two guys was the right thing in another reality maybe.

Haven returned to the couch and sat next to her. "I'm disappointed, obviously, but I'm not walking away."

"Really?" Her heart did that soft, slow waltz again.

He cupped her chin in his hand and drew her close. His minty scent drifted around her. The waltz in her heart sped up. Was he going to kiss her? Did she want him too?

Oh, yeah.

But he released her chin and stood. "I plan on winning your heart, Ms. Corliss Morgan, but I intend to do it the right way."

But a kiss would certainly help sway her, wouldn't it?

He stuffed his hands in his front pockets. "I'm busy this coming weekend, but . . . have you ever walked across the Mississippi?"

"No, I've always wanted to."

"Perfect. A week from Saturday I'm making a trip up to Itasca State

Park. The *Tour Minnesota* magazine has commissioned me to shoot some scenery, if you can believe that."

"Really? I knew you liked to take pictures, but I didn't realize you were that serious."

"There's a lot you don't know about me." He kicked at her carpeted floor.

Although he was looking downward, it wasn't enough to hide the pain in his eyes. Pain she wanted him to share with her. Pain she wanted to soothe. "I'd like to learn."

He raised his chin and his lips edged upward. "Well, if you're free, would you care to join me?"

"I'd love to."

"Good." He leaned over and kissed her forehead. "I'll see myself out."

The hummingbirds were back in her stomach. Remaining on the couch, she watched him leave. The door shut softly behind him. No tantrum, just a promise to pursue her. She stretched out on the couch and kneaded a budding headache. Who knew matters of the heart could be so confusing? "God," she prayed aloud, "if you're the missing piece in this heart equation, I'd like to know what you want me to do."

She closed her eyes and listened.

Nothing but silence. She'd have to make the decision all on her own.

Chapter Fourteen

Lissa pulled out a vinyl-upholstered chair, set her notebook and pen on the break room/meeting room table. Sitting, she pulled out a chair for Rita. "What do you suppose this is about?"

"Beats me." Rita plopped down beside her, her Pop Rocks crackling at a sprinter's pace. Seconds later they were joined by Haven's—make that Tyler's—assistant, the department secretary, and the bank's three other collection agents.

A Friday afternoon meeting in August was precisely what they didn't need to begin the weekend with. Now, if it would only end problem free. Fat chance since Tyler had taken over. Tyler strutted in, his chin held high and mouth tilted in a smirk, carrying a stack of folders half a foot high.

"Oh, brother." Rita didn't even try to cover her disdain.

"Excuse me, Ms. Dunlap?" Tyler dropped the papers onto the table. The thud echoed throughout the room and papers sashayed to the floor.

Lissa pushed her chair from the table. "Let me help."

"That's all right, Ms. Morgan. Don't expect me to fall for your bootlicking as our previous supervisor did. You won't get the same benefits from me."

Her jaw dropped, and gasps and snickers bounced off the walls. How dare he insinuate such a thing! "I'll have you know—"

"Methinks thou dost protest too much."

Lissa dropped back in her chair. To think she had to survive another half a year, possibly, with this pompous jerk. If a promotion wasn't a possibility, she'd be looking for a new employer as soon as the work day ended. But until then—

Whoa . . . That was exactly what he wanted her to do!

If he could get her out of his way, the promotion was a cinch for him. Well, that wasn't happening. All she had to do was keep performing her duties with the skill and care she always had, without reacting to Tyler's obvious digs.

The room fell eerily silent around her, and she scooted her chair back to the table and folded her hands over her notebook. No way was she going to allow him to get to her.

Tyler cleared his throat and splayed a hand over the top of the paper stack. Loose papers still lay scattered on the table and floor. "Actually, I'd like to thank Ms. Morgan for helping me make my point today."

Rita leaned over and whispered in Lissa's ear. "Here it comes."

"Ms. Dunlap, didn't your parents teach you any manners?"

She snapped her candy. "If that means respecting my elders, I guess you certainly qualify."

Soft chuckles echoed around the room.

Tyler held up his hands. "Fine. You've all had your laughs, now it's time we get down to business." Again, he slapped his hand over the stack of files. "This is unnecessary, all this paper waste, trees cut down for no good reason, when we could eliminate this altogether."

"We're finally going paperless?" Lissa held back her grin. Haven had been trying to convince the bank board for years that all those files were a waste. Finally, they listened to him.

"Very astute, Ms. Morgan. I'm certain that's a system you'll appreciate given your latest foibles. In fact, it's because of you that I brought this matter to the board."

Fire ignited in Lissa's gut. It was just like Tyler to take credit for something he had no control over. She pursed her lips, holding in a sassy remark.

Tyler dragged a file from the bottom of the pile. "Missing customer files will be a thing of the past, Ms. Morgan." He skidded the file across the table to Lissa.

No.

Swallowing hard, she glanced at the name on the file. Jonathan C.

Johnson. "Where . . . ?" Did she even want to hear his answer?

He nodded toward the refrigerator. "The janitorial staff found it on the top when they were dusting. Interesting filing system you have, Ms. Morgan. My question is, why didn't I hear about this missing file?"

The top of the fridge? How in the world did it get there? There was no doubt that this was a set up. Clenching her jaw she glared at Tyler—the snake—and picked up her pen, rotating it through her fingers. Say nothing. Don't give him any ammunition to fire.

"Well, consider yourself on probation, Ms. Morgan."

"Probation!" She gripped the arms of her chair to keep from jumping up and making more of a scene that she was already doing.

"Trust, Ms. Morgan, it's all about trust. If I can't trust you to keep our customers' information confidential, then it's time you look for a position where confidentiality isn't an issue."

How dare he? She clutched the pen between her middle and forefingers. *Don't let him get to you.* "You can count on me." To tell Haven all about this nasty trick. He still had influence over the bank board and he could make them see how power hungry Tyler was.

"I certainly hope I can trust you in the future." He pointed at the wayward file. "By the way, that gentleman needs a call. He's late."

Oh, Jonathon Johnson would get a call all right. Taking her frustrations out on a customer was a lot healthier for her career than talking back to the boss.

Following the meeting, she strode from the room to her desk and slapped the folder down. How dare Tyler make her a scapegoat! She punched in Mr. Johnson's number and it rang . . . and rang. Twenty times before she gave up. No surprise there. Debtors relied on caller I.D. and rarely had answering machines or voice mail.

She puffed out a breath and sighed. Thank God no one answered. Considering the scathing words she'd thought of using, could she blame debtors for hiding? If she wasn't careful, she'd turn into Tyler the Belligerent and any chance of promotion would zing out the door.

And Tyler would win. The scum had played her perfectly and to think she fell for it.

Oh, she'd keep trying to reach Mr. Johnson, and when she did she'd slather him with such syrupy sweetness that he'd come current in minutes. With such winning results, promoting Tyler wouldn't be a consideration.

Yesterday's call from the bank still had Caleb sweating. Caller I.D. was a marvelous invention. He didn't need to talk with them to know what they—probably Lissa—wanted. He set down his nail gun and stared at the envelope screaming from the sawhorse table. Ten days late wasn't the end of the world. But that was when the letter had been sent. Now his mortgage was fifteen days late and his bank account had a hollow echo to it. He couldn't keep hiding from them. Today he'd return that call to Lissa—not to confess, but to lay the groundwork for that confession.

The problem was, his spare time was committed to Aiden and Yvette's basement right now. It would be three weeks before he had enough open time to tell her the truth. That needed to be done in person so she could visibly experience what his home meant to him. Maybe she'd see how desperately he needed to keep his home and find some miracle solution. Right. That was about as likely as it was for Lissa to take up ski-jumping.

Three weeks . . . His mind drifted to that man he'd seen her hug a week ago. What was their relationship? It sure hadn't looked like a brotherly hug. Caleb squeezed the back of his neck. Would three weeks' absence make her heart grow fonder for him or would it secure another man's arms around her?

What he'd give for a spare evening, but that time belonged to Aimee. Between job hunting and working on this basement, she was missing enough of him as it was.

God, what can I do?

Tell the truth. It wasn't an audible answer, but his gut knew that was the right thing, even if it meant waiting. He pulled out his prepaid cell phone, a cheap one he'd picked up after cancelling his home phone, and planned to use for all the creditor calls. Lissa would never associate this number with his home number. His gut twisted. Was that a lie? What was he teaching his daughter?

He leaned against the newly sheetrocked wall and slid down until he sat on the cold concrete. Make the call now before his guilt grew worse, before his in-laws and Aimee returned from Como Zoo and sensed that guilt. With the fan blowing his hair, he dialed her number.

One ring, two, three. "Hello."

"Hey Lissa."

"Caleb!"

What a beautiful sound it was to hear her jubilant exclamation of his name. "Thanks again for the tubing trip. It was a fun day."

"You had fun going with a scaredy cat?"

He chuckled. "Ahh, you're braver than you give yourself credit for."

"I never thought I'd hear someone tell me that. You should talk to my cube mate."

"Maybe someday I will." But that step was miles down the road. "How about something tamer next time?"

"Tame, huh?" He closed his eyes and pictured her biting her lower lip and gold glimmering from her brown eyes. "What if I'm ready for more adventure?"

"Really?" Now that was a surprise, a good one at that. And it gave him an even better idea. "I know just where to take you."

"What have you got in mind?"

"Not gonna tell you."

"What?" A nervous edge tinged her voice.

Good. Now, to let her hang over that edge a little bit longer. "And I'm afraid I'm busy till the first Saturday in September."

"Three weeks?" Too bad he wasn't there in person to see her lip sticking out, but his imagination did a fine job of filling in her picture.

"Yeah, I've got a side construction job and my clients . . ." He shot a glance toward the stairwell. His in-laws wouldn't appreciate the deception, but telling Lissa he was fired needed to be said in person, not over the phone. "They want this job completed ASAP so I'm gonna be working weekends to get it done." Once his father-in-law made up his mind about something, he wanted it done now and disappointing him wasn't an option.

"You realize I'm going to be a nervous wreck wondering what

adventure you're dragging me on."

"That's the whole point. Anticipation is half the fun."

She groaned. "If you plan on taking me on one of those alpine slides, you can forget—"

"Hey, that's a good idea." For sometime down the road. By then, she'd be begging for even greater adventures.

"I'm zipping my lips."

"Oh, you want to try a zip line? I know a great one—"

"Not on your life!"

Caleb chuckled. "Okay. No zip line." This time, anyway. "You mind if I call you in the meantime?"

"You better. Three weeks is a very long time."

"Tell me about it, but it'll give us that much more to look forward to."

"And more time to back out."

"Nope. Won't happen. Now that you've tasted the wild side, you can't help but crave more."

"You're nuts, you know that."

Nuts about her? Maybe he was, but truth needed to be told before he could share his feelings. "I better get back to work—that is, if I want to see you soon."

"Call me."

"I will." He hit 'End' and glanced around the room under construction. It was taking on a new shape—like the remodeling being done on his heart. Three weeks from now, he'd have a new job. He had to. Culver's, K-Mart, anything to catch up on his house payment and calm his worries. Then he could enjoy the time with Lissa and maybe dare to plan a new future.

Chapter Fifteen

With one foot resting on a water-covered rock, Lissa glanced out over Lake Itasca then at the twenty-foot channel that was the beginning of the mighty Mississippi River. It was hard to believe that this narrow creek extended over twenty-three hundred miles with depths reaching over two hundred feet. Was that how love began? A trickle that blossomed and flowed with unimaginable intensity?

Haven's promise to speak with the bank president about Tyler's shenanigans fed that trickle. Getting that first kiss from him today wouldn't hurt either. And they had the perfect setting for it too.

"Stay there." He waved at her from several feet away and aimed his camera.

Donning a smile, her heart did a little dance. Not more than a little two-step though.

"Perfect." He rested his camera against his chest. The strap circling his neck held it in place.

She crossed her arms. "I thought you were supposed to take pictures of nature, not me."

"I am, but I'd say you certainly enhance nature."

If this was his attempt at winning her heart, he might succeed. She nodded to the rocks lining the mouth of the river and the water rushing over them. Slippery stepping-stones to the other side. A few months back, she would have hesitated to cross them, but now, thanks to Caleb . . .

Something brushed her arm. "Are you all right?"

Startled, Lissa looked at Haven's hand resting on her forearm. She nodded. "I'm fine." Just daydreaming about the other man in her life. "Shall we go?"

He held out his hand. "Need some help?"

"Actually, I think I can do it on my own." And if she fell, well, she'd get wet and they'd have a good laugh. Couldn't be worse than landing on her backside in mud.

She placed a bare foot on top of the next closest stone. Her toes slipped and her arms flung out. She teetered and regained her balance. No giving up. With arms still held out from her sides, she aimed for another rock, a foot farther away, but one that rose above the water. Her foot landed and gripped the surface. She released the breath she didn't realize she was holding. Now, the left foot. Leaning forward a smidgen, she lifted her other leg and brought it even with the right. Yes! No wobbling. Only perfect balance. She glanced ahead. Twenty-some steps to go yet.

Again, she stretched her right leg forward until it gained purchase on a stone. Left, right, and left—one stone conquered at a time until her bare feet landed firmly on the sandy ground on the opposite side of the river. Grinning, she glanced back as Haven tottered on a rock. She'd done it! Walked across the mighty Mississippi without a hand to help her! Wait until she told Caleb. He'd be thrilled.

But what he had planned for her probably was a lot more intense than this. Her heart boogied at the thought. Why did that excite her so?

Caleb . . . She combed her fingers through her bangs and watched the river water course away from Lake Itasca. How could he be on her mind when Haven was giving her a perfectly wonderful day?

"Hey Lissa, lost you again."

"Huh?" She turned to see Haven standing behind her, hands pocketed behind his back. "Oh, just in my happy place."

"Really?" He took her arm and led her away from the river rocks on a dirt path bordered with marsh grass.

"Really." She reached over and squeezed his hand. "I'm having an amazing day."

"Hmm." Hands linked together, they stepped onto a wooden

footbridge that led them back across the Mississippi. They stopped in the middle and looked out toward the tree-framed lake. Some tourists waded through the flowing waters while others attempted the rock bridge she'd crossed. Wading would have been easier. But far less fun. Perhaps Caleb had the right attitude about life.

Haven sat on the footbridge, dangling his feet above the water, and patted the spot next to him.

She sat beside him.

Maintaining silence, he raised his camera and captured the headwaters on the LCD lens. He snapped a picture of a toddler being helped across the slippery rocks, and lowered his camera. "Look at the trust that child has in her father."

A smile, brimmed with sunshine, filled the little girl's face; her arms stretched upward clinging to a man whose smile echoed the child's. Lissa once looked at her own father that way. "Beautiful, isn't it? A child should be able to trust her father." To do the right thing.

"Yes. They should." Haven raised his camera again and began snapping random pictures. "My dad was never like that. He would have pushed me forward and made me cross on my own. It worked, I guess. I learned that after you mess up and fall, you get back up, dry yourself off, and pray you didn't hurt too many people with your screw up."

"Sounds like you wanted some help along the way."

He shrugged. "I know what I would do now. Doesn't make sense to second-guess the past. My mistakes have made me who I am today."

Lissa latched her arm around his. "I guess I can't complain. I happen to like who you are."

"Do you?" He turned to her and his eyes examined hers.

"Very much so. I always have. Ever since Dad introduced me to you. I guess you could say I had ulterior motives when I accepted the internship at the bank."

"Something beyond your framed list?"

"That little list has been my inspiration for years. It doesn't exactly say 'date a gorgeous guy', but I think it's implied."

"Gorgeous, huh?" He waggled his brows above eyes that matched Itasca's water. Eyes that closed as he narrowed the distance between himself and Lissa.

And she leaned toward him—

"Watch out!" A woman yelled and cold water sprayed Lissa's legs, lap, and arm.

Squealing, Lissa pulled away from Haven and glanced down at a splashing, giggling toddler.

Haven chuckled.

"I am so sorry. Turner, tell the nice people you're sorry." The woman attached to the warning voice waded toward the boy and scooped him out of the water. "He can't stay out of mischief. Turner, say you're sorry."

"Don't worry." Lissa wiped the dampness from her arm and squeezed it from her shirt. "It's only water."

"I know, but you two . . ." Red faced, the woman averted her eyes toward her child. "Turner, say you're sorry."

"Sowwy." Accompanied with more giggles.

"You're forgiven." Grinning, Lissa patted his head. The mom and child waded toward land and Lissa sighed. Would she ever know the taste of Haven's lips? She glanced over at him. His camera rested on his lap as he dried it with his shirt. "Is it okay?"

Lips scrunched, he raised it up and glanced at the LCD screen. "Should be fine. Just got a little damp." He pointed the camera at her and depressed the shutter. A second later he grinned. "Fine indeed."

"Oooh, let me see." She grasped the camera from his hands and wrinkled her nose at the picture of her half smile, half grimace, and partially closed eyes. Lovely. "How do I delete this?" She studied the plethora of buttons on the back.

"Uh-uh." Haven grabbed the camera. "You never know when I might need this."

"You are so lucky you're holding that camera, because otherwise, you'd be taking a bath in the river."

"Sounds like a threat."

"Hmmph." She flapped her peasant blouse, attempting to dry it. "Just you wait."

"I've got something to look forward to." Standing, he offered his hand. "I think I've got enough shots—"

"One too many, you mean." She ignored his hand and strode down a wooded path toward the parking lot.

"The perfect amount of shots from this location."

Hands on hips, she turned around and stuck out her tongue.

He laughed. "Yep, you've changed, all right."

"What are you talking about?" Her hands remained on her hips as he lessened the gap between them.

He stopped within kissing distance and whispered. "Once upon a time, I knew this beautiful woman and admired for her dedication, her focus, her tender heart, but . . ."

The dance resumed in her heart. "But?" The word squeaked out.

He stroked her cheek. "But she was this timid thing, afraid to veer off her scheduled track."

Giggles sounded behind her, and she backed away. No way was she going to share Haven's first kiss with strangers. "Come here." She grabbed his hand and led him past a family to a break in the woods that looked like a deer trail. Did she dare? Even with Haven's hand enveloping hers, tension tingled in her fingers at the very thought of breaking a rule.

Caleb wouldn't think twice about going off the path.

Caleb? How could she even think of him with Haven so close? Well, there was one sure fire way to drown his name completely. She tugged on Haven's hand and turned off the people path.

He held her back. "We're not supposed to go there."

"Really?" She brought a finger to his lips and traced them. "Are you sure?"

A bead of sweat appeared on his brow, but he didn't say no.

She tugged his hand again. This time he followed down a path normally travelled by wildlife. She stomped on a cigarette butt and kicked a beer can. Some human wildlife too, apparently. After walking fifty paces or so, she glanced back toward civilization. Nothing but trees, birds, gophers, wildflowers. Perfect.

Apparently Haven thought so too as he released her hand and wrapped his arms around her back and pulled her tight against him. "As I was saying, I once knew this timid thing, afraid to go off the track."

Lissa's heart beat against his chest. Was she ready? She backed away a few inches only to be stopped by a tree. "What happened to her?" she whispered, resting her back against the trunk. Now she had no way out. It was finally going to happen.

"Hmm. Let's see." He cupped his hands on her cheeks and leaned forward, closing his eyes.

A sharp pain stung her back and she jumped forward, slamming her forehead into Haven's mouth. Another sting bit her forearm.

Haven grabbed her arm and tugged her away as a swarm of bees charged from the tree trunk announcing their attack with a high-pitched hum.

With a scream, she followed Haven as he flew down the wildlife path, the sharp pain in her back and arm escalating.

"Are you allergic?" Haven yelled while running.

"No!" But the stings made her eyes tear. That was worsened by the sting of another missed opportunity.

Breathing hard, they arrived at the manmade path.

"Are you all right?" Haven raised her arm, and she grimaced at the growing welt.

She nodded. "It hurts like the dickens, though."

"I'm sure it does." He drew his wallet from his back pocket and slid out a credit card. With its edge, he scraped the stinger out. "Any more?"

"One." She turned her back to him and lifted her shirt.

"Ouch."

She felt his card scrape at her skin and more tears threatened. "I'm sorry, Haven. I thought . . ."

"Shhh. Don't worry about it. If you recall, I didn't object too loudly."

"I know, but—"

"But nothing. Let's get you to first aid, and get something on that."

"You're right." She clasped Haven's hand and hustled down the dirt path. One more opportunity crushed. *God, what are you trying to tell me?* Try harder? Or forget it?

They arrived at the visitor center without her hearing an obvious answer. She downed two aspirin with a drink of water and applied ice to the sting.

Haven held a cube to his lips, swollen from her head butting into them. Within thirty minutes her pain had abated. They'd applied the perfect first aid.

Too bad Haven didn't realize it wasn't the bee stings that required first aid, it was her heart. She studied his luscious blue eyes, tender with concern, and held in a sigh. If only his lips were swollen from their kisses instead, maybe then she'd have an answer to the Caleb/Haven predicament. Maybe then she'd know whether Mr. Perfect was Mr. Right or Mr. Very Very Wrong.

If Haven was perfect for her, why did her heart long for Caleb? Lissa dove onto her bed and lay there, her face pressed into the pillow. A headache pulsed in her temple and her fingers trembled, aching for that hand to mouth action. Longing to taste the bitter smoke. *God, help me please.*

The tingling cravings escalated. Just like her cravings to spend more time with Caleb. Everyone knew cravings were bad. If only Haven had kissed her, then maybe she'd be lying here still savoring the warmth of his lips, not wishing Caleb would call.

Where was that neighborhood cat when she needed him? He always relieved stress. And why was she stressed by having two wonderful men vying for her? Rita would be reveling in this quandary. She was the one person who would encourage her, not judge. Though it was nearly midnight, that was still early for Rita. Lissa pushed herself up, grabbed her phone from the nightstand, and reclined against her headboard.

The phone rang three times before Rita answered. "Hey sweets, what's up?"

Lissa massaged her throbbing temple. "Man problems."

"Oooh, the best kind to have. Can you hold a sec? I've got my own man issues and he doesn't need—"

"Rita, no. If you've got someone there, I don't mean to interrupt. This can wait."

"Uh-uh, sweets. You don't call me at midnight and leave me hanging. Not happening." A squeak of springs and a thud sounded over the phone. "Be right back, babe." Rita's voice was muffled. A thump, like a door closing, sounded in the background. "Now dish. I need to know everything."

Terrific. Lissa sunk lower on the bed. It didn't take much imagination to know what this phone call had interrupted. What a life her friend led. "Do I know this guy?"

"I ain't telling. Besides, you called me with your problem. Monday, I'll fill you in on mine."

And Rita's details would be far more colorful than Lissa's, that was for certain. With a sigh, Lissa closed her eyes and recounted the day with Haven.

"So you're telling me, the man still hasn't laid lips on yours?"

Lissa sighed and muttered, "No." She picked at lint on her comforter. "The thing is, I don't know if I really want to kiss him. I like him—"

"Like? You've been drooling over him for years, sweets."

"Really like him, okay? And he's treated me to the most beautiful days, but now that I think back, kissing him today—or trying to—seemed forced, as if I was out to prove something to myself." As if that would expunge Caleb from her thoughts.

"Sweets, you've got it bad, you know that?"

"If that's true, why am I confused? If I've got it so bad, why am I conflicted about kissing him?"

Rita snorted. "You are clueless."

"Gee, thanks. So, why don't you fill me in?"

"Sometimes, you gotta figure things out for yourself."

"Rita . . ."

"Nope. Not gonna tell you. When are you seeing Mr. Reckless again?"

"He's not reckless."

Rita laughed.

"Fine. Two weeks from now. And what we're doing is a surprise."

"A surprise? Whoa, girl, you are in major trouble. The dude's probably got you going up in a helicopter or—"

"Or windsurfing, or climbing rock walls, or—"

"Out on his Harley maybe."

"Harley? Huh! No, no, no. Caleb doesn't do Harleys. He and his wife used to have matching souped-up cycles."

"Ah, you mean donorcycles 'cause their riders often end up donating their body parts."

Lissa groaned. "Thanks for that image."

"This dude likes you?"

"Go figure."

"And you still don't know what to do with your love life."

Lissa pressed her head into the pillow and released a growl.

"Well, sweets, in two weeks, if you haven't puzzled it out by then, maybe I'll clue you in. But for now, I've got one gorgeous hunk of man waiting for me."

Lissa banged her head against the pillow. "Go." And be stupid with some guy. Rita was going to get herself in big trouble some day.

At least Lissa's problem was with two Christian guys who respected her. She tossed the phone onto her bed. Two weeks. To be honest, she didn't need two weeks to decipher what her heart was telling her. But maybe it was enough time for her head to convince her heart otherwise. She clenched her twitching fingers into fists and tucked them beneath her arms.

What she'd give for one cigarette. Just one to stop the shaking.

No, no, NO! No giving in. She grabbed her journal off her end table and wrote, "I care for Haven, not Caleb." Maybe, in two weeks, seeing the words repeated every day would engrave them on her heart and she'd finally be able to let Caleb go. And, if she was lucky, her cigarette cravings would fly away with him.

Chapter Sixteen

Where are we going?"

Caleb tore his gaze from the tree-sided road and snuck a peek at Lissa seated next to him in his pickup. She was doing that cute thing with her lip again. "It's a surprise."

"Let me guess. You just turned south on 494 so it's not the State Fair."

"Right."

"Please, please tell me we're not going to Valleyfair."

He grinned, picturing the two of them on a rollercoaster. "Okay, we're not. Although it wouldn't be a bad idea."

"Waterskiing?"

"Did you bring your suit?"

"Oh, guess not."

"Hot air balloon?"

"It's on my bucket list."

"You're not going to give me any hints, are you?"

"Now, would that be any fun?"

Her foot tapped rhythmically on the floor. "I've been going insane these past three weeks. You've got my stomach so tied up in knots wondering what death-defying adventure you're taking me on."

"I've done my job well."

"Oh, you."

He glanced over at her again. The mock anger on her face was beyond adorable. "For the record, these past three weeks have been long for me too, but not for the same reasons."

"And those reasons are?"

"Just one. I missed you." And his musings had centered more on Lissa than Jeanette. Queasiness still unsettled his stomach somewhat at the thought of dating again, but his heart—and his in-laws—said it was the right thing. But first, he had to be honest about who he was and that would happen later today. After he'd shown her what his home meant to him. And after he watched her spread her wings one more time. Then . . .

He swallowed the clog in his throat. "Lissa?"

"Yeah?"

"I need to stop at my house, if you don't mind. I left our tickets there." On purpose. But she didn't need to know that.

"Tickets?"

He grinned. "You'll never guess to what."

"Hmmph."

The car in front of him slowed and Caleb veered into the left lane. "Does that mean you're not upset about the delay?"

"Hardly. I'd love to see your place."

Just the response he was looking for. "Good. It's only a few miles off the interstate so it'll take us twenty, maybe twenty-five extra minutes."

"Will I get to meet your daughter?"

Someday, hopefully. "She's at her grandparents'. Besides, I still don't like the idea of introducing you until I know you'll be a permanent part of my life."

"Oh." Her voice tailed off.

"It's nothing against you. But if I introduce you two, I know you'd fall in love with each other, then if I stopped seeing you, it'd be like losing her momma all over again. I can't do that to her."

Lissa's hand rested on his forearm. "I understand."

"I knew you would." At least, he hoped she would. He steered off of 494 onto the Bass Lake Road exit and hung a right. They drove a few miles, past older residential areas and finally to his newer subdivision, a scant five years old. The road wound through the eclectic neighborhood where no two homes looked alike. Finally he turned into his cul-de-sac and waved at the pre-teens riding their bikes around the street. This was the perfect location to raise children.

He drove up the short cobblestone driveway. It had taken him one entire summer to complete the project. That was back when Heart of the Home Kitchen Designs' services were in high demand, relegating his personal home updates to the bottom of the priority list. It had been worth the work.

Lissa helped herself out of the truck. "Your place is beautiful."

He met her by the sidewalk he'd paved with the same brick outlining the driveway. "Thanks. Jeanette and I designed it ourselves and I did a lot of the work to save money." And to make sure it was built to top standards.

She ran her hand down the stone facing on the front of the split-entry house. "Limestone?"

"Sure is." He walked ahead and unlocked the front door. "Come on in."

But she stayed back beneath the overhang, her brows narrowed in puzzlement. "I could swear I've seen your house before."

"Really?" He swallowed and massaged the back of his perspiring neck. "It's a one-of-a-kind. You've been in the neighborhood before?"

"No." She shook her head and shrugged. "But I see so many pictures, they all start to blend together."

"That must be it." If only that were true. The second missed payment notice he received from her yesterday probably imbedded his house in her mind. Well, she needed to see how important his home was so the bank couldn't take it away. He held the door for her. "Would you like a tour?"

"I'd love one."

He kicked off his tennis shoes on the tiled entry and led her down a short flight of stairs. To his left was the family room they'd finished right before Jeanette died. Her strawberry body splash still seemed to permeate the room. He prayed it would never leave. Although the house was barely five years old, it held an older home appeal with its wide baseboards and moulding stained dark brown.

A large window opened up to their tree-filled backyard. With parkland in back of them, they never had to worry about filling the view with other houses. They'd been so blessed to find this location.

Certainly God wouldn't let it slip away. After today, he prayed Lissa would be on God's side.

He rested a hand on the back of his curved sectional and pointed to a fireplace framed in by oak cabinets and bookshelves. "Stone from Lake Superior. Jeanette loved this room. We'd sit down here and read, feed Aimee, relax . . ." And love each other.

Lissa gave his hand a squeeze and walked past him, over pecan-brown carpeting soft enough to baby Aimee's knees, to the shelving. He wiped his nose and watched her run her hands over the vine he'd whittled into the bookshelves' facing, along with the Bible verse, "Let love and faithfulness never leave you; bind them around your neck, write them on the tablet of your heart." Proverbs 3:3. Jeanette had loved and lived that verse. And that was all he'd tried to do since she died.

At least until he met Lissa. Was dating her breaking his covenant of faithfulness? His head screamed no, but his heart . . . ?

"This is exquisite." A tremor shook her quiet voice. "You did this too, I assume. Like your picnic box."

"Yeah. It's mine."

"You've got a gift Caleb. One that should be shared."

"Thank you." He walked to Lissa's side and took her hand. She squeezed it and held on. It felt right, protecting her hand with his. Jeanette was most likely grinning.

Breaking his covenant? Maybe his heart was finally convinced it was time to let go.

Lissa ran her teeth over her lower lip. What was it about Caleb's hand that exuded strength? Safety? And why didn't Haven's feel the same way? Regardless, she wasn't about to release Caleb from his grip. "Why don't you show me the rest of your house?"

"Sure thing." Keeping their fingers entwined, he led her down a short hallway, pointing out a full bath and two bedrooms. Six-panel doors guarded each room. "They're bare, but we'd hoped someday . . ."

She clung to his hand tighter and walked into a bedroom. Like in the living room, dark-stained moulding framed-in walls painted a bamboo color. Caleb was right, not a stick of furniture decorated these rooms. Not that the sectional in the family room, with the triangular chaise lounge at one end, constituted much in the way of furnishings. A clean slate for her to decorate. Although, that couch called to her. All she needed was a fire, a good book . . . and Caleb snuggled against her.

She shook off the image and walked out of the bedroom, pulling Caleb along with her.

"Like it?"

"It's a dream. I love your old-fashioned touches. Reminds me of my grandparents' old Tudor in Minneapolis."

"That's exactly what we were going for." He led her to the foyer and up another short flight to the living room. "We both wanted to build, but didn't like the modern look, and we wanted to craft something that would complement God's creation, not steal from it."

"I'm not sure what you mean."

He pulled her down a short hallway lined with pictures, past a bath, to Aimee's room. Painted forest scenes and wildlife colored the walls, and glow-in-the-dark stars dotted her ceiling. Six-panel doors hung here too. He ran his hand down the walnut finish. "With a few exceptions, we tried to re-use building materials. These doors, for instance, came from a home someone was renovating. The shelves downstairs, I created from scrap wood. The kitchen cabinets, a wrong order by someone else."

"So you take someone else's rejects and engrave it to make it yours."

"Exactly." He grinned that sexy, squinty-eyed smile and the butterflies polkaed in her heart. Why was she doing this to herself, letting her heart rule the head? That was what got people into trouble.

She pulled her hand from his and glanced toward the master bedroom, the place where Caleb and his wife had probably shared their most intimate moments. She didn't need to see that room, but he pointed to the door frame.

Three vines wound around the verse, "A cord of three strands is not easily broken." Ecclesiastes 4:12. "It was always a reminder to us to keep God at the core of our marriage."

"You still love her, don't you?"

His face blanched and he rubbed a hand over his whiskers. "I do. I always will, but I'm also learning to let her go. If I meant that God was the center of our marriage, then I have to give Jeanette up to him and live again. With you"—He ran a hand down Lissa's cheek—"I feel like it's finally happening. You've breathed life into my heart again in a way that's very different from Jeanette, but equally as good."

Her breath quickened and her gaze stopped on his lips, her own lips tingling with hope. He leaned toward her, his hands resting on her hips, and she closed her eyes, breathing in his woodsy cologne.

But his hands sprang from her hips and she felt him move away. Disappointment thudded in her stomach as she opened her eyes. He leaned against the wall across from her, his wedding picture grazing his right shoulder.

"I'm sorry." His Adam's apple bobbed. "I don't mean to take advantage."

By all means, take advantage! The declaration lodged in her throat. "You weren't." She reached for him, but he walked away.

"Let me show you my favorite room."

With a sigh, she followed him into the kitchen. Cherry Shaker cabinets hung from the walls; the upper corner cabinet had more of Caleb's carvings. Stuffing her frustration from the near kiss, she walked toward the cabinet and traced his etchings with her finger. Vines again wove among calligraphied words, "I am the vine; you are the branches. If a man remains in me and I in him, he will bear much fruit; apart from me you can do nothing." John 15:5.

"That's beautiful, Caleb. Why don't you do this for a living?"

"It was a hobby. If I made it my job, I'm afraid I'd stop liking it."

Made sense. Still, this man's artwork needed to be seen by the rest of the world. There had to be a way to help him.

He rested his forearms on the island angled opposite his stove and refrigerator. The perfect kitchen triangle.

"We called it the kitchen heart," he said as if reading her mind. "It just made sense, considering the name of our business . . . and this." His finger traced an outline of red etched into the granite.

"A heart!"

"Hard to believe, huh? When Jeanette and I saw it, we couldn't pass the piece up, no matter the cost. I think God made it just for us."

"It is perfect. Just like your house. This kitchen. You've created a warm haven that people yearn for."

"Thanks. That's what we strived for."

"You still design kitchens, don't you?"

"I would, if the economy would let me."

"That blasted economy."

"That, and the fact that I'm an artist not a bookkeeper. I have no sense for numbers."

"Hmmm." She chewed on her lower lip. With her head for business and her connections . . . "Let me help you."

"You'd do that?"

"Of course. How about we sit down next week and go over your business plan. If I can save people's homes, maybe I can save your business too."

His cheeks flexing, he looked down. "You don't know what that means to me. And to Aimee."

"I think I do." She walked around the island, circled her arms around his waist and rested her head on his chest. His arms surrounded her with strength. Now wasn't the time to try for that kiss, but later?

Why did Caleb have such a grip on her heart when Haven was made for her? Maybe today would tell. When Caleb dropped her off tonight, if he didn't kiss her, then she'd know he wasn't ready to move on and date. Then she could gently let him go and be free to date Haven.

So why did the thought of not seeing Caleb again weigh in her stomach like wadded up Wonder bread?

Lissa hummed along with the radio, but kept her eyes alert looking for any hint of where Caleb was taking her. And if that meant off-road four-wheeling or rock-climbing, somehow she knew she'd be safe. She was ready for whatever heart-thumping thrill ride he would throw at her.

The blinker pinged and Lissa glanced at the sign on the side of the road. "Arboretum?"

"Is that okay?"

She fluttered her hands in front of her face and sniffled. "I love this place." A thousand-plus acres of flowers and vegetation with miles of walking paths. It had to be a glimpse of heaven.

"I figured as much." He drove down the zigzagging, tree-shadowed road and parked close the visitor center. "Want to picnic here or while we're out walking?"

"Another picnic?"

"Sorry. Someday I'll be able to treat you to a formal—"

"I wasn't complaining. As a matter of fact, your picnics are so much better than anything we could get at a restaurant. I can't wait to taste what you've brought today, so let's eat out there somewhere."

"The funny thing is, Jeanette was the exact opposite. She got bored with her dad's cooking and my sandwiches and begged to go out. She'd be thrilled that I found someone who enjoys my picnics." He grabbed the insulated backpack from the seat and stepped out of his pickup. Lissa followed suit and they walked side by side to the grey-blue two-story building.

Wood carvings and etchings by local artisans filled the atrium-like room in the visitor center. Caleb took her hand and led her to the closest piece. A human profile, a tear-filled relief engraved in a paper-sized piece of maple, and waves of sunset sinking behind the face. Amazing how a simple wood carving could evoke such emotion. Lissa wanted to reach out and brush the tear away. What had happened to stir up such sadness?

"Beautiful, isn't it?"

Lissa just nodded.

"And so is the price." Caleb pointed out the tag with the artist's and artwork's name. "This would take care of a month's mortgage."

Lissa felt her eyes widen. "Whoa."

"Exactly." They strolled to a larger piece entitled "Hope" that showed a garden of tulips sprouting next to a snowman with the snowman's stick arms reaching to pluck a flower from its snow bed.

The detail and depth of the scene was astounding. "And this one would pay two months' worth."

"So, what's stopping you from doing this?" She splayed her arms toward the dozen other pieces showcased around the room.

"Ever hear of the starving artist? Well, that's how all these got their start. Chances are it took years to hone their talent, and establish a presence. Besides, for me, that would take the joy out of it."

"Hmmm. I suppose you're right."

For the next hour, they walked from one woodcarving to another. It didn't matter what Caleb said, his talent equaled, even surpassed these artists. There had to be a way to market his talent. It needed to be shared with the public, not stored away for his viewing only.

They left the room and walked down a hallway where oil paintings of vibrant-colored flowers were hung. If she weren't saving to buy a house, she'd be tempted to purchase artwork for her home.

That was it!

That was how she'd begin to promote Caleb's talent. She'd be his first customer. For him, she'd even splurge a little. Her mom wouldn't be able to resist, and with her mom's connections . . .

"Hey, Lissa, where'd you go?"

"What?" Lissa blinked her eyes back into focus. This daydreaming around the men in her life had to stop. "I get lost in my happy place a lot."

"Happy place, huh? I think I like that."

With a contented smile, Lissa curled her arm around his.

Caleb led her outside where a smorgasbord of floral scents and warbling birds greeted them. "You up for a long walk?"

Here? With Mr. Thrill Ride turned Peaceful Romantic? "I could walk for forever." But what about Haven? She clung tighter to Caleb as they entered the Japanese garden with its stone lanterns lighting the pathway that circled a waterfall. Then on through a hosta garden and over a path that cut between azaleas. From there they walked past roses and irises to groves of willow, pine, larch, poplar, and linden trees.

"You like mazes?" He pointed at a floral labyrinth bordered with pines, and its pathway hedged with junipers, azaleas, lattice, bamboo, and fabric walls.

"As long as you let me lead." Without waiting for an answer, she took his hand and dragged him through the maze she'd traversed so many times, past giant bug sculptures, carved by Minnesota artists, that seemed to crawl right out of the ground. She led the way to the center, back out again with barely a wrong turn, and plopped down on a wooden bench to view the maze's next victims.

"Done this before, huh?" Caleb nudged her over and sat dangerously close.

Her stomach flip-flopped and growled simultaneously, and she glanced at her watch. Two hours already? Where had the time disappeared to?

"I take it you're hungry."

Her face must have turned stoplight red. "Gee, how'd you guess?"

He grinned, wrapped his hand around hers, and stood. "I think we'll have to find a cozy place for a picnic."

"Cozy, huh?"

"Well, uh . . ." His face bloomed a shade that had to equal hers.

"Don't worry." She patted his hand. "You can trust me."

He winked. "You had me worried there." They walked down a paved road protected by gnarly oaks. The oaks bowed out to ornamental grasses that introduced giant heart-shaped-leaf catalpa trees. "Mind if we sneak off the path?"

"With you, I wouldn't expect any less." They walked until path and people disappeared. Caleb pulled a blanket from his backpack and spread it in a tree's shade. Lissa sat, crossing her legs beneath her while Caleb divvied up pulled pork sandwiches, an array of sliced vegetables, and chocolate-dipped strawberries. Absolutely delectable.

Everything about this day was delicious. Now, if only Caleb would cap it off right, then she'd know he was the one for her.

But what about Haven?

She bit into a strawberry and studied Caleb across from her, leaning against a catalpa's trunk, with its heart leaves draping over him. Beautiful. Too bad she didn't have her camera, but her phone would do. Then she could actually prove to Rita she wasn't exaggerating about this hunky man. She pulled her phone from her purse and snapped a candid shot of him biting into his sandwich. She'd get more later, posed among the flowers, or on a bridge, or in front of a waterfall, or all of the above.

Caleb finished his sandwich and cleaned his hands with a wet wipe. "Now, it's my turn."

He reached into his backpack and pulled out a book-sized piece of wood and a chisel.

Lissa steepled her hands over her mouth and blinked back tears. To be the object of an artists' eye was a priceless gift.

His lips quirked to one side as he dragged the chisel over the wood.

"Do I need to sit still?"

"Nah, you'll be fine."

Hardly. She fingered away tears, trying not to move. Concentration narrowed his eyes and furrowed his brows. He wiped the rogue curls from his forehead, but they rebelled. That was okay. Rebellion looked mighty sexy on him.

A shadow slunk low on his face as the next hour passed and he finally held up his artwork. Failing to halt her quivering chin, she accepted the portrait. It was almost like looking in a mirror. The fine details of her hair and lashes, even the light reflecting off her eyes with her head dipped slightly, and teeth raking her lower lip, was a masterpiece.

"I love that look on you."

Goodness. She wiped more tears off her cheeks.

"I take it you like it."

"It's exquisite, Caleb."

"It's yours."

"No. Really? I can keep it?" She'd never been given such a precious gift.

He shrugged. "That's why I made it."

With a sniffle, she set the portrait down on the blanket and inched toward Caleb, the dance in her heart speeding from polka to rock 'n roll. He pressed his back further against the tree trunk, and his normally slit eyes grew wide as rose petals.

So, the man could jump from airplanes, but was afraid of her. Well, that was about to change. She took his hand and knelt next to him, her eyes locking with his.

"Lissa, I don't . . ."

"Shhh." Her lips puckered perfectly with the sound as she lowered her head and brushed her lips against his. She pulled away enough to see his eyes. "That was to say thank you." She brushed the stray curl from his forehead and embraced her hands over his whiskered cheeks, turning his head her way. "And this is to say, well, I'll let you figure it out."

Her lips whispered against his then pressed deeper, sending her heart into an irregular jazz beat. Caleb's arms circled her back and he pulled her down on his lap, his lips mirroring her intensity, his heart dancing arm in arm with hers.

So this was what free-falling into love felt like. Danger never felt so good.

Chapter Seventeen

C aleb was the one.

Lissa practically giggled as she squinted into the evening sun, looking ahead as Caleb steered his pickup down her street. Tonight, she had no intentions of letting him drop her off and leave. That kiss of his meant the day was just beginning.

The curb in front of her townhome was bare, her driveway unoccupied. She slowly released her breath. The last time she and Caleb had made the trek down this road a surprise had awaited her. Not that she'd minded seeing Haven at that time, but now? The timing would be awful considering what she had to tell him. Whoever would have figured that she'd be the one breaking Haven's heart and not vice versa?

The pickup pulled tight to the curb and Lissa peeked at Caleb. That alone propelled her heartbeat. He couldn't leave yet, not with God's gift of a sunset waiting to be unwrapped.

"Caleb, do you think—"

"—Lissa, how about—"

Lissa laughed and reached over to grasp Caleb's hand still clinging to the steering wheel. How ironic to see Mr. Risk Taker so terrified. "I'd really like it if you'd stick around a bit longer. Catch the sunset from my steps."

He loosened his grip on the steering wheel and took her hand. "I'd like that."

They got out of the truck and Caleb's strong hand embraced hers while he escorted her to the townhome steps. Keeping their hands entwined, they sat and she rested her head against his shoulder. The stares and wry smiles from her neighbors walking past didn't bother her. She closed her eyes and listened to kids playing soccer in the middle of the street, the wind rustling leaves, birds singing to their mates, and a bell chiming out a tune.

The kids' game grew quiet and Lissa opened her eyes. The bell's tune crescendoed and the children added hollered words to the melody.

Shouts of "Ice cream truck!" echoed down the street.

"An ice cream truck?" Caleb sounded as excited as the preteens.

"Yeah. It comes through about once a week. The kids go nuts over it." She rolled her eyes. Didn't parents realize what a problem childhood obesity was nowadays?

Caleb squeezed her hand. "How about it?"

"You're kidding, right?" Did he know how many calories and how much cholesterol was in those bars? The artificial ingredients alone could cause cancer.

"I'm dead serious."

Dead was right. That was exactly what they'd be with an ice cream diet. "I think I'll pass."

"Aww, come on. One won't hurt you." He stood and pulled her up with him.

Lissa, don't be a hypocrite. She gave Caleb's hand a slight tug, but he threw her his squinty-eyed grin. The man didn't know how to play fair. "Okay, but if my cholesterol rockets, I know who to blame."

He stopped and took her other hand. His gaze landed on her lips. "Honey, if your cholesterol rockets, I think we could blame that sweet little kiss."

Honey? Did he just call her Honey? First the grin, followed by the endearment, and now topping it off with a reminder of their not-so-little, and definitely more than sweet kiss? Oh, not fair at all. "You realize that you are single-handedly corrupting me, don't you?"

"I hope so." With a wink, he nodded to the kids pouring out of homes and cascading down the street toward the tinny music. He released one hand and pulled her along with the throngs.

Just one ice cream treat. Caleb was right. One wouldn't hurt her, or would it? They waited behind the mob of children all waving their dollar bills and hollering out "Snow cone," "Fudgesicle," and "Cotton candy swirl."

"Know what you want?" Caleb nodded toward the sign on the side of the truck.

She shook her head. The peanut butter cup bar did sound good, but what would her stomach say?

"Aimee would have the Dora the Explorer bar, but I think I'll be a bit more sophisticated." He handed the truck driver a five. "I'll have a Spiderman pop, and my girlfriend will have . . ."

Her eyes widened, staring at him. Girlfriend? Not fair. Absolutely unfair! "I'll take a peanut butter cup bar."

"That's my girl." The driver handed Caleb change and the bars.

Lissa unwrapped hers and Caleb stuffed both wrappers into his back pocket. She stared at the artery-hardening treat and gave it a slight lick.

"Aw, come on. You can do better than that. Bite into it, savor the flavor." He bit off Spiderman's forehead and moaned his pleasure.

Well, here it goes. She bit into the bar. Chocolate and peanut butter exploded on her taste buds, and she echoed Caleb's delighted moan. If her mom saw her now, she'd never live this down.

They returned to her steps and finished off their treats. One a year wouldn't hurt.

Figures Caleb would get her to take another—

That sneak! "You always manage it, don't you?" If she didn't know better, she'd think he alone enticed that ice cream truck to roll down her street at this precise time.

"What?" He backhanded the reddish drip trailing down his chin.

"Our dates." Curbing her smile, she leaned toward him, daring him to come closer, wanting him to make the next move. "You always get me to step out of my comfort zone. So today, I'm expecting you to take me parasailing or on some other death-defying date and we end up at the Arboretum. You couldn't let the day pass without adding some risk to my life, could you?"

What she'd give to taste his strawberry and lemon sweetened lips. His chest undulated with breath, but he kept pulling away. What was wrong? Was it her? Didn't he find her attractive?

He thumbed what must have been ice cream off her cheek then licked his thumb. "You're beautiful, do you know that?"

Then kiss me.

A cloud muted the sun and Caleb increased the distance between them. "There's something I need to tell you."

Dread curdled in her stomach. "What?"

He turned from her, planted his feet on the steps and massaged the back of his neck. "I realized something right before our last date, and I wanted to tell you, but when I dropped you off, some other guy . . ."

Whew. She blew out a relieved breath. Caleb was jealous. That was the problem. "That was Haven, my former boss. He and I—"

"That wasn't the problem. I wanted to tell you something and I lost the opportunity. Now, I'm scared to death."

Caleb scared? No way could this be good. Lissa removed his hand from his neck and wove her fingers with his. "I'm listening."

He huffed out a breath. "This morning, when you said you recognized my house, there was a reason for it."

She shrugged. "Tell me."

"My full name. My legal name is Jonathan Caleb Johnson. You probably recognize my house from a file you keep at work."

Her mind searched through her mental files. Johnson, Jonathan. She and Rita had recently laughed over absurd names. Why was his so familiar? She closed her eyes, imagining the files, trying to picture the name typed on the corner. Johnson, Jonathan.

Okay, she could see it now, in her hands, on her desk. Open.

And a phone call.

From a French-accented man whom she felt very sorry for. A man who'd lost his business, his wife, and was not about to lose his home.

A man just like Caleb.

No, it couldn't be. He wouldn't use her like that, would he? "You didn't call me, pretending you were French, did you?" Please say no.

He sighed. "That was a mistake."

"A mistake?" She jumped up and glared down at him. "That was you?" Her chin quivered as his betrayal—his deception slammed into her heart.

"I'm sorry."

"Sorry? You're sorry? How dare you?" Her anger squeaked out then strengthened. "How dare you use me?!" All this time, she thought he cared when all he wanted was that stupid house. How could she not have seen this before?

"I'm sorry, Lissa, I—"

"Don't." She tugged on her screen door. If the bank found out about this, her job would be at stake, much less her promotion.

"Lissa, please . . ."

Ignoring his sad plea, she fumbled with her keys. Finally grasping the right one, she shoved it into the keyhole. She flung the door open, stepped inside, and spun back around.

Caleb still stood there, red-faced, his hands buried in his pockets. "Can't we talk?"

"I want you to leave. Now. And the next time I see you, it better be at the bank with a cashier's check covering your whole amount past due. If you don't, you can kiss that house goodbye, and I won't feel one ounce of guilt for taking it away from you." She slammed her door shut, and leaned against it.

Heaving sobs tore from her as gravity tugged her to the ground. She flexed her itching fingers and breathed in, trying to placate lungs begging for that lethal yet seducing smoke. If ever she had a reason to give in, now was it. She wiped her eyes and sniffled.

No one would recognize her at that hole-in-the-wall convenience store a few miles away. Five minutes there, five back. Peace was only ten minutes away. She hurried through her home to her car. Today, not even God would blame her for giving in.

With music blaring from the truck's speakers, Caleb pounded the steering wheel as he turned onto his in-laws' street. How could he convince Lissa to listen to him? Without evicting him from his home?

He zoomed the truck onto Aiden's moonlit driveway and turned down the volume on his radio. With his luck, he'd probably get cited for disturbing the peace. And that was exactly what he'd be doing by stopping at his in-laws'. But he couldn't return to his empty home. Tonight he needed to know he was worth loving. A quiet home sent the exact opposite message.

A few years back, he'd have taken his bike out for an adrenaline-blitzing spin. If only he still had a bike. Maybe he could call the friend who bought it, borrow it for a day. He pulled out his cell phone and scrolled through the numbers. His thumb hovered over his friend's number. No. That wouldn't solve anything and, considering his current state-of-mind, it might leave Aimee without a dad. He wouldn't do that to her.

He retrieved his backpack from behind his seat and trudged toward the house. A light shone from a basement window, Aidan's new man cave. He was probably watching ESPN or some TV movie. Caleb would join him in the mindless venture. He entered the house, taking care to be soundless. If Aimee heard him, she'd run to see him regardless of the time of day.

With his backpack straddled over his left shoulder, he walked down the stairs. He didn't have to feign a smile when he saw Aiden. The man was reclined in his leather chair as if he'd spent a lifetime there. And the chair was the perfect man chair with controls for heat and massage on one side, and a cooler, glass, and remote holder on the other. The only thing he'd have to get up for was a bathroom break.

"You're liking your room, I take it." Caleb walked past Aiden and plopped down on the couch, dropping his backpack on the floor.

Grinning, Aiden diverted his gaze from a baseball replay. "Yvette likes it even better. Now I'm not in her way anymore. When she gets tired of me, she shoos me downstairs." Aiden cupped his hands behind his head. "This is the life."

"Glad you're enjoying it."

"You outdid yourself. Yvette and I are very grateful for this gift."

"It's the least I could do." Caleb slipped his shoes off and stretched out on the couch. "You mind if I sack out here tonight? Home without Aimee is a little too quiet."

"You're always welcome and now you've even got a bedroom to sleep in. Your mother-in-law made the bed up just in case."

"She knows me too well."

"That she does."

Caleb nodded to the LCD screen. "How'd the Twins do tonight?"

"Another win. Looks like they're play-off bound."

"Bet you're excited."

Aiden pushed down the foot rest and sat up. "Caleb, son, why don't you get to the point?"

"What do you mean?"

"When you start talking about things you have no interest in, I know you have something on your mind."

"I like baseball."

"Caleb."

Caleb groaned and sat up. "It was a perfect day. She absolutely loved the Arboretum. I took her home and we talked and had ice cream. I was beginning to believe this was it. Maybe God was giving me another chance for love, and . . ." He rested his elbows on his knees and cuffed his hands behind his head.

"You finally told her."

Caleb nodded and swiped his arm across his nose. "She accused me of using her to save my home. Now she's threatening to take it away."

"I see. Why don't you give her a few days to sort things through, then go talk with her. Right now she's justifiably hurt and angry."

"She said the next time she sees me, I better have a check in hand. Aiden, I don't know that I can afford to pay my electric bill this month. How can I convince her that my feelings for her had nothing to do with my house?"

"I believe Yvette would recommend offering an olive branch."

Caleb rolled his eyes and shook his head. "What could I possibly offer . . . ?"

Wait, maybe there was something. He zipped open his backpack and blew out a relieved sigh. Lissa hadn't taken it with her. "You know, Aiden, I think I have just the thing." Caleb pulled out his portrait of Lissa and studied it. He could add more detail, some dimension and depth to the sketch. He passed the engraving to Aiden. "What do you think?"

"Now that, my son, will make a perfect olive branch."

Lissa pulled her car into the garage and hit the remote. The door squealed shut behind her. With her heart beating too fast to be healthy, she grabbed the brown bag off the passenger seat and strode out of the garage into her side yard. Even walking through the house would take too long. Clutching the bag, she thrust open her squeaking gate and it slammed against the fence. She closed her eyes and clenched her fists. "Cool it, Lissa," she whispered. She was alone. No one would ever have to know. One little cigarette would calm her nerves and strip Caleb from her thoughts.

After inhaling a calming breath, she hurried to her step hidden between the arborvitae trees and pulled out the coffee can. A loud meow cut through the night followed by the cat climbing onto the steps. Tiger. He always picked the worst times to show up. "It's not going to work this time, buddy." She ran her hand over his soft fur as he brushed against her leg. "Uh-uh." Apparently sensing he wasn't wanted, Tiger leapt off the steps and disappeared into the night. Thank you, G—

Oh boy, that was one thank you God didn't want to hear. He probably sent Tiger to rescue her. Well, not tonight. She had no desire to be rescued.

Her hands shook as she removed the coffee can lid and retrieved her lighter. They trembled more as she fought the plastic on the pack.

God wasn't going to make this easy for her, was he? Didn't matter. Finally, she won the battle with the plastic and deposited it in the can.

For the first time in two months, she cradled the cancer stick between her fingers. That action alone was soothing. She brought it to her mouth, her lips caressing it as she flicked the lighter. Once. Twice. On the third try, a small flame broke the night's blackness. She lit the cigarette and seconds later the end flickered with red sparks. After a moment she inhaled, and the sweet smoke curled its way to her lungs. She exhaled through her nose then took another drag. Her fingers calmed and she relaxed against the door, forcing down accusing words: stupid, weak, unlovable.

How could Caleb do that to her? Didn't he realize that her seeing him was a clear conflict of interest? Didn't he realize it could cost her her job?

Was saving a house worth the cost of breaking her heart?

She wiped away tears and inhaled again. Well, she'd learned her lesson, that was for sure. That was what she got for taking a risk. Hadn't she learned anything from her dad? From now on, her choices would be strictly by the book. Get her promotion, a house, then a husband. Someone like Haven.

Why had she ever strayed from that plan? Because she'd stupidly followed her heart, that was why. That was a sure-fire way to get burned.

Tomorrow, she'd salve that burn, get back on the track she'd paved years ago, one both parents even approved of.

She sucked in more nicotine and blew a ring from her mouth while tapping the cigarette against the coffee can snuggled between her feet. Red lightening bug ashes flit downward. How could something so pretty be so deadly? And why was she chained to something so lethal? If only this habit was as easy to break as was sending Caleb away.

"Lissa?"

What? No! Coughs spasmed from her mouth. She dropped the cigarette into the can and slowly glanced up. Haven stood in front of her, mouth agape.

Of all the times for him to stop by, why did it have to be now?

"Lissa?" His voice rasped like the hinge on her gate, the very gate she left open behind herself when she hurried to her step.

"I can explain," she coughed out. Sure, she could explain. But it wouldn't matter. Not for someone as perfect as Haven.

Chapter Eighteen

She could explain? How, when it didn't make sense to her? Lissa backed into the screen door, wanting desperately to disappear. With the trees on either side of her, escape was impossible. The very place where she had always sought refuge now caged her in.

Her chin tucked at her chest, she glanced upward through misty eyes and sniffled. Haven's arms hung loosely at his side, and in the dark, his facial expression was unreadable. He raised his arm a few inches and flicked his hand as if to say move over.

Keeping her head down, she moved away from the door and inched to the edge of the cold concrete steps. He squeezed next to her. His breathing was deep and steady, adding a solid beat to the crickets' chirp.

Out of the corner of her eye, she saw him glance at the cigarette dangling between her fingers. This was it. She'd not only lost Caleb, Haven would never ask her out again.

He laid a hand on her arm and pointed to the cigarette. "I understand."

"You do?" Coughing, she reached for her coffee can before her fingers burned.

"I know what it's like to need that one thing to calm your nerves, to help you through the day, through the rough spots, and even celebrating the highlights."

What was he talking about? "I don't understand."

"I was fourteen when my mom died." His voice was low, melancholy. "A pretty vulnerable time for a young boy."

She looked over at him, but he was gazing outward, his chin raised, and his hands clutching his thighs.

"Now I love my dad, and I respect him for doing the best he could, but the time was rough for him too. After I went to bed, he'd take solace with the bottle. Usually cheap beer. But when you're trying to forget, who cares what losing yourself tastes like? What Dad didn't know was that I watched him . . . and mimicked him."

What?

"When Mom died, I felt hollow, deserted by her and Dad, and needed something to fill their space. I didn't know then that was God's spot." He shook his head. "It wasn't terribly difficult to get my hands on booze, not when I hung with the wrong people." He turned toward her, his eyes meeting hers. "The point is, I know what it's like to be addicted."

"Addicted?" she whispered.

"Big shock, huh?" Haven itched his nose. "Yeah, I know the gossip about me, but that's all it is. Rumors. Falsehoods. People have me perched up on this pedestal of righteousness that I don't deserve."

People like her.

"That's part of the reason why I left Hennepin Bank. I couldn't possibly live up to everyone's beliefs. The minute I made one little mistake, one error in judgment, I would hurt God's kingdom. I couldn't be responsible for that so I fled to a place where I can be human."

"But being too human's what killed my dad, don't you see?" She picked up the pack of cigarettes. "Even this was his fault."

"He felt awful about that, you know."

"What? You knew?" If Haven knew, who else did? Could this day get any worse?

"Your dad was my mentor and, toward the end, I was his sounding board, his confidant. He had a lot of regrets about his fathering skills, about his health choices, but have no doubt about how much he loved you and how proud he was of you."

But he didn't love her enough to change his lifestyle for her, did he? Lissa wiped tears from her cheeks.

"Hey, it's okay." Haven wrapped his arms around her and tugged her close to him, tucking her head beneath his chin. "I'm glad I stopped by."

She sniffled. "Why? What are you doing here anyway?"

His hands caressed her back. "I needed to talk with someone so I wouldn't end up pacifying myself with my addiction." He pulled her tighter against his chest and she felt him shudder. "Sometimes playing piano helps, but not today. Not with this. And my accountability partner's on his honeymoon. I didn't think he'd appreciate a call right now, so I thought of you."

She leaned back to see his eyes, but they were hooded with wetness leaking from beneath his lashes. "Haven, what's wrong?"

He heaved a sigh and sniffled. "I had to put Schroeder down today."

Lissa pinched her eyes shut and pressed her head to Haven's chest. She was so stupid, spending a day making out with Mr. Sham when she could have been consoling someone who truly cared for her. She pulled away and peered up at his red veined eyes. "I am so sorry. I know how you loved him."

"I had him for over half of my life." He wiped a hand below an eye. "It's true what they say. A dog is a man's best friend."

And he'd had to suffer through losing that best friend all on his own. Lissa caressed Haven's arm. "Why didn't you call me? I'd have been there with you."

"I tried calling all day, but you wouldn't answer."

She tugged her phone from her pocket, scrolled through the list of received calls, and mentally kicked herself. "My phone was on mute." So her day with Caleb would be uninterrupted. What an idiot she'd been.

"That explains it. I was concerned so I drove over to check things out. When I saw the gate open . . . It scared me to death."

"So you come back and see me like this." No one was ever supposed to know. Especially Haven.

"I found you needing a friend too." He rested his hand on her arm. "Anything you care to talk about?"

She held up the offensive pack and squeezed it. "How do I stop? I hate that this habit rules me. I hate that it makes me feel better."

"Addictions are like that. They seduce you with comfort, then jail you."

"That's it. That's exactly how I feel. So how do I break out of this cell?"

"Tonight's a beginning. It's not hidden anymore. For me, that was a first step, admitting I had a problem. Then there was treatment, counseling, AA. It helps to talk with people who understand."

"So, I join Smoker's Anonymous? There are groups, you know."

"That would be a great idea."

And admit to a bunch of strangers that she couldn't say *no* to nicotine? How pathetic could she get? The idea made her want to smoke more. "I don't know."

"Talk to your doctor. There's the patch, gum . . . You can call me when you're feeling weak. But the most effective tool I've found is prayer. I begin each day asking God to walk beside me because I know something's going to happen that I'll want to drink away. The devil loves playing to our weaknesses. The key is letting God fill that hole in your heart. It's worked for six years now."

"You were twenty-four?"

"God gave me a wake-up call."

She studied his eyes, but he turned his head toward her garden. What exactly prompted that call?

"That's a discussion for another time." He rubbed his hands over his thighs.

He read her thoughts! That was a sure sign that he was the one for her, right?

He kissed her forehead. "Assuming you'd like to have more discussions . . ."

Biting her lip, she nodded. "Your competition is out of the picture." A fiery mass burned up her throat. Losing Caleb shouldn't hurt this badly.

"Does that mean . . . ?"

She peered into eyes searching hers and nodded. A grin slowly spread from his mouth to the upward crinkle by his eyes, eyes that seemed to focus on her mouth.

That wasn't happening. Not now, with her nicotine-tainted breath. She snuggled back against his chest. She wanted him to remember their first kiss with fondness, not disdain.

His arms surrounded her again and gently squeezed his understanding.

She nestled closer, cradled with mint and strength. Right where she belonged.

Safe.

Why had it taken her so long to recognize it? Oh, the heart was a cruel deceiver. Well, she wouldn't listen to it anymore.

Chapter Nineteen

Forcing a hum, Lissa yanked Caleb's—make that Jonathan Johnson's—file from her drawer. She glanced at the now-familiar picture of his house and her gut seethed. To think that she'd been gullible enough to fall for his spiel. The man had to be an actor too. Well, effective today, she'd hand his file to someone else and be officially finished with him. She wouldn't let him hurt her again. She'd even sic Tyler on him, not Rita. Rita would fall for Caleb's line quicker than Lissa had.

She laid his file on the top of her desk and her hand pulled away with a sticky residue. "Ewww." A reddish fingerprint dotted the edge of the file.

Candy crackled behind her. "Got a problem, sweets?"

"Just someone leaving their gummy remnants." Wrinkling her nose, Lissa pumped hand sanitizer into her palm and rubbed her hands together. The germs these folders carried could wipe out the office if they weren't careful. It was amazing they weren't sick more often.

"That is nasty."

"Tell me about it." Lissa picked up the file, pinching it between two fingers. "I'll clean this up, then pass it on to someone else. I need to wash my hands of this mess." Literally, now.

"Yeah? What's the deal?"

Lissa rolled her eyes. "Mr. Thrill Chaser, the one you kept pushing me toward. Well, he got his thrills all right. Turns out, he's someone I've been sending notices to. The guy's been using me to save his house. The nerve of him."

"And you didn't recognize the name?" Rita grabbed the file. "You're slipping, sweets."

"That's because I knew him by his middle name. I can't believe he used me like that." She wiped a tear. *I can't believe I fell for him.* At least she had Haven. "But one good thing did come out of this mess."

"Tell me."

"I saw Haven Saturday night and now we've got a standing Friday night date with a few Saturdays and Sundays thrown in. He's even invited me up to his dad's place in Duluth in early October, just in time to see the leaves at their peak. He's got a photography assignment for some Midwest magazine. With Mr. Deceiver out of the picture, I can give my full attention to Haven. He likes me, and he really cares for me even though he knows my biggest issues."

Rita moaned and slunk in her chair. "So Mr. Bore-me-to-death knows that you once ate half a Milky Way bar. Yep, you two are perfect for each other."

"As a matter of fact, we are." Lissa stood and snatched the file from Rita and held it like a dirty diaper. Now to clean this off, and let someone else deal with its future messes.

"Hey Lissa!" The bank's pregnant receptionist, Jordan, waddled toward Lissa, carrying a shirt box. "An incredibly adorable hunk of a man dropped this off for you. He opened it for me, so I know it's safe."

Scrunching her brows, Lissa stopped in the cube entry and accepted the box. An envelope addressed to Lissa was taped on top. Incredibly adorable did describe Haven, but the receptionist would obviously know him. "What did this guy look like?" Not that it mattered. Considering the architect-type printing on the envelope, it was obvious whom this was from.

"I'd say six footish. Dark, wavy hair. He's got that day old beard thing going, and he wears it well." She fluttered a hand in front of her face. "If I weren't married . . ."

"Well, looks are deceiving." Still clinging to Caleb's file, she shoved the box toward Rita. "Here. You want adventure? Then go for it."

"Don't mind if I do."

"Seriously?" Jordan splayed a hand over her heart. "Look at it, Liss.

The man obviously has it bad for you."

Lissa huffed. "I guess that's his problem, isn't it?"

With a shrug, Jordan waddled back to the front of the bank.

Groaning, Lissa glanced at the ceiling and her shoulders drooped. Just because she was in a bad mood didn't mean she should take it out on everyone. *Sorry*, she whispered upward. She'd make it up to Jordan later. After getting rid of the file and the gift.

"Sweets, I think you should look at this."

"Uh-uh. It's going to be some kind of bribe that my stupid heart will pitter-patter over and I'll forgo all sensibility. That's what he does, you know. He played me like a master cellist." She took a step toward the restrooms.

"Lissa. Look."

Lissa sighed. "Fine." She turned on her heel and peeked into the box. Caleb's file slipped to the floor, scattering the pages, and she covered her mouth with her hand. Her heart didn't pitter-patter. It tangoed. "Oh, my." She plopped down on her chair and lifted his gift from the box. The picture he'd engraved while at the Arboretum. But it was different, as if he'd added another dimension with fine details highlighting strands of hair and eyelashes. Somehow he'd captured the light glinting from her eyes. She ran her hand over the surface and moisture fogged her eyes. How dare he bribe her with this?

"Would you like me to read his note?"

Keeping her gaze trained on the engraving, she nodded to Rita. Whatever he had to say wouldn't change a thing. No way.

Rita cleared her throat. "'Dear Lissa, I'm sorry. So very sorry. I didn't give thought to our relationship hurting your job. I'm not wired that way, but I should have considered it. I realize now that I put you in a precarious position. Should your employer find fault with you, direct them to me. The blame is mine alone. You had no way of knowing.'"

Rita quieted.

With Lissa's heart still doing the traitorous dance, she glanced at Rita. "Is that it?"

"No," Rita whispered. "I'm with Jordan, this man has a thing for you and if you're too blind to see it—"

"Thank you, Oprah. I didn't ask for your advice now, did I?" Lissa grabbed the note from Rita and read to herself.

I realize this isn't a check. I'd send one if I could, but I lost my job two months ago and have no money coming in. I know what that means for my future in this house, but I have faith that God will provide a way. He always does. Just like He showed my heart how to beat again. For that I have you to thank. I will cherish our friendship—if that was all it was—for a lifetime. Watching you spread your wings was a glorious sight, and I am blessed for having witnessed your flight. I pray you continue to leap from the nest, trusting Him to catch you. You're beautiful when you fly.

Lissa snatched a tissue and blotted tears from her cheeks as she continued reading.

I wish you well in all your future adventures. Caleb.

Thank goodness he didn't add "love" before his signature. That would have been more than she could handle. Besides, Caleb was wrong. She wasn't born to fly. He'd have to find some other patsy. Her feet belonged firmly rooted to the ground, and Haven was the one who realized that.

"Ladies, I'm not seeing a lot of work going on, and what's with this mess on the floor?"

Tyler! Lissa dropped the box and note on her desk and knelt to gather the papers. "I'm sorry. I got a delivery and it"—Wrung the tears from her heart? Made her miss . . . long for the man who clearly wasn't made for her?

"I don't care about your personal neuroses. What I need to see is you on the phone, bringing owed money into the bank." He picked up the note from Lissa's desk. "Since you're reading this on bank hours, I'm presuming this is work related."

"Tyler, no!" She jumped up and grabbed at the paper.

He backed out of her reach, his eyes moving from side to side, a smirk lifting his lips.

God, please let him see the words as Caleb meant them.

"Does this say what I think it does?" He folded the letter and pocketed it inside his suit coat. "That you are in a relationship with a client?"

"*Was* in a relationship. Was. I didn't know he was a client. I only found out this past weekend."

He grunted. "Likely story. You probably had lover boy write this just to get you off the hook. Sorry, Ms. Morgan. It didn't work. This is a clear conflict-of-interest violation and I don't expect the bank board will look kindly at this. I'd say you've hammered one more nail into your promotional coffin."

"Tyler, please."

He patted his suit coat where he'd stuffed the letter. "By the way, I received word that the bank is going to post *my* supervisory position. I'll be permanent by the New Year and you, well, perhaps it's time to update your résumé. Unfortunately, in the light of your recent behavior and lack of organization, Hennepin Bank won't be able to offer a good recommendation, in spite of Haven Carlysle's attempt to slander me to them."

"You knew Haven talked with them?"

"Well, of course, when I had to answer all their allegations, it didn't take a genius to figure out who the accuser was. I would deduce that Haven may still offer you a good recommendation, unless, of course, he was aware of your dalliance with a client. If not, I might have to tell him." Tyler tipped his head. "Good day, Ms. Morgan."

Lissa dropped onto her chair and cradled her face in her hands. This was what she got for stepping outside of God's plan, for dating two guys when only one was right for her, for leading Caleb on. *I'm sorry, God. Forgive me?* Oh, He'd forgive her, but that didn't mean she wouldn't suffer the consequences for her disobedience.

Chapter Twenty

It was time to celebrate. Caleb pumped his fist and laid his cell phone on the mountain of bills heaped on his kitchen island. *Thank you, Jesus.* A job offer. Finally. So what if it was a temporary Christmas position at the local big box department store? Being it was the first of October, that gave him three months of full-time employment. Who knew, it might lead to something permanent. His dream of keeping his and Jeanette's home might not be squashed after all.

Problem was, it would be another month before he got a paycheck. Until then, he'd have to rely on Aiden and Yvette for food and childcare. Thank God for gracious in-laws. With his first check, he could catch up on the utilities, but the mortgage? That still required a miracle, not that God was incapable.

And why couldn't a miracle happen to him? Whistling, he walked to Aimee's room. She lay tummy down, head up, on the floor, creating Picasso-esque art with crayons. No coloring books for his daughter. She loved free-hand drawing, like Dada. He squatted next to her and twirled the ponytail sprouting like a fountain on top of her head. "Hey, Aimee-doodles, looks like you're going to be the next Grandma Moses."

"I no grandma. I little."

"Grandma Moses was a great artist, just like you." He bopped her nose. "Hey, what do you say about going out for Dairy Queen? Dada got a job and I want to celebrate with my bestest girl."

"Yeah, yeah, yeah!" Aimee dropped her crayons, jumped up, and skipped around her bedroom.

"I take it that's a yes."

"Go now." She grabbed his hand and tugged him toward her door.

"Hey, slow down, Doodles. You need something covering those little piggies." He tickled her toes and she giggled. "Find some socks and your shoes and bring them to me. I'll help you put them on."

"Okay, Dada."

"I'll be in the kitchen." Attempting to conquer that mountain of overdue bills. But Jeanette would be mad at him for ignoring it. With a job, now he wouldn't have to.

He returned to the kitchen, sat by the island, and fanned through the pregnant mail pile. The latest letter from the bank lay unopened on top. Why bother opening it? He already knew what it said. Pay up or leave. Didn't matter to them that he had no money. Yet. But God had a miracle awaiting him. He had to believe.

With a pocket knife, he sliced open the letter and glanced at the signature inked on the bottom. No longer Corliss A. Morgan's swooping cursive that somehow gave him hope, but some man named Tyler Abernathy's angry angular penmanship. The Notice of Intent to Foreclose said exactly what Caleb anticipated, but in polysyllabic lawyer-speak. Still, bile burned in his throat. This was a real warning. A threat. Pay up this impossible amount or lose your house.

Technically, he knew he had until the first of February to pay in full, plus any late fees, lawyer fees, and whatever other kind of fee they could imagine. Four measly months. It would take a miracle to come up with the kind of cash he needed, but who was he to put limits on God? Until that front door closed and locked permanently behind him, his dream was still breathing.

"I ready, Dada." Aimee ran to him holding one red toe sock, a tie-dyed anklet, and her patent leather church shoes.

With a chuckle, he hefted her onto his lap and kissed her velvety cheek. "Absolutely perfect, Doodles." He wouldn't dream of squelching the artist in his daughter. Crushed dreams were hard enough for adults to live with.

Today, they'd finally have their perfect date. Lissa sat on a damp lava-formed boulder on the edge of Gooseberry River and smiled at Haven.

"Now chin up a tad, and turn your head a titch to your right."

She turned her head slightly, looking away from Haven, and jutted her chin. With the cold mist from Gooseberry Falls tumbling mere feet behind her, it was tough to tame the shivers, but she smiled anyway. It wasn't difficult. Haven would never let her down.

"Atta girl. Perfect." Haven pointed his camera. With his tongue sticking out and his brows tented together, he repeatedly pressed the shutter for what seemed minutes, but was probably only seconds. "Okay. Done." He lowered the camera and offered his hand, helping her leap slick stones to dry ground.

She shuddered and hugged her sweatshirted arms. "It's beautiful here, but that water is frigid."

"Sorry about that." Wincing, Haven removed his maroon hoodie with the University of Minnesota-Duluth bulldog embroidered on the front and offered it to her. "I get so caught up in capturing the moment, logic escapes me."

"Thank you." She shrugged into his sweatshirt, covered her head with the hood, and warmed her hands beneath her upper arms. Still her teeth chattered. "M-much b-better."

He circled his arm around her and led her away from the water. "No more water pictures. I promise."

"I'll hold you to it."

"But you've got to admit . . ." He raised up the camera and displayed the pictures on the LCD screen. "The scenery is amazing." He held it in front of her. "What do you think?"

He revealed his last shot, with her seated in the foreground. A sense of déjà vu filled her. What was it? She pinched her eyes closed and ran a slide show through her head. No. She moaned.

"What's wrong?" Haven squeezed his arm tighter on her shoulders.

"Just a memory." Of the wedding picture hanging on Caleb's wall with Gooseberry Falls in the background. "No big deal."

"You sure? You seemed to freeze up for a second."

"I'm fine. Let's check out the rest of your photos." Maybe that would chase the memory.

She watched the screen as he scrolled through the remaining pictures and shook her head. "Stunning." Haven had a gift for capturing light, shadow, and color. With the trees bordering the falls, all in their October glory of reds, oranges, and yellows, she couldn't imagine a more picturesque location.

"Thanks. I appreciate it."

"Well, it's the truth. You could do this for a living."

He shrugged. "Someday, maybe. Right now it's more a dream, an expensive hobby that brings in a couple bucks a month." He released her, turned off his camera, and offered his arm. "But for now, I think it's time to pack this away and find a place for lunch. If you're up for a walk, there's a trail that takes us along the river, right to Lake Superior. It's only a few miles and should warm you up, but it's rather hilly."

"Sounds like a perfect hike." And exactly like a trek Caleb would take her on, had probably walked with his new bride. She shook her head, driving away his image. Why, after four weeks, and several evenings spent with Haven—perfectly beautiful, albeit kiss-less evenings—why did memories of Caleb insist on intruding?

Because Rita was right. Haven's lips were virgin. That was the only answer. Well, that would be remedied today on this trek through God's garden. There wasn't a better place for romance to flourish.

She followed Haven on a dirt path cloaked with falling leaves. The trail coursed east of the falls, up and down craggy hills, curving around century old trees whose gnarly roots leaped above the surface. This had to be a glimpse of Heaven. Was this the type of scenery that greeted her father each day? It was hard to believe Heaven could be more beautiful than this.

The path curved, gracing them with a view of the falls thundering beyond the valley. Marvelous. "Can we picnic here?" She called to Haven who'd continued up the path.

He turned around and shrugged. "Guess so." He walked back to her and his eyes widened, apparently noticing the sweeping scene for the first time. "Amazing," he whispered and lifted the camera that hung from his neck. "I've walked this so often, I must have tunnel vision."

"I'll set up our lunch while you take some shots . . . and I don't mean of me."

With a grin, he slipped the backpack off his shoulders and handed it to her. "My assignment is to capture beautiful scenery and you, my dear, fit that description perfectly."

Attempting to hide the crimson she knew painted her face, she removed the blanket from the backpack and spread it over the ground. She sat, crossing her legs, and pulled out the paper sack that held their meal. She had a lot to learn about creating a romantic picnic meal. Just organic peanut butter and strawberry jelly on seven grain, and a bag of finger veggies: carrots, celery, broccoli, and cauliflower. Although she'd spent a little extra time on the fruit kabobs, spearing strawberries, apples, grapes, pineapple, and cantaloupe on a wooden skewer. Somehow, though, it didn't come close to Caleb's creations.

She patted the blanket and looked up as Haven pointed his camera at her. "That's enough, already. Sit and eat."

"Good idea." He removed the camera strap from around his neck and laid the camera on the blanket. "I get carried away, seeing things through the lens. It's such a different point of view, capturing snippets of God's art studio, I forget I need to eat." He picked up a sandwich, bit into it and his eyes rolled up. "This is heavenly."

"You must be hungry. It's not that great." Not if compared to Caleb's. Arghh. Why couldn't she move beyond him? Especially when seated across from Haven, someone who would never hurt her. Picking up a fruit kabob, she glanced across the valley at the river tumbling over the falls and racing to the big lake. From here, its purpose was evident, not like it had been up close. But seeing the falls up close carried its own detailed beauty with the miniscule droplets of water creating a kaleidoscope of color, along with rocks huddled beneath the river's surface, smoothed by the water's power.

This panoramic scene told the bigger story, revealing the truth.

She sucked a grape off the kabob, and her stomach soured. Had Caleb told the truth?

That night he admitted who he was, hadn't he said he'd tried to tell her on that evening when Haven showed up unannounced? She dropped the kabob onto her paper plate. And in his note, he'd apologized. Sincerity rang through the apology, not deceit. She folded her hands in front of her face. Time, like distance, had a way of smoothing the details and bringing the entire picture into a clearer and truer perspective.

She owed him an apology.

But that didn't mean they were meant to be together.

"These kabobs are to die for." Haven reached for a second one and flashed her a grin.

How did Caleb worm his way into her head when the perfect man sat across from her, continuously throwing out sincere and unsolicited compliments? A man with a job. A house. A secure and planned-out future. She picked up his camera and snuck a shot of Haven with berry juice dribbling down his chin. It didn't hurt that Haven's face was camera friendly.

"I think it's my turn to capture some of the scenery." She focused and snapped the shutter again, this time snaring his grin. "You need to send these to me. My workspace needs brightening up, especially with Tyler the tyrant throwing his power around."

"That bad?"

"I swear, he sits outside my cube waiting for me to mess up. Between those missing files he's framing me for, and then that mess with Caleb, he's right there recording it, promising to prove to the bank board I'm unfit for my job, much less the promotion. If he becomes permanent supervisor, I can't imagine staying."

"But you've applied, right?" He wiped cantaloupe juice from his chin.

"Right away. We'll see how it goes."

"Wish I could help you more, but my input only goes so far and I'm afraid that our current relationship won't help matters either."

"I know. I've thought of that." She leaned back, resting her weight on her arms "Sorry. I didn't mean to grumble about work. I'm here to have fun." A mass of birds flew above the trees. Hawks? She nodded toward them. "Don't hawks fly solo?"

"Not always. They fly in kettles, not flocks, and not in formation either so they're still independent."

So much like Caleb.

She blinked the thought away and concentrated on the birds. "The sky's been busy today. You should get a picture."

"I know. I've thought of it, and now's a great time with all the hawks heading south. But with this tree cover it's hard to get a decent shot. When we head home, we'll stop near Duluth, a place called Hawk Ridge. I don't think there's a better place on earth to watch the birds."

Lissa glanced upward and around. Below them was the valley leading to the river, behind them a treed, but steep embankment that led to what looked like a small clearing. It was off the path, but . . .

She looped the camera around her neck and grabbed Haven's hand. "I have an idea."

"Uh-oh. Why do I have a feeling I'm not going to like this?"

"I think you will." She packed their picnic into the backpack, gave it to Haven, then dragged him across the path, stopping in front of the embankment. Steep, but not unconquerable. She handed the camera back to Haven. That was his baby to break. She grabbed a low hanging tree branch, stepped onto the bank, and pulled herself up. This wouldn't be hard at all. She glanced back at Haven who stood shaking his head.

"Well, are you coming?"

"Do I have a choice?"

Lissa grinned and reached for another branch. Moments later, she stood at the top of the hill and pumped her fists over her head. She lay down and stared up at the blue sky frequently speckled with a variety of winged creatures instinctively making their way to warmer climates. God truly was amazing.

Seconds later, Haven joined her, set his camera and backpack on the ground then laid down dangerously close to her. His minty cologne was faint, but it still drowned out the pine scents surrounding her. Perhaps in its subtlety, it made her crave more. She reached for his hand and he wove his fingers with hers. A perfect match. Yes, God was definitely good.

She closed her eyes and felt Haven scoot closer. The warmth of his closeness gave her goose bumps. His hand embraced her cheek and guided her head to the side, his breath caressing her face. "Lissa, have I told you how beautiful you are."

The waltz played in her heart and her breathing danced along. She opened her eyes and Haven leaned toward her, eyes hooded, lips parted ever so slightly. His lips whispered against hers and the heart's orchestra sped up. He tipped her chin and his eyes apprehended hers. "May I?" His voice came out low, heavy.

She nodded and rose up on her side, leaning toward him. Their lips met, tentative, searching. His arm circled her, pressing her against him, deepening the kiss, tasting berries, grapes, and longing. Rockets soared behind the orchestra in her heart for what seemed an eternity. If this was his first kiss, she couldn't wait until he had experience.

Haven jerked away, his chest heaving. He sat up and wiped his mouth. "I'm sorry."

"Sorry?" She grinned and reached for him, but he backed away.

Perspiration beaded on his forehead, and his lips slowly curved to one side as he rubbed his hands over his thighs. He cleared his throat but his voice still came out husky. "I'm thinking we might need a chaperone."

She blew out a breath and bit her lip, the waltz finally slowing. "That might be wise."

Haven stood, wiping dirt, grass, and leaves from his T-shirt and jeans. "I suppose I should get some shots while we're up here." He retrieved his camera, focused on her and, as she opened her mouth to object, he clicked the shutter. "A little something for me to remember this day by." He winked and aimed upward in time to capture a kettle of hawks.

Smiling, Lissa lay back, resting her head on her hands, and closed her eyes. Perfection. The man was absolute perfection. And to think she'd worried about his kissing ability. She moistened her lips. Not anymore, that was for sure.

"Hey sleepyhead, shall we go?"

Her eyes fluttered open. She'd fallen asleep? She blinked her eyes into focus and grabbed Haven's extended hand. Warm. Secure. Safe. As it should be. He helped her up and she followed him to the embankment.

Grasping onto tree trunks, Haven lowered himself down.

Lissa waited until his feet hit the trail, then she reached for a trunk and slowly lowered one foot until it had firm purchase on the ground.

Fear twirled in her stomach. She could do this. Swallowing a deep breath, she stepped with the other leg and found an embedded stone. Just keep going. Slowly, alternating legs, she climbed down the cliff. Only three, maybe four feet to go. She glanced down and Haven opened his arms. An invitation. Who was she to decline?

She launched from the hillside, but Haven's arms didn't stop her descent. She landed on a stone and kept going down. Something popped in her knee before she landed and it popped back as her bottom clunked on the path.

"Lissa! Are you okay?" Haven knelt next to her and laid his camera case on the ground.

She rubbed her knee. No pain, but numb. That must mean she was okay, right? She stretched her leg out and tried flexing it, but it refused to bend. Maybe it didn't hurt, but something was definitely wrong.

"Lissa, talk to me." He kissed her forehead and his hands caressed her arms. "Are you hurt?"

In more ways than one.

Caleb never would have allowed her to fall. He would have kept her safe. She shook her head at Haven and whispered. "You didn't catch me."

Chapter Twenty-One

Lissa clapped a hand to her mouth. She hadn't said that aloud, had she?

"Say what?" Haven froze and his eyes clouded over.

Oh no, she obviously had let it slip. "I'm sorry. I must be delirious." Going home and getting rest would be the perfect remedy. It had to be.

Worry wrinkled his forehead. "You are hurt. Tell me where." He pressed the back of his hand to her forehead.

The man was clueless. "It's my knee. It won't bend."

His gaze landed on her jean-covered knee and his hands followed, gently caressing the area. "Does it hurt?"

"Not really." She shook her head. "It feels funny, like something popped out of place and back in."

"I think it might be swelling." Frowning, he pulled out his cell phone and groaned. "No reception. What about yours?"

"It's in the backpack."

He shrugged the backpack off his shoulders, unzipped the front pouch, and took out her phone. "No bars." With a deep sigh, he rested his chin on his chest and his forehead on his fingers. "Okay. We have to get to the visitor center." He stood and looked up and down the trail. "If someone would come by . . ." His jaw twitched back and forth.

You could carry me.

"But I can't rely on that happening. The visitor center is maybe a mile back. I could get there in fifteen, twenty . . ."

You could carry me.

His mouth scrunched to the side. "Will you be okay here?"

No. *Caleb would carry me.* She reached for Haven and attempted to stand.

"Lissa, don't even try. It may be nothing, but we don't know that. The only option I see is getting to a phone ASAP."

"You could carry me." Whew. She said it.

He stared at her blankly, then his shoulders drooped. "I considered that, but think about it, we'd have to splint your leg first. Any movement could make it worse. I don't want to take the chance of ruining your knee for life." He knelt again and caressed her cheeks. "I've done enough damage already. I couldn't live with hurting you more."

God, forgive my stupidity. "You're right. Of course. I'm just scared."

"I know. I'll be quick. I promise." He set the backpack next to her and pulled out an energy bar and water bottle. "You'll be fine." But worry furrowed his blond brows. He brushed a kiss over her lips and then jogged off.

Lissa wrapped Haven's hoodie tightly around herself and crossed her arms. How had she been so stupid to erect Haven up on some pedestal as her savior? What kind of Christian was she anyway, putting her faith in men? They could never live up to her standards.

She rubbed her swelling knee. Yeah, resting was the remedy, resting in God, not in others. Especially not in herself.

"Surgery!" Lissa's mom jumped up from the chair angled by Lissa's front window.

"On Friday." Securing both hands on her blue-cushioned leg brace, Lissa lifted her leg and rested it on the ottoman in front of her. "Would you mind getting me a pillow or two from my bedroom? I'm supposed to keep this elevated." And then she'd encourage her mom to leave. It was the only way she'd get some rest.

"Darling, of course. If you'll tell me what the doctor said."

"I promise." Then, hopefully, her mom would go home. Not that she didn't appreciate her mom's company, but Lissa was craving some alone time. Thank goodness, without a secret stash of cigarettes, smoking wasn't even an option. Maybe this was God's way of getting her to stop.

She relaxed into the couch's back as her mom hurried from the room. Of all the lousy times to have surgery. How would she ever convince the bank board that she was the most capable person for the supervisory job if she missed a week of work or even more right now? Not to mention, how was she supposed to get to work if she couldn't drive?

"Here you go, darling." With her mom's help, Lissa lifted her leg and settled it on the pillows. "What can I offer you to drink? Do you have lemonade? Do I need to make some up?"

"Mom, I'm not an invalid." Yet.

That didn't stop her mom. She was off to the kitchen and returned a minute later with a glass of pink lemonade and a plate of celery sticks filled with peanut butter. Comfort food. She set them on the end table next to Lissa. "You need to keep up your energy, darling."

"I'm fine, really."

"That's why you're having surgery, because you're fine." She sat beside Lissa and crossed one leg elegantly over the other.

"Sarcasm doesn't suit you."

"And false heroism doesn't fit you either." She patted Lissa's hand. "I'm your mother. Appease me, won't you? Allow me to baby you again."

Lissa rolled her eyes, but couldn't stop her grin. "Fine. Baby away, although Haven's already been doting on me since it happened. Insisted on taking yesterday off for my MRI. The technician told us to give it a few days for the results. Huh. Doctor called last night and had me schedule surgery. Haven's a basket case. He thinks it's his fault."

And who's to blame for that? Lissa grabbed her glass of lemonade and sipped. Sour. Just like she'd treated Haven after he'd been so sweet.

"He wanted to hang around today, make sure I didn't take any more unnecessary risks. I had to force him to go to work. He only agreed when I promised to call you."

"Darling, are you serious about Haven?" Her mom picked up a framed picture of Haven standing in the middle of the Mississippi River. That day had been so much fun . . . until the bees attacked.

With Haven there was always an *until*. Lissa worried her lip. "I think I am." *But you're not certain, are you?*

"Then don't let him go like you did that young man from the auction." Was that disappointment in her mom's voice? Couldn't be. She'd always liked Haven.

"I don't plan on letting Haven go." So, why did she feel relieved when he left last night, as if she could finally breathe?

"Now, do tell me, what did the MRI reveal?"

That she was an idiot. "When I fell—when I jumped, that is—I tore my ACL and meniscus."

"ACL? Men-iss-what? Darling, please speak English."

"Anterior cruciate ligament. It helps stabilize the knee. And the meniscus, it's cartilage that acts like a shock absorber between your knee bones. I tore them both, not an uncommon occurrence."

"So how do they repair them? Will you be scarred?" She slapped a hand over her mouth and spoke through it. "Disabled?"

Lissa chuckled at her mom's dramatics. "It happens all the time with athletes and they go on to have strong careers. The surgery is arthroscopic. They make a couple of little incisions and fix the knee through that. I'll barely have a mark."

"Darling, that's terrible. Well, I'll take some time off—"

"Mom, please!" The thought of spending a month or even just a week with her mom made Lissa's stomach whirl. "Haven's promised to help out. I can probably even drive within a week or three, depending on how well I do with therapy, and I plan on working very hard at it. Honestly, I hear therapy's worse than the surgery. Four times a week to begin with. They say it's painful."

But she'd do whatever she could to get back to work. The good thing was, she wouldn't be tempted to drag herself outside on crutches to have a smoke. Maybe this accident would finally cure her.

"What time shall I pick you up on Friday?"

"You don't have to."

"Nonsense. My only child's having surgery." She splayed a hand over her heart. "What kind of mother would I be if I weren't there for you?"

Lissa clamped her eyes closed. Why did it always take something bad to make her realize the blessings she had? "Thanks, Mom. I have to be at the Maple Grove hospital by six a.m."

"I'll pick you up at four thirty."

"Five, please? Give me another half hour of sleep?"

"Five it is. Now in the meantime." Her mom stood and glanced around the living room. "I think I'll tidy up your place—"

"Mo-om—"

"Tut tut." She wagged her finger. "That's enough. You're supposed to keep your leg up, and you can't do that if you're wandering around your home dusting."

"Yes, Mother." Lissa leaned back and closed her eyes. She had no choice but to take advantage of this forced respite.

"Darling, where did you have this done?"

Lissa raised an eyelid and peeked at her mom standing by the other end of the couch, holding up Caleb's etching. Rats! Why hadn't she stuffed that away in a drawer like she planned?

"This is exquisite. You must let me know who did this. All the Red Hatters would gush over this work."

"Caleb," Lissa said under her breath.

"What's that, darling?"

Lissa sighed and readjusted her leg. "Caleb did it."

"Oh, yes, that handsome young man from the auction, the one you floated down the river with." Her mom cocked her head while staring at the carving. "Hmm, you were quite . . ." She set the etching down and turned to Lissa, a single brow raised, the rest of her face devoid of expression. "Sensible in choosing Haven over him."

Was sensible a good thing? Lissa adjusted the straps on her brace. Why didn't the very mention of Haven's name ignite fireworks in her heart?

"Well, if you don't mind, I would love to have his phone number. Perhaps we can send a little business his way."

Lissa twisted at her waist and picked up the phone up from the end table. She scrolled through the listings and offered the phone to her mom. "I'm certain he'd be thrilled to have your business."

Then he'd be able to pay off some of his mortgage.

As a matter of fact, maybe she should give him a call, apologize for her snotty behavior that day he'd taken her to the Arboretum. He might not be the one for her, but he still didn't deserve her scorn either. Maybe after the surgery, when she could use some company. They could start over again, this time as friends.

A proud swagger colored Caleb's stride as he walked out the big box department store employees-only door. Amazing how nearly three months of unemployment changed his perspective on working. Nearly three months of being looked down upon as unmotivated, lazy. Nearly three months of not being the proper provider Aimee deserved in a father. He'd check his phone for messages, and then it was time for a little ice cream celebration with his three favorite people.

Wearing a confident smile, he walked across the pothole-laden parking lot to his pickup. He got inside and pulled his cell phone from the glove box. Five messages. Two demanding payment. He deleted those. They'd get their payment as soon as he got his check. One message from Aimee singing, "I wuv you, Dada." That one, he saved.

The final message set him thinking. Could he . . . ? Should he say yes to this woman he'd met only once? Was this the break he'd been praying for? Well, there was one way to find out. He hit 'Send' and his phone redialed Adelaide Morgan's number. He rubbed the back of his neck waiting through three rings before a woman answered.

"Hello."

"Uh, yes, this is Caleb Johnson. I'm returning a call to Adelaide Morgan."

"Wonderful. This is Adelaide. I'm thrilled that you returned my call. You have a rare artistic gift, Caleb, and my friends are very eager to pay for your services."

"I'm flattered, Mrs. Morgan, but I'm not sure what to say. I've never engraved for payment before. It's something I've done to pass the time."

"Well, that must change, now, mustn't it? A talent like yours needs to be flaunted, not hidden, and I would be more than happy to help you jumpstart your career."

Career? Wouldn't that steal the fun from his art? "Mrs. Morgan, I appreciate your offer, but—"

"I wouldn't be so quick to say no, Caleb dear. The remuneration we plan to offer will certainly give you a step out of your financial hole."

Oh boy. So Lissa had talked about his financial woes with her mother. He kneaded his neck harder and swallowed his pride. It didn't hurt to listen to her offer. "Okay. I'm not saying yes. Yet. Before you make your offer, there are a few things you should know. I can't work from pictures; I need to see the model in person in order to see all dimensions and understand their personality."

"That would not be a problem."

"The sessions would have to fit around my work schedule and not cut into family time."

"I wouldn't have it any other way."

"Also, I don't have a studio to work in and the costs to rent a place would more than eat anything I'd make."

"My home is available. I have this perfect little garden hut that would make an ideal studio. You should drop by to see it. I'm certain you won't be disappointed."

"Well—"

"Corliss said you were a risk-taker, Caleb, and all I'm hearing is hesitation. Perhaps a dollar figure would help persuade you." Adelaide quoted a number that made Caleb's mouth hang open.

"But that's too—"

"Cost is relative, dear, and my friends are eager to pay you for the privilege of owning an original piece."

Caleb swallowed a lump that had massed in his throat. How could he say no now? This could absolutely be the answer to his prayers. Still, he needed time's perspective, plus an evening to pray over his decision. "Can I get back to you tomorrow?"

"That would be fine, dear. I will anticipate your call."

Caleb ended the call and tossed the phone onto the passenger side.

He pressed his back against the seat, curved his hands over the steering wheel, and closed his eyes. *What do you think, Jeanette?* He chuckled. She was probably doing handstands. Literally.

He turned the key in the ignition and set out for his in-laws'. Over ice cream, Aiden and Yvette would offer discerning advice. They were gifted at separating emotion from wisdom in decision-making matters. Because right now, his emotions screamed, "Accept Adelaide's offer." But did that mean he'd run into Lissa? Not that it mattered. If he did accept the offer, it would be for Aimee's sake. His feelings for Lissa had no place in his decision.

Caleb steered his ancient pickup between manicured hedges onto a paver-block driveway that was guarded by rows of towering oaks. Precisely cut grass carpeted the yard beyond the trees. He parked directly in front of a four-car garage and blew out a breath. Adelaide Morgan's mansion of a home on Lake Minnetonka was miles above his pay grade. These people could certainly pay well to have him etch portraits.

But what would the financial elite—those who could afford to purchase a Mercedes on impulse—what would they possibly see in his work? But if they were interested, who was he to complain? Telling Adelaide Morgan yes could be an answer to prayer.

He rubbed his hand over his whiskers. Maybe he should have shaved it all off, gone for the clean look. But people would see his baby face and not take him seriously. No, keeping the stubble was the right thing. Besides, Jeanette had loved it.

So had Lissa.

Man, what was he doing here where her image was certainly displayed?

Because of Aimee.

Breaking his heart again and again was worth it as long as he could be a good father.

Grabbing his small bag of engraving tools, he got out of the pickup and strode up the stone walkway that journeyed beneath the oaks. Limestone-covered columns stood guard to a covered porch. He stopped at the crystal-etched door and rang the doorbell.

A slender woman with Lissa's gold-brown eyes, probably fiftyish, answered the door. The very woman who had placed that outrageous bid months ago at the bachelor auction.

He held out his hand. "Hi, I'm Caleb Johnson and—"

"Please, Caleb"—she wound her arm around his back and tugged him over the threshold—"do come in."

As if he had any choice.

She led him over what appeared to be Brazilian ebony hardwood floors, and through a living room furnished in white. Aimee would not be allowed in here. Especially with that wall made entirely of windows fronting the lake. Her little hand and nose prints would require daily cleaning. But with the windows, Adelaide had no need for manmade artwork with God's azure blue tinting the water, and with oak leaves gilded with burnt reds and oranges.

Why would Lissa give up this beauty?

"Lovely, isn't it?" Adelaide circled her arm around his and led him out on a wood deck that spanned the length of the home.

"Stunning." He could sit on this deck all day with etching or sketching tools. Maybe learn to paint the sailboats flying past in the summer and the fish houses that created a temporary city on ice in the winter. That would be the life.

Adelaide pointed to a cottage bordering the lake, a smaller version of the mansion, but big enough for the average family to be comfortable in. "And that is my garden hut."

Hut? "That's a hut?"

She laughed. So much like Lissa's. "Well, I admit that wasn't its initial purpose. Lissa's father and I built it with the intention that Lissa would live there until she could afford her own home. But our daughter insisted on being independent and rented that monstrosity in carbon copy land."

Whoa. His thought exactly. How could she give this up? But in doing so, she'd spread her wings long before he'd come along. Her mother clearly didn't understand the beauty in that. "With all due respect, Mrs. Morgan, Lissa has made her home unique and I applaud her for stepping out. It probably wasn't easy for her."

Adelaide patted his hand. "You are so right, young man. I like that you see that in her. Now, let's go take a look at your art studio."

My art studio? He hadn't agreed yet. But this woman would make saying no awfully difficult. He shook his head and followed her down wooden steps, across a plush yard Aimee could easily tumble around on and not get hurt. They stepped onto the cottage's pillared porch that overlooked the lake. Slatted swings hung on each end. It was easy to visualize Lissa seated on one, her lower lip tucked, and her gaze cast toward the water.

"Do you approve?"

Oh, yeah. He nodded.

"Would you care to see the inside?"

"I'd love it."

They stepped into a living room that actually encouraged living. Not like that child-unfriendly main home. Slate blue paint covered the walls and bookshelves flanked an oak fireplace. A cushy taupe sofa with a matching recliner were angled to take in the lake and the fireplace. "You call this a hut?"

"That was Theodore's word for it. Since Lissa didn't wish to stay here, this became his refuge."

Probably from a sterile house. "I'd be working in here?"

"If you wish. The main is also available if you would rather—"

"No, no. I think this is absolutely perfect."

"You've decided to accept my offer."

Oh, the woman was sneaky. Truthfully, when he arrived, his answer wasn't clear. Perhaps, now it was. The compensation she was offering, plus the opportunity to create in this nature-blessed atmosphere, made it hard to turn her down. But he still had one important question, a possible deal-breaker. "I do have one request that's non-negotiable. I fully understand if you refuse."

"Certainly." She ran a finger across the carved mantel. "I must have Katrina dust this place before you set up."

Assuming his answer was yes. "When I work, I need to bring my daughter with me."

Adelaide turned on her heel and raised a single eyebrow. "And this will not impede your work?"

"Actually, I find that she spurs my creativity. More important, I won't sacrifice my time with her. She's lost her mother, I can't take away her dada too."

Pursing her lips, Adelaide nodded. "Then you shall bring her along for the sittings."

Whew. Thanks, God. He'd eliminated the final hurdle. This had to be right. "I accept your offer."

"Wonderful." Adelaide clasped her hands together. "One more detail." She glided to a window and looked out. "With Lissa's surgery, I will—"

"Surgery?" What had happened? "What's wrong?"

Adelaide laughed softly and continued to gaze out at gently lapping waves. "She spent this past weekend with Haven."

The whole weekend? No wonder she'd dumped Caleb so easily. This Haven was likely affluent, and had waited around for her to get smart. Caleb crossed his arms, squeezing out his bruised ego. Lissa needed surgery and here he was worrying about himself. "And she hurt herself?"

"At Gooseberry Falls. For some reason, my child decided she could fly."

A smile crept to his lips.

"And unfortunately, her young man was unable to catch her."

I never would have let her fall.

"She messed up her knee something fierce. And it'll take weeks of recovery. I don't know how she's going to manage. She won't let me help, and Haven has his own career to worry about."

"I'm very sorry to hear that, Mrs. Morgan. Is there anything I can do to help?"

She turned around and faced him. "Precisely the question I was waiting for." She pointed to the sofa. "Please, have a seat."

He sat at one end, and Mrs. Morgan perched at the other end, one leg crossing the other like a TV celebrity. "Haven is a dear young man. He was a favorite of my late husband's, and Lissa has had a crush on him for years. The only problem is, now that they're dating I see him from a different perspective. The man cocoons Lissa too much. I fear if she stays with him, he'll drain the spirit from her, the spirit that prompted her to move out on her own."

The very spirit he'd witnessed on their dates, when he'd viewed her flight and started to care for her. Caleb squirmed on the couch. "Why are you telling me this?"

Adelaide curved a manicured hand over his. "Dear, isn't it obvious? My daughter may think Haven is the one for her, but I see her expression when she talks about you. It's you who has given her wings. It's you she cares for. She's afraid to admit it."

Caleb wiped perspiration from his brow. "I don't know what to say. That's not the impression I got."

"Darling, that was the impression of a young woman afraid to fly." She pulled a wicker-framed picture from off an end table. A toddler dressed as Tinker Bell.

"Lissa?"

Adelaide nodded. "My question to you is, what are you going to do about restoring her wings?"

He swallowed hard, gripping the picture. Perhaps it was time for him to fly again too. "I guess I might pay her a visit."

Crutches braced beneath her arms, Lissa studied the two steps leading into her home. Two measly steps. With that leaden weight bracing her repaired knee, it might as well be Mount Everest. Making the short trek up her crumbling sidewalk had been hard enough, and already had her perspiring in October's cool morning sun. But she'd conquered the walk, now it was time to conquer that mountain.

Caleb would have loved that analogy.

"Lissa, let me help you." Haven stopped at her side and set a copy-paper box overflowing with flowers, balloons, and stuffed animals on the ground.

"No." She set her jaw. She could defeat this mountain on her own. But how to do it? Her brief crutches' lesson had taught her to grab on to a railing. That would work well if these steps had a railing.

"You don't have to be such a hero." Irritation edged his voice. A tone she'd never heard before. "Let me carry you inside. You can do it from there."

I will not be carried! Making certain her crutches were planted on firm concrete, not the broken pieces, and with her injured leg suspended slightly behind her, she tried leaping to the first step. Her foot hit the front of the step and she screamed as she tilted forward. Haven's arms surrounded her, breaking her fall.

A tear trailed down her cheek and he kissed it away. "I'll carry you."

She shook her head. "No."

"Stubborn woman," Haven muttered.

"So what if I am?" She pinched her eyes closed. How could she be so lousy to him when he was just trying to help? She looked him in the eye. "I need to learn to do this, Haven. Otherwise, how'll I get around?"

He raised his hands in surrender. "I guess I'll be here to catch you."

Will you?

Oh, she was nasty. How could one little fall destroy her faith in him? Well, perhaps it wasn't so small, but still, it wasn't his fault she decided to practice flying. "Okay, how about this? I use you as my guardrail, and go up the steps like they taught me."

"Let's do it." He stepped to her side and raised his left arm.

She handed him one crutch, which he secured under his right arm. Perspiration seemed to ooze from every pore in her body as she held on to Haven. This was not how she imagined being close to him. Steeling the left crutch, she hopped off her right leg and, with Haven's help, she landed securely on the first step.

"I did it!"

"Way to go!"

Wow. Such enthusiasm for one teensy little step. It was interesting how God put things in perspective.

"You ready?" Haven clapped his right hand over her arm.

"Absolutely." She leaned against Haven, secured her crutch, and hopped. Again landing without a hitch, but it completely wiped her out. She'd get inside, lie down, and not move.

Haven handed over her other crutch and pulled open her screen door. After unlocking the inside door, he pushed it open.

Seeing the raised threshold, she moaned. One more stupid step. Well, this one she'd conquer on her own. She rested a crutch inside the door, grabbed the door frame and hopped. Her wobbly landing wouldn't win her any grace points, but who cared.

"You trying to break your neck?" Obviously, Haven cared.

"Sorry, I needed to prove to myself that I could do it and I did."

He shook his head. "I don't know what's gotten into you."

"You don't like me being independent?" With crutches in place, she inched toward the resting refuge of her couch.

"Whoa, don't be putting words in my mouth." He stayed close to her side as she moved, but didn't touch her. "I happen to like it very much, but I feel I should be doing more for you. If it weren't for me, you wouldn't be . . ."

"You had nothing to do with my being an idiot." No, it wasn't his fault, but . . . "Tell you what. I'll make it to the couch, then you can wait on me. How's that sound?"

"Until noon anyway. I wish I didn't have to leave. Maybe I could talk to the publisher and ask to meet her next week instead."

"I'm not going to let you change your plans. Mom's coming for the week." Oh, joy. There couldn't be a better incentive for her to get better. She inwardly rolled her eyes. "In between all her volunteer hours, of course, which will give me time to breathe."

"And I can come after work."

"You don't have to." She reached the couch and stared down at it. Boy, it was a long way down.

"I want to."

"Okay. I'd like to see you." But every day? Did she really want to?

Holding both crutches in one hand, she grabbed the back of the couch and slowly lowered her body onto it. Relief. Now, to raise that two-ton leg. She grasped her leg between her hands and pulled it onto the sofa. Time to rest. She laid her head back on the armrest, closed her eyes, and listened to Haven bustling about her living room.

Seconds later she felt her leg being raised then lowered onto a hill of pillows. "Remember to keep your knee above your heart."

"Mm, hmm." Her body, worn from that little walk, melded with the sofa.

Haven spread a blanket over her and tucked a stuffed animal into her arms. She opened an eye and peeked at the cuddly monkey he'd given her yesterday. The box holding her other gifts sat on the floor next to the couch.

"I'll put together a little lunch for you, we'll do your exercises, then I should get going."

Not those infernal exercises. Giving birth had to be easier. She opened her eyes and pouted using her best puppy-dog face. "Can't we skip the therapy? Just for today?"

"Really? Where did that independent, brave woman go?"

"She ran away as soon as you mentioned torture."

"Slight exaggeration."

"That's what you think."

Haven chuckled. "This—" He cleared his throat. "—torture is doctor prescribed. Start retraining those muscles right away, and get the knee moving again so all that scar tissue doesn't lock your knee up, so you can go back to rock climbing."

"Yes, Nurse Ratched."

He kissed her lips. "You were saying?"

She stared into his bottomless blues. To think this gorgeous, perfect man liked her, and she'd been so rotten to him. She touched a finger to his lips. "Tell you what, if you can promise me more of that, I'll refrain from calling you names."

"Promise?"

She drew an X over her chest. "Cross my heart."

He kissed her again. "I'll go make lunch."

Probably wouldn't be as good as Caleb's. She balled her hands into fists. How dare Caleb intrude on this beautiful moment?

She reached down into the gift box and pulled out a book. Charles Martin. Hadn't heard of him before, but from the back cover explanation, it sounded like a romance. The perfect thing to whisk her thoughts away. She started reading as Haven clunked around her kitchen.

"Your cupboard is pretty bare." Haven opened a TV tray and set it next to the couch. He placed a water glass and filled plate on it.

Romaine lettuce and spinach topped with mandarin oranges and sprinkled with walnuts. Not exactly fresh, but that was what she got for being grounded from walking for a week. Regardless, it looked delicious. Better than hospital food any day.

She pushed herself up into a sitting position and adjusted the pillows beneath her leg. It would take too much effort to lower it to the floor and then lift it back up.

Haven squatted next to her gift box and pulled out a vase that had a color-bursting mix of roses, chrysanthemums, and carnations. "Where would you like all your flowers?"

She glanced around the room. "How about over there?" She pointed to a round table, dressed with a lace tablecloth, that sat in front of her picture window. A reading lamp and her Bible rested on top. Her favorite place to read, but it might be a while before she could sit for prolonged periods without elevating her leg. In the meantime, that table was in the perfect location for her to enjoy the three flower arrangements and two balloon bouquets. One would think she'd spent a week in the hospital, not one night.

Haven spent several minutes sorting the arrangements, sometimes moving them millimeters. Finally, he stepped back, and cocked his head to the side. "How's that?"

"Perfect." She forked the remaining piece of salad and downed it with lemon water. For a guy, he really did have a keen eye. Perhaps that was what made him such a good photographer.

"Good." He glanced back at her. "You all done?"

"For now. Mom's bringing groceries when she comes."

Haven cleared the TV tray and moved it to the side. "Well, I've got a few minutes before I have to take off. Just enough to get that knee bending a bit."

A groan slid from her mouth. "Can't we just say we did?" Man, she was a wimp.

"What do you think?"

With a huff, she scooted down on the couch until she was lying flat. "I better not see one smile while you're hurting me."

He ran a hand over his mouth and kept it there. "I'll do my best. Let's get that knee bending again, okay?"

"Fine."

She steeled herself as he lifted her leg about a foot off the couch, then slowly pushed on her foot, forcing the knee to bend.

Tears fogged her eyes as nerve-slashing pain shot through her leg with each hair of movement. "Stop!"

"Hold it, Liss, you'll be fine."

He held her leg at that angle for what seemed like hours. "Okay, now straighten."

She pushed against his hands. At least that wasn't as painful.

"Now, press down, get that leg straight."

Clenching her fists and squeezing her eyes, she tried to press her leg flat. Pain sliced through her leg, but it wasn't as sharp as when bending the knee.

"Good. Now hold."

She held her breath and counted to ten.

"And rest."

Thank you, Jesus.

"Now, breathe." He handed her a tissue and she wiped her tears.

"Ready?"

"No."

"Let's do it."

She stuck out her tongue.

Ignoring her, and probably sucking in a grin, he lifted her leg and pushed. It looked like the leg barely moved, but the knives piercing it said otherwise. Her trickle of tears turned into a flood.

"Liss, hey I'm sorry. I hate doing this, you know. Go ahead and push."

Gladly. He was lucky this thing weighed as much as a boulder, otherwise her leg would become a weapon. "Isn't that enough? Please? I promise I'll work on it tonight, okay? Mom'll help me."

"Lissa . . ." He rested her leg.

"No, really. I'm tired and sore and cranky."

"But—"

"But I'll do better tonight and tomorrow. I promise."

"Twice a day, remember? All the exercises, not just this one."

"I promise." She nodded. "Mom'll make me."

"I'm sure she will." He frowned at his watch. "Well, I suppose I need to get going. As long as you promise."

"I do."

"Okay. But in the meantime . . ." He hustled to the kitchen and returned with a blue ice bag and timer, then he pulled a heating pad from the hospital box and set it all on the TV tray. "Ice twenty, heat twenty. Keep that swelling down."

"Yes, sir." She saluted.

"You're not taking this seriously."

"Sorry. You're right."

He scurried around more, gathering a water bottle, a bowl of carrots, her phone, and the television remote and crowded them on the TV tray. "What am I missing? Anything?"

"Your appointment, if you don't get moving."

"You'll call if you need anything?"

"Stop babying me. This isn't your fault."

"Could've fooled me."

Arghh. Would he never forget her accusing words? Was he trying to make up for not catching her? She was the idiot who jumped. "Haven, I'll be fine. Seriously. And I appreciate you being there for me through all of this. I do. But Mom's coming shortly. Until she gets here, I'm going to rest, but I won't get any rest if you don't get out of here."

"You're right. You're right. I'm off." He leaned down and kissed her. "Take care of yourself, now. I'll see you on Monday."

She grasped his hand as he turned away. "Sorry I'm so crabby. I'll miss you, you know?"

The crinkles by his eyes appeared with his smile. "Love you." He kissed her hand and walked out her door.

Finally. Releasing a relieved sigh, she sank into the couch. She thought he'd never leave. Wait a second. He didn't say love, did he? Oh my gosh, he did! Why didn't that make her heart do a Snoopy dance?

And why was she so relieved when he left?

Morning sun beamed through Lissa's bedroom window, directly onto her face. The way she usually liked it.

Not today. Not when she had to go to the bathroom but couldn't get there without her mom's help. Well today, even if her mom protested, she'd throw away that dependence and learn to walk, to handle life on her own again.

How dare the sun smile when she felt so rotten? She moaned and tears congregated in her eyes as she attempted to lift her leaden leg. The surgeon hadn't warned her that her leg would feel like it carried a Mack truck. She backhanded her tears and tightened the Velcro securing the knee brace to her leg. She stabilized her leg between both hands, the brace adjusting for the narrowest of angular movements, and guided her foot to the floor.

Success. And on her own too. She reached for the crutches propped next to her headboard and stole a glance at the doorway. Silence, and no sign of her mom. Good. Lissa could do this by herself. Holding both crutches' middle padding with one hand, she grasped the headboard with one arm and pushed up.

A curse flitted through her mind but didn't pass her lips. Yet. And on Sunday of all days. Church certainly wasn't an option today. She sniffled, wiped away another tear, and tried again.

"Corliss Adelaide Morgan, what do you think you're doing?"

Lissa fell back on the bed, her leaden leg weighted to the floor. "I need to use the bathroom. I can't do that?"

"Darling, why didn't you ask?"

Lissa dropped the crutches and clenched hair in her fists. "I hate being helpless."

"Today, you can feel helpless." Her mom bent over, retrieved the crutches, and handed them to Lissa. "Tomorrow, you'll wish you were helpless when you start sessions with your physical therapist."

She shivered. The exercises she did yesterday with Haven and her mom were bad enough. Lissa sat back up, kicked at the ground with her right foot and mumbled, "Mom, will you help me?"

"Darling, we'll work on that robotic plea later, but yes, I would be glad to help."

Lissa breathed in, then forced it out before clutching the crutches and the headboard. With a continuous grunt, she pushed up with her good leg and arms while her mom supported her back. Victory! Never again would she take standing for granted.

She secured a crutch below each arm and glanced down at her legs. Okay, now what was she supposed to remember? No pressure on knee. Extend crutches first, think of them as additional legs. Keeping the weight on her good leg, and her left leg extended forward slightly, she swung the crutches ahead half a foot, and used them for support as she inched her good leg in front of the crutches. At this rate, it would take an hour to get to the bathroom.

"You're doing well, darling." Her mom stayed at her side, but didn't interfere.

Lissa swung her crutches forward again, another half a foot, then she stepped with her good leg. Woo hoo. A whole four inches this time. At least she didn't have to go up steps to the bathroom. Thank goodness for little things.

This time, she'd go for more. Six inches with the crutches. No problem. She swung her right leg forward an extra two inches and landed with a thud, jarring her body, sending spasms through her left leg and rocking her backward. She screeched, but her mom's body braked Lissa's fall. A creek trickled from her eyes. "I can't do this."

"Yes you can, and you will. And, I have it on very good authority that a sumptuous lunch is on its way. You'll want to be up and dressed by the time it gets here."

"What time is it?" Lissa stepped into the hallway. One milestone reached.

"Eleven thirty."

"What?" No way had she slept that long. "Are you sure?"

"Keep moving forward, darling."

"Right." There was no retrieving the lost morning. Okay. Only two more feet to the bathroom. Crutches. Right foot. Crutches. Right. Yes! She'd conquered the hallway. But now . . . she looked at the toilet and whimpered. Why did today seem harder than yesterday?

"You can do it, dear." Her mom's hand rested on her back.

Lissa gritted her teeth. "I'll holler if I need help."

Twenty minutes later she stood in front of the mirror in her bedroom, dressed in a T-shirt and cut-off sweatpants, with padded crutches chafing her armpits. The cost of victory. It was worth it. She was going to make it.

Balancing on her crutches, she looped her hair into a ponytail. Today, it didn't matter what she looked like. With Haven out of town, she could be completely comfortable.

The doorbell rang. Must be lunch, which, considering that her mom ordered out, would be extravagantly delicious. Her mom never went half way.

Lissa turned toward her bedroom door. Now for the trek out the door, down the hallway, to the couch. She might as well be running a marathon. But even that began with one foot, then the other, and repeat.

"Darling," her mom hollered from the living room. "I'm stepping out for a moment. This nice young man will help you."

Say what? *Mom, you've gone absolutely nuts!* It was probably some waiter she'd gotten to know at one of her fine dining establishments. Some kid eager to make a whopper of a tip. Well, today he'd earn it.

The ping of aluminum rang from the kitchen. Lissa slogged down the hallway, enticed by the delectable aromas of peppery steak and orange and oregano. Funny, this hallway always seemed so short before. She didn't even bother looking in the kitchen when she passed it. That would take too much extra effort, and she planned on obeying her mom today.

Finally, she reached the couch. Having her mom wait on her suddenly sounded like a good idea. Exhausted, she dropped down on the sofa, lifted up her braced leg and rested it on a mountain of pillows. For the rest of the day, minus a bathroom break or two, this would be her home.

She lay back on the pillow and closed her eyes. Moving was too much work. Hopefully, the meal would restore her energy.

"Are you hungry?"

What? Lissa's eyes popped open and she stared directly into squinty, toffee-brown eyes. Gorgeous, familiar eyes. Her mom set this up? That didn't make any sense. "Wh-what are you doing here, Caleb?"

Chapter Twenty-Two

’m bringing you lunch." Caleb's dreamy eyes smiled down on Lissa, stealing her voice and sending her heart into an erratic jazz beat.

This was so wrong. She was acting like a lovesick teenager, so she averted her gaze and closed her eyes. Get the words out, thank him for the food, and ask him to leave.

"Your mother is very persuasive."

Her eyes popped open. "M-my mom?"

With a nod, he erected a folding tray next to the couch.

"No, you must be wrong." She pointed toward the door. Her shaky finger matched her voice. "You can't mean Adelaide Morgan, that woman who just left this house. We cannot be talking about the same person."

"One and the same." Caleb grinned.

How dare he do that? She covered her fluttering heart with a hand. Her pain meds must be making her bonkers.

"I need to thank you for telling her about my artwork." He covered the TV tray with a purple tablecloth that cascaded to the ground. "The least I can do is say thanks with a meal."

"So this isn't some game, you're not trying to get back together again, because if you are, you need to know there is someone—"

"Yes, yes, admittedly I'm not happy about it, but I shouldn't expect less when I hurt you."

With quivering fingers she played with the Velcro straps on her brace. "And I overreacted." Just as her two-timing heart was doing now.

"All we can do is move forward from here, and that means serving one of Chez Amélie's most requested meals."

No wonder her mouth was watering. "You shouldn't have. That's way too expensive." He clearly hadn't learned a thing about money. Which was exactly why he was wrong for her. Her heart finally listened and slowed to its normal pace.

"There are some privileges to having their sous chef as your father-in-law. And now, it's my privilege to serve you."

Her belly flip-flopped as he disappeared into the kitchen. It had to be from the luscious aromas wafting from there. Hummingbirds dancing in her belly were no longer allowed for Caleb.

He returned, a purple towel draped over his arm, balancing a large round tray on one hand. Obviously, he'd learned more from his father-in-law than French cooking. The tray didn't wobble as he removed a water goblet with a lemon wedge clinging to the top. He set down a China plate with food arranged so artistically, she didn't want to touch it. He framed the food art with a white cloth napkin and silverware. The savory scent of peppercorn drifted from the steak au poivre, and her stomach growled. Proof that her tummy's churning was caused by physical rather than heart hunger.

She dropped her right leg to the floor, and swung her left around, slowly lowering it.

Caleb adjusted the tray around her legs so she could reach the food better. "If you clean your plate, there's dessert."

She couldn't help grinning. "Sounds like a dad speaking." But there was no doubt she'd eat every morsel and maybe ask for seconds. She sliced off a bite of the filet mignon, brought it to her mouth, and held it there. "Will you join me?"

"Do you mind?"

"I'd like that. Really. I wasn't very kind to you last time I saw you, and I've been meaning to give you a call to apologize, but my ego has stopped me. I guess in person is better than over the phone."

"I'll be right back." He hurried to the kitchen and returned with a second TV tray and an everyday plate filled with food and sat in her Queen Anne chair. No fancy presentation for him.

By the time he settled, half her steak was gone, as was the radicchio and mashed potatoes. "This is phenomenal."

"I'll extend your compliments to the chef. He's praying for a swift recovery . . . So am I." He looked down at his plate and carved off a slice of meat.

She dropped her knife. How could she have doubted his sincerity? "Caleb, I'm terribly sorry about the way things ended between us."

A sliver of sunlight sliced between her drapes, cutting the carpeted floor between her and Caleb in half.

He set his fork down and wiped his mouth with a paper napkin. "I should have made the time to talk to you. I shouldn't have played games that day by showing you the house beforehand. Your reaction was just."

"But my conclusion was still wrong. And now . . ." There's someone else. Someone better suited to her.

"Now, I've learned a very sad lesson. But I'm still a better man for knowing you."

"Could you, would you consider being my friend?"

His lips curved up and his eyes squinted. "I'd like that very much, but first I need to be completely honest about my intentions."

"There can't be an us, Caleb."

"That's not where I was going."

"I'm sorry. Please continue."

"I've come with a very selfish request."

"O . . . kay."

He leaned back in the chair, his food barely touched. "Jeanette was the numbers person in our family, our business. Me? I can't add two plus two unless you're talking architectural dimensions—then I can visualize it."

Lissa nodded. Knowing Caleb, that actually made sense.

He massaged the back of his neck. "You obviously know about my house, that I'm three payments behind."

"There's nothing special I can do for you, Caleb. I thought I made that clear."

"No, that's not what I meant. I'm not asking for special treatment. What I want is your financial expertise. You offered before to help me create a business plan, to help me organize my checkbook. I've got a job now. It's only a temp position at a department store, but they like me. I'm hoping to get hired on permanent. With that and with the work your mom brought me, I think I might be able to make it, but I need help with a game plan."

Lissa spooned potatoes to her mouth and washed them down with water. Sure, she could help him, but would her heart fall for him again? Could she afford taking that risk? "I'm not sure."

"How about if I throw in a little incentive? Your mom said you needed rides this week to physical therapy so she doesn't have to cancel her volunteering. She said you've got morning appointments. I'm scheduled to work in the evening."

"My mom told you that?"

"Yep."

Lissa shook her head. What was her mom up to? The woman was giving her a headache. "For this week only, okay? If you can bring over your finances tomorrow, I'll take a look, but I'm not promising we'll find a way to save your house."

"All I ask is a chance."

"That's all I can offer." She shook her fork at him. "After this week, I plan on driving myself."

"I don't doubt that you will."

And she definitely had incentive to drive. Any more than one week around Jonathan Caleb Johnson and she'd certainly lose perspective on their relationship again.

Ignoring her pleas for help, Caleb stood behind Lissa as she tackled the steps to her townhome. Offering an arm would only make her dependent. The sooner she learned to climb the steps on her own, the better for her.

Maybe today, once Lissa looked over his paperwork, she could keep him from falling, from losing his home. All his papers were in his truck waiting for her perusal. What he needed now was a miracle.

She hopped up and fell back, right into his arms.

Lord have mercy. He breathed in her floral scent and wished he could hold her forever, and to catch her whenever she fell. "Good try," his voice pitched higher. Still holding her, he cleared his throat. "You'll do it next time."

"That's easy for you to say," she mumbled.

"Yeah, I suppose it is." He braced her until she stood upright. Still, letting go wasn't easy. "Go ahead, try again."

She rotated her shoulders. "You're as bad as that physical terrorist."

"She was nasty, wasn't she? But look at how far your knee bends already. Before you know it you'll be rock-jumping again. But first, let's conquer these steps."

She mumbled something he didn't think he wanted to hear, and he chuckled. She had more spirit than she gave herself credit for.

"I'm behind you, Lissa, go for it."

Her shoulders rose and fell and her fingers whitened on the crutch handles. She pushed off the ground and her right foot landed on the concrete step. "Yes!"

"Victory feels good, doesn't it?"

"I'm not there yet."

"You can do it."

Her shoulders tensed, she pushed off the step, and came down on the landing. "I made it!"

"And on your own, too." He opened both doors and held them. With barely a hesitation, she crossed the threshold. What beautiful determination. Too bad saving his house wasn't as easy as this. Maybe, for Lissa, it might be.

Slowly, she crossed the carpet to her couch, where she plopped down and elevated her leg. "Thank you for bringing me today. You don't know how I've appreciated your encouragement."

"Glad I could help. So, now if you wouldn't mind . . ." He scratched the back of his neck.

"I'd love to look over your books, see how I can help."

Caleb hurried out to his pickup and returned with a plastic file carrier. "Here's my life in a nutshell. Bills due are up front." He pulled a sheet of paper from his pocket. "Here's what I'm anticipating from the commissioned artwork and from my temporary position."

She took the sheet and grimaced.

"Yeah, I know, it's pathetic, but it's all I've got to work with."

She blew out a breath. "I've got a calculator, pen, and paper in my top drawer next to the stove. Would you mind getting them?"

"Sure." He retrieved them and set up a TV tray. "Do you want me to hang around, answer questions maybe? Or should I go for a jog, get out of your way?"

Eyes squinting, she scratched the side of her head. "Answer a few questions first, okay?"

"Fire away."

She rummaged through the folders, pulling former clients' files. "Your business, you designed kitchens for new homes only?"

"Yep."

"Never remodeling?"

He shrugged. "Never gave it much thought."

"Perhaps you should. People aren't moving, but they're remodeling. Hennepin Bank's approved a ton of home improvement loans."

"I suppose I could. I recently finished off my in-laws' basement, but I'd be starting from scratch as far as clientele goes."

"You're starting from scratch anyway, aren't you?"

"I guess."

"Well, consider it. After seeing the work in your house, I've no doubt about your ability." She held up a picture of a kitchen he and Jeanette had designed and built with cabinets he'd crafted by hand in his garage. "This is beautiful. I can foresee a demand for your skills, but more so in the remodeling industry now. New homebuilders, even for more expensive builds, are streamlining everything, using less original cabinetry. But people looking to remodel instead of moving might love this."

Caleb tucked his hands in his back pockets. "But how do I begin again? I'm broke and even I know capital is required to start a business."

"Well, let me study your paperwork and see what I come up with." She chewed on her lower lip. "Now's probably a good time to go for that jog. Give me an hour and I'll see what I can do."

"I appreciate this, Lissa." He pulled on his tennis shoes and went for a jog around her neighborhood, breathing in the crisp fall air. Young trees now stood bare and autumn leaves danced on postage-stamp yards that offered nowhere for a toddler to run or fly. He jogged past character-free townhomes to the neighborhood playground and relaxed on a swing. Aimee would love the diverse selection of entertainment: swing sets, slides, molded plastic tunnels, and climbing walls. Still it wasn't the same as having it in her own back yard.

He backpedaled in the swing then lifted his feet, propelling him forward. He pumped and the swing carried him higher with each pendulum swing. Then he leapt and landed on his feet.

Just as he knew he would do once Lissa guided his finances in the right direction.

He jogged from the park and turned in a cul-de-sac surrounded with single-family homes that had no more personality than the townhomes. The whole area was depressing, but if he couldn't keep his house, this was what he had to look forward to. He checked his watch. Forty-five minutes had passed already. Time to head back.

After stretching his leg muscles, he jogged back to Lissa's home with jumping beans partying in his stomach. She had to have good news for him. If anyone could save his home, Lissa could.

He reached her door and paused for a breath before knocking and letting himself in. The party escalated in his gut as he glanced at Lissa. Her eyes were red rimmed and a slight pout curved her lips. Not what he wanted to see.

"I take it, it's not good." He hung by the door and tucked sweaty hands in his jean pockets.

Looking down, she shook her head. "I wish I had something good to tell you." Her chin lifted, but her gaze still didn't meet his. "Hennepin Bank detests taking people's homes away. It's cheaper for us to work with people, to offer discounts, refinancing, whatever it takes to keep the owners in their home. Within reason."

"There's nothing you can do?"

She sighed and readjusted her ponytail. "Your current income, temporary income, will barely cover three-quarters of your mortgage and that's without paying other bills. That's without eating, buying gas. And you're in arrears on your bills too, although by just a month."

"But I'll catch up as soon as I get paid. After that I can worry about the mortgage."

With a groan, she leaned her head back. "What's more important to you? The house or heat?"

He dropped into the Queen Anne and stared at the floor. "The house, of course."

"Why pay the other bills first? The first bill you should pay every month is your mortgage. You can live without a phone, even electricity and gas, although they can't cut that in winter around here, but you need a home. Do you see what I'm saying?"

"I suppose." He'd never thought of it that way. "So, that's what I do? I ignore the utilities?"

She puffed out a breath. "If your financial situation was better, I'd suggest that you prioritize paying your mortgage, but as it stands, that wouldn't catch you up."

"I've got time though, don't I? Maybe I'll get hired on permanent. Maybe get a raise."

"Maybe, Caleb, maybe. Banks don't survive on maybe. And yes, you've got time to catch up, but in the meantime penalties are accruing, a lawyer will be retained, not to mention interest. With what I'm looking at, catching up will take a miracle."

"I believe in miracles."

She laughed through a frown. "Well, maybe God's miracle isn't yours. Maybe you're supposed to make a different choice."

No way. He swallowed the grapefruit-sized knot in his throat. God wouldn't take his home away. "What do you suggest?"

"Come over here." She lowered her legs to the floor. "Let me show you what I've got. It's not all bad."

He walked across her carpet, shuffling his feet through its fibers, and sat next to her.

With the pen she pointed at his mortgage total. "Here's what we can work with. Unlike a lot of homeowners nowadays, you actually have escrow. Even with the down market, I can see you making this amount." She pointed at a number penned below the mortgage. "When you sell the home."

He jumped up. "Who said I'm selling?"

"You asked for my help. Are you going to listen or not?"

Sounded like his mother-in-law. He plopped back down and muttered, "I'm listening."

"Now, assuming you sell, you could probably make this amount, maybe even more. That means you rent for a bit, save, and build again."

But he already had the home he wanted. "And if I don't want to sell?"

"Barring a miracle, within a year you'll lose your home and whatever good credit you may have left. Then try to build a business."

This isn't the answer I wanted, God. "Can I think about it?"

"You know the ramifications. It's your decision, but I wouldn't wait too long. When you sell, the lawyers will take the first bite, and they have voracious appetites, believe me."

He rubbed the back of his neck. "I appreciate your help."

"I'm so sorry." She rested her hand on his arm. "I know what your home means to you; it's evident how much of yourself you've poured into it."

Why did her hand have to feel so good? He walked over to the window table scented with her hospital floral arrangements. *God, what do I do now? Will you tear the last piece of Jeanette from me?*

"Caleb?"

He turned toward her, and kicked at the carpet. "I should get going. I need to give Aimee-doodles a hug."

"Before you go, I hate asking this, but would you mind doing me a favor? It's either you or my mom."

"Sure." He avoided her eyes? "What."

"Help me with one of my exercises? It's easier doing them with someone. And you get to take your frustrations out on me."

He chuckled. "I'd be glad to."

"Take out your frustrations?"

"No. Help. Torn ligaments aren't a foreign thing to me. Rock climbers and skydivers have their share of injuries."

"I don't know if that reassures me."

"I'll be kind. I promise. What do you need me to do?"

"Hold my foot and push, then I try to stretch it straight."

"Sure thing."

She lay down on the couch and he gripped her foot. "Ready?"

"No, but go ahead anyway."

Slowly, he pressed her leg forward. Her face reddened with each centimeter and tears glossed her eyes.

"Enough," she squeaked out.

"A tad more." He pressed a little harder and tears tracked down her cheeks. "Now count." Keeping one hand on her foot, he reached for the pen and a piece of paper. He rested it against the side of her knee and recorded the angle. "Now, let's bring it back."

She pushed her leg outward and tried flattening it.

"Don't worry, it'll come."

"It shouldn't be so hard."

"You've traumatized your knee. It's rebelling. Shall we go again?"

"Do we have to?"

He grinned and lifted her leg, pushing.

Tears crawled from beneath her pinched eyelids as she gripped the sofa's fabric, her fingers whitening. "Enough."

"Nope. A little more." He shoved a little harder.

"Stop, Caleb!"

"Count to ten, okay?"

A river flowed over her cheeks. "It hurts."

"I know." He released his pressure. "Press it back down."

They repeated the process seven more times. "Okay. This is the last one. Let's—"

"You're evil, Caleb, plain evil."

He smirked and picked up her leg. "Let's go for a record, okay?"

"I don't want to break a record!"

"Pull, Lissa, pull." He pushed her leg, the knee protested but slowly bent. More tears crept out. He hated to see her in pain, but healing was never pain free.

"That's enough!"

"Another inch. You can do it, Lissa. I know you can." Well, maybe half an inch, but it was still progress. "Hold it, let those muscles adjust." He retrieved the paper with the first bend mark, set it against her knee and grinned. "And release."

She pushed against his hand and tried to flatten her knee against the couch. Not there yet, but it would come, especially if she kept working this hard.

"Why don't you sit up?" He handed her a water bottle. "I've got good news."

"You're leaving and never coming back?"

He chuckled. "That too." He showed her the piece of paper with her progress. "Look at this. A whole ten degree improvement from your first push to the last."

"Really?" A grin broke through her tears as she studied the paper. "Will you help me tomorrow too?"

"Absolutely." He tapped the paper. "Keep it up, and you'll by flying again in no time."

She waved a hand in front of her mouth and sniffled. "I will be flying, won't I?"

If he hadn't blown it with her earlier, he'd be a front seat witness to her flight.

Chapter Twenty-Three

A brisk November wind howled outside Adelaide's so-called hut as Caleb packed up his carving tools. He hated leaving this cottage, but the carvings were all complete, and it was time to go. He'd retrieve Aimee from the back bedroom and head home.

Home. He sighed. Just in time for another lonely holiday.

The forecast for tomorrow said it could be the coldest Thanksgiving on record. Frankly, they'd all been cold since Jeanette's death, even though the temperature sometimes said otherwise.

He clenched his fists and steeled his jaw. Jeanette would ream into him for this pity party, but she had no clue how lonely the holidays were. With this being the third Thanksgiving without her, maybe it was time to give thanks that he'd had her at all. His mother-in-law would call that a thought in the right direction. Now, to turn that thought into action.

Which meant moving on. Letting Jeanette go. Lissa too. Working in her mother's lake cottage had only intensified his longing for her. Well, as of today, he was done. He took one last glance around his temporary art studio. No wood shavings littered the hardwood floor. The kitchen's granite countertop sparkled and the stainless steel sink shined. It was time to say goodbye to this cottage many people would love to have as their permanent home.

Adelaide Morgan had been more than generous in offering this space for the commissioned portraits, now all complete. But what fun he'd had creating them. Perhaps Jeanette—and Lissa—were right. Maybe this was a skill he could market.

But marketing a new business took money.

Money the bank demanded from him. And now lawyers. He massaged the back of his neck. It didn't matter that he paid as much as he could on the mortgage. It was like using a tablespoon to dig out from under a pile of dirt while the bank and attorneys used a front-end loader to heap more on.

But a miracle could still happen.

He flipped the switch on the fireplace, turning it off, and walked down a short hallway past a bath and a den to a bedroom. Aimee lay cuddled beneath a puffy down comforter. Still sound asleep. And completely at peace.

How could he disturb that? He kissed her cheek and smoothed copper strands from her face. "Dada loves you, my Sleeping Beauty." She didn't stir. Maybe he should lie down next to her, see if some of that peace would rub off on him via osmosis. He pulled back the comforter and a knock sounded on the outside door.

He jogged to the door and opened it. "Good afternoon, Mrs. Morgan." He waved her into the room and closed the door behind her. "I just finished cleaning, but Aimee's still napping. I hate to wake her."

"By all means, don't. Let the sweet child rest."

"Thank you, Mrs.—"

"Adelaide, dear, please call me Adelaide. You should know that by now." She shrugged out of her lamb's-wool jacket and hung it on the coat tree next to the door. "That will give us a moment to chat." Clutching her purse with one hand, she pointed to the curved leather couch facing the corner fireplace. "Please have a seat."

Oh boy. He sat on the far end of the couch, keeping a cushion between them. Having a talk was never a good sign. Maybe her friends weren't pleased with his job. Could he have engraved some with greater detail? Did they want their money back? If so, they'd have to wait in line behind the bank and the utilities.

"Dear." She reached over and patted his arm. "I see that worry on your face. I assure you that my friends are all ecstatic with your artwork and I have a feeling that you will be hounded with more calls once word gets out."

He released a relieved sigh. "I've enjoyed it, and I can't tell you how much I appreciate having the use of this cottage."

"You can express your appreciation by continuing to use it when the need arises."

"But—"

"No, no buts. It's my pleasure to host an up-and-coming artist, and a handsome one at that. I rather enjoy my friends' envy and being the subject of juicy gossip."

He glanced down at the floor, hoping to hide his blush. It didn't take a physicist to figure out what that gossip was about. Maybe using this studio wasn't such a good idea.

"Dear Caleb, don't you worry about that gossip. As much as they've flattered me, I've quelled the rumors."

"Thank you." A tarnished reputation would be more difficult to fix than his money problems. Even with Lissa's help last month, he was no closer to saving the house. But she'd warned him about that, hadn't she?

"I wish to thank you for encouraging Corliss in her exercises. I was concerned when she returned home from the hospital, but you found some miraculous way to spur her on, and for that I'm very grateful."

"She's doing well?" It may have been weeks since he'd seen her, but those weeks had been peppered with the memory of her victorious smile. Working in the cottage built specifically for her had only enhanced his longing to see her again. His daily prayers to remove her from his heart had been ignored just like his prayers to save his home.

"She's doing perfectly marvelous."

"Good. I've been praying for her."

"Your prayers have been heard, as have mine."

Caleb blinked. Until now, he and Adelaide had avoided any talk of prayer or God. Finally a prayer was being answered with a yes.

"She nearly has full extension on her knee and a wonderful range of movement and is hoping to throw away her crutches next week."

"I'm sure she will."

"Caleb." Adelaide patted his leg. "I absolutely adore your can-do attitude, and I thank you for inspiring Corliss."

"I just gave her a little nudge."

"I appreciate your nudge and, as a thank you, I would love to have you and Aimee join Corliss and me for Thanksgiving dinner on Saturday."

"Saturday?"

"Yes, dear. Corliss and I serve Thanksgiving meals at her church tomorrow, a tradition her father started years ago. It's always a very humbling experience. It's difficult for me to imagine not having the financial means to make a meal, much less Thanksgiving."

Sounded like something Lissa would do. "Thank you, but I already have commitments on Saturday." What he'd give to join Lissa tomorrow and Saturday. Working with her that first week following her surgery, watching her push past the pain and seeing her joy after each milestone reached had only deepened his feelings for her. He hated turning Adelaide down, especially with all she'd done for him, but at least he had a good excuse.

"Is it family? They're welcome to join us, too. I'm afraid my celebrations are rather silent with only Lissa and me, and Haven, of course."

Sounded like the invitation came with ulterior motives. He'd rather cliff-dive into shark-infested waters. "Thank you, but Saturday afternoon I'm participating in another heart disease awareness fundraiser." A brand new adrenaline-inducing experience. He couldn't wait. "And I work Saturday morning." And probably every day up until Christmas. He'd be lucky to tuck Aimee in every night. But it was a job. If he wanted to save his house . . .

"Well, I'm very sorry to hear that. Perhaps after Christmas you'll have more time."

Too much time, probably, unless the store found him indispensible. So far he'd done his best to promote their products, and offer painting advice the customer normally wouldn't get there. "We'll see what the New Year brings." He slapped his hands on his thighs. "I suppose I should wake Aimee and get going. Thank you again for all you've done for me."

She waved her hand. "It's been my pleasure and, before you go." She reached into her purse and pulled out a letter envelope. "I'd like to offer you this gift of my appreciation."

With narrowed eyes, he accepted the envelope. "What's this?"

She patted his leg and stood. "Have a nice holiday, Caleb. I do hope you and Aimee will not be strangers."

What in the world could it be? Clutching the envelope, he walked her to the door.

She donned her jacket and peered up at him, her eyes misty, and embraced his hand between hers. "You've got a precious child back there. Love her, Caleb, but don't clutch her too tight. You must let her breathe. The heart needs oxygen in order to keep pumping."

He opened his mouth, but his mind had gone blank. Wordlessly, he held the door for Adelaide and shut it behind her. Was he suffocating Aimee? No. He loved her free spirit and encouraged it. But what would his in-laws say? That was a discussion for another day. For now, he'd go snuggle against her and steal a brief rest before the madness of the Christmas season.

Christmas. It was going to be bleak this year. Even twinkling lights weren't in his budget. He walked back to Aimee's room. Still sound asleep, her precious lips puckered into a smiling heart. Gently, he sat next to her and glanced at the envelope from Adelaide with Caleb written in precise cursive. Using his finger, he sliced open the envelope and peeked inside.

Dear God, she didn't. His heart pumped faster and his hands shook as he pulled out the contents and read the brief note: *Treat Aimee to something special.*

Special? How about grandiose?

He fanned the bills in his hand. Ten one-hundred-dollar bills.

"Dishes are done."

Lissa put her book down and glanced up at Haven standing in her mom's kitchen doorway. Savory scents of turkey remnants wafted around him. He looked perfectly adorable with the dishtowel draped over his shoulder and a frilly apron tied around his waist. She patted the spot next to her on the loveseat and glanced over at her mom reclining on a chaise near her gas fireplace. Her mom didn't even have the decency to put her book down or lower the volume on the television. How could the woman be so rude?

Lissa had had enough. As soon as Haven was ready to go, they were leaving, and she might bang the door on the way out. That would get her mom's attention.

Haven raised a finger, telling Lissa one minute, then crossed her mom's family room, stopping next to the tufted chaise. "Mrs. Morgan, thank you so much for the delectable meal. Your pumpkin pie was the best I've ever eaten."

Her mom barely peered up from her book and flipped her hand. "Yes, dear, I'm glad you could make it."

Lissa rolled her eyes and mouthed "sorry" to Haven. The least her mom could do was say thank you for cleaning up instead of treating Haven like hired help.

"It's okay," he mouthed back.

No it wasn't. And come tomorrow her mom would get an earful. But not today, not in front of Haven. He probably couldn't wait to flee this place.

"Haven, the weather isn't looking great. We should get going." Before she spewed something she'd regret.

Haven glanced toward the window plastered with heavy snowflakes. "I suppose you're right." He untied the apron and disappeared into the kitchen. Seconds later, he returned to the family room with her winter jacket.

Her knee screamed as she tried to get up. Apparently, she'd done too much standing today. Tonight she'd baby it while watching a simple chick flick. Gritting her teeth against the pain, Lissa took Haven's offered hand and stood. He helped her into her jacket then picked her crutch up off the floor. Next week she'd say goodbye to the crutches for good. The one she still used got in her way more than it helped. Never would she take walking, or even standing, for granted again.

"Ready?" Haven slipped his calf-length peacoat on.

"Let's go." Six hours at her mom's house should qualify Lissa and Haven for sainthood, especially with her mom's incessant gloating about Caleb's wood engravings. And right in front of Haven. Clearly her mom had been abducted by aliens and replaced with a doppelganger.

With the crutch secured beneath her arm, she worked her way across the family room to her mom. Haven walked alongside, ever protective. Her mom finally set down the Charles Martin novel Lissa had loaned to her, peeled the quilted throw off her lap and legs, and stood to give Lissa a hug and kiss.

"Thank you for coming, darling. I had a wonderful afternoon."

Could have fooled me. "I'll see you soon." Christmas would be soon enough.

Her mom sat back on her chaise, covered up with the throw, and picked up her book. "Drive safely now. I'll be here keeping warm." She nodded to the television. "Unlike those fools."

Lissa glanced at the TV and shook her head. Fools was right. Anyone who jumped into freezing waters had to have a nut or two loose.

"But they are raising funds for heart disease awareness." Her mom increased the volume. "What a lovely gesture."

"I suppose." That didn't erase the fact that they were half crazy. "Let's go, Haven."

"Wait." He curved a hand over hers. "That guy, he looks familiar. Where have I seen him before?"

The TV displayed footage of a bathing suit clad man standing outside on a frozen lake. A parka-wearing audience surrounded him. The shirtless man perched on the edge of a rectangular deck that framed in a large hole—about the size of a pickup—cut into the ice. Breath clouds blew from his mouth.

A mouth she knew intimately.

Oh my! She yelped as Caleb cannon-balled into the water, spraying a shower upward. Volunteers dressed in orange climate suits reached out to him with a pole. He ignored it and swam to the end of the hole where he climbed a ladder, and another volunteer wrapped him in a towel.

Victory shined from his grin.

Maybe he wasn't crazy after all. Maybe that would actually be fun.

Gnawing her lip, she peered up at Haven. "Maybe we should try that sometime.”

He tapped her nose and chuckled. “Honey, you’ve got a warped sense of humor.”

Her shoulders drooped, but she forced a smile for him. “It was a silly idea, wasn’t it?”

With Haven anyway, but Caleb? Why did that thought make her heart tap dance?

Caleb stepped into the foyer of his house and shut the garage door. An enticing aroma of Aidan’s salmon crepes baking wafted around him and his mouth watered. He shrugged out of his winter jacket and followed the savory scent up the stairs to his kitchen. No Aidan or Yvette. Aimee’s giggle bounced from down the hallway. Must be in her bedroom. He inhaled and held it. He’d get in his much-needed hug after looking at the dreaded mail.

He picked up an envelope from Hennepin Bank and Trust and laughed at the irony of a broke—and about to be homeless—man having a French chef personally create meals for him. God hadn’t forgotten him, in spite of what this letter might say.

His hands trembled as he slit open the letter dated December 5. Yesterday. He read through it, and pinched his eyes shut. Merry Christmas, Caleb. A sheriff’s sale date had been set. In two short months, this home would be sold to the highest bidder, a bidder who would never appreciate all the memories this home had kept alive for him. Two months to come up with an impossible amount of money. His eyes still closed, he tilted his head toward the ceiling. *God, I’m running out of time.*

But two months was plenty of time for a miracle.

Slapping the notice in his hand, he walked down the hall and peeked into Aimee’s bedroom. Yvette sat in a wooden rocker holding Aimee on her lap while reading *The Very Hungry Caterpillar*. Caleb remained in the doorway and listened to the end of the story where the caterpillar pushed its way out of the cocoon and spread its wings.

Absolutely beautiful.

Like Lissa.

He soundlessly backed away from the door and aimed for his bedroom. It had been weeks since he'd seen Lissa. He prayed she was still spreading her wings, that her boyfriend wasn't clipping them. His cell phone rang as he closed his bedroom door. Tensing, he pulled it from his pocket and glanced at the caller I.D. Judith Nickels? The name was unfamiliar, so it was probably a collection agent. He let it go to voice mail.

After switching out of his work clothes into jeans and a sweatshirt, he listened to the message. "Hello. I hope I have the right number. I'm looking for a Caleb Johnson who worked at Home Mart. I talked with him this past summer and he drew the most fabulous cabinet design for me. I've just now found his business card and am very interested in hiring him on for my kitchen makeover. No one else has come close to creating my dream kitchen. No one but him. If this is Caleb, please call me. I assure you, it will be worth your while."

Caleb plopped down on his bed, and tried to slow his racing heart. Finally, here was the miracle he'd been praying for. He looked toward the ceiling and pumped his fist. "Thank you." He'd call Ms. Nickels back tonight once his excitement calmed down so he'd be able to speak with her on a professional level.

But Yvette would love to share in his excitement. Armed with his phone and the bank letter, he strode back to Aimee's room. Aimee remained on her grandmother's lap, but Aimee held her artist pad, the one she'd filled with her own crayon creations, while reading her own made up story to her grandma.

He cleared his throat and stepped into the room, spreading his arms out. "Hey little miss Louisa May Alcott, why don't you come see your dada?"

"Dada!" A grin blossomed on her face. She tossed her book on the floor, slid from Yvette's lap, and ran toward him.

He knelt and she bowled into him, knocking him backward. With a pretend yelp, he clutched Aimee's waist and fell on his back, lifting his daughter in the air while strangling the bank letter in his hand.

"I fly!" She spread out her arms and paddled her legs.

"You sure do, Doodles." He lowered her and pressed a kiss to her lips. "Now how about you fly to Papi?" Caleb lifted his gaze to Yvette who remained in the rocker. "Is he downstairs?"

Yvette nodded. "He is watching some football game or some other such nonsense."

That's right. Thursday night football. Packers versus the Vikings. Caleb would even enjoy that match up. He lowered Aimee to the ground and she galloped out of her bedroom. "One second." He raised a finger to Yvette then hurried to catch up to Aimee who crawled down the stairs head first. The little stinker had inherited 100% of her parents' adventure genes.

Then he returned to Aimee's room where Yvette sat on the floor cleaning up Aimee's artwork. "Do you have a moment?"

"You wish to talk, *mon cher*?"

"If you don't mind." Caleb plopped down on Aimee's car-shaped toddler bed and waved the bank envelope. "I've got bad news." With a grin, he held up his cell phone. "And good." He told her about the sheriff's sale and the kitchen design offer. "It's the miracle I've been waiting for."

Yvette shook her head though, and scowled.

"What? I thought you'd be thrilled for me."

Her lips pursed, she joined him on the bed and patted his leg. "This is good news, yes. You do for kitchen design what Aidan does with food. It is artistry. This Judith Nickels will be pleased."

But apparently, Yvette wasn't. "So, what's the problem?"

"You plan on keeping your house, yes?"

"It's the miracle I've been praying for. I'll do her kitchen and she'll tell her friends, and I'll get more business—"

"Caleb, dear, do not rush ahead. You do not know that this will generate more business. You do not even know that this will help you out of your hole."

"I have faith that it will." Why wasn't she excited for him? Why did she want to puncture a hole in his faith?

"Perhaps it is best that you do not keep the house."

"What?" He bounded from the bed and glared at his mother-in-law. "How can you say that? How can I throw away all I've got left of

Jeanette?"

"*Mon cher*, you still have Jeanette here"—She patted the left side of her chest—"and downstairs." She gestured to the walls. "This is wood, stone, and paint but you have made it a shrine. You clutch Jeanette so tight to your heart that her memory cannot breathe, and you leave no room for love to enter. By selling this house, you would not be throwing away what you have left of Jeanette, but you would finally be surrendering her to God. Is that not where she belongs? Is that not what you wish to teach Aimee? What would Jeanette wish you to do?"

Caleb turned away from Yvette, squeezed a hand over his mouth and blinked. Is that what he'd been doing? Smothering Jeanette? Cocooning her so the memories couldn't soar?

Yvette was right. This house had become a shrine to Jeanette.

And a morgue for him.

He felt Yvette's hand on his shoulder.

"Do you not think it is time for you to live?"

With a sigh, he clasped Yvette's hand. "Yes, it's time."

Lissa glanced at the digital clock at the corner of her monitor and moaned. How could it be only nine o'clock? She'd been at work for what seemed hours already. Fridays were naturally slow, but today was worse than normal. The bank's announcement about who would take over Haven's job could come anytime. She breathed in, held it, then blew out. Focusing on her work and ignoring distractions would help the time pass quicker. She hoped.

"Got a problem, sweets?" Rita said with the ever-present and annoying crackle of Pop Rocks.

Lissa spun around, tensing her fists. "I hate this waiting. They said we'd know today. Do they really think I can get any work done?"

"So you think you still got a chance, I mean with the paperwork problems and all?"

"I think the board knows me well enough to see past Tyler's shenanigans, don't you?"

Rita shrugged. "Guess we'll find out, won't we? But hey, are you gonna be okay if you don't get the job?"

Lissa forced a smile. "Of course, why wouldn't I be?" She swiveled back toward her desk and read her framed list of goals.

"I hear a 'yeah-but' in there." Rita wheeled her chair next to Lissa's.

"Yeah-but? Excuse me?"

"You know, yeah, you'll be fine, but . . . Come on, sweets, as your best bud, I know you, and there's something you're not telling me."

Lissa rocked back in her chair and drummed her fingers on her desk. Worrying her lower lip, she picked up the framed picture of Haven she'd placed right beside her goals. He looked so handsome with Gooseberry Falls rumbling in the background. What a day that had been. He'd finally kissed her and . . . and then he'd dropped her.

She stretched out her leg, forcing it to go straight, then bent it back. Not perfect yet, but getting there. At least the crutches and brace were now memories, even if physical therapy wasn't.

"Sweets." Rita grabbed Haven's photo. "Please, please don't tell me, Mr. Never Been Kissed will dump you if you don't get the job."

"He has too kissed me!" Lissa snatched back the photo. "As a matter of fact, I think he's getting serious. We're going out tonight and I think he might . . ." Propose? Why did that frighten her? Shouldn't the thought make her heart waltz as it had when he'd kissed her?

"Well, it's about time. You two have been making googly eyes for forever."

"But I can't—"

"But?"

"—say yes if I don't get the promotion."

"Un-tootin-believable. You mean to tell me that you'd turn down his proposal all because he doesn't fit into your sixth grade master plan?"

Would she? Lissa read over the list of goals again: graduate from high school and college, find a job, become a boss, buy a home, get married, have children. It was sensible, the right way to do things.

Her cell phone rang from inside her purse. Lissa retrieved her purse from beneath her desk and dug out her phone. Her heart did a traitorous tango as she stared at the caller I.D. Caleb? She'd call him back later, away from the office and eavesdropping ears. She laid the phone on her desk, but Rita snatched it up. Lissa reached for it, but Rita backed away and answered.

"Hello." Rita waggled her eyebrows. "Nope, this is the right number. Lissa's right here, she was busy for a sec." With a smirk she handed the phone to Lissa. "It's for you."

"Gee, thanks." Lissa grabbed the phone and hobbled out of their cubicle. Rita didn't need to hear this conversation. "Hi Caleb, how's it going?"

"Good. Awesome even. That's why I'm calling. I was wondering if I could take you to lunch today, so I can—"

"Not a good idea, Caleb." She limped into the empty break room and plopped down on a chair. "It's time you move on." So she could move on and finally get over him.

"Actually, that's what I'm doing. I want to say thank you, but I'd rather do it in person. My treat."

So the guy still didn't understand the wise use of money. "The best way to say thanks is to put that money toward one of your bills."

She heard him blow out a breath. "Lissa, that's no longer a problem," he said so softly she barely heard him. "Please. Just this once. No strings attached."

"Today?"

"If that works for you."

Well, maybe it wasn't a bad idea to get away from the office for an hour. Maybe two. She certainly wasn't getting any work done. "Okay. Where and when?"

"How about Dave and Buster's."

Figured, he wanted to go to the adult-sized Chuck E. Cheese. "Sure. Why not?"

"Noon okay?"

"Can we make it eleven thirty? And I'll meet you there."

"Eleven thirty it is. See you later."

"Yeah." Lissa closed her phone and put a hand over her heart, trying to slow its dance as she walked back to her cube. Thankfully, Rita was occupied on her phone. Now, if Lissa could bring up the information on her next client and get on the phone before Rita was off, she'd avoid more conversation. She logged on to her computer and studied her client's profile. Two months late. Before that, he had always paid on time and had impeccable credit. He'd obviously run into some hardship. Determined to help, she picked her headset off her desk.

"Hey, that was the dangerous one, wasn't it?"

Clutching the headset, she turned at the waist. "Don't you think we should get some work done before Tyler comes by and finds more reason to complain?"

"Sweets, you are so clueless." Rita pointed at Lissa's cell phone lying on her desktop. "I know why you can't say yes to Mr. Never-Been-Kissed. You've got the hots for Mr. Skydiver, don't you?"

"Get back to work, Rita." Lissa raised the headset. "And mind the bank's business, not mine."

"Yeah. You're right. Gotta do things the right way, don't you? Well, who says living out a sixth grade fantasy is the right way, huh? Maybe it's time you grew up and realized life doesn't come in a tidy package."

"Rita . . ."

"Aw, forget it. Go ahead, live your boring life. See what I care."

Rita's wheels screeched as she scooted her chair back across the cubicle.

Sixth grade fantasy? Lissa secured the headset and punched in her customer's phone number. That sixth grade wisdom had gotten her this far, hadn't it? At least, she wasn't stuck in some home she couldn't afford. And, unlike her father, her heart wouldn't give out from abuse. If that was boring, so be it. She wouldn't change a thing.

She stole a glance at Haven's picture. The perfect catch. So, why did thinking of a future with him make her stomach queasy?

Lissa tugged on the door to Dave & Buster's. Go in, eat, and leave. Most importantly, don't let Caleb get to her.

Ear-pounding rock and roll greeted her as she stepped into the entry. Not exactly the best place for a conversation. What was Caleb thinking?

Squinting, she glanced around the restaurant lit with muted bar lights. To her left sat '50s style tables and chairs. Pool tables and an array of flashing video games hemmed in the seating. The bar area, with over a dozen flat screen televisions suspended from the ceiling, was directly in front of her. This wasn't a place Haven would consider going.

"Lissa." Caleb's voice came from her right. He jogged toward her and gave a short wave. Did he have to look so gorgeous? "I got a table for us back over here where it's a bit quieter."

So, he had considered the noise. She should know better than to jump to conclusions where Caleb was concerned. Without speaking, she followed him past square wooden tables and chairs to a corner that gave them a view of the snowy landscape outside.

He drew out her chair, helped her out of her coat, and hung it on the back of the chair. She sat and he gently pushed her in. Did he have to be such a gentleman? He rounded the table and sat with his back to the window.

"Thanks for coming." He pulled two silverware-filled cloth napkins from a tin beer bucket centered on the table and handed one to her.

"I guess I'm curious as to your situation change." It was vital to keep the discussion detached, professional, like she'd treat a client. She removed the silverware and spread the napkin over her lap.

He grinned and her heart danced a salsa. Why didn't Haven's grin have the same effect? She'd have to avoid looking at Caleb, that was all. She stared across the room, beyond the bar, into the game room area. The blinking lights should hold her focus.

"I took your advice."

Her gaze shot back to Caleb.

"Can I get you something to drink?"

Lissa startled and looked up at the waitress. "Uh, yeah, a lemon water please."

"I'll take a Coke."

She watched the waitress walk toward the bar, then she turned her attention back to Caleb. "What advice?"

"You know, about the house." His grin slid into a smile, but his half-opened eyes gave away his true feelings. "I decided that the house was expendable and put it on the market."

"Caleb, I'm so sorry."

He shrugged. "Hey, it was the right thing to do. And God apparently agreed because I had an offer within a week."

Her eyes closed, hemming in tears. Sure, it was the right decision financially, but that didn't take away the sting of what he'd done.

And she was to blame. She reached across the table and covered his hand with hers. "Are you doing okay?"

Another shrug. "It's only a building."

Literally etched with memories he couldn't take with him. "How long do you have?"

"I close on New Year's Eve." He turned his hand over and clasped hers. "Perfect, huh? I'll start the New Year with a clean slate."

"So soon? Where are you going to live?" Her mom's cottage! And the way her mom boasted about Caleb, she'd probably let him stay rent free. Perfect. "I have a suggestion."

"Actually, that's taken care of too."

"Oh?"

"I have the best in-laws. I think they knew all along that I'd sell. Aidan had me finish his basement . . . for me and Aimee. Built-in babysitters and a gourmet chef. Can't get much better than that. I'm mostly moved in already. I figured, why wait. I'm ready for a fresh start."

"I'm proud of you, Caleb."

"Thanks. That means a lot, especially coming from you. And, that's not my only news."

His true smile returned. Maybe he'd found someone else. Maybe that was what convinced him to make the changes. Her stomach soured at the idea.

"But I better decide what I want first." He picked up the menu.

And leave her hanging? Men. She paged through the menu. Not exactly heart-healthy meals. Have to settle for a salad.

The server returned with their beverages. "Are you ready to order?"

"Lissa?"

"Yeah. I'll have the grilled chicken salad."

"Salad? Really? You should try their peppercorn steak. It's unreal."

"Salad." She nodded to the waitress.

"If that's what you want. I'll take the peppercorn sirloin. You can try mine. See what you're missing. And for dessert we'll have—"

"No dessert."

"—the Belgian chocolate fondue."

She rolled her eyes but smiled. The man was hopeless.

The waitress walked away.

What had they been talking about? Oh, right, he had good news. "So, what's your news?" Please, let it not be another woman.

A glint shone from his eyes. "I've been contracted for a kitchen remodel. I get to custom build some cabinets."

Whew.

Whoa. She was relieved? How could her heart betray Haven like that? She swallowed. "I'm happy for you. Sounds like things are finally turning around."

"They are, and I have you to thank."

Right. She twirled the straw in her water, watching the vortex swirl deeper. All she had done was convince him to sell the last tangible memories of his life with his wife. How heartless could she get?

"I mean it, Lissa." He touched her arm. "Look at me, okay?"

Keeping her chin tucked, she peered through her lashes at Caleb. "What have I done for you other than lead you on, and take away your home?"

"That's not what you did."

"I—"

"Lissa, listen." He took her hand and leaned toward her. "Once upon a time I was an adrenaline-junky, a big risk-taker. When we had Aimee, she was our next adventure and we wanted to live for her and that meant parking the motorcycles and no skydiving for a while. That was fine. Then Jeanette died, and making it through each day was adventure enough for me. I was content to live in the past."

Lissa squeezed his hand. "That's not what I've seen."

"Exactly. I've had the most fun watching you try new things, seeing this amazing joy on your face, and you convinced me—you convinced my heart that it's time to soar again. You helped me realize that love isn't bound by four walls. By holding on to the house, I was strangling my heart. By letting go, I'm able to breathe again. You, Lissa, you taught me that it's okay to love again."

Love? She tugged her hand from his and stood. "If you'll excuse me, I need to go to the restroom." Without waiting for a response, she limped away from the table and searched for the bathroom. How dare he come here being so nice and looking so sexy and . . . and making the right financial decisions? She backhanded a tear and shoved open the restroom door. If she killed enough time in here, they could avoid filling the space with more conversation. They'd eat, then say goodbye. It had to be for good.

Several minutes later, she returned to the table, now filled with food. Good. That part of her plan went well anyway. Her salad tasted okay, but couldn't compare to his steak. Three little bites wouldn't hurt her. And the fondue? She dipped a strawberry into the dark chocolate sauce and took a bite. Her eyes rolled back and she sighed. It had to be a touch of heaven, and Caleb was thoughtful enough to save the fruit for her while he ate the cheese and crackers.

"What do you say to a few games?" Caleb skewered a marshmallow and dipped it.

She savored one last banana slice and glanced at her watch. Only twelve forty-five, and she said she'd be out till one thirty. With a fifteen-minute drive, that gave her thirty minutes to spare. What would it hurt to play a few games? Then she could say goodbye and wish him a good life and she could go on with hers. "Sure, why not?"

They left their jackets at the table and she led him to the game area filled with rows of video and virtual games, pool tables, skee-ball, and air hockey. Even Pac Man. She'd never played any of the games.

"What do you want to play?"

She shrugged and walked past a crane game where the winner would receive a stuffed animal. No. The worst thing she should do was to take home a cuddly teddy bear won by Caleb. "Hey, how about that?" She pointed at the two-person Dance Dance Revolution. Now, that would be a heart-healthy activity. If her knee held out.

"Perfect." He swiped a card in the machine and they each stood in the center square of separate nine-square pads. He selected a song.

"Ready?"

"No."

He chuckled. Music thumped and the screen lit up with arrows indicating where and when to step. She stepped onto the left middle square and her knee yelped. Well, that wasn't going to stop her. With her right leg, she stepped twice on the square behind her and once on the square to the right. Yes! She hit it perfect.

She kept going, usually hitting the squares late, judging by Caleb's steps. The music ended, and, breathing hard, Lissa stepped off the pad. She leaned over and rested her hands on her knees. "That's the best work out I've had since surgery." And now she had to go back to work all sweaty. Real smart, Lissa.

Caleb took her hand and led her to a ride simulator: piloting a commercial aircraft. "I always wanted to learn to fly. This is as close as I've gotten. Why don't you give it a try?"

"No, you go ahead. I'll watch."

"You'll love it. Seriously."

She studied the screen in front of the ride. It looked harmless enough. When would she ever do this again? Certainly never with Haven. This was her one-time shot. "Oh, why not?"

"Atta girl."

She sat down at the controls, grabbed the wheel, and Caleb swiped his card, starting the ride. The runway sped past and she tugged on the wheel, bringing the virtual nose up on the screen. Seconds later she was airborne. Clouds puffed past and then she was above them. She could almost feel the air blowing her hair. All too soon, the runway appeared below and she pushed on the wheel, lowering the nose. The plane bumped and skidded on landing. Didn't matter. She'd flown. All by herself.

She climbed off and threw her arms around Caleb's broad shoulders. His beard tickled her forehead. Oh, big mistake. She jerked away her arms and looked down at her foot drawing imaginary circles on the floor. "Sorry."

He tipped up her chin. "Don't ever be sorry about that."

"You know, I think I better get back to work." Away from temptation.

"Just one more."

"Caleb."

"Please?"

"You sound like a little child, you know that?"

Grinning, Caleb took her hand and led her to a virtual motorcycle ride. "I don't have my bike anymore, so this is second best. What do you think?"

"Be my guest."

He straddled the seat. "Climb on behind me, like you would a real bike."

And be that close to him? Was he nuts?

"Come on." He tugged on her arm. "Then you can leave. I promise."

"One time." Even that would be too much. She sat behind him, trying to keep space between them, but she kept sliding off the back of the seat. She inched forward, melding her body with his, and grabbed the seat.

"You've never been on a bike before, have you?"

She shook her head, her chin scraping the back of his sweatshirt that smelled like the winter breeze.

"Hold on to me."

"I'm fine."

"If you don't want to fall off and have another surgery, hold on."

Did he know what he was doing to her? She released the seat and cuffed her hands on his waist.

He chuckled and grabbed her hands, pulling her arms forward, wrapping them around toned abs.

Her breath quickened as he started the ride. She peeked over his shoulder at the screen. Obstacles flew by on the virtual road as Caleb squeezed the throttle.

"Lean with me," he shouted above the engine's roar.

She closed her eyes and clutched him tight as the bike angled sideways, straightened, leaned the other direction, and continued back and forth. It was amazing how their bodies remained in sync as if they'd been riding together for years. What a thrill this would be on an actual bike, with the breeze cruising past while she soaked up the warmth and security from his body. Maybe sometime in the future they could . . .

Lissa! She loosened her grip and rested her head against his shoulder. An eon—or seconds—later, the motor quieted, and the cycle righted itself. She sprang from the bike and grimaced as she landed on her bad leg.

He caught her waist and helped her stand. His eyes lasered into hers. "You okay?"

"Yeah." Her knee was fine, anyway. She tried to look away, but his eyes had some magnetic pull. It was her heart, tap dancing at record speed, that concerned her as he pulled her in closer so she could feel his heart beating against her.

His lips parted slightly and hers followed, disobeying orders from her brain. His lips brushed hers, leaving behind a hint of chocolate, making her crave more. He pulled his arms away and backed up.

"I'm sorry, Lissa." He rubbed the back of his neck and focused on the floor. "You're right, it's time to go. I'll go get your coat."

As if she needed it right now. The ten-degrees-below temperature might be precisely what she needed to expunge Caleb from her thoughts and hopefully freeze him from her heart.

"Morgan, you're late."

Tyler. The jerk. "Sorry." Not really. Not with the decision already made about whom the bank was hiring. Now it was just a matter of waiting for the bank to tell her who they chose. It better not be Tyler. She wasn't a quitter, but she couldn't imagine working for him.

She dropped her purse beneath her desk, crossed her arms, and turned to face him. She didn't have to kiss up to him any longer. "What do you want, Abernathy?"

He smirked. "The bank pres wants to see you. I had to explain that you were late. Keep up the good work, Morgan. I appreciate you making my promotion so easy."

Lissa clenched her jaw and her fists. Good thing she was at work. And even if she were home, she'd thrown out her last pack of cigarettes back when Haven caught her, and had resisted temptation ever since. Tyler would not be her downfall now. She raised her chin and brushed past Tyler. *Please, God, let it be good news.*

She hobbled down the hallway, past the break room, and stopped at the president's door. Even with Tyler undermining her, she stood a good chance at this promotion. She'd known the bank president her whole life and he knew she wasn't a cheat.

She stopped at his door, inhaled a deep breath and blew it out, then knocked.

"Come in."

Lissa opened the door and forced a smile. "Good afternoon, Mr. Malachek."

He closed his laptop and folded his hands over it. "Lissa. Please, have a seat." No hint of a smile or affirmation.

Her hands shaking, she sat across from him. Words were as frozen in her thoughts as the lakes outside.

"Now, you know how much respect I had for your father. And for you."

Not a promising start. She nodded. If she spoke, he'd hear her tremble.

"And I'm continually impressed with your work in collections. No one has the track record you do for bringing accounts current, and I want to assure you, that hasn't gone unnoticed."

Yeah, but . . .

"But—"

Lissa squeezed her hands together.

"—we believe at present, Tyler is a better fit for the supervisory position."

I knew it. She blinked and coerced a smile while hiding shaking hands in her lap. "I understand." *Liar!* The whole office knew she was better qualified, with the exception of time spent on the job. His extra years in collections hadn't groomed him for a supervisory position.

"I knew you would." Mr. Malachek winked. "You keep up the good work. We're proud to have you here at Hennepin Bank and Trust."

"Thank you. I'm glad to be here." *Liar!* In a daze, she walked from his office to the restroom. The door closed behind her and she sniffled.

It was okay. This was just a minor setback. After all, six months ago a promotion wasn't even a thought. She wiped her eyes and studied her reflection in the mirror. Her makeup looked good. No touch up was needed.

She drew in a breath and heaved it out before donning her professional demeanor to show Tyler Abernathy the proper way to face defeat. Squaring her shoulders and lifting her chin, she strode from the restroom, down the hall, to Haven's former office. Now Tyler's permanent office. She knocked on the glass door.

He looked away from his computer. A smirk grew on his face as he leaned back in his chair and crossed his arms over his chest. Guess that meant enter.

She opened the door, stepped in, and closed the door behind her. "I want to be the first to congratulate you on your new position. I'm sure you'll do a fine job." Okay, so that was a little lie, but at least she'd taken the high road.

Tyler secured his hands behind his head and crossed his feet on top of his desk. "Sucking up won't help you, Morgan. I could fire you right now, but the years you've spent being a lapdog for the bank board play in your favor. Yet. But you can be assured that as soon as possible, you'll be kissing your job goodbye."

How dare he! She strode forward and slapped his feet off his desk. Caleb would be proud of her. Tyler's eyes grew wide, but his perpetual sneer returned. "Sounds like you've declared war, Abernathy, and you can be assured, I plan to win."

How, she didn't know, but it was time Tyler got the medicine he deserved. Quitting wasn't an option. She refused to give him that satisfaction.

"No way am I quitting." With Haven's hand warming hers, they rode down the escalator in Macy's in downtown Minneapolis. Spending the evening with him going through the Santaland display was the perfect antidote to Tyler's gloating. Tyler would not ruin her evening too.

"That's my girl." Haven squeezed her hand as they left the warmth of the building. He nodded to the building across the street. "There's a Caribou over there. Care for a coffee before heading on?"

"Not a bad idea." Considering that in a few minutes they'd be walking several blocks outside in single-digit temperatures to the Holidazzle Village. Only in Minnesota would people find that an enjoyable experience.

Caleb would love it.

She shook her head. How could she think of Caleb when she was holding hands with Haven? Clutching his hand tighter, they crossed the street and found the coffee shop filled with holiday shoppers. Businesses like this had to love freezing weather.

"What would you like?" Haven removed his pea coat and slung it over his arm. "I'll bring it to you."

Pursing her lips, she studied the fat-laden menu. Everything screamed heart attack. "Guess I'll have a chai tea latte with skim milk, no whipped cream."

"Living dangerous, huh?"

"As dangerous as I get." She hobbled to an open table, removed her jacket, and plopped down. Minutes later, Haven returned with their steaming drinks, his a dark chocolate cocoa topped with whipped cream and mini chocolate chips.

She sipped her latte and relaxed in the chair. The stress from the day's events oozed away, if only for a moment. "This is a wonderful idea."

"The coffee?"

"Well, that too, but I was talking about Holidazzle. I've never been."

"Me neither, though I used to watch the parade every year." He looked at his watch. "By the way, did I mention I hired a limo to take us there?"

She blinked. "A limo?" Why wasn't she thrilled? Was she insane? "Isn't freezing part of the experience?"

"I'm sure it is. Just not an experience I need."

"I see," she mumbled and stared down at her drink. Caleb would never take a limo to avoid the cold. A horse-drawn carriage maybe.

Now that would have been romantic. And a limo wasn't? Sheesh, she was still a snob. "A limo ride sounds lovely. Thank you."

"He's picking us up in thirty minutes." Haven stirred his cocoa. "I wanted to treat you to something special after what the bank did. I still can't believe they chose Tyler over you. They must be blind."

"When he took my files, that sort of nailed my coffin shut."

"Are you certain it was Tyler? I know he can be a jerk, but a cheat? I never saw that in him."

"You haven't been around him for these past six months either. With the job at stake, he did everything imaginable to discredit me. Obviously, it worked." And without that promotion, what would she say if Haven wanted to take their relationship to another level? Was Rita right? Was she afraid to grow up?

Haven spooned a dollop of whipped cream off his drink. A drop remained on the side of his mouth.

What would he say if she kissed it off? Would that be too dangerous an experience as well? Probably. Public displays of affection weren't his style.

She took another sip of her drink and glanced around the crowded room. Off in the corner, a couple shared a lingering kiss. She counted to five before they broke it off. Five whole seconds. In public. She wasn't anti-PDA, but five seconds? With a roll of her eyes, she started to turn away, but then glimpsed their faces and her back stiffened. No. It couldn't be. She filtered out the voices in the room and honed in on the couple. The woman giggled and threw something into the man's mouth.

Lissa's heart rate doubled as the truth smacked her.

Now the disappearing files made sense. And the sticky residue on Caleb's file. How could she have been so blind? "Haven, I see some people we know." Her voice low, attempting to hide her anger, she pointed at the couple, entwined once again. "I'd like to go say hi."

Haven glanced over and recognition fired in his eyes. "You've got to be kidding." Madder than she'd ever seen him, he shoved away from the table making tea and cocoa leap from their cups. Didn't matter, her appetite was ruined.

Tyler being involved with the missing files wasn't a surprise, but her best friend? No, make that her former best friend. Tyler's apparent cohort in crime.

How could Rita do this to her?

Lissa swore steam blew from Haven's ears as he strode to Rita and Tyler's table. She followed right behind. He stopped at their table and cleared his throat. "Excuse me."

Simultaneously, Rita and Tyler glanced up. Both were struck mute.

"Mind if we join you?" Haven pulled out a chair for Lissa then grabbed one from another table and straddled the back. "Imagine finding you two here. Together. Boss and co-worker. I thought the bank frowned upon fraternization."

"Liss, I didn't want you to know." Rita reached for Lissa's hand, but Lissa crossed her arms over her chest. How dare Rita ruin Lissa's career over . . . over Tyler of all people.

Tyler's gaze darted everywhere but toward Haven and Lissa. "I can explain."

"You better bet you will. On Monday. To the bank board. Both the affair and the files. And if you don't . . ." Haven leaned toward Tyler and lowered his voice. "You can believe I will."

"Now come on. You're going to complain about me and Rita when you and Miss Perfect here were having your own little fling?" A cocky grin grew on Tyler's face. He lifted his coffee off the table and nodded it toward Haven. "The board already knows about that."

"Haven and I didn't date until after he left. I'll have no problem convincing Mr. Malachek of the truth, especially when they hear about the files."

"The files." Tyler stirred his coffee and chuckled. "You know, I don't think you'll be saying too much." He relaxed in his seat and winked at Rita. "Don't worry. Your job is safe."

Rita's brows knitted. "How can you be sure? Tyler, I can't lose my job."

"So you wreck mine instead?" Lissa cuffed her hands on her hips. "I thought we were friends."

"Well, it's not like you need the job, sweets. You can always crawl to Mommy."

"That's enough." Haven stood and grasped Lissa's hand. "We're going to go enjoy our evening and celebrate Lissa's upcoming promotion."

Lissa's hand never felt so secure in Haven's, and her heart did a little jig—not a waltz this time—as they walked away. He'd truly protected her.

"Reece." Tyler's voice sneered behind them.

Haven froze and his hand went limp. Slow as ice melts in December, Haven turned back toward Tyler and Rita. "What did you say?" Gravel grated in his voice.

Tyler raised his cup. "You know, I don't think you will say anything or I might have to expose your little secret."

His secret? "Haven, what's he—?"

"Not now, Lissa," Haven growled. Shoulders stooped, he shuffled toward Tyler. "How do you know?"

"I have my ways, and unless you want the world to know about Reece, I'm guessing my job's secure."

Haven remained mannequin-still, resting his forehead on his fist. "You win," he whispered and took Lissa's arm. He gathered their jackets and pulled her out of the coffee shop into the frigid air.

"I don't understand." Lissa shook off his hand once they cleared the doors. While waiting for a reply, she put on her jacket and gloves. "What aren't you telling me? Who's Reece?"

"Not here, Lissa." He hurried down the block and around the corner away from the holiday crowd.

She followed and found him leaning against a building, his hands covering his face. She strode over to him and pulled his hands down. "Who is Reece?"

"I was going to tell you, later tonight." His shoulders hunched forward. Never had she seen him look so defeated, but she was tired of men keeping secrets.

"Who. Is. Reece?"

With a sigh that breathed a frozen cloud, Haven retrieved his billfold from his back pocket. He flipped it open, pulled out a crinkled wallet photo, and handed it to Lissa. "This is Reece. My son."

Chapter Twenty-Four

Haven's son? "But I thought . . ." Lissa blinked back tears and turned away from Haven. And here she'd been foolish enough to believe his *lips* were virgin. Ha! Who was this man?

"I've been wanting to tell you."

She fingered her eyes and spun around. "Why haven't you? It's not like you haven't had the time."

"I know." He tucked his hands beneath his armpits. "But how do you tell the woman you're in love with, you used to be a scoundrel?"

Did he just say love? After he throws this secret in her face? "And you're not a fraud now?"

"Perhaps I am, but I wanted to protect you. Your dad always said I should be honest about who I am, that my ugly past made me the man I am today."

Lissa clenched her fists. Her dad knew about Haven but still pushed her toward him? She should have known her dad was wrong about Haven too. "Well, I don't know if I like the man you are now."

"Let me tell you the whole story. It'll make it worse, but I guess that's a risk I have to take, one I should have taken when we first started dating."

Worse than him hiding a son? Did she even want to know? Maybe not, but she needed to hear him out. Wasn't that the Christian thing to do? "Let's go inside first." With Haven trailing behind, she hurried to the main street as fast as her gimpy leg allowed her, and then limped a block and a half to a pub that would provide the anonymity they both needed.

Shortly after being shown to their seats, the server came by and told them about drink specials. Lissa asked for a lemon water, but Haven hesitated as his eyes followed another server carrying a tray of alcoholic drinks.

"I'll have, uh." His gaze jerked back to her as he rubbed a hand over a perspiring face. Perspiring in the middle of December? He cleared his throat, but he words still eked out. "I'll have a Coke."

The server walked away as Lissa mentally cuffed herself. Of all the places in Minneapolis, she had to choose one that would tempt Haven, especially when he was already under duress. She gathered her purse and jacket. "I'm sorry, we can go somewhere else."

"I'm fine." He shook his head. "I won't deny a drink sounds very appealing, but today I'm not giving in."

Did that mean tomorrow he would? And if he did, would it be her fault?

"Lissa, I know what's going on your head, and no you're not driving me to drink. I've made it six years without giving in, and I've had hundreds of tough days. I don't plan on blowing that streak now. Telling you about Reece might just make this day easier."

Oh how she wished she could reach over and take his hand, to tell him everything would be okay. Maybe later she could, but now that wasn't a possibility.

The server delivered their drinks and asked if she could bring them anything else.

"This is all." Haven spoke to his glass, swirling it as the server walked away. "I used to live with someone."

Her body tensed. Live with? "A woman?"

He nodded.

"And you thought I didn't need to know that little tidbit?" He was right, his story did get worse. She took a long swallow of her water.

"I told you something happened that gave me a wake-up call when I was drinking."

Her throat constricted. All she could do was nod for him to continue.

"I was twenty-four. Things were going great—or so I thought. I had a great girlfriend, a beautiful two-year-old son, a new home. I'd just gotten my first promotion at the bank I worked at in Duluth. I wanted to celebrate my promotion with Amanda, but she'd already made plans with her sister and needed me to stay with Reece. Being the selfish cad I was back then, I wasn't happy with her, so when a drinking buddy invited me out, I couldn't tell him no."

He sniffled and dragged an arm over his face. "I got the neighbor girl to babysit, and she took Reece down to the lake. He loved climbing the rocks, and there was this freak accident. One of the massive boulders shifted, trapping his foot."

"No." Lissa slapped a hand over her mouth, imagining where this was heading, and she didn't like the ending. "What happened?"

"His foot was crushed, mutilated." He sniffled. "They had to amputate my little boy's foot. All because I chose drinking over spending an evening him."

A tear trailed down his cheek, and she reached over to take his hand. She couldn't begin to imagine how he must feel.

Blinking, Haven stared at the ceiling. "I'd passed out at my buddy's place so I didn't even know about it until the next morning, after the surgery."

Lissa wiped away her own tears. "How is he doing now?"

Haven's eyes closed and he heaved several breaths before whispering, "I don't know."

"You don't know?" How could a man injure his son then abandon him? She shook off his hand and reclined against the hard back of the booth. How could she have been so fooled by this man?

Haven stared at his untouched beverage. "The community viewed it as a tragic accident, but I knew the truth. I was a drunk who chose booze over my son. I didn't deserve to be a dad, and my son deserved someone who could keep him safe. Amanda kicked me out and told me never to come near them again. If I did, she'd sic her attorney dad on me. I didn't know then that I had a choice, not until I met your father. Back then, I thought leaving was the best thing for all of us, but now . . ."

A sob leapt from his throat. "I haven't seen Reece in nearly six years and it's killing me."

Lissa's shoulders felt as if they carried sacks of lead. Knowing

Haven's tender heart, the pain he must feel on a daily basis had to be excruciating. His son was alive, but Haven had lost him anyway.

Perhaps the easiest way to endure losing Reece had been to avoid talking of him, by storing his memory in a forbidden compartment in the brain. She could forgive Haven for that, couldn't she?

What was ironic was that Lissa couldn't think of anyone better suited to be a father than Haven. Yes, he'd lost a son, but that son lost the opportunity to know a good man. She wasn't ready to forgive him for keeping this secret, but she could understand it. What Haven needed more than anything now was a confidant. Apparently, he'd had one in her father, and with her father's passing, they'd both lost someone they loved.

She reached for his hand again. "I'm here for you."

He laughed. "Do you think that's wise? I failed to protect him. And I failed Amanda. Now I've hurt you too. Again. What kind of man am I that I can't protect the people I love?"

"You're a man who cares deeply." She squeezed his hand and physical pain flashed through her chest. Was it possible for the heart to physically feel her emotional hurt? "And I think your son deserves to know you. I think he'd be proud of the man you've become."

"You mean that?"

"Absolutely." But it didn't mean she was ready to forgive Haven for hiding the truth, just as Caleb had done. She rubbed where the pain has slashed through. Maybe she'd be better off if she crossed "Get married" off her Goals list. Her heart would be much happier and healthier without men.

Lissa stepped up to her front door, unlocked it, and stuffed her gloved hands into her coat pockets. Her heart hurt from this miserable day, from her reckless attraction to Caleb, to losing the promotion, to discovering her best friend—former best friend—was behind that loss. And now, discovering Haven's secret . . . It was too much for her heart to take, and the physical ache affirmed that.

Keeping her hands in her pockets, she turned to face Haven. No longer the perfect man, and no longer her safe haven, but a broken man. And the stoop in his once-proud shoulders underscored his brokenness. He needed her forgiveness. That would come. But not tonight. Tonight she needed to escape from the world and sleep. If that were possible.

"Thanks for bringing me home." Neither attempted a hug, much less a goodnight kiss.

He looked down and kicked at her concrete step. "Will you let me call you again?"

A winter breeze nipped at her cheeks and she hugged herself. "Give me a few days, okay?"

"I can do that." He glanced up and caressed her jaw line. "I am sorry."

She covered his hand with hers. "I know." She turned from him, entered her home, and leaned against the closed door. Silence greeted her. She massaged the center of her chest. Even the answering machine light held steady, unblinking. She couldn't call Rita and vent anymore. Sure, she could always call her mom, but she would lecture rather than listen. Besides, her mom was visiting friends in Fargo. She didn't need to be burdened with Lissa's problems.

Good thing she'd thrown out her remaining cigarettes three months ago when Haven had caught her, or today's events would provide all the excuse she needed to say "just one more." Not even she would brave the slick roads for a smoke. Besides, her back step would be too cold to sit on tonight, the air too biting. Winter always made it easier to stare down temptation.

It was time to go to bed and end this miserable day. Tomorrow she could sleep in. Maybe a night's rest would give her a fresh perspective. She tugged off her boots, hung her jacket in the entry closet, and limped to her bedroom. Even her leg hurt more tonight. She pulled open her top dresser drawer and dug out her flannel footie pajamas from the back. A single, unattached person could wear flannel footies.

She undressed then slipped one foot into a pajama leg, followed by the other. Something wedged beneath her right foot. She pulled her foot out and dug into the footie.

Uh-oh. Her heart beat a bit faster as she pulled out the cigarette. She caressed it between her fingers and her mouth ached to taste the menthol flavoring. But that meant going outside, shoveling off her back step, and sitting in the below zero air. Not even she would do that.

She aimed for her wastebasket, but held back. Did she have to go outside? Maybe if she opened her window a crack and blew out. No one ever came into her bedroom anyway. One wouldn't hurt. It would get her through the worst evening in her life. Well, not quite the worst. The day her dad died had been worse, but this was definitely in second place. If anyone had an excuse to smoke, it was her.

Now, to find a lighter. She hobbled to the kitchen, took a book of matches from her junk drawer and a soup can from her recycle bin, then returned to her bedroom. She sat on the edge of her bed, facing the open window, and rotated the stress from her shoulders. There was still time to say "no."

With the cigarette hugged between fingers, she wiped sweat from her brow. Perspiring with the window open in the dead of winter? One deep inhale should take care of that. She struck a match and held it to the end of the cigarette. Red embers sparkled. Peace enveloped Lissa as she brought the stick to her lips and inhaled, drawing the nicotine clouds down into her sated lungs. For a second she held it, then she leaned close to the window and blew wispy tendrils through her nose.

A sharp pain knifed through her chest and she jerked upright. The smoke stuck in her throat and she coughed to eject it. Her coughing ceased and she caressed the sting in her chest. Was this more than a broken heart?

It couldn't be. She ate healthy and exercised and did everything right. She brought the cigarette to her lips again and stopped before inhaling.

She stared down at the cigarette. No, she didn't do everything right. She wrenched the stick from her mouth and limped to the bathroom, her breath labored. It couldn't be her heart. She was too young. The smoke had to be causing her pain. She hurled the cigarette into the toilet and flushed it. Never again. Maybe this would finally be what cured her.

Certainly, she'd feel better after a good night's sleep. With invisible hands squeezing her chest, she lay down and covered up. The pain skyrocketed. Coughing, struggling for breath, she sat up with the pain escalating.

Tears leaked from her eyes as she reached for her bedside phone and dialed 911.

The operator answered after one ring. "911, what's your emergency?"

Lissa coughed and kneaded her chest as the words strained from her lips. "I think . . . I'm having . . . a heart attack."

Chapter Twenty-Five

Walking the sterile hospital hallway, Caleb clutched a box of dark-chocolate truffles in one hand and a vase filled with yellow freesia in the other. Simple gifts that didn't hold hidden meanings. The chocolate was Aiden's gift—Lissa never turned down Aiden's cooking—and the flower simply meant friendship. He prayed she was sleeping; that way he could sneak in and out without further heartbreak.

He spotted room 231. The door was open. Holding his breath, he stepped inside and stopped. Straight ahead sat Caleb's competition—rather, the winner of the fight for Lissa's heart. The man's elbows were perched on his knees and his forehead rested on fists. His hair was tousled as if it hadn't seen a comb for days. Ugly jealousy burned in Caleb's gut. Though he hated hospitals, he still wished he were the one sitting there praying over loved ones. But he'd forfeited that right.

He backed out of the room and turned toward the hallway. Someone at the nurses' station could deliver his gifts. Lissa would know he still cared anyway.

"It's Caleb, right?" The victor's voice sounded behind him.

Gritting his teeth, Caleb looked back into the room.

"Haven Carlysle." The rival extended his hand, then his gaze flitted to the gifts Caleb carried and he pulled his hand back.

"Caleb Johnson." He raised the gifts. "I'll drop these off." He glanced at Lissa sleeping as he squeezed his gifts onto a bedside table already loaded down with flowers and cards. A monitor beeped out a steady heart rhythm, and an IV delivered medicine to her arm.

Otherwise she looked normal, peaceful even.

"I'm sure she'd like you to stay."

That wasn't happening. Caleb nodded toward her. "How is she doing?"

"Good. Grateful that it wasn't a heart attack. She'll be going home today."

Thank you God. "That's great news." Losing Lissa to heart disease would have been more than he could take. During a phone conversation with Lissa's mom earlier in the day, he'd learned the diagnosis was pericarditis—an inflamed membrane around the heart. Anti-inflammatory medicine would ease the swelling and the heart-attack-like pain.

He stuffed his hands in his front jeans pockets. "Tell her I said hi. I wish you both the best." Well, Lissa anyway.

He aimed for the door.

"It was my fault."

Caleb stopped in the doorway. The smart thing would be to keep going. God would forgive him. After all, he wasn't a counselor or a friend. Enemy was too strong, but fit better and felt true. But his conscience forced him to turn back.

"I broke her heart." Haven moved from the chair to the window and shook his head. "Her father asked me to protect her. I failed. Like I failed my son."

His son?

Haven turned around and pinned Caleb with his gaze. "Yeah, Lissa didn't know either." He nodded to the bed. "I drove her to smoke and—"

"Smoke?" Caleb blinked. No, that couldn't be right. Not Lissa.

"I don't know if she'll ever forgive me."

"You're right, Haven." Lissa's weak voice broke into their conversation like a cannon shot. "As a matter of fact, I want you both to leave."

"Lissa, please—"

"Now, Haven."

"Fine. Leaving." His shoulders drooped as he trudged from the room.

"Lissa, he's—"

"What part of *now* don't you understand, Caleb?"

"Okay, I'm going. Enjoy my father-in-law's truffles." He strode out the door and brushed past Lissa's mom.

"Caleb, wait." Manicured fingers grasped his arm.

He shook his head. "She needs you." He trekked down the hallway following Haven. The doctors might have a solution to mend her physical heart, but her emotional one? After what the men in her life put her through, that would take a miracle.

Tonight he would get on his knees. Thank goodness he knew the creator of miracles.

"Corliss Adelaide Morgan!"

Lissa covered her face with a pillow. Wasn't it bad enough that she'd kicked two gorgeous and godly men out of her hospital room? Now she had to listen to her mom's preaching? No thank you.

All she wanted was time alone, to contemplate what she'd just heard. She hated the despair she'd heard in Haven's voice. Despair she'd put there. How could she possibly face him now?

The pillow lifted from her face. "There will be no hiding, do you understand?"

"Yes, Mother." With a groan, Lissa tried sitting up.

"Let me help you." Her mom pushed the button on the side of the bed and the head slowly rose.

Lissa felt only a slight pinch in her chest and her breath flowed without a coughing interruption. She glanced at the clock. Three in the afternoon. Hard to believe that a few hours ago, that same heart was racked with pain.

Her mom towered over the bed, her arms crossed. "Would you mind telling me what that was all about?"

Yes, she would mind, but if she didn't talk to her mom she'd face the pain of enduring another lecture. Well, Lissa would make her mom understand. "Okay, I'll tell you." She told her mom about the worst Friday ever, about Caleb's kiss, Tyler's promotion, Rita's duplicity, and then the final and most painful betrayal: Haven had a son.

"Why do people keep lying to me? Caleb, Rita, and now Haven. Am I that gullible that people think they can take advantage of me?"

"Gullible? You think you're a victim here?"

"You don't?"

"Darling." Lissa's mom sighed and patted her daughter's hand. "Did you ever consider the fantasy standards you hold everyone to? Your father ate poorly and didn't exercise. Caleb is too dangerous. Rita, you never took seriously, and Haven? My goodness, you had him hoisted up on this pedestal of perfection. The poor man likely didn't know how to get down without hurting you."

Lissa resisted the temptation to shrink back into her pillow. Her mom was wrong. Lissa wasn't about to concede defeat. She sat up straight and crossed her arms. "Did you know about Haven, that he had a son?"

An eye roll accompanied her mom's headshake. "Of course I did, but it wasn't my place to tell you. Besides, I knew this would be your reaction. I'm certain Haven did too. If anyone is owed an apology, it would be him."

"But—"

Her mom pointed toward the empty doorway. "But that man stayed with you all night long in that wretched chair, praying, even after the way you treated him. Yes, I've been pushing you toward Caleb, but now I see that I'm wrong. Haven's a gem and, if you can't see that, you don't deserve him or Caleb."

Lissa opened her mouth, but silence came out. Her mom couldn't be right, could she? Was Lissa that rigid, that legalistic, that others feared speaking the truth around her?

All except her mom, that is.

A mom she hid her own secrets from.

Her chin quivered and she covered her mouth. Her mom was right. Lissa had created an unwinnable situation for Haven. When she got home later today, she'd give him a call. Invite him over. Apologize. It was bad enough she'd lost Caleb, she couldn't lose Haven too.

But for now, she needed to tell her mom the truth. She coughed and her throat felt raw. "Can you pour me some water?"

"Certainly." Her mom walked around to the other side of the bed where the moving bed tray stood. She poured water into a Styrofoam cup.

Lissa downed the beverage and held a few cool drops in her mouth before allowing it to glide down her scratchy throat. "Mom, I need to confess something."

"Darling, don't worry about that now. I'm sorry I came down so hard on you."

"You were honest with me, and I appreciate that. It's time I was honest with you." Her thoughts returned to the previous evening. "When I got home last night, I had no one. You were out of town. I obviously couldn't talk to Rita. It hurt physically to feel so alone. At least that's what I thought I felt."

"And you didn't try praying?"

Lissa coughed. Her mom suggested praying? "Excuse me?"

"Darling, don't be so shocked. If you would call me occasionally, you would know that I've been attending church. Caleb persuaded me to go. I think I finally understand your father's final years."

Unreal. Lissa scratched her forehead. All the years Lissa and her dad had tried to convince her mom to go to church, and it took a parasailing widower to convince her. Lissa couldn't stop a chuckle. "I'm happy for you."

"That's nice, but you didn't answer my question. It sounds like God provided the perfect opportunity for you to talk to Him last night. I'm wondering if you took advantage of it."

Lissa pressed down on the mattress, wishing she could disappear into the bed. Prayer hadn't even peeked into her thoughts. "No," she whispered. Convicted about prayer by her mom. The world had to be turning off-kilter.

She picked at the blanket's fleece. "It gets even worse." Her mom would be so disappointed. "Mom . . ." It was so hard to admit imperfections.

"Yes, darling." Her mom patted her hand. "I promise to listen and not lecture."

But promises were easily broken. Lissa looked off to the side, at bare trees and blue skies outside the hospital window. She didn't want to see her mom's disappointment. "Mom, I smoke."

All Lissa heard was the beep of the monitor by her bedside. Biting her lip, she slowly turned back to her mom.

"That's it? That's your big confession? Darling, I knew years ago."

Lissa blinked. "You did? You never said anything."

"What good would it have done? Would you have listened to me? When have you ever listened to what I've said? I wasn't nearly as nice to your father about it though."

"I . . ." What? Her mom knew this whole time and never judged her. "I'm sorry. It's so . . . so embarrassing. I feel like the weakest person on earth."

"Nonsense. You're an imperfect person, like the rest of us. I'd love to see you quit, but your smoking does not, in any way, diminish my love for you."

Lissa wished she could say the same about her feelings toward her dad. And now toward Caleb and Haven and even Rita. "I'm a jerk," she muttered.

"We all have our moments. Myself included." Her mom fidgeted with her purse handle and sat next to the bed. "I need to apologize for playing games with your affections."

"No you—"

"Hush for a moment. This isn't easy for me."

Oh so true. Her mom apologize? Had that ever happened before?

Her mom's smile was bittersweet. "Darling, I was out of line in dealing with your beaus. The truth is, both gentlemen are worthy, God-fearing men. I behaved rudely toward Haven at Thanksgiving and intend to apologize to him. You would do well to have him as a husband, and I would be proud to claim him as son-in-law. You already know how pleased your father would be."

Husband? Lissa blinked several times. Is that what she wanted?

"Mom, I was so mean to him last night, and then today." She sniffled. "If marriage was Haven's intention, I don't think it is anymore."

"You may be surprised." Her mom patted her hand. "I believe the man will respond very well to an apology."

Yeah, Haven likely would. But he wasn't the only one she needed to apologize to. "Mom, I'm sorry."

"Whatever for?"

Lissa pressed back into her pillows, her chin shaking. "About Dad. His death. It was my fault."

Her mom sat up straight. "Darling, whatever are you talking about? Your father's death had nothing to do with you."

"If I'd have listened to him, if I'd have moved into the cottage like he wanted me to and not insisted on having my own place, he wouldn't have been so stressed. If I would have stayed home like I was supposed to, he'd still be around."

"Is that truly what you believe?"

"Think about it. He had the heart attack a week after I moved out. Mom, I. Broke. His. Heart." She fisted her chest with each word.

"Darling, I never realized you felt that way. Now, I understand." Keeping Lissa's hand, her mom stood. She leaned over the bed and kissed and hugged her daughter, her tears washing Lissa's cheeks. "Corliss, dear, your father was proud of how you spread your wings, of how you chose to make your way in life without our money. If anything, your independence gave him extra time on Earth, not less."

"Dad was proud of me for moving out?"

"He bragged about it constantly, that his precious butterfly didn't need my family money."

Lissa covered her mouth with her hand. "I always thought . . ."

"If I would have known you blamed yourself . . ."

Lissa waved a hand in front of her face attempting to stave off tears. Her mom had presented her with the most precious gift possible. "Thank you." Lissa squeezed her mom's hand. "If you wouldn't mind, I'd like to spend more time with you, get to know you better."

Silence answered. Another miracle. Her mom always had an answer. "Mom, could I stay at your place for a little while?"

Her mom's eyes closed, and a tear trickled from the corner of one eye. She bent over and hugged Lissa, their tears blending.

"Excuse me, ladies, I hate to interrupt."

Her mom pulled away as the nurse walked toward the bed. "I'm afraid it's time to take those vitals again."

"Nurse, I believe you'll find my daughter's heart to be in perfect condition."

Lissa smiled as the nurse wrapped the blood pressure cuff over her arm. Her mom wasn't completely right. Her heart wasn't healed. Yet. First she had to forgive Haven. Maybe they still had a chance at a future together.

She should be excited about that.

So why wasn't she? Why did her broken heart still pine for Caleb?

Chapter Twenty-Six

Yes!" Lissa pumped her fist. One more home saved for a family. The bank would be very glad she came back into work on December thirtieth, even if it was the only day she worked this week. The more families who could face the new year unafraid of losing their homes, the better, for both sides of the business.

Maybe not getting the promotion was the best thing for her. When she sat at this desk, she personally impacted people's lives. As a supervisor, she'd lose that personal contact and become a paper pusher. God did know best, didn't He?

She glanced at the clock. Quarter to five. Time for one more call? Why not? She'd give one more family hope for the new year. If only she hadn't promised Haven that she'd spend the day with him tomorrow, she could have come in then too.

She brought up the next name on her computer files and clicked to their information. Whether she liked to admit it or not, Tyler had been wise in implementing this paperless system. It was far more efficient than paper files. At least he'd done one thing right.

It didn't even hurt admitting that. Amazing. She dialed the first three digits of the client's phone number.

"Lissa?" Crackling Pop Rocks accompanied her name.

Just like that, her joy fled and her stomach soured. All day she'd managed to avoid her former friend. Why couldn't it last a few more minutes? With so many co-workers taking the day off, Rita had worked in a different cubicle today, thank goodness. Lissa knew she needed to forgive, but now wasn't the right time. "Rita." She dialed two more digits. "I'm busy."

"Lissa, please, I have something important to tell you."

"Fine." Lissa spun in her chair. "Make it quick. I've got one more phone call to make." Technically, it could wait until after the new year, but why prolong a family's agony?

Rita sat in her old chair and played with a pink strip of hair. The Pop Rocks were actually silent. "I just finished talking with the bank president. I told him everything."

"What?" Had she heard right? "Everything?"

Rita nodded. "Tyler. Your files. I couldn't live with myself anymore and I'm so sorry, sweets. You've been the best friend a girl could ask for and I pull this junk on you." She reached over and touched Lissa's hand. "I miss you."

Lissa tugged her hand away. "Why? Why did you do it?"

Rita drew a circle on the floor with her foot. "I fell in love with Tyler. I know, I know. How could someone love Tyler, but he's different outside the bank, and he actually cares for me, quirks and all. It was totally my idea to take your files."

"But he didn't object."

"No. And with you coming from money, I didn't think the promotion would matter so much, but I was wrong. I was stupid. I don't want to lose your friendship. That's way more important than Tyler."

Lissa sighed and relaxed. Yes, she could forgive Rita, but restore a friendship? That she couldn't guarantee. "Rita, I'm not condoning what you did, but I forgive you."

"You do? Really?"

"But you'll have to earn my trust—my friendship—back. To be honest, that could take a while."

"You won't have to worry about running into me here at work." She pulled an empty copy paper box from beneath her desk and began filling it with personal items. "I've been dismissed."

Lissa pinched her eyes shut. It didn't surprise her, but she hated seeing Rita lose a job she performed so well. "If there's any way I can help, maybe offer a reference?"

"Hey, that's cool. I appreciate it." Rita picked up the full box.

"What about Tyler?" Was the supervisor position now available? Did she even want it?

"I don't think he's gonna like me too much anymore, but I can live with myself. Catch ya later, sweets." Rita turned to leave.

"Rita, one second." Lissa reached for Rita's arm. "You need a friend, call me, okay?"

"I'll do that."

They exchanged a hug and Rita walked from the office, her shoulders squared and head held high. Doing the right thing hurt, but now Rita would hopefully live with a clean conscience.

Lissa watched the exodus of employees from the office. That meant it was five and time to go home. Her mom would expect her to be on time or else. How nice to have her mom dote on her.

She took one last look at her computer, at tomorrow's schedule. Jonathan C. Johnson popped up. Caleb . . . Tomorrow morning he was losing his dream. She worried her teeth over her lip. Wasn't there anything else she could do for him? Some way he could take a remnant of the house along with him?

Something to think about. She logged off her computer, shut it down, and gathered her purse and winter coat from her cubicle.

"Ms. Morgan." Mr. Malachek's voice came from the hallway behind her.

She froze. Was this about the supervisor position? She swallowed the lump in her throat and turned around. "Good evening, Mr. Malachek."

"It's nice to see you doing well, Ms. Morgan. I spoke with your mother earlier and she didn't seem pleased that you insisted on returning to work so soon."

Was he reprimanding her? "I had clients dangling and I wanted to touch base with them before New—"

"Now, Ms. Morgan, please, I'm thrilled to have an employee with a passion for her job, and I've come to make amends for an earlier poor decision. Would you care to step into my office?"

"Certainly." Lissa clutched her purse, trying to calm her hands as she limped toward his office.

She sat in the cushiony leather chair opposite his desk.

"Coffee?" He poured a cup from his coffee maker.

"No thank you."

He carried his cup to the desk and sat down, folding his hands on top of the desk. "New information has come to light regarding other employees of Hennepin Bank and Trust, and we've reversed our decision to hire Tyler Abernathy as the Collections Supervisor."

This was it. Her big break. She held her breath.

"We'd like to offer you the position in his stead." He handed her a sheet of paper with the offer written out.

Yes! With the raise she could afford to move into an actual standalone home. She bit her lip, trying to stop her overanxious grin. Now was the time for professionalism. "May I have a few days to think about it?"

"Of course, of course. Take until Monday if you wish." He winked. "I'm confident of your answer."

As was she. "Thank you, Mr. Malachek."

Lissa left his office, trying her hardest not to do a little jig down the hallway. At her desk she picked up her framed sixth grade list of goals and read them over, mentally marking "become a boss" off the list. This was what she always wanted.

Wasn't it?

What would happen to her clients, people she'd grown to care about? Would she be able to establish the same type of relationships in the supervisory position?

Was living her sixth grade dream what she wanted to do? She squeezed the framed list into her purse. Maybe Rita was right. It was time to grow up and add a little heart to the process, let her head communicate with her heart. And with God.

Heart. Caleb. Yes! There was something she could do to help him. Lissa picked up the phone and called his in-laws. Ten minutes, and a few phone calls later, the plan was put into action. It cost her a pretty chunk of change, but it was worth every penny.

Chapter Twenty-Seven

It was time to say goodbye to the place that held so many tender memories. For the last time ever, Caleb inserted the key into his home's deadbolt. His home for another three hours and then, at noon, he'd sign the papers and hand over the key to the new owners. They could create warm memories here.

His hand shook as he pushed open the door. Moving shouldn't be this difficult. This was the right thing to do. As long as he lived here, he'd hang onto Jeanette and he needed to let her go.

He walked downstairs first, to the fireplace, and ran his finger over the verses etched into the wood bookshelves. This could be his witness to the next family. He walked through the two bedrooms and bath on the lower level, mentally saying his goodbyes. It wasn't too difficult since these bedrooms remained empty. Upstairs would be a different story.

He climbed the stairs to the foyer, then the steps to the main living area. Even with snow blowing outside, perspiration broke out on his forehead. He walked down the hallway once decorated with pictures. Ugly holes remained where the hangers had been. In Aimee's room, no stars clung to the ceiling anymore, but the painted forest scene and wildlife lived on.

He wiped sweat from his forehead and stopped in the doorway of his and Jeanette's room. Their former room. With tears trickling over his cheeks, he caressed the etching over the door. The three-stranded cord that had bound him and Jeanette with God hadn't broken easily, but it had severed, never to be repaired. Now, another couple could grow their love here. He brought his hand to his lips, kissed his fingers, and blew the kiss into the air. "I love you." His voice raked over raw vocal cords.

Sniffling, he walked down the empty hallway into the living room. A new family would find life and love here. He could be happy for them, couldn't he?

All he'd leave behind was paint and wood and carpet surrounded by four manmade walls.

All replaceable.

But could he say the same for the heart of the home? He shuffled his feet over the hardwood floor and stepped onto the kitchen's ceramic tile. Clenching his jaw, he looked up at the cabinets. He walked to the corner cabinet and smoothed his hand over the vine and branches etched into the wood. Another family would find heart and bear fruit in this kitchen. They'd cook and talk and eat and share their lives with each other.

He turned around to the island and blinked. His heart quickened as he rushed to the kitchen centerpiece. No! Black granite still covered the island, but it didn't have the heart. This countertop was not his and Jeanette's piece. How could this have happened? The new owners didn't have access yet. The bank?

Who? Why?

Why did it even matter? In a few hours it would no longer be his anyway. Still, its disappearance hurt, robbing him of one final opportunity to say goodbye.

He anchored his elbows on the new granite and rested his forehead on fisted hands.

God? Pinching his eyes closed, he angled his head toward the ceiling.

Surrender.

But I have!

Have you?

Had he?

He ran a hand across the cold surface. It was just stone.

Replaceable.

Unlike Jeanette. Aimee. His in-laws . . .

Lissa.

He dried his eyes and strode from the kitchen, through the living room, down the stairs, and out the door. For the very last time, he locked the deadbolt.

It was time to officially say goodbye.

Butterflies flitted past Lissa in the Mall of America exhibit. Today's date with Haven would end differently from their other dating disasters. It had to. On Christmas Eve he'd graciously accepted her apology. Today was a fresh start, a re-birth in their relationship. Nothing would go wrong today.

Could it?

A brownish butterfly perched on Lissa's hand and spread its wings, displaying what looked like four enormous eyes. What an amazing creature! Lissa grinned at Haven who had arrived separately after an early morning meeting. "Just think, if God took the time to paint this little guy, imagine how much time He spent on us."

"Especially you, Lissa." Haven snapped a picture.

She blushed and glanced around the exhibit, at the hundreds of butterflies winging past or clinging to a netted wall or even perching on a rotten banana. "This place is remarkable. I had no clue it was here."

She grabbed his hand and led him on the concrete path around tropical greenery, all encompassed within a netted circular home. Outside the netting lived an entirely different indoor world of roller coasters, carousels, and Ferris wheels. Lissa pointed to a metal box with a glass window. She peeked into the box's window at the dozens of cocoons waiting to break open and release their reborn captives to a new world of flight. To think that God could take a caterpillar, cocoon it, and create an entirely different creature.

Haven gestured to a padded bench not far from the cocoon box. "So we can sit and talk."

Talk. Why did that singular word make her nervous? She'd forgiven

Haven, and in return asked for his forgiveness. Putting him on a pedestal had been unintentional, but she was still guilty of it.

She sat beside him and eyed the brown butterfly that looked like it had a giant eye on its wing, a God-built defense against predators.

"Things have changed over these past weeks." Haven rubbed his palms over his thighs. "You got me thinking about my son, about missing him—him needing to know me."

She curved her arm around his. "He does need to know you. Maybe not as the daddy who's always there, but as a man of integrity, someone who's taken a sad life and turned it into something beautiful." Just like these butterflies. "Reece needs to see that."

"You're right. God's helped me see that too, so I've made some drastic changes, some sacrifices . . . for Reece. My needs aren't important anymore."

Sacrifices? She didn't like the sound of that. She took his hand, offering him assurance.

"I've quit my job, Lissa."

"You quit?" How could he give up his dream job? Was that a sacrifice or stupidity?

He held out his camera, focused, and clicked the shutter. "A Minnesota nature monthly has contracted with me for the next year. It's based in Duluth."

"Duluth? That means . . ." He'd be moving away.

Her heart quieted. *She* was his sacrifice.

"It's an opportunity I couldn't pass up. I'll be close to my son. The challenge will be getting Amanda to agree to my seeing him, but I won't give up. My lawyer says I have every legal right. The last thing I want to do is drag her into court, and I pray I can avoid that, but I won't run anymore either. Reece is too important. I want him to see that men stand up and take responsibility."

Lissa studied a black butterfly on a nearby plant, its wings closed. The wings flung open displaying a gemlike blue. "I'm proud of you. Dad would be proud too."

"I know he would be. Actually, it was your dad who pointed me in this direction." He reached into his jeans pocket, pulled out something, and squeezed his fingers around it. He took her hand and tipped up her chin, his gaze meeting hers. He opened his fist, displaying a velvet box. "I'd like you to come with me."

"You . . . you're proposing?" Her stomach flip-flopped.

He nodded and half grimaced. "I'm sorry, that wasn't very eloquent."

"No, no. It was beautiful." But completely unexpected.

And exactly what she'd always wanted.

"May I?" Without waiting for an answer, she tugged at the box's cover. The circular solitaire sat on a band of white gold. Simple yet elegant.

He removed the ring from the box and slid it onto her trembling finger. "I promised your dad I'd take care of you."

She rotated the ring on her finger, studying it, then lifted her gaze to the box of cocoons. Beyond the box and the netting, a roller coaster streamed, appearing out of control. A tear drifted down her cheek, followed by another. First the promotion, now a proposal. Even with his past, Haven was perfect. He was who she always wanted.

Life happening in her sixth grade planned order.

So why wasn't her heart dancing a jig? And where were the hummingbirds in her stomach?

Lord, what do I do?

One of the cocoons wiggled, a butterfly straining to break free.

Just like her.

She wiped a tear. Haven wanted to cocoon her, keep her safe, protect her like he hadn't protected his son. But she needed to break out of the cocoon, spread her wings, and enjoy life's roller coaster.

With Haven, there would be no roller coasters, no churning rapids, no climbing trees off nature-made paths. There was only one person who would do that with her.

She wiped another tear. God was pointing her toward a new path, not one she had planned for, yet one that was immensely better for her. It was time to let go of her sixth grade list and its constraints and listen to God.

Haven might be who she always wanted, but he wasn't who she needed.

Her hand shaking, she slid the ring from her finger, placed it in

Haven's hand, and gently closed his fingers around it. "I'm so sorry."

Confusion narrowed his eyes and moisture rimmed their edges.

Such a gentle soul. If only she could love him. But he deserved to be loved with her heart, not just her mind.

"I thought so." He chuckled sadly and stuffed his hand into his pocket, keeping his gaze on his lap. "It's that other guy yet, isn't it?"

More tears fell and she nodded. "He gave me flying lessons."

"He did, didn't he?" Tears glossing his eyes, Haven ran a hand over his mouth then kissed her forehead. "Do you know that you're beautiful when you fly?"

"Haven, don't be so nice."

"I'm releasing you, Lissa. Spread your wings. I'll be fine. I've got my son to live for. Go."

"Now?"

"Why wait?"

She peeked at her watch. Twelve fifteen. If she hurried, maybe she'd arrive in time. She stood and glanced back at Haven.

He gave her a sad smile and a thumbs up.

"Haven, your son's going to love you." And someday, so would some other very lucky woman.

Was she being a fool?

Her head screamed Yes! On paper, Haven was perfect for her and Caleb completely wrong. But her heart told her Haven was a dear friend and nothing more.

Caleb was the man who taught her to spread her wings again, who taught her that life was about more than a set of rules written on paper. And that sometimes the best lessons were learned when veering off that narrow path.

God, what do you think? She studied the cocoons, at a butterfly breaking free.

Yes, it was time to fly.

One fifteen already. Lissa had time yet. Mortgage closings never occurred on a timely basis. She leapt from her car and limped, as fast as she dared, across the icy parking lot toward the bank's title company office. If she could stop Caleb from signing—from selling his dream—with her promotion she could now afford it and then . . .

Would he consider sharing it with her?

She reached the city sidewalk and hobbled past eclectic shops selling fat-loaded bakery goods, second-hand children's clothing, and avant-garde beauty salons. Only one block to go. The glass door opened at the title company and Caleb walked out. She waved, but he turned in the opposite direction.

Come on leg, go faster. "Caleb," she yelled, but a horn drowned out her voice. She cupped her hands around her mouth. "Caleb!"

He didn't slow one bit. The man must be deaf. He jogged across the street, avoiding patches of ice, and climbed into his truck. Seconds later he backed out of the parking spot.

She waved frantically, hoping he'd see her in his rearview mirror, but he drove off without a single hesitation.

He couldn't be done already, could he? Last she heard his scheduled closing time was one. Paperwork was never signed that quickly.

Maybe the offer fell through. Maybe he came to his senses and decided to stay in his home.

That had to be it. Please let it be so. She tugged open the door of the title company and walked in. The receptionist was someone she'd worked with often and who would be able to give Lissa the information she needed.

Lissa limped to the woman's desk, her leg feeling the stress from the extra walking this morning. "Good morning, Amber."

"Hey, Lissa, what are you doing down here? And on New Year's Eve of all days?"

"I was in the area and had a few questions about a client I worked with. He said he was closing today and that he would be paying off his mortgage." She nodded toward the outside door. "I believe he just walked out of here. The name's Cal . . . make that Jonathan C. Johnson."

"Of course. What a sweet guy and such a sad story. Quite the looker too."

Amber didn't know the half of it. "I know. That's when I hate my job, when I have to ruin someone's dreams."

"Well, he didn't seem too upset. He was even whistling when he left."

"Why? Didn't he close?" *Please say no.*

"Oh, he closed. He was nice enough to reset his appointment at the last minute for an hour earlier."

No. Lissa's hand flew to her mouth and she blinked away tears. She was too late.

In spite of her quavering chin, Lissa forced a smile. "Good. I assume I can close the book on him." Businesswise, anyway. She prayed that personally he'd consider reopening their book, though he had little reason to, not with the way she'd treated him. "Thanks for the info."

"Hey, no problem. Hope you have a good New Year."

Yeah. She did too.

It was time for Plan B. She got in her Volvo, called Caleb's in-laws and told them about her failed plan and her new one. Maybe Caleb no longer had his dream home, but a home was more than four walls and wood and paint, wasn't it?

She prayed he'd see it that way.

Caleb walked up the quiet hill, over crunchy snow, past grave markers long forgotten by family and friends. If Jeanette had walked here, she probably would have stopped to drop a flower at each one, to show they weren't forgotten. Next time. Today was about saying goodbye to Jeanette.

He breathed in the scent from the bouquet he carried: pink carnations and dainty blue forget-me-nots. No, he could never forget his first love.

But . . .

He stopped at her granite headstone and read, "Jeanette Louise McCarthy Johnson. Beloved wife, mother, and daughter. She lived everyday as if it were God's precious gift to her. She was God's gracious gift to us. She lived joyously. Psalm 68:3."

And now it was time for him to live again.

He squatted down, brushed the snow from the gravesite's vase and arranged the bouquet in it. "I did it, Jeanette. Just like you wanted me to, and you know what? I'm happy. I even found someone else, but lost her because I didn't have the courage to let you go." With a gloved finger, he snatched a frozen tear from his face. "You'd have been friends with her, Jeanette. Lissa's got this youthful joy whenever she tries something new."

He removed his glove and rubbed his hand over the granite's frosty surface. "I won't forget you, and no one will ever replace you, but it's time for me to move on, to live again. Lissa taught me how."

A tear froze to his cheek as he kissed his fingers then laid them on top of the stone. "I'm releasing you. You don't have to worry about me anymore. Go. Fly with the angels. See if they can keep up with you."

With a chuckle, he stood up and walked back through the snow.

And unlike every other time he made this lonely walk, this time his heart didn't break.

It rejoiced.

Caleb hesitated at the door of his in-laws' home. Change that—his and Aimee's new home. Out of respect, he'd always knocked before entering. Was that still proper? They'd probably think it was foolish. They would be right.

He turned the knob and opened the door to his new life.

Aimee greeted him with a knee hug.

"Hey Doodles, how's my big girl?"

"I got a new 'nocerus."

"A rhinoceros, huh?" He lifted her up, kissed her, and rubbed his nose against hers. "Isn't that a bit big for your bedroom."

"It a baby."

"Ah, I see."

She wiggled out of his grip and grabbed his hand. "Come see."

"In a second, Doodles. How about if you let me take off my boots first so Mémé doesn't scold me."

"Okay." Ignoring the railing, Aimee hopped down the steps one at a time and ran off to her room.

He removed his boots and squeezed them into the foyer's closet along with his coat. A closet made for two, not four. But at least he had a home to go to. Not everyone facing foreclosure had the same blessing.

"Dada, come on!"

"I'm coming, I'm coming." He jogged down the stairs and took a right into a short hallway, and an immediate left into Aimee's room. Green stars clung to this ceiling now, and fluffy animals inhabited almost every inch of her toddler bed.

She jumped on the bed at the foot, bounced over the animals toward the headboard, and picked up a burgundy rhinoceros. "See Dada. I love it." She gave it a squeeze hug and held it out for him.

"Does it bite?"

"No, silly."

"If you say so." He accepted the animal, hugged it, and gave a little yelp. "It bit me."

"Dada, it don't have no teeth."

"Silly me." He crouched next to her bed.

"Silly Dada."

He raised the rhino to his ear and nodded and rolled his eyes back and forth. "Uh-huh. Yep." He cradled the animal in his arm. "Do you know what rhino says?"

"Uh-uh."

Grinning, Caleb tickled Aimee's stomach with the rhino's horn. "He says gwaba, gwaba, gwaba." Giggling, she flounced back on her bed.

A knock sounded on the door. "Are you dear children having fun?"

Caleb glanced back at Yvette with a sheepish smile. "What's it look like?"

"Like a young man who is happy to be free."

Such a wise woman. He underhanded the animal back to Aimee. "I am."

"Aimee, may I speak with your dada alone for a moment, *sil vous plait*? You may play with your new toy."

"*Oui, oui*, Mémé."

"So, Mémé's teaching you French now."

"A child learns languages much easier when they are young."

Caleb followed Yvette out the door and shut it behind him.

"This time together will be very good for Aimee and for you."

"As long as it's temporary." It was important for a man to make it on his own. The sooner he could move on, the better.

Yvette led him to his little kitchen and stopped beside the bar area that jutted out from the wall.

His hand rested on the bar and he did a double take. "What? How?" Blinking, he glanced up at the ceiling and back down at the familiar slab of granite with the God-hewn heart etched in the center. It wasn't gone for good. He ran his hand over the top, tracing the heart's outline.

Yvette kissed his cheek. "The new homeowners are very gracious, but more importantly, there is a young lady who cares very much for you. She even turned down a marriage proposal because of you."

"Turned it down?" His heart beat a Samba. "Because of me?"

"*Oui.* I do not doubt that she loves you." She placed her hand on top of Caleb's as he traced the granite's heart.

"She loves me?"

"*Oui.* I am French. I know these things. Her eyes very much say she is in love. As do yours. What are you going to do about this?"

"Do?" He scratched his head. "What am I—?"

"Go. She is home."

"I—"

She perched manicured hands on delicate hips. "Where is the young man my Jeanette fell in love with? The one willing to take any risk?"

Caleb studied the red heart-shape etched permanently into stone. Could he risk loving again?

Jeanette would push him out the door, tell him to get his derrière moving.

Yes, if he was going to live again, like he promised Jeanette, that meant taking a risk. And if his heart was broken again, well, he'd learned that it does heal.

He kissed his mother-in-law on both cheeks. *"Merci beaucoup."* Thank you very, very much. He jogged to Aimee's room, knocked on the door, and let himself in. "Doodles, let's go for a ride."

Lissa hunched down on her couch and picked up the television remote. Was Caleb home yet? If so, what did he think about her housewarming gift? Would he take the hint? Maybe she should have been less subtle and left a note declaring her feelings, feelings beyond the sadness over him losing his house. Or, she could call now, see if he was home. What she'd give to bring in the new year with a kiss from Caleb. She picked up her phone from the end table and began dialing.

But maybe she assumed wrong. Maybe he didn't really care for her. Would Haven forgive her for saying no?

"Arghh." She hurled a throw pillow across the room. Caleb would tell her to take a chance. She dialed the remaining numbers to Caleb's cell. It rang the same time as her doorbell. She ended the call. Whoever was at her door, she'd send them off and try Caleb again.

Her leg protested as she limped to the door. Too much running today.

She squinted into her peephole and gasped. He'd understood? Not even trying to conceal her smile, she flung open the door. Caleb stood, one hand in his jeans pockets, the other holding a bouquet of red tulips and calla lilies, looking way too sexy with his intentional stubble and squinty eyes.

"Hey there." His mouth tipped into a smile.

She bit her lower lip. "Hey yourself."

"I, uh, I wanted to say thank you. Having that granite slab means the world to me."

"I know. Won't you come in?"

"Well . . ." He glanced back at his pickup then at Lissa. "First, I have a question I need to ask."

Her heart stopped. No dance. No life at all. Was she reading him wrong? Her voice stuck in her throat so she nodded.

"Well, you see, in February the local chapter of the American Heart Association is holding another fundraiser. It's a Sweetheart Dinner Dance catered by my father-in-law. Anyway, I have a problem. I'm looking for someone to be my sweetheart. Someone who makes my heart dance, someone who gave me flying lessons."

Her heart jumpstarted.

He stepped close enough so his minty breath warmed her cheeks. "There's this woman I really like, I mean, I think I love her, but I don't know if she feels the same way about me."

He loved her? She swallowed the lump rising in her throat and nodded.

Cupping his hand over her cheek, he came closer and his cold jacket brushed her overheated heart. She swore steam rose between them. "This sweetheart I'm looking for . . . is someone I could spend a lifetime with."

Even with the freezing temperatures, her face burned. "A lifetime?"

"I know it's fast, but there are some things I don't want to risk, and one of them is losing you."

Words couldn't express her proper answer so she leaned forward, into the cold, and brushed her lips over his. He groaned and wrapped his arms around her, drawing her tight to him, deepening the mint-flavored kiss that probably melted all the snow surrounding them. She certainly didn't miss a jacket.

An eternal second later, she pulled back and gnawed on her lower lip. He kissed that too and grinned. "Does that mean yes?"

She nodded, too stunned, too exhilarated to say anything.

He whooped, picked her up, and twirled her around. When he set her down just inside the house, she dove in for another kiss, but his finger blocked the way. "One more thing."

"What?"

"You'll see." He hurried back to his pickup, opened the passenger door, and a toddler wearing a bright pink snowsuit and tasseled hood jumped from the truck. She landed with a summersault on the snow covered grass.

Lissa's eyes widened and she took a step onto the cold concrete and pulled back. "Is she all right?"

Caleb just laughed as the child got up without his help then hopped up the sidewalk. He caught up to her, swooped her into his arms, then threw her in the air.

"Caleb!" Lissa gasped and covered her mouth.

He grinned as the giggling child fell safely into his arms. The smile remained on his face as he carried the squirming toddler up the steps then into the house.

After closing the door behind him, Lissa swatted his arm. "Does everything have to be an adventure with you?"

"You want me to change?"

"Never."

"Then I think we need to add one more to this adventure." He kissed the little girl's cheek then rubbed his nose against hers. "Aimee-doodles, I'd like you to meet Lissa. She's a very special lady to your dada. She likes adventure, just like you and me, and she's taking a chance on loving both of us."

Without warning, Aimee leapt from Caleb's arms into Lissa's and Lissa snuggled the adorable child to her chest. Caleb was wrong, Lissa wasn't taking a chance on love. Risking love with Caleb and his daughter was no real risk at all, rather it was the beginning of a heart-pounding life adventure, and she couldn't wait to start!

THE END

Read Haven's story in *Capturing Beauty*, coming February 2017!

Dear Reader,

Thank you for reading Lissa and Caleb's story. I hope you enjoyed getting to know them as much as I did. And Haven's story, about getting to know his son, will continue in Capturing Beauty, due to come out in February 2017.

Reviews are vital for authors, so when you get a moment, I'd greatly appreciate it if you'd share a review on your blog or on any of the popular book sites. The review doesn't have to be long or eloquent, just honest.

For the latest information on upcoming releases, contests, recipes, what I'm reading, and more, sign up for my e-newsletter. Opt in at:

http://eepurl.com/MoZZr

You can also stay in touch via my website:

http://brendaandersonbooks.com/

And via social media:

https://www.facebook.com/BrendaSAndersonAuthor/
https://twitter.com/BrendaSAnders_n
https://www.pinterest.com/brendabanderson/
https://www.goodreads.com/BrendaSAnderson/

I also love hearing from readers as you are the reason we write! You can send a note to:

Brenda@BrendaAndersonBooks.com

Thank you for joining me on this writing journey!

In Him,
Brenda

ACKNOWLEDGEMENTS

Putting out a book is never a solo effort, and I'd be remiss not to mention those who've helped bring *Risking Love* to readers.

Thank you to ...

~ My team of Book Boosters who eagerly spread the word about my books!

~ My many critique partners, Stacy Monson, Stephanie Prichard, Lorna Seilstad, Shannon Taylor Vannatter, and Jerri Lynn Ledford for helping to make this story shine. And thank you for convincing me it was worth seeing beyond my computer.

~ My sister Gayle Balster for being an honest first reader, top cheerleader, and final proofreader. None of my books would exist without you!

~ Lesley Ann McDaniel, for your keen-eyed editing.

~ John Martin Keith of Edenbrooke Productions for producing the beautiful trailer for *Risking Love*!

~ George at Think Cap Design Studios for continuing to capture the essence of my stories in your cover design!

~ Gay Hartfiel of Portraits from the Heart for always making me look good in my author photos. You are amazing!

~ My daughter, Sarah, for not only supporting me on this writing journey, but also for stepping into the role of proofreader, which you've performed admirably!

~ My sons Bryan and Brandon, both gifted authors, for enduring so many macaroni and cheese meals while I stare down the computer.

And special Thank You to my husband, Marvin, who cheers louder than anyone, and supports my writing habit 100 percent. God blessed me richly with your love!

And the ultimate thanksgiving and praise goes to the One who convinced me not only that I can write, but that I should write. All glory goes to You!

Coming Soon!

Capturing Beauty
(Where the Heart Is book #2)
coming February 2017

Planting Hope
(Where the Heart Is book #3)
coming May 2017

Coming Home Series

Pieces of Granite (prequel)

Chain of Mercy (book #1)

Memory Box Secrets (book #2)

Hungry for Home (book #3)

Brenda S. Anderson writes authentic and gritty, life-affirming fiction. She is a member of the American Christian Fiction Writers and is currently President of the ACFW Minnesota Chapter, MN-NICE. When not reading or writing, she enjoys music, theater, roller coasters, and baseball, and she loves watching movies with her family. She resides in the Minneapolis, Minnesota area with her husband of 29 years, their three children, and one sassy cat. Learn more about Brenda at www.BrendaAndersonBooks.com